PENGUIN BOOKS

THE TORTILLA CURTAIN

T. Coraghessan Boyle was born in New York's Hudson Valley and now lives near Santa Barbara, California. He is the author of the novels *East is East*, *World's End*, which was winner of the 1988 PEN/Faulkner Award, *Budding Prospects*, *Water Music* and *The Road to Wellville*, as well as *Without a Hero* and three other collections of short stories.

The Tortilla Curtain

T. CORAGHESSAN BOYLE

PENGUIN BOOKS

PENGUIN BOOKS

Published by the Penguin Group
Penguin Books Ltd, 27 Wrights Lane, London W8 5TZ, England
Penguin Books USA Inc., 375 Hudson Street, New York, New York 10014, USA
Penguin Books Australia Ltd, Ringwood, Victoria, Australia
Penguin Books Canada Ltd, 10 Alcorn Avenue, Toronto, Ontario, Canada M4V 3B2
Penguin Books (NZ) Ltd, 182–190 Wairau Road, Auckland 10, New Zealand

Penguin Books Ltd, Registered Offices: Harmondsworth, Middlesex, England

First published in the USA by Viking Penguin 1995
Published in Great Britain in Penguin Books 1996
1 3 5 7 9 10 8 6 4 2

Printed in England by Clays Ltd, St Ives plc

For Pablo and Theresa Campos

They ain't human. A human being wouldn't live like they do. A human being couldn't stand it to be so dirty and miserable.

—**John Steinbeck,** *The Grapes of Wrath*

Acknowledgments

The author would like to thank Bill Sloniker, Tony Colby and James Kaufman for their assistance in gathering material for this book.

PART ONE
Arroyo Blanco

1

AFTERWARD, HE TRIED TO REDUCE IT TO ABSTRACT terms, an accident in a world of accidents, the collision of opposing forces—the bumper of his car and the frail scrambling hunched-over form of a dark little man with a wild look in his eye—but he wasn't very successful. This wasn't a statistic in an actuarial table tucked away in a drawer somewhere, this wasn't random and impersonal. It had happened to him, Delaney Mossbacher, of 32 Piñon Drive, Arroyo Blanco Estates, a liberal humanist with an unblemished driving record and a freshly waxed Japanese car with personalized plates, and it shook him to the core. Everywhere he turned he saw those red-flecked eyes, the rictus of the mouth, the rotten teeth and incongruous shock of gray in the heavy black brush of the mustache—they infested his dreams, cut through his waking hours like a window on another reality. He saw his victim in a book of stamps at the post office, reflected in the blameless glass panels of the gently closing twin doors at Jordan's elementary school, staring up at him from his omelette aux fines herbes at Emilio's in the shank of the evening.

The whole thing had happened so quickly. One minute he was winding his way up the canyon with a backseat full of newspapers, mayonnaise jars and Diet Coke cans for the recycler, thinking nothing, absolutely nothing, and the next thing he knew the car was skewed across the shoulder in a dissipating fan of dust. The man must have been crouching in the bushes like some feral thing, like a stray dog or bird-mauling cat, and at the last possible moment he'd flung himself across the road in a mad suicidal scramble. There was the astonished look, a flash of mustache, the collapsing mouth flung open in a mute cry, and then the brake, the impact, the marimba rattle of the stones beneath the car, and finally, the dust. The car had stalled, the air conditioner blowing full, the voice on the radio nattering on about import quotas and American jobs. The man was gone. Delaney opened his eyes and unclenched his teeth. The accident was over, already a moment in history.

To his shame, Delaney's first thought was for the car (was it marred, scratched, dented?), and then for his insurance rates (what was this going to do to his good-driver discount?), and finally, belatedly, for the victim. Who was he? Where had he gone? Was he all right? Was he hurt? Bleeding? Dying? Delaney's hands trembled on the wheel. He reached mechanically for the key and choked off the radio. It was then, still strapped in and rushing with adrenaline, that the reality of it began to hit him: he'd injured, possibly killed, another human being. It wasn't his fault, god knew—the man was obviously insane, demented, suicidal, no jury would convict him—but there it was, all the same. Heart pounding, he slipped out from under the seat belt, eased open the door and stepped tentatively onto the parched strip of naked stone and litter that constituted the shoulder of the road.

Immediately, before he could even catch his breath, he was brushed back by the tailwind of a string of cars racing bumper-to-bumper up the canyon like some snaking malignant train. He clung to the side of his car as the sun caught his head in a hammerlock and the un-air-conditioned heat rose from the pavement like a fist in the face, like a knockout punch. Two more cars shot by. He was dizzy. Sweating. He couldn't seem to control his hands. "I've had an accident," he said to himself, repeating it over and over like a mantra, "I've had an accident."

But where was the victim? Had he been flung clear, was that it? Delaney looked round him helplessly. Cars came down the canyon, burnished with light; cars went up it; cars turned into the lumberyard a hundred yards up on the right and into the side street beyond it, whining past him as if he didn't exist. One after another the faces of the drivers came at him, shadowy and indistinct behind the armor of their smoked-glass windshields. Not a head turned. No one stopped.

He walked round the front of the car first, scanning the mute un-revealing brush along the roadside—ceanothus, chamise, redshanks—for some sign of what had happened. Then he turned to the car. The plastic lens over the right headlight was cracked and the turn-signal housing had been knocked out of its track, but aside from that the car seemed undamaged. He threw an uneasy glance at the bushes, then worked his way along the passenger side to the rear, expecting the worst, the bleeding flesh and hammered bone, sure now that the man must have been trapped under the car. Stooping, palm flat, one knee in the dirt, he forced himself to look. Crescendo and then release: nothing there but dust and more dust.

The license plate—PILGRIM—caught the sun as he rose and clapped the grit from his hands, and he looked to the bushes yet again. "Hello!" he cried suddenly over the noise of the cars flashing by in either direction. "Is anybody there? Are you okay?"

He turned slowly round, once, twice, as if he'd forgotten something—a set of keys, his glasses, his wallet—then circled the car again. How could no one have seen what had happened? How could no one have stopped to help, bear witness, gape, jeer—anything? A hundred people must have passed by in the last five minutes and yet he might as well have been lost in the Great Painted Desert for all the good it did him. He looked off up the road to the bend by the lumberyard and the grocery beyond it, and saw the distant figure of a man climbing into a parked car, the hard hot light exploding round him. And then, fighting down the urge to run, to heave himself into the driver's seat and burn up the tires, to leave the idiot to his fate and deny everything—the date, the time, the place, his own identity and the sun in the sky—Delaney turned back to the bushes. "Hello?" he called again.

Nothing. The cars tore past. The sun beat at his shoulders, his neck, the back of his head.

To the left, across the road, was a wall of rock; to the right, the canyon fell off to the rusty sandstone bed of Topanga Creek, hundreds of feet below. Delaney could see nothing but brush and treetops, but he knew now where his man was—down there, down in the scrub oak and manzanita. The high-resin-compound bumper of the Acura had launched that sad bundle of bone and gristle over the side of the canyon like a Ping-Pong ball shot out of a cannon, and what chance was there to survive that? He felt sick suddenly, his brain mobbed with images from the eyewitness news—shootings, stabbings, auto wrecks, the unending parade of victims served up afresh each day—and something hot and sour rose in his throat. Why him? Why did this have to happen to him?

He was about to give it up and jog to the lumberyard for help, for the police, an ambulance—they'd know what to do—when a glint of light caught his eye through the scrim of brush. He staggered forward blindly, stupidly, like a fish to a lure—he wanted to do the right thing, wanted to help, he did. But almost as quickly, he caught himself. This glint wasn't what he'd expected—no coin or crucifix, no belt buckle, key chain, medal or steel-toed boot wrenched from the victim's foot— just a shopping cart, pocked with rust and concealed in the bushes beside a rough trail that plunged steeply down the hillside, vanishing round a right-angle bend no more than twenty feet away.

Delaney called out again. Cupped his hands and shouted. And then he straightened up, wary suddenly, catlike and alert. At five-foot-nine and a hundred and sixty-five pounds, he was compact, heavy in the shoulders and with a natural hunch that made him look as if he were perpetually in danger of pitching forward on his face, but he was in good shape and ready for anything. What startled him to alertness was the sudden certainty that the whole thing had been staged—he'd read about this sort of operation in the Metro section, gangs faking accidents and then preying on the unsuspecting, law-abiding, compliant and fully insured motorist . . . But then where was the gang? Down the path? Huddled round the bend waiting for him to take that first fatal step off the shoulder and out of sight of the road?

He might have gone on speculating for the rest of the afternoon, the vanishing victim a case for *Unsolved Mysteries* or the Home Video Network, if he hadn't become aware of the faintest murmur from the clump of vegetation to his immediate right. But it was more than a murmur—it was a deep aching guttural moan that made something catch in his throat, an expression of the most primitive and elemental experience we know: pain. Delaney's gaze jumped from the shopping cart to the path and then to the bush at his right, and there he was, the man with the red-flecked eyes and graying mustache, the daredevil, the suicide, the jack-in-the-box who'd popped up in front of his bumper and ruined his afternoon. The man was on his back, limbs dangling, as loose-jointed as a doll flung in a corner by an imperious little girl. A trail of blood, thick as a finger, leaked from the corner of his mouth, and Delaney couldn't remember ever having seen anything so bright. Two eyes, dull with pain, locked on him like a set of jaws.

"Are you . . . are you okay?" Delaney heard himself say.

The man winced, tried to move his head. Delaney saw now that the left side of the man's face—the side that had been turned away from him—was raw, scraped and flensed like a piece of meat stripped from the hide. And then he noticed the man's left arm, the torn shirtsleeve and the skin beneath it stippled with blood and bits of dirt and leaf mold, and the blood-slick hand that clutched a deflated paper bag to his chest. Slivers of glass tore through the bag like claws and orange soda soaked the man's khaki shirt; a plastic package, through which Delaney could make out a stack of *tortillas* (*Como Hechas a Mano*), clung to the man's crotch as if fastened there.

"Can I help you?" Delaney breathed, gesturing futilely, wondering whether to reach down a hand or not—should he be moved? Could he? "I mean, I'm sorry, I—why did you run out like that? What possessed you? Didn't you see me?"

Flies hovered in the air. The canyon stretched out before them, slabs of upthrust stone and weathered tumbles of rock, light and shadow at war. The man tried to collect himself. He kicked out his legs like an insect pinned to a mounting board, and then his eyes seemed to sharpen, and with a groan he struggled to a sitting position. He said something then in a foreign language, a gargle and rattle in the throat, and Delaney didn't know what to do.

It wasn't French he was speaking, that was for sure. And it wasn't Norwegian. The United States didn't share a two-thousand-mile border with France—or with Norway either. The man was Mexican, Hispanic, that's what he was, and he was speaking Spanish, a hot crazed drumroll of a language to which Delaney's four years of high-school French gave him little access. *"Docteur?"* he tried.

The man's face was a blank. Blood trickled steadily from the corner of his mouth, camouflaged by the mustache. He wasn't as young as Delaney had first thought, or as slight—the shirt was stretched tight across his shoulders and there was a visible swelling round his middle, just above the package of *tortillas*. There was gray in his hair too. The man grimaced and sucked in his breath, displaying a mismatched row of teeth that were like pickets in a rotting fence. *"No quiero un matasanos,"* he growled, wincing as he staggered to his feet in a cyclone of twigs, dust and crushed tumbleweed, *"no lo necesito."*

For a long moment they stood there, examining each other, unwitting perpetrator and unwitting victim, and then the man let the useless bag drop from his fingers with a tinkle of broken glass. It lay at his feet in the dirt, and they both stared at it, frozen in time, until he reached down absently to retrieve the *tortillas,* which were still pinned to the crotch of his pants. He seemed to shake himself then, like a dog coming out of a bath, and as he clutched the *tortillas* in his good hand, he bent forward woozily to hawk a gout of blood into the dirt.

Delaney felt the relief wash over him—the man wasn't going to die, he wasn't going to sue, he was all right and it was over. "Can I do anything for you?" he asked, feeling charitable now. "I mean, give you a ride someplace or something?" Delaney pointed to the car. He held his fists up in front of his face and pantomimed the act of driving. *"Dans la voiture?"*

The man spat again. The left side of his face glistened in the harsh sunlight, ugly and wet with fluid, grit, pills of flesh and crushed vegetation. He looked at Delaney as if he were an escaped lunatic. "Dooo?" he echoed.

Delaney shuffled his feet. The heat was getting to him. He pushed the glasses back up the bridge of his nose. He gave it one more try: "You know—*help*. Can I help you?"

And then the man grinned, or tried to. A film of blood clung to the jagged teeth and he licked it away with a flick of his tongue. "Monee?" he whispered, and he rubbed the fingers of his free hand together.

"Money," Delaney repeated, "okay, yes, money," and he reached for his wallet as the sun drilled the canyon and the cars sifted by and a vulture, high overhead, rode the hot air rising from below.

Delaney didn't remember getting back into the car, but somehow he found himself steering, braking and applying gas as he followed a set of taillights up the canyon, sealed in and impervious once again. He drove in a daze, hardly conscious of the air conditioner blasting in his face, so wound up in his thoughts that he went five blocks past the recycling center before realizing his error, and then, after making a questionable U-turn against two lanes of oncoming traffic, he forgot himself again and drove past the place in the opposite direction. It was over. Money had changed hands, there were no witnesses, and the man was gone, out of his life forever. And yet, no matter how hard he tried, Delaney couldn't shake the image of him.

He'd given the man twenty dollars—it seemed the least he could do—and the man had stuffed the bill quickly into the pocket of his cheap stained pants, sucked in his breath and turned away without so much as a nod or gesture of thanks. Of course, he was probably in shock. Delaney was no doctor, but the guy had looked pretty shaky—and his face was a mess, a real mess. Leaning forward to hold out the bill, Delaney had watched, transfixed, as a fly danced away from the abraded flesh along the line of the man's jaw, and another, fat-bodied and black, settled in to take its place. In that moment the strange face before him was transformed, annealed in the brilliant merciless light, a hard cold wedge of a face that looked strangely loose in its coppery skin, the left cheekbone swollen and misaligned—was it bruised? Broken? Or was that the way it was supposed to look? Before Delaney could decide, the man had turned abruptly away, limping off down the path with an exaggerated stride that would have seemed comical under other circumstances—Delaney could think of nothing so much as Charlie Chaplin walking off some imaginary hurt—and then he'd vanished round the bend and the afternoon wore on like a tattered fabric of used and borrowed moments.

Somber, his hands shaking even yet, Delaney unloaded his cans and glass—green, brown and clear, all neatly separated—into the appropriate bins, then drove his car onto the big industrial scales in front of the business office to weigh it, loaded, for the newspaper. While the woman behind the window totted up the figure on his receipt, he found himself thinking about the injured man and whether his cheekbone would knit properly if it was, in fact, broken—you couldn't put a splint on it, could you? And where was he going to bathe and disinfect his wounds? In the creek? At a gas station?

It was crazy to refuse treatment like that, just crazy. But he had. And that meant he was illegal—go to the doctor, get deported. There was a desperation in that, a gulf of sadness that took Delaney out of himself for a long moment, and he just stood there in front of the office, receipt in hand, staring into space.

He tried to picture the man's life—the cramped room, the bag of second-rate oranges on the streetcorner, the spade and the hoe and the cold mashed beans dug out of the forty-nine-cent can. Unrefrigerated *tortillas*. Orange soda. That oom-pah music with the accordions and the tinny harmonies. But what was he doing on Topanga Canyon Boulevard at one-thirty in the afternoon, out there in the middle of nowhere? Working? Taking a lunch break?

And then all at once Delaney knew, and the understanding hit him with a jolt: the shopping cart, the *tortillas*, the trail beaten into the dirt—he was camping down there, that's what he was doing. Camping. Living. Dwelling. Making the trees and bushes and the natural habitat of Topanga State Park into his own private domicile, crapping in the chaparral, dumping his trash behind rocks, polluting the stream and ruining it for everyone else. That was state property down there, rescued from the developers and their bulldozers and set aside for the use of the public, for nature, not for some outdoor ghetto. And what about fire danger? The canyon was a tinderbox this time of year, everyone knew that.

Delaney felt his guilt turn to anger, to outrage.

God, how he hated that sort of thing—the litter alone was enough to set him off. How many times had he gone down one trail or another with a group of volunteers, with the rakes and shovels and black plastic bags? And how many times had he come back, sometimes just days later, to find the whole thing trashed again? There wasn't a trail in the Santa Monica Mountains that didn't have its crushed beer cans, its carpet of glass, its candy wrappers and cigarette butts, and it was people like this Mexican or whatever he was who were responsible, thoughtless people, stupid people, people who wanted to turn the whole world into a garbage dump, a little Tijuana . . .

Delaney was seething, ready to write his congressman, call the sheriff, anything—but then he checked himself. Maybe he was jumping to conclusions. Who knew who this man was or what he was doing? Just because he spoke Spanish didn't make him a criminal. Maybe he was a picnicker, a bird-watcher, a fisherman; maybe he was some naturalist from South of the Border studying the gnatcatcher or the canyon wren . . .

Yeah, sure. And Delaney was the King of Siam.

When he came back to himself, he saw that he'd managed to reenter the car, drive past the glass and aluminum receptacles and into the enormous littered warehouse with its mountains of cardboard and paper and the dark intense men scrabbling through the drifts of yesterday's news—men, he saw with a shock of recognition, who were exactly like the jack-in-the-box on the canyon road, right down to the twin pits of their eyes and the harsh black strokes of their mustaches. They were even wearing the same khaki workshirts and sacklike trousers. He'd been in Los Angeles nearly two years now, and he'd never really thought about it before, but they were everywhere, these men, ubiquitous, silently going about their business, whether it be mopping up the floors at McDonald's, inverting trash cans in the alley out back of Emilio's or moving purposively behind the rakes and blowers that combed the pristine lawns of Arroyo Blanco Estates twice a week. Where had they all come from? What did they want? And why did they have to throw themselves under the wheels of his car?

He had the back door open and was shifting his tightly bound bundles of paper from the car to the nearest pile, when a shrill truncated whistle cut through the din of machinery, idling engines, slamming doors and trunks. Delaney looked up. A forklift had wheeled up beside him and the man driving it, his features inscrutable beneath the brim of his yellow hard hat, was gesturing to him. The man said something Delaney couldn't quite catch. "What?" he called out over the noise of the place.

A hot wind surged through the warehouse doors, flinging dust. Ads and supplements shot into the air, *Parade, Holiday, Ten Great Escapes for the Weekend.* Engines idled, men shouted, forklifts beeped and stuttered. The man looked down on him from his perch, the bright work-polished arms of the vehicle sagging beneath its load of newsprint, as if it were inadequate to the task, as if even sheet metal and steel couldn't help but buckle under the weight of all that news.

"Ponlos allá," he said, pointing to the far corner of the building.

Delaney stared up at him, his arms burdened with paper. "What?" he repeated.

For a long moment, the man simply sat there, returning his gaze. Another car pulled in. A pigeon dove from the rafters and Delaney saw that there were dozens of them there, caught against the high open two-story drift of the roof. The man in the hard hat bent forward and spat carefully on the pavement. And then suddenly, without warning, the forklift lurched back, swung round, and vanished in the drifts of printed waste.

"So what'd you hit—a deer? Coyote?"

Delaney was in the showroom of the Acura dealership, a great ugly crenellated box of a building he'd always hated—it didn't blend with the surrounding hills, didn't begin to, not at all—but somehow, today, he felt strangely comforted by it. Driving up with his cracked lens and disarranged signal housing, he'd seen it as a bastion of the familiar and orderly, where negotiations took place the way they were supposed to, in high-backed chairs, with checkbooks and contracts and balance sheets. There were desks, telephones, the air was cool, the floors buffed to brilliance. And the cars themselves, hard and unassailable, so new they smelled of wax, rubber and plastic only, were healing presences arranged like heavy furniture throughout the cavern of the room. He was sitting on the edge of Kenny Grissom's desk, and Kenny Grissom, the enthusiastic moon-faced thirty-five-year-old boy who'd sold him the car, was trying to look concerned.

Delaney shrugged, already reaching for the phone. "A dog, I think it was. Might have been a coyote, but kind of big for a coyote. Must have been a dog. Sure it was. Yeah. A dog."

Why was he lying? Why did he keep thinking of shadowy black-and-white movies, men in creased hats leaning forward to light cigarettes, the hit-and-run driver tracked down over a few chips of paint—or a cracked headlight? Because he was covering himself, that's why. Because he'd just left the poor son of a bitch there alongside the road, abandoned him, and because he'd been glad of it, relieved to buy him off with his twenty dollars' blood money. And how did that square with his liberal-humanist ideals?

"I hit a dog once," Kenny Grissom offered, "when I was living out in Arizona? It was this big gray shaggy thing, a sheepdog, I guess it was. I was driving a pickup at the time, Ford half-ton with a four-sixty in it, and my girlfriend was with me. I never even seen the thing—one minute I'm cruising, and the next minute my girlfriend's all in tears and there's this thing that looks like an old rug in the middle of the road in back of me. I don't know. So I back up and the dog like lurches to his feet, but he's only got three legs and I thought like holy shit I blew his leg right off, but then Kim gets out and we kind of look and there's no blood or anything, just a stump."

Kenny's face was working, as if there were something trapped under the skin trying to get out. "Friggin' thing only *had* three legs to begin with," he suddenly shouted, "no wonder he couldn't get out of the way!" His laugh reverberated through the vast hollow spaces of the room, a salesman's laugh, too sharp-edged and pleased with itself. And then his face came back to the moment, sober suddenly, composed round the pale tawny bristle of his mustache. "But it's a bitch, I know it is," he observed in a sort of yodel. "And don't you worry, we'll have your car for you any minute now, good as new. Feel free to use the phone."

Delaney just nodded. He'd dialed Kyra at work and was listening to the number ring through.

"Hello?" Her voice was bright, amplified, right there with him.

"It's me, honey."

"What's wrong? Is it Jordan? Something's happened to Jordan?"

Delaney took a deep breath. Suddenly he felt hurt, put-upon, ready to let it all spill out of him. "I had an accident."

Now it was her turn—the sharp insuck of breath, the voice gone dead in her throat. "Jordan's hurt, isn't he? Tell me, tell me the worst. Quick! I can't stand it!"

"Nobody's hurt, honey, everybody's okay. I haven't even gone to pick Jordan up yet."

A numb silence, counters clicking, synapses flashing. "Are you all right? Where are you?"

"The Acura dealer. I'm getting the headlight fixed." He glanced up, lowered his voice, Kenny Grissom nowhere in sight: "I hit a man."

"*Hit* a *man?*" There was a flare of anger in her voice. "What are you talking about?"

"A Mexican. At least I think he was a Mexican. Out on the canyon road. I was on my way to the recycler."

"My god. Did you call Jack?"

Jack was Jack Jardine, their friend, neighbor, adviser and lawyer, who also happened to be the president of the Arroyo Blanco Estates Property Owners' Association. "No"—Delaney sighed—"I just got here and I wanted to tell you, to let you know—"

"What are you thinking? Are you out of your mind? Do you have any idea what one of these shyster personal-injury lawyers would do to get hold of something like this? You *hit* a man? Was he hurt? Did you take him to the hospital? Did you call the insurance?"

Delaney tried to gather it all in. She was excitable, Kyra, explosive, her circuits so high-wired she was always on the verge of overload, even when she was asleep. There were no minor issues in her life. "No, listen, Kyra: the guy's okay. I mean, he was just . . . bruised, that was all. He's gone, he went away. I gave him twenty bucks."

"Twenty—?"

And then, before the words could turn to ash in his mouth, it was out: "I told you—he was *Mexican*."

2

HE'D HAD HEADACHES BEFORE—HIS WHOLE LIFE was a headache, his whole stinking worthless *pinche vida*—but never like this. It felt as if a bomb had gone off inside his head, one of those big atomic ones like they dropped on the Japanese, the black roiling clouds pushing and pressing at his skull, no place to go, no release, on and on and on. But that wasn't all—the throb was in his stomach too, and he had to go down on his hands and knees and vomit in the bushes before he'd even got halfway to the camp in the ravine. He felt his breakfast come up—two hard-cooked eggs, half a cup of that weak reheated piss that passed for coffee and a tortilla he'd involuntarily blackened on a stick held over the fire—all of it, every lump and fleck, and then he vomited again. His stomach heaved till he could taste the bile in the back of his throat, and yet he couldn't move, that uncontainable pressure fighting to punch through his ears, and he crouched there for what seemed like hours, hypnotized by a single strand of saliva that dangled endlessly from his lips.

When he got to his feet again, everything had shifted. The shadows had leapt the ravine, the sun was caught in the trees and the indefatigable vulture had been joined by two others. "Yes, sure, come and get me," he muttered, spitting and wincing at the same time, "that's all I am—a worn-out carcass, a walking slab of meat." But Christ in Heaven, how it hurt! He raised a hand to the side of his face and the flesh was stiff and crusted, as if an old board had been nailed to his head. What had happened to him? He was crossing the road, coming back from the grocery after the labor exchange closed—the far grocery, the cheaper one, and what did it matter if it was on the other side of the road? The old man there at the checkout—a *paisano,* he called himself, from Italy—he didn't look at you like you were dirt, like you were going to steal, like you couldn't keep your hands off all the shiny bright packages of this and that, beef jerky and *nachos* and shampoo, little gray-and-black batteries in a plastic sleeve. He'd bought an orange soda, Nehi, and a package of *tortillas* to go with the pinto beans burned into the bottom of the pot . . . and then what? Then he crossed the road.

Yes. And then that pink-faced *gabacho* ran him down with his flaming *gabacho* nose and the little lawyer glasses clenched over the bridge of it. All that steel, that glass, that chrome, that big hot iron engine—it was like a tank coming at him, and his only armor was a cotton shirt and pants and a pair of worn-out *huaraches.* He stared stupidly round him—at the fine tracery of the brush, at the birds lighting in the branches and the treetops below him, at the vultures scrawling their ragged signatures in the sky. América would help him when she got back, she'd brew some tea from manzanita berries to combat the pain, bathe his wounds, cluck her tongue and fuss over him. But he needed to go down the path now, and his hip was bothering him all of a sudden, and the left knee, there, where the trousers were torn.

It hurt. Every step of the way. But he thought of the penitents at Chalma, crawling a mile and a half on their knees, crawling till bone showed through the flesh, and he went on. Twice he fell. The first time he caught himself with his good arm, but the second time he tasted dust and his eyes refused to focus, the whole hot blazing world gone cool and dark all of a sudden, as if he'd been transposed to the bottom of the ocean. He heard a mockingbird then, a whistle and trill in the void, and it was as if it had drowned in sunlight too, and then he was dreaming.

His dreams were real. He wasn't flying through the air or talking with the ghost of his mother or vanquishing his enemies—he was stalled in the garbage dump in Tijuana, stalled at the wire, and América was sick with the *gastro* and he didn't have a cent in the world after the *cholos* and the *coyotes* had got done with him. Sticks and cardboard over his head. The stink of burning dogs in the air. Low man in the pecking order, even at the *dompe. Life is poor here,* an old man—a garbage picker—had told him. *Yes,* he'd said, and he was saying it now, the words on his lips somewhere between the two worlds, *but at least you have garbage.*

América found him at the bottom of the path, bundled in the twilight like a heap of rags. She'd walked nearly eight miles already, down out of the canyon to the highway along the ocean where she could catch the bus to Venice for a sewing job that never materialized, and then back again, and she was like death on two feet. Two dollars and twenty cents down the drain and nothing to show for it. In the morning, at first light, she'd walked along the Coast Highway, and that made her feel good, made her feel like a girl again—the salt smell, people jogging on the beach, the amazing narrow-shouldered houses of the millionaires growing up like mushrooms out of the sand—but the address the Guatemalan woman had given her was worth nothing. All the way there, all the way out in the alien world, a bad neighborhood, drunks in the street, and the building was boarded up, deserted, no back entrance, no sewing machines, no hard-faced boss to stand over her and watch her sweat at three dollars and thirty-five cents an hour, no nothing. She checked the address twice, three times, and then she turned round to retrace her steps and found that the streets had shuffled themselves in the interim, and she knew she was lost.

By lunchtime, she could taste the panic in the back of her throat. For the first time in four months, for the first time since they'd left the South and her village and everything she knew in the world, she was separated from Cándido. She walked in circles and everything looked strange, even when she'd seen it twice, three times over. She didn't speak the language. Black people sauntered up the street with plastic grocery bags dangling from their wrists. She stepped in dog excrement. A *gabacho* sat on the sidewalk with his long hair and begged for change and the sight of him struck her with unholy terror: if he had to beg in his own country, what chance was there for her? But she held on to her six little silvery coins and finally a woman with the *chilango* accent of Mexico City helped her find the bus.

She had to walk back up the canyon in the bleak light of the declining day while the cars swished by her in a lethal hissing chain, and in every one a pair of eyes that screamed, *Get out, get out of here and go back where you belong!*—and how long before one of them tore up the dirt in front of her and the police were standing there demanding her papers? She hurried along, head down, shoulders thrust forward, and when the strip of pavement at the side of the road narrowed to six inches she had to climb over the guardrail and plow through the brush.

Sweat stung her eyes. Burrs and thorns and the smooth hard daggers of the foxtails bit into every step. She couldn't see where she was going. She worried about snakes, spiders, turning her ankle in a ditch. And then the cars began to switch on their lights and she was alone on a terrible howling stage, caught there for everyone to see. Her clothes were soaked through by the time the entrance to the path came into sight, and she ran the last hundred yards, ran for the cover of the brush while the cold beams of light hunted her down, and she had to crouch there in the bushes till her breath came back to her.

The shadows deepened. Birds called to one another. *Swish, swish, swish,* the cars shot by, no more than ten feet away. Any one of them could stop, any one. She listened to the cars and to the air rasping through her lips, to the hiss of the tires and the metallic whine of the engines straining against the grade. It went on for a long time, forever, and the sky grew darker. Finally, when she was sure no one was following her, she started down the path, letting the trees and the shrubs

and the warm breath of the night calm her, hungry now—ravenous—
and so thirsty she could drink up the whole streambed, whether
Cándido thought the water was safe or not.

At first, the thing in the path wasn't anything to concern her—a
shape, a concert of shades, light and dark—and then it was a rock, a pile
of laundry, and finally, a man, her man, sleeping there in the dirt. Her
first thought was that he was drunk—he'd got work and he'd been drinking, drinking cold beer and wine while she struggled through the nine
circles of Hell—and she felt the rage come up in her. No lunch—she
hadn't had a bite since dawn, and then it was only a burned tortilla and
an egg—and nothing to drink even, not so much as a sip of water. What
did he think she was? But then she bent and touched him and she knew
that she was in the worst trouble of her life.

The fire was a little thing, twigs mostly, a few knots the size of a fist,
nothing to attract attention. Cándido lay on a blanket in the sand
beside it, and the flames were like a magic show, snapping and leaping
and throwing the tiniest red rockets into the air round a coil of smoke.
He was dreaming still, dreaming with his eyes open, images shuffled
like cards in a deck till he didn't know what was real and what wasn't.
At the moment he was replaying the past, when he was a boy in Tepoztlán, in the south of Mexico, and his father caught an opossum in
among the chickens and he hit it with a stick—*zas!*—just above the
eyes. The opossum collapsed like a sack of cloth and it lay there, white
in the face and with the naked feet and tail of a giant rat, stunned and
twitching. That was how he felt now, just like that opossum. The pressure in his head had spread to his chest, his groin, his limbs—to every
last flayed fiber of his body—and he had to close his eyes against the
agonizing snap and roar of the fire. They skinned the opossum and
they ate it in a stew with hominy and onions. He could taste it even
now, even here in the North with his body crushed and bleeding and
the fire roaring in his ears—rat, that's what it tasted like, wet rat.

América was cooking something over the fire. Broth. Meat broth. She'd laid him here on the blanket and he'd given her the crumpled bill he'd earned in the hardest way any man could imagine, in the way that would kill him, and she'd gone up the hill to the near store, the one run by the suspicious Chinamen or Koreans or whatever they were, and she'd bought a stew bone with a ragged collar of beef on it, a big plastic bottle of aspirin, rubbing alcohol, a can of *gabacho*-colored Band-Aids and, best of all, a pint of brandy, E & J, to deaden the pain and keep the dreams at bay.

It wasn't working.

The pain was like the central core of that fire, radiating out in every direction, and the dreams—well, now he saw his mother, dead of something, dead of whatever. He was six years old and he thought he'd killed her himself—because he wasn't good enough, because he didn't say his "Hail Marys" and "Our Fathers" and because he fell asleep in church and didn't help with the housework. There was no refrigeration in Tepoztlán, no draining of the blood and pumping in of chemicals, just meat, dead meat. They sealed the coffin in glass because of the smell. He remembered it, huge and awful, like some ship from an ancient sea, set up on two chairs in the middle of the room. And he remembered how he sat up with her long after his father and his sisters and brothers and uncles and aunts and their *compadres* had fallen asleep, and how he'd talked to her through the glass. Her face was like something chipped out of stone. She was in her best dress and her crucifix hung limp at her throat. *Mamá*, he whispered, *I want you to take me with you, I don't want to stay here without you, I want to die and go to the angels too*, and then her dead eyes flashed open on him and her dead lips said, *Go to the devil*, mijo.

"Can you drink this?"

América was kneeling beside him and she held an old styrofoam coffee cup to his lips. The smell of meat was strong in his nostrils. It nauseated him and he pushed her hand away.

"You need a doctor. Your face . . . and here"—she pointed to his hip, then his arm, a gentle touch, the rag soaked in alcohol—"and here."

He didn't need a doctor. He didn't need to put himself in their hands—his bones would knit, his flesh would heal. What would he say to them? How would he pay? And then when they were done with him, the man from *La Migra*—the Immigration—would be standing there with his twenty questions and his clipboard. No, he didn't need a doctor.

The firelight took hold of América's face and she looked old suddenly, older than the girl she was, the girl who'd come to the North with him though she'd never in her life been farther than the next village over, older than his grandmother and her grandmother and any woman that had ever lived in this country or any other. "You have to go to the doctor," she whispered, and the fire snapped and the stars howled over the roof of the canyon. "I'm afraid."

"Afraid?" he echoed, and he reached out to stroke her hand. "Of what? I'm not going to die," he said, but even as he said it, he wasn't so sure.

In the morning, he felt worse—if that was possible. He woke to fog and the inquisition of the birds, and he didn't know where he was. He had no recollection of what had happened to him—nothing, not a glimmer—but he knew that he hurt, hurt all over. He staggered up from the damp blanket and pissed weakly against a rock, and that hurt too. His face was crusted. His urine was red. He stood there a long while, shaking his prick and watching the leaves of the tree above him emerge incrementally from the mist. Then he felt dizzy and went back to lay himself down on the blanket in the sand.

When he woke again, the mist had burned off and the sun stood directly overhead. There was a woman beside him, black eyes bleeding through a wide Indian face framed in blacker hair, and she looked familiar, terrifically familiar, as familiar as the *huaraches* on his feet.

"What's my name?" she asked, her face leaning anxiously into his. "Who are you? Do you know where you are?"

He knew the language and the voice, its rhythms and inflections, and he understood the questions perfectly. The only problem was, he couldn't answer them. Who was she? He knew her, of course he did, but no name came readily to his lips. And what was even stranger was the question of his own identity—how could he not know himself? He began to speak, began to feel the shape of the words on his lips—*Yo soy*, I am—but it was as if a cloud had suddenly obscured the sun and the words were hidden in darkness. *Where are you?* That one he could answer, that was easy. "Abroad in the wide world," he said, grinning suddenly.

América told him later that he'd been out of his senses for three hours and more, gibbering and raving like one of the inmates of the asylum on Hidalgo Street. He gave a speech to the President of the United States, shouted out snatches of songs popular twenty years ago, spoke in a whisper to his dead mother. He chanted, snarled, sobbed, screeched like a pullet with five fingers clamped round its throat; and finally, exhausted, he'd fallen into a deep trancelike sleep. América was mortified. She cried when he couldn't say her name, cried when he wouldn't wake up, cried through the long morning, the interminable afternoon and the eternal night. He slept on, inanimate as a corpse but for the breath scratching through his ruined nostrils.

But then, in the heat of the afternoon on the second day, when she'd lost all hope and could think only of forcing her head under the surface of the creek till she drowned herself or leaping from one of the high crags and smashing her body on the rocks below, he surprised her. "América," he called suddenly—from out of nowhere, from sleep, from the husk he'd become—"are there any of those beans left?"

And that was that. The fever was gone. He was lucid. He remembered the accident, the *tortillas,* the twenty dollars the *gabacho* had given him. And when she came to him with wet cheeks and threw her arms round his neck and sobbed her heart out, he knew everything about her: she was seventeen years old and as perfect and beautiful as an egg in its shell; she was América, hope of the future, his wife, his love, mother-to-be of his first child, the son who was even now taking shape in that secret place inside of her.

She had to help him to his feet so he could find a spot to relieve himself, and he needed her shoulder to make his way to the blanket again, but at least he was back among the living. After that, he ate— *tortillas* out of the package, pinto beans, the broth she'd been simmering for two days to keep it from going bad. He ate slowly, thoughtfully, one spoonful at a time, but he kept it down and that was a good sign. Still, the pain never left him—it was sharp and unremitting, like a nerve rubbed raw—and he fought it down with the chalky little tablets of aspirin, chewing them by the handful, his jaws working ruminatively beneath his battered cheekbone.

For the rest of the afternoon he sat in the shade on the blanket and considered the situation, while América, exhausted from her vigil, slept with her head in his lap. He'd suffered a concussion, that much was clear, and his left cheekbone was crushed, staved in like the flesh of a rotting pumpkin. He couldn't see himself—there was no mirror out here in their crude camp—but his fingers told him how ugly his face was. A hard crusted scab ran from his jaw to his hairline, his left eye was swollen shut and his nose was tender to the touch—he must have looked like a fighter on the losing end of a fifteen-round bout or one of those monsters that crawl out of moonlit graves in the movies. But that was all right. He would live. And who cared how ugly he was as long as he could work?

No, his face was nothing—it was the rest of him he was worried about. His left arm didn't seem to want to do anything—it just hung there uselessly in the sling América had made from his shirt—and his hip was bothering him, drilling him with pain every time he got to his feet. He wondered if there was a fracture somewhere in the socket or the ridge of bone above it. Or if he'd torn a ligament or something. Any way you looked at it, he couldn't work, not for the time being— hell, he could barely stand, and that was his bad luck, his stinking *mala suerte* that had got him robbed at the border and thrown up against the bumper of some rich man's car. But if he couldn't work, how would they eat?

And then the thing happened that he didn't want to happen, the thing he'd been dreading: América got up at first light on the fourth day after the accident and tried to slip off up the hill before he'd aroused himself. It was some sixth sense that made him wake when he did—she was silent as a cat, so he couldn't have heard her. She stood off a bit in the mist, insubstantial in the pale rinsed-out light, and he saw her arms go up over her head as she shrugged into her dress, the good one, the one with the blue flowers against the beige background that she wore when she wanted to make a good impression. But oh, she was silent, pantomiming the motions of a woman getting dressed. *"¿Adónde vas, mi vida?"* he said. "Where are you going, my love?"

"Hush," she whispered. "Go back to sleep."

The dew lay heavy on the blanket, on his shirt and the sling that cradled his arm. The day breathed in and out, just once, and then he repeated himself: "I said, where are you going? Don't make me ask again."

"Nowhere. Don't trouble yourself."

"You haven't started the fire," he said.

No answer. The mist, the trees, the birds. He heard the sound of the creek running beneath its mats of algae to the sea, and in the background, the faint automotive hum of the first commuters coming down the canyon to work. A crow called out just behind them, harsh and immediate. And then she was there, kneeling before him on the blanket, her face fresh-scrubbed, hair brushed, in her good dress. "Cándido, *querido,* listen," she said, milking his eyes, "I'm going up the road to the labor exchange to see if I can't . . . see if I might . . . find something."

Find something. It was a slap in the face. What was she saying— that he was useless, impotent, an old man fit for the rocking chair? *Viejo,* his friends called him because of the gray in his hair, though he was only thirty-three, and it was like a prophecy. What good was he? He'd taken América from her father so they could have a better life, so they could live in the North, where it was green and lush the year round and the avocados rotted on the ground, and everyone, even the poorest, had a house, a car and a TV—and now he couldn't even put food in her mouth. Worse: *she* was going to earn *his* keep.

"No," he said, and his tone was final, clamped round the harshness of the negative like a set of pliers, "I won't have it. I didn't want you to go out the other day on that wild-goose chase just because some woman gave you a tip—and you got yourself lost, didn't you? Admit it. You were nearly separated from me—forever—and how would you expect me to find you, eh? How?"

"I'm not going to the city," she said quietly. "Just to the exchange. Just up the street."

He considered that scenario—his wife, a barefoot girl from the country who didn't know a thing about the world, out there among all those men, those lowlifes who'd do anything for a buck—or a woman—and he didn't like it. He knew them. Street bums who couldn't keep their hands in their pockets, sweaty *campesinos* from Guerrero and Chiapas who'd grown up abusing their livestock, *indios* from Guatemala and Honduras: coochie-coochie and hey baby and then the kissing noises. At least in the garment trade she'd be among other women—but up there, at the labor exchange, she'd be like a pot of honey with a hundred bees swarming round her.

They'd been living in the canyon three weeks now—there was no way he would expose her to life on the streets, to downtown L.A. or even Van Nuys—and though they didn't have a roof over their heads and nothing was settled, he'd felt happy for the first time since they'd left home. The water was still flowing, the sand was clean and the sky overhead was his, all his, and there was nobody to dispute him for it. He remembered his first trip North, hotbedding in a two-room apartment in Echo Park with thirty-two other men, sleeping in shifts and lining up on the streetcorner for work, the reek of the place, the roaches and the nits. Down here was different. Down here they were safe from all the filth and sickness of the streets, from *la chota*—the police—and the Immigration. Twice he'd gotten work, at three dollars an hour, no questions asked—once from a contractor who was putting up a fieldstone wall and then from a *rico* in a Jaguar who needed a couple of men to clear the brush from a ravine out back of his house. And each morning when he went out looking, not knowing whether he'd be back at noon or after dark, he'd warned América to douse the fire and keep out of sight.

He hadn't wanted to frighten her, but he knew what would happen if any of those *vagos* from above discovered her down here while he was away. It would be just like that girl in the dump at Tijuana. He could see her now, skinny legs, eyes like pits. She was a child, twelve years old, and her parents poor people who were out working all day, sifting through the mountains of trash with broomsticks fitted with a bent nail at one end, and the drunks in the place had come after her. The girl's parents had a shack made out of wooden pallets nailed together, a surprisingly sturdy little thing set amid a clutter of tumble-down shanties and crude lean-tos, and when they went off in the morning, they padlocked the girl inside. But those animals—they howled outside the door and pounded at the walls to get at her, and nobody did a thing. Nobody except Cándido. Three times he snatched up a length of pipe and drove them away from the shack—junkies, *cementeros*, bottle suckers—and he could hear the girl sobbing inside. Twelve years old. One afternoon they managed to spring the lock, and by the time Cándido got there, it was all over. The sons of bitches. He knew what they were like, and he vowed he'd never let América out of his sight if he could help it, not till they had a real house in a real neighborhood with laws and respect and human dignity.

"No," he said. "I can't let you do it. I was worried sick the whole day you were gone—and look at the bad luck it brought us." He patted his arm in its sling by way of illustration. "Besides, there are no jobs for women there, only for men with strong backs. They want *braceros*, not maids."

"Listen," she said, and her voice was quiet and determined, "we have maybe a cup of rice left, half a twelve-ounce sack of dry beans, six corn *tortillas*—no eggs, no milk. We have no matches to start the fire. No vegetables, no fruit. Do you know what I would do for a mango now—or even an orange?"

"All right," he snarled, "all right," and he pushed himself up from the blanket and stood shakily, all his weight on his good leg. The aspirin bottle was nearly empty, but he shook half a dozen tablets into his palm and ground them between his teeth. "I'll go myself. Nobody can tell me I can't feed my own wife—"

She wasn't having it. She sprang to her feet and took hold of his forearm in a grip so fierce and unyielding it surprised him. "Maybe tomorrow," she said. "Maybe the next day. What happened to you would have killed an ordinary man. You rest. You'll feel better. Give it a day or two."

He was woozy on his feet. His head felt as if it were stuffed with cotton. The crow mocked him from an invisible perch. "And what do you plan to do for work?"

She grinned and made a muscle with her right arm. "I can do anything a man can do."

He tried for a stern and forbidding look, but it tortured his face and he had to let it go. She was tiny, like a child—she *was* a child. She couldn't have weighed more than a hundred and five pounds, and the baby hadn't begun to show yet, not at all. What could she hope to accomplish at a labor exchange?

"Pick lettuce," she said. "Or fruit maybe."

He had to laugh. He couldn't help himself. "Lettuce? Fruit? This isn't Bakersfield, this is L.A. There's no fruit here. No cotton, no nothing." His face tightened on him and he winced. "There's nothing here but houses, houses by the millions, roof after roof as far as you can see . . ."

She scratched at a mosquito bite on her arm, but her eyes were alive, shining with the image, and her lips compressed round a private smile. "I want one of those houses," she said. "A clean white one made out of lumber that smells like the mountains, with a gas range and a refrigerator, and maybe a little yard so you can plant a garden and make a place for the chickens. That's what you promised me, didn't you?"

She wanted. Of course she wanted. Everybody who'd stayed behind to dry up and die in Tepoztlán wanted too—hell, all of Morelos, all of Mexico and the Indian countries to the south, they all wanted, and what else was new? A house, a yard, maybe a TV and a car too—nothing fancy, no palaces like the *gringos* built—just four walls and a roof. Was that so much to ask?

He watched her lips—pouting, greedy lips, lips he wanted to kiss and own. "Well?" she demanded, and she wasn't teasing now, wasn't bantering or joking. "Didn't you?"

He'd promised. Sure he had. He'd held up the lure of all those things, washing machines, vacuum cleaners, the glitter of the North like a second Eden; sure, a young girl like her and an old man like himself with gray in his mustache—what else was he going to tell her? That they would get robbed at the border and live under two boards at the dump till he could make enough on the streetcorner to get them across? That they'd hide out like rats in a hole and live on a blanket beside a stream that would run dry in a month? That he'd be hammered down on the road so he could barely stand or make water or even think straight? He didn't know what to say.

She let go of his arm and turned away from him. He watched the morning mist enclose her as she began to pick her way over the boulders that cluttered the ravine like broken teeth. When she got to the foot of the trail she swung round and stood there a moment, the mist boiling beneath her. "Maybe somebody will need a floor mopped or a stove cleaned," she said, the words drifting down to him over the hum of the invisible cars above.

It took him a long moment, and when he spoke it was as if the air had been knocked out of him. "Yeah," he said, sinking back down into the blanket. "Maybe."

3

HIGH UP THE CANYON, NESTLED IN A FAN-SHAPED depression dug out of the side of the western ridge by the action of some long-forgotten stream, lay the subdivision known as Arroyo Blanco Estates. It was a private community, comprising a golf course, ten tennis courts, a community center and some two hundred and fifty homes, each set on one-point-five acres and strictly conforming to the covenants, conditions and restrictions set forth in the 1973 articles of incorporation. The houses were all of the Spanish Mission style, painted in one of three prescribed shades of white, with orange tile roofs. If you wanted to paint your house sky-blue or Provençal-pink with lime-green shutters, you were perfectly welcome to move into the San Fernando Valley or to Santa Monica or anywhere else you chose, but if you bought into Arroyo Blanco Estates, your house would be white and your roof orange.

Delaney Mossbacher made his home in one of these Spanish Mission houses (floor plan #A227C, Rancho White with Navajo trim), along with his second wife, Kyra, her son, Jordan, her matching Dandie Dinmont terriers, Osbert and Sacheverell, and her Siamese cat, Dame Edith. On this particular morning, the morning that Cándido Rincón began to feel he'd lost control of his wife, Delaney was up at seven, as usual, to drip Kyra's coffee, feed Jordan his fruit, granola and hi-fiber bar and let Osbert and Sacheverell out into the yard to perform their matinal functions. He hadn't forgotten his unfortunate encounter with Cándido four days earlier—the thought of it still made his stomach clench—but the needs and wants and minor irritations of daily life had begun to push it into the background. At the moment, his attention was focused entirely on getting through the morning ritual with his customary speed and efficiency. He was nothing if not efficient.

He made a sort of game of it, counting the steps it took him to shut the windows against the coming day's heat, empty yesterday's coffee grounds into the mulch bucket, transform two kiwis, an orange, apple, banana and a handful of Bing cherries into Jordan's medley of fresh fruit, and set the table for two. He skated across the tile floor to the dishwasher, flung open the cabinets, rocketed the plates and cutlery into position on the big oak table, all the while keeping an eye on the coffee, measuring out two bowls of dog food and juicing the oranges he'd plucked from the tree in the courtyard.

Typically, he stole a moment out in the courtyard to breathe in the cool of the morning and listen to the scrub jays wake up the neighborhood, but today he was in a rush and the only sound that penetrated his consciousness was a strange excited yelp from one of the dogs— they must have found something in the fenced-in yard behind the house, a squirrel or a gopher maybe—and then he was back in the kitchen, squeezing oranges. That was what he did, every morning, regular as clockwork: squeeze oranges. After which he would dash round the house gathering up Jordan's homework, his backpack, lunchbox and baseball cap, while Kyra sipped her coffee and washed down her twelve separate vitamin and mineral supplements with half a glass of fresh-squeezed orange juice. Then it was time to drive Jordan to school, while Kyra applied her makeup, wriggled into a form-fitting skirt with matching jacket and propelled her Lexus over the crest of the canyon and into Woodland Hills, where she was the undisputed volume leader at Mike Bender Realty, Inc. And then, finally, Delaney would head back home, have a cup of herbal tea and two slices of wheat toast, dry, and let the day settle in around him.

Unless there was an accident on the freeway or a road crew out picking up or setting down their ubiquitous plastic cones, he would be back at home and sitting at his desk by nine. This was the moment he lived for, the moment his day really began. Unfailingly, no matter what pressures were brought to bear on him or what emergencies arose, he allotted the next four hours to his writing—four hours during which he could let go of the world around him, his fingers grazing lightly over the keyboard, the green glow of the monitor bathing him in its hypnotic light. He took the phone off the hook, pulled the shades and crept into the womb of language.

There, in the silence of the empty house, Delaney worked out the parameters of his monthly column for *Wide Open Spaces*, a naturalist's observations of the life blooming around him day by day, season by season. He called it "Pilgrim at Topanga Creek" in homage to Annie Dillard, and while he couldn't pretend to her mystical connection to things, or her verbal virtuosity either, he did feel that he stood apart from his fellow men and women, that he saw more deeply and felt more passionately—particularly about nature. And every day, from nine to one, he had the opportunity to prove it.

Of course, some days went better than others. He tried to confine himself to the flora and fauna of Topanga Canyon and the surrounding mountains, but increasingly he found himself brooding over the fate of the pupfish, the Florida manatee and the spotted owl, the ocelot, the pine marten, the panda. And how could he ignore the larger trends—overpopulation, desertification, the depletion of the seas and the forests, global warming and loss of habitat? We were all right in America, sure, but it was crazy to think you could detach yourself from the rest of the world, the world of starvation and loss and the steady relentless degradation of the environment. Five and a half billion people chewing up the resources of the planet like locusts, and only seventy-three California condors left in all the universe.

It gave him pause. It depressed him. There were days when he worked himself into such a state he could barely lift his fingers to the keys, but fortunately the good days outnumbered them, the days when he celebrated his afternoon hikes through the chaparral and into the ravines of the mist-hung mountains, and that was what people wanted—celebration, not lectures, not the strident call to ecologic arms, not the death knell and the weeping and gnashing of environmental teeth. The world was full of bad news. Why contribute more?

The sun had already begun to burn off the haze by the time Jordan scuffed into the kitchen, the cat at his heels. Jordan was six years old, dedicated to Nintendo, superheroes and baseball cards, though as far as Delaney could see he had no interest whatever in the game of baseball beyond possessing the glossy cardboard images of the players. He favored his mother facially and in the amazing lightness of his hair, which was so pale as to be nearly translucent. He might have been big for his age, or maybe he was small—Delaney had nothing to compare him to.

"Kiwi," Jordan said, thumping into his seat at the table, and that was all. Whether this was an expression of approval or distaste, Delaney couldn't tell. From the living room came the electronic voice of the morning news: *Thirty-seven Chinese nationals were drowned early today when a smuggler's ship went aground just east of the Golden Gate Bridge . . .* Outside, beyond the windows, there was another yelp from the dogs.

Jordan began to rotate his spoon in the bowl of fruit, a scrape and clatter accompanied by the moist sounds of mastication. Delaney, his back to the table, was scrubbing the counter in the vicinity of the stove, though any splashes of cooking oil or spatters of sauce must have been purely imaginary since he hadn't actually cooked anything. He scrubbed for the love of scrubbing. "Okay, buckaroo," he called over his shoulder, "you've got two choices today as far as your hi-fiber bar is concerned: Cranberry Nut and Boysenberry Supreme. What'll it be?"

From a mouth laden with kiwi: "Papaya Coconut."

"You got the last one yesterday."

No response.

"So what'll it be?"

Kyra insisted on the full nutritional slate for her son every morning—fresh fruit, granola with skim milk and brewer's yeast, hi-fiber bar. The child needed roughage. Vitamins. Whole grains. And breakfast, for a growing child at least, was the most important meal of the day, the foundation of all that was to come. That was how she felt. And while Delaney recognized a touch of the autocratic and perhaps even fanatic in the regimen, he by and large subscribed to it. He and Kyra had a lot in common, not only temperamentally, but in terms of their beliefs and ideals too—that was what had attracted them to each other in the first place. They were both perfectionists, for one thing. They abhorred clutter. They were joggers, nonsmokers, social drinkers, and if not full-blown vegetarians, people who were conscious of their intake of animal fats. Their memberships included the Sierra Club, Save the Children, the National Wildlife Federation and the Democratic Party. They preferred the contemporary look to Early American or kitsch. In religious matters, they were agnostic.

Delaney's question remained unanswered, but he was used to cajoling Jordan over his breakfast. He tiptoed across the room to hover behind the boy, who was playing with his spoon and chanting something under his breath. "Rookie card, rookie card," Jordan was saying, dipping into his granola without enthusiasm. "No looking now," Delaney warned, seductively tapping a foil-wrapped bar on either side of the boy's thin wilted neck, "—right hand or left?"

Jordan reached up with his left hand, as Delaney knew he would, fastening on the Boysenberry Supreme bar just as Kyra, hunched over the weight of two boxes of hand-addressed envelopes—Excelsior, 500 Count—clattered into the kitchen in her heels. She made separate kissing motions in the direction of her husband and son, then slid into her chair, poured herself half a cup of coffee lightened with skim milk—for the calcium—and began sifting purposively through the envelopes.

"Why can't I have Sugar Pops or Honey Nut Cheerios like other kids? Or bacon and eggs?" Jordan pinched his voice. "Mom? Why can't I?"

Kyra gave the stock response—"You're not other kids, that's why"—and Delaney was taken back to his own childhood, a rainy night in the middle of an interminable winter, a plate of liver, onions and boiled potatoes before him.

"I hate granola," Jordan countered, and it was like a Noh play, timeless ritual.

"It's good for you."

"Yeah, sure." Jordan made an exaggerated slurping sound, sucking the milk through his teeth.

"Think of all the little children who have nothing to eat," Kyra said without looking up, and Jordan, sticking to the script, came right back at her: "Let's send them this."

Now she looked up. "Eat," she said, and the drama was over.

"Busy day?" Delaney murmured, setting Kyra's orange juice down beside the newspaper and unscrewing the childproof caps of the sturdy plastic containers that held her twelve separate vitamin and mineral supplements. He did the little things for her—out of love and consideration, sure, but also in acknowledgment of the fact that she was the chief breadwinner here, the one who went off to the office while he stayed home. Which was all right by him. He had none of those juvenile macho hang-ups about role reversal and who wore the pants and all of that—real estate was her life, and he was more than happy to help her with it, so long as he got his four hours a day at the keyboard.

Kyra lifted her eyebrows, but didn't look up. She was tucking what looked to be a small white packet into each of the envelopes in succession. "Busy?" she echoed. "Busy isn't the word for it. I'm presenting two offers this morning, both of them real low-ball, I've got a buyer with cold feet on that Calabasas property—with escrow due to close in eight days—and I'm scheduled for an open house on the Via Escobar place at one . . . is that the dogs I hear? What are they barking at?"

Delaney shrugged. Jordan had shucked the foil from his hi-fiber bar and was drifting toward the TV room with it—which meant he was going to be late for school if Delaney didn't hustle him out of there within the next two minutes. The cat, as yet unfed, rubbed up against Delaney's leg. "I don't know," he said. "They've been yapping since I let them out. Must be a squirrel or something. Or maybe Jack's dog got loose again and he's out there peeing on the fence and driving them into a frenzy."

"Anyway," Kyra went on, "it's going to be hell. And it's Carla Bayer's birthday, so after work a bunch of us—don't you think this is a cute idea?" She held up one of the packets she'd been stuffing the envelopes with. It was a three-by-five seed packet showing a spray of flowers and printed with the legend *Forget-Me-Not, Compliments of Kyra Menaker-Mossbacher, Mike Bender Realty, Inc.*

"Yeah, I guess," he murmured, wiping at an imaginary speck on the counter. This was her way of touching base with her clients. Every month or so, usually in connection with a holiday, she went through her mailing list (consisting of anyone she'd ever sold to or for, whether they'd relocated to Nome, Singapore or Irkutsk or passed on into the Great Chain of Being) and sent a small reminder of her continued existence and willingness to deal. She called it "keeping the avenues open." Delaney reached down to stroke the cat. "But can't one of the secretaries do this sort of thing for you?"

"It's the personal touch that counts—and moves property. How many times do I have to tell you?"

There was a silence, during which Delaney became aware of the cartoon jingle that had replaced the voice of the news in the other room, and then, just as he was clearing Jordan's things from the table and checking the digital display on the microwave for the time—7:32—the morning fell apart. Or no: it was torn apart by a startled breathless shriek that rose up from beyond the windows as if out of some primal dream. This was no yip, no yelp, no bark or howl—this was something final and irrevocable, a predatory scream that took the varnish off their souls, and it froze them in place. They listened, horrified, as it rose in pitch until it choked off as suddenly as it had begun.

The aftereffect was electric. Kyra bolted up out of her chair, knocking over her coffee cup and scattering envelopes; the cat darted between Delaney's legs and vanished; Delaney dropped the plate on the floor and groped for the counter like a blind man. And then Jordan was coming through the doorway on staccato feet, his face opened up like a pale nocturnal flower: "Delaney," he gasped, "Delaney, something, something—"

But Delaney was already in motion. He flung open the door and shot through the courtyard, head down, rounding the corner of the house just in time to see a dun-colored blur scaling the six-foot chain-link fence with a tense white form clamped in its jaws. His brain decoded the image: a coyote had somehow managed to get into the enclosure and seize one of the dogs, and there it was, wild nature, up and over the fence as if this were some sort of circus act. Shouting to hear himself, shouting nonsense, Delaney charged across the yard as the remaining dog (Osbert? Sacheverell?) cowered in the corner and the dun blur melded with the buckwheat, chamise and stiff high grass of the wild hillside that gave onto the wild mountains beyond.

He didn't stop to think. In two bounds he was atop the fence and dropping to the other side, absently noting the paw prints in the dust, and then he was tearing headlong through the undergrowth, leaping rocks and shrubs and dodging the spines of the yucca plants clustered like breastworks across the slope. He was running, that was all he knew. Branches raked him like claws. Burrs bit into his ankles. He kept going, pursuing a streak of motion, the odd flash of white: now he saw it, now he didn't. "Hey!" he shouted. "Hey, goddamnit!"

The hillside sloped sharply upward, rising through the colorless scrub to a clump of walnut trees and jagged basalt outcroppings that looked as if they'd poked through the ground overnight. He saw the thing suddenly, the pointed snout and yellow eyes, the high stiff leggy gait as it struggled with its burden, and it was going straight up and into the trees. He shouted again and this time the shout was answered from below. Glancing over his shoulder, he saw that Kyra was coming up the hill with her long jogger's strides, in blouse, skirt and stocking feet. Even at this distance he could recognize the look on her face—the grim set of her jaw, the flaring eyes and clamped mouth that spelled doom for whoever got in her way, whether it was a stranger who'd locked his dog in a car with the windows rolled up or the hapless seller who refused a cash-out bid. She was coming, and that spurred him on. If he could only stay close the coyote would have to drop the dog, it would have to.

By the time he reached the trees his throat was burning. Sweat stung his eyes and his arms were striped with nicks and scratches. There was no sign of the dog and he pushed on through the trees to where the slope fell away to the feet of the next hill beyond it. The brush was thicker here—six feet high and so tightly interlaced it would have taken a machete to get through it in places—and he knew, despite the drumming in his ears and the glandular rush that had him pacing and whirling and clenching and unclenching his fists, that it was looking bad. Real bad. There were a thousand bushes out there— five thousand, ten thousand—and the coyote could be crouched under any one of them.

It was watching him even now, he knew it, watching him out of slit wary eyes as he jerked back and forth, frantically scanning the mute clutter of leaf, branch and thorn, and the thought infuriated him. He shouted again, hoping to flush it out. But the coyote was too smart for him. Ears pinned back, jaws and forepaws stifling its prey, it could lie there, absolutely motionless, for hours. "Osbert!" he called out suddenly, and his voice trailed off into a hopeless bleat. "Sacheverell!"

The poor dog. It couldn't have defended itself from a rabbit. Delaney stood on his toes, strained his neck, poked angrily through the nearest bush. Long low shafts of sunlight fired the leaves in an indifferent display, as they did every morning, and he looked into the illuminated depths of that bush and felt desolate suddenly, empty, cored out with loss and helplessness.

"Osbert!" The sound seemed to erupt from him, as if he couldn't control his vocal cords. "Here, boy! Come!" Then he shouted Sacheverell's name, over and over, but there was no answer except for a distant cry from Kyra, who seemed to be way off to his left now.

All at once he wanted to smash something, tear the bushes out of the ground by their roots. This didn't have to happen. It didn't. If it wasn't for those idiots leaving food out for the coyotes as if they were nothing more than sheep with bushy tails and eyeteeth . . . and he'd warned them, time and again. You can't be heedless of your environment. You can't. Just last week he'd found half a bucket of Kentucky Fried Chicken out back of the Dagolian place—waxy red-and-white-striped cardboard with a portrait of the grinning chicken-killer himself smiling large—and he'd stood up at the bimonthly meeting of the property owners' association to say something about it. They wouldn't even listen. Coyotes, gophers, yellow jackets, rattlesnakes even—they were a pain in the ass, sure, but nature was the least of their problems. It was humans they were worried about. The Salvadorans, the Mexicans, the blacks, the gangbangers and taggers and carjackers they read about in the Metro section over their bran toast and coffee. That's why they'd abandoned the flatlands of the Valley and the hills of the Westside to live up here, outside the city limits, in the midst of all this scenic splendor.

Coyotes? Coyotes were quaint. Little demi-dogs out there howling at the sunset, another amenity like the oaks, the chaparral and the views. No, all Delaney's neighbors could talk about, back and forth and on and on as if it were the key to all existence, was gates. A gate, specifically. To be erected at the main entrance and manned by a twenty-four-hour guard to keep out those very gangbangers, taggers and carjackers they'd come here to escape. Sure. And now poor Osbert— or Sacheverell—was nothing more than breakfast.

The fools. The idiots.

Delaney picked up a stick and began to beat methodically at the bushes.

The Arroyo Blanco Community Center was located on a knoll overlooking Topanga Canyon Boulevard and the private road, Arroyo Blanco Drive, that snaked off it and wound its way through the oaks and into the grid of streets that comprised the subdivision. It was a single-story white stucco building with an orange tile roof, in the Spanish Mission style, and it featured a kitchen, wet bar, stage, P.A. system and seating for two hundred. The hall was full—standing room only—by the time Delaney arrived. He'd been delayed because Kyra had been late getting home from work, and since it was the maid's day off, there'd been no one to watch Jordan.

Kyra was in a state. She'd come in the door looking like a refugee, her eyes reddened and a tissue pinned to the tip of her reddened nose, grieving for Sacheverell (Sacheverell it was: she'd been able to identify the surviving dog as Osbert by means of an indisputable mole clinging to his underlip). For an hour or more that morning she'd helped Delaney beat the bushes, frantic, tearful, her breath coming in ragged gasps—she'd had those dogs forever, long before she'd met Delaney, before Jordan was born even—but finally, reluctantly, she'd given it up and gone off to work, where she was already late for her ten o'clock. She'd changed her clothes, reapplied her makeup, comforted Jordan as best she could and dropped him off at school, leaving Delaney with the injunction to find the dog at all cost. Every half hour throughout the day she called him for news, and though he had news by noon— grim, definitive news, news wrapped up in half a dozen paper towels and sequestered even now in the pocket of his windbreaker—he kept it from her, figuring she'd had enough of a jolt for one day. When she came home he held her for a long moment, murmuring the soft consolatory things she needed to hear, and then she went in to Jordan, who'd been sent home early from school with chills and a fever. It was a sad scene. Just before he left for the meeting, Delaney looked in on them, mother and son, huddled in Jordan's narrow bed with Osbert and Dame Edith, the cat, looking like survivors of a shipwreck adrift on a raft.

Delaney edged in at the rear of the auditorium beside a couple he didn't recognize. The man was in his forties, but he had the hips and shoulders of a college athlete and looked as if he'd just come back from doing something heroic. The woman, six feet tall at least, was around Kyra's age—mid-thirties, he guessed—and she was dressed in black Lycra shorts and a USC jersey. She leaned into her husband like a sapling leaning into a rock ledge. Delaney couldn't help noticing the way the shorts cradled the woman's buttocks in a flawless illustration of form and function, but then he recalled the thing in his pocket and looked up into a sea of heads and the harsh white rinse of the fluorescent lights.

Jack Jardine was up on the dais, along with Jack Cherrystone, the association's secretary, and Linda Portis, the treasurer. The regularly scheduled meeting, the one at which Delaney had stood to warn his neighbors of the dangers of feeding the local fauna, had adjourned past twelve after prolonged debate on the gate issue, and Jack had convened tonight's special session to put it to a vote. Under normal circumstances, Delaney would have stayed home and lost himself in John Muir or Edwin Way Teale, but these were not normal circumstances. Not that he was indifferent to the issue—the gate was an absurdity, intimidating and exclusionary, antidemocratic even, and he'd spoken against it privately—but to his mind it was a fait accompli. His neighbors were overwhelmingly for it, whipped into a reactionary frenzy by the newspapers and the eyewitness news, and he didn't relish being one of the few dissenting voices, a crank like Rudy Hernandez, who liked to hear himself talk and would argue any side of any issue till everyone in the room was ready to rise up and throttle him. The gate was going up and there was nothing Delaney could do about it. But he was here. Uncomfortably here. Here because tonight he had a private agendum, an agendum that lay hard against his hip in the lower pocket of his windbreaker, and his throat went dry at the thought of it.

Someone spoke to the question, but Delaney was so wound up in his thoughts he didn't register what was being said. There would be discussion, and then a vote, and for the rest of his days he'd have to feel like a criminal driving into his own community, excusing himself to some jerk in a crypto-fascist uniform, making special arrangements every time a friend visited or a package needed to be delivered. He thought of the development he'd grown up in, the fenceless expanse of lawns, the shared space, the deep lush marshy woods where he'd first discovered ferns, frogs, garter snakes, the whole shining envelope of creation. There was nothing like that anymore. Now there were fences. Now there were gates.

"The chair recognizes Doris Obst," Jack Jardine said, his voice riding out over the currents of the room as if he were singing, as if everyone else spoke prose and he alone spoke poetry.

The woman who rose from a seat in the left-front of the auditorium was of indeterminate age. Her movements were brisk and the dress clung to the shape of her as if it had been painted on, yet her hair was gray and her skin the dead bleached merciless white of the bond paper Delaney used for business letters. Delaney had never laid eyes on her before, and the realization, coupled with the fact that he didn't seem to recognize any of the people he was standing among, produced a faint uneasy stirring of guilt. He should be more rigorous about attending these meetings, he told himself, he really should.

". . . the cost factor," Doris Obst was saying in a brooding, almost masculine tenor, "because I'm sure there isn't a person in this room that doesn't feel our fees are already astronomical, and I'm just wondering if the board's cost analysis is accurate, or if we're going to be hit with special assessments down the line . . ."

"Jim Shirley," Jack sang, and Doris Obst sank into her seat even as a man rose in the rear, as if they were keys of the same instrument. To his consternation, Delaney didn't recognize this man either.

"What about the break-ins?" Jim Shirley demanded, an angry tug to his voice. There was an answering murmur from the crowd, cries of umbrage and assent. Jim Shirley stood tall, a big bearded man in his fifties who looked as if he'd been inflated with a bicycle pump. "Right on my block—Via Dichosa?—there've been two houses hit in the last month alone. The Caseys lost something like fifty thousand dollars' worth of Oriental rugs while they were away in Europe, and their home entertainment center too—not to mention their brand-new Nissan pickup. I don't know how many of you sitting here tonight are familiar with the modus operandi, but what the thieves do is typically they pry open the garage door—there's always a little give in these automatic openers—then they take their sweet time, load your valuables into your own car and then drive off as if they were entitled to it. At the Caseys' they even had the gall to broil half a dozen lobster tails from the freezer and wash them down with a couple bottles of Perrier-Jouët."

A buzz went through the crowd, thick with ferment and anger. Even Delaney felt himself momentarily distracted from the bloody evidence in his pocket. Crime? Up here? Wasn't that what they'd come here to escape? Wasn't that the point of the place? All of a sudden, the gate didn't sound like such a bad idea.

Delaney was startled when the man beside him—the athlete— thrust up his arm and began to speak even before Jack Jardine had a chance to officially recognize him. "I can't believe what I'm hearing," the man said, and his long-legged wife nuzzled closer to him, her eyes shining with pride and moral authority. "If we'd wanted a gated community we would have moved to Hidden Hills or Westlake, but we didn't. We wanted an open community, freedom to come and go— and not just for those of us privileged enough to be able to live here, but for anyone—any citizen—rich or poor. I don't know, but I cut my teeth on the sixties, and it goes against my grain to live in a community that closes its streets to somebody just because they don't have as fancy a car as mine or as big a house. I mean, what's next—wrist bracelets for I.D.? Metal detectors?"

Jack Cherrystone made an impatient gesture at the president's elbow, and Jack recognized him with a nod. "Who are we kidding here?" he demanded in a voice that thundered through the speakers like the voice of God on High. Jack Cherrystone was a little man, barely five and a half feet tall, but he had the world's biggest voice. He made his living in Hollywood, doing movie trailers, his voice rumbling across America like a fleet of trucks, portentous, fruity, hysterical. Millions of people in theaters from San Pedro to Bangor churned in their seats as they watched the flashing images of sex and mayhem explode across the screen and felt the assault of Jack Cherrystone's thundering wallop of a voice, and his friends and neighbors at Arroyo Blanco Estates sat up a little straighter when he spoke. "I'm as liberal as anybody in this room—my father chaired Adlai Stevenson's campaign committee, for christsakes—but I say we've got to put an end to this."

A pause. The whole room was riveted on the little man on the dais. Delaney broke out in a sweat.

"I'd like to open my arms to everybody in the world, no matter how poor they are or what country they come from; I'd like to leave my back door open and the screen door unlatched, the way it was when I was a kid, but you know as well as I do that those days are past." He shook his head sadly. "L.A. stinks. The world stinks. Why kid ourselves? That's why we're here, that's why we got out. You want to save the world, go to Calcutta and sign on with Mother Teresa. I say that gate is as necessary, as vital, essential and un-do-withoutable as the roofs over our heads and the dead bolts on our doors. Face up to it," he rumbled. "Get real, as my daughter says. Really, truly, people: what's the debate?"

Delaney found himself clutching at the thing in his pocket, the bloody relic of that innocent dog, and he couldn't restrain himself any longer, not after the onslaught of Jack Cherrystone's ominous tones, not after the day he'd been through, not after the look on Kyra's face as she slumped across that narrow bed with her son and her terrified pets. His hand shot up.

"Delaney Mossbacher," Jack Jardine crooned.

Faces turned toward him. People craned their necks. The golden couple beside him parted their lips expectantly.

"I just wanted to know," he began, but before he could gather momentum someone up front interrupted him with a cry of "Louder!" He cleared his throat and tried to adjust his voice. His heart was hammering. "I said I just wanted to know how many of you are aware of what feeding the indigenous coyote population means—"

"Speak to the question," a voice demanded. An exasperated sigh ran through the audience. Several hands shot up.

"This is no trivial issue," Delaney insisted, staring wildly around him. "My dog—my wife's dog—"

"I'm sorry, Delaney," Jack Jardine said, leaning into the microphone, "but we have a pending question regarding construction and maintenance of a gated entryway, and I'm going to have to ask you to speak to it or yield the floor."

"But Jack, you don't understand what I'm saying—look, a coyote got into our backyard this morning and took—"

"Yield the floor," a voice called.

"Speak to the question or yield."

Delaney was angry suddenly, angry for the second time that day, burning, furious. Why wouldn't people listen? Didn't they know what this meant, treating wild carnivores like ducks in the park? "I won't yield," he said, and the audience began to hiss, and then suddenly he had it in his hand, Sacheverell's gnawed white foreleg with its black stocking of blood, and he was waving it like a sword. He caught a glimpse of the horror-struck faces of the couple beside him as they unconsciously backed away and he was aware of movement off to his right and Jack Cherrystone's amplified voice thundering in his ears, but he didn't care—they would listen, they had to. "This!" he shouted over the uproar. "This is what happens!"

Later, as he sat on the steps out front of the community center and let the night cool the sweat from his face, he wondered how he was going to break the news to Kyra. When he'd left her it was with the lame assurance that the dog might turn up yet—maybe he'd got away; maybe he was lost—but now all of Arroyo Blanco knew the grisly finality of Sacheverell's fate. And Delaney had accomplished nothing, absolutely nothing—beyond making a fool of himself. He let out a sigh, throwing back his head and staring up into the bleary pall of the night sky. It had been a rotten day. Nothing accomplished. He hadn't written a word. Hadn't even sat down at his desk. All he'd been able to think about was the dog and the gnawed bit of bone and flesh he'd found in a hole beneath a dusty clump of manzanita.

Inside, they were voting. The windows cut holes in the fabric of the night, bright rectilinear slashes against the black backdrop of the mountains. He heard a murmur of voices, the odd scrape and shuffle of hominid activity. He was just about to push himself up and go home when he became aware of a figure hovering at the edge of the steps. "Who is it?" he said.

"It's me, Mr. Mossbacher," came the voice from the shadows, and then the figure moved into the light cast by the windows and Delaney saw that it was Jack Jardine's son, Jack Jr.

Jack Jr. swayed like a eucalyptus in the wind, a marvel of tensile strength and newly acquired height, long-limbed, big-footed, with hands the size of baseball mitts. He was eighteen, with mud-brown eyes that gave no definition to the pupils, and he didn't look anything like his father. His hair was red, for one thing—not the pale wispy carrot-top Delaney had inherited from his Scots-Irish mother, but the deep shifting auburn you saw on the flanks of horses in an uncertain light. He wore it long on top in a frenzy of curls, and shaved to the bone from the crest of his ears down. "Hello, Jack," Delaney said, and he could hear the weariness in his own voice.

"They got one of your dogs, huh?"

"Afraid so." Delaney sighed. "That's what I was trying to tell them in there—you can't feed wild animals, that's about the long and short of it. But nobody wants to listen."

"Yeah, I know what you mean." Jack Jr. kicked at something in the dirt with the toe of one of his big leather hi-tops. In this light, the shoes seemed to grow out of the ground and meld with his body, trunks to anchor the length of him. There was a pause during which Delaney again contemplated pushing himself up and heading home, but he hesitated. Here was a sympathetic ear, an impressionable mind.

"What they don't realize," Delaney began, but before he could finish the thought, Jack Jr. cut him off.

"By the way—the other night? When you came to see my father about the Mexican?"

The Mexican. Suddenly the man's face floated up again to press at the edges of Delaney's consciousness, fill him up like some pregnant ghost with images of rotten teeth and stained mustaches. The Mexican. What with Sacheverell, he'd forgotten all about him. Now he remembered. The boy had been stretched out on the sofa like a recumbent monarch when Delaney had gone over to Jack's to confer with him about the accident, and Delaney had thought it odd that Jack didn't offer to take him into another room or out on the patio where they could talk in private. Jack took no notice of his son—he might just as well have been part of the furniture. He put an arm round Delaney's shoulder, made him a drink, listened to his story and assured him that he had nothing to worry about, nothing at all—if the man was legal, why would he refuse aid? And if he was illegal, what were the chances he'd find an attorney to represent him—and on what grounds? "But Jack," Delaney had protested, "I didn't report the accident." Jack had turned to him, calm and complicitous. "What accident?" he said, and he was the most reasonable man in the world, judge, jury and advocate all rolled into one. "You stopped and offered to help—the man refused assistance. What more could you do?"

Indeed. But now Jack Jr. wanted to know, and the thought of it made Delaney's stomach sink. There were five people in the world who knew what had happened out on that road, and by luck of the draw Jack Jr. was one of them. "Yeah?" he said. "What of it?"

"Oh, nothing. I was just wondering where it happened—you said they were camping and all."

"Out on the canyon road. Why?"

"Oh, I don't know." Jack Jr. kicked at something in the dirt. "I was just wondering. I see an awful lot of them down there lately. You said it was down below the lumberyard, right? Where that trail cuts off into the ravine?"

For the life of him Delaney couldn't grasp what the boy was getting at—what was it to him? But he answered the question almost reflexively—he had nothing to hide. "Right," he said. And then he got to his feet, murmured, "Well, I've got to be going," and strode off into the darkness fingering the sorry lump of flesh in his jacket pocket.

He made a mental note to put it in the freezer when he got home. It would begin to stink before long.

4

THE MORNING AFTER AMÉRICA CLIMBED UP OUT OF
the canyon to offer herself at the labor exchange—futilely, as it turned
out—she insisted on going again. Cándido was against it. Vehemently.
The day before, he'd waited through the slow-crawling morning till the
sun stood directly overhead—twelve noon, the hour at which the labor
exchange closed down for the day—and then he'd waited another hour,
and another, torn by worry and suspicion. If she'd somehow managed
to get work she might not be back till dark, and that was almost worse
than if she hadn't, what with the worry—and worse still, the shame.
He kept picturing her in some rich man's house, down on her knees
scrubbing one of those tiled kitchens with a refrigerator the size of a
meat locker and one of those dark-faced ovens that boil water in sixty
seconds, and the rich man watching her ass as it waved in the air and
trembled with the hard push of her shoulders. Finally—and it must
have been three in the afternoon—she appeared, a dark speck creeping
over the sun-bleached rocks, and in her hand one of those thin plastic
market bags the *gringos* use once and throw away. Cándido had to
squint to see her against the pain that filmed his eyes. "Where were
you?" he demanded when she was close enough to hear him. And then,
in a weaker voice, a voice of apology and release: "Did you get work?"

No smile. That gave him his answer. But she did hand him the bag
as an offering and kneel down on the blanket to kiss the good side of

his face like a dutiful wife. In the bag: two overripe tomatoes, half a dozen hard greenish oranges and a turnip, stained black with earth. He sucked the sour oranges and ate a stew made from the turnip and tomatoes. He didn't ask her where she'd gotten them.

And now she wanted to go again. It was the same ritual as the day before: slipping up from the blanket like a thief, pulling the one good dress over her head, combing out her hair by the stream. It was dark still. The night clung to them like a second skin. No bird had even begun to breathe. "Where are you going?" he croaked.

Two words, out of the darkness, and they cut him to the quick: " To work."

He sat up and railed while she built a fire and made him coffee and some rice pap with sugar to ease the pain of his chewing, and he told her his fears, outlined the wickedness of the *gabacho* world and the perfidy of his fellow *braceros* at the labor exchange, tried to work the kind of apprehension into her heart that would make her stay here with him, where it was safe, but she wouldn't listen. Or rather, she listened—"I'm afraid," she told him, "afraid of this place and the people in it, afraid to walk out on the street"—but it had no effect. He forbade her to go. Roared out his rage till his indented cheekbone was on fire, got up on unsteady legs and threatened her with his balled-up fist, but it did no good. She hung her head. Wouldn't look him in the eye. "Someone has to go," she whispered. "In a day or two you'll be better, but now you couldn't even get up the trail, let alone work—and that's *if* there's work."

What could he say? She was gone.

And then the day began and the boredom set in, boredom that almost made him glad of the pain in his face, his hip, his arm—at least it was something, at least it was a distraction. He looked round the little clearing by the stream, and the leaves, the rocks, the spill of the slope above him and even the sun in the sky seemed unchanging, eternal, as dead as a photograph. For all its beauty, the place was a jail cell and he was a prisoner, incarcerated in his thoughts. But even a prisoner had something to read, a radio maybe, a place to sit and take a contemplative crap, work—they made license plates here in *Gringolandia,* they broke rocks, but at least they did something.

He dozed, woke, dozed again. And every time he looked up at the sun it was in the same place in the sky, fixed there as if time had stood still. América was out there. Anything could happen to her. How could he rest, how could he have a moment's peace with that specter before him?

América. The thought of her brought her face back to him, her wide innocent face, the face of a child still, with the eyes that bled into you and the soft lisping breath of a voice that was like the first voice you'd ever heard. He'd known her since she was a little girl, four years old, the youngest sister of his wife, Resurrección. She was a flower girl at the wedding, and she looked like a flower herself, blossoming brown limbs in the white petals of her dress. He took the vows with Resurrección that day, and he was twenty years old, just back from nine months in *El Norte,* working the potato fields in Idaho and the citrus in Arizona, and he was like a god in Tepoztlán. In nine months he had made more—and sent half of it home via *giros*—than his father in his leather shop had made in a lifetime. Resurrección had promised to wait for him when he left, and she was good to her word. That time, at least.

But each year the wait got longer, and she changed. They all changed, all the wives, and who could blame them? For three quarters of the year the villages of Morelos became villages of women, all but deserted by the men who had migrated North to earn real money and work eight and ten and twelve hours a day instead of sitting in the *cantina* eternally nursing a beer. A few men stayed behind, of course—the ones who had businesses, the congenitally rich, the crazies—and some of them, the unscrupulous ones, took advantage of the loneliness of the forlorn and itching wives to put horns on the heads of the men breaking their backs in the land of the *gringos.* "Señor Gonzales" is what they called these ghouls of the disinterred marriage, or sometimes just "Sancho," as in "Sancho bedded your wife." There was even a verb for it: *sanchear,* to slip in like a weasel and make a *cabrón* out of an unoffending and blameless man.

And so, after seven seasons away and six cold winters at home during which he felt like half a man because Resurrección would not take his seed no matter what they tried—and they tried Chinese positions, chicken fat rubbed on the womb during intercourse, herbs and potions from the *curandera* and injections from the doctor—Cándido came home to find that his wife was living in Cuernavaca with a Sancho by the name of Teófilo Aguadulce. She was six months pregnant and she'd spent all the money Cándido had sent her on her Sancho and his unquenchable thirst for beer, *pulque* and distilled spirits.

América was the one who broke the news to him. Cándido came to the door at his father-in-law's place, bearing gifts, jubilant in his return, the all-conquering hero, benefactor of half the village, the good nephew who'd built his mother's sister a new house and had a brand-new boombox radio in his bag for her even now, and there was no one home but América, eleven years old and shy as a jaguar with a pig clenched in its jaws. "Cándido!" she screamed, throwing herself in his arms, "what did you bring for me?" He'd brought her a glass Christmas ball with the figure of a *gabacho* Santa Claus imprisoned in it and artificial snow that inundated him with a blizzard when you turned it upside down— but where was everybody? A pause, release of the limbs, a restrained dance round the room with the inverted Christmas ball: "They didn't want to see you." What? Didn't want to see him? She was joking, pulling his leg, very funny. "Where's Resurrección?"

Then came his season in hell. He took the first bus to Cuernavaca, sought out Teófilo Aguadulce's house and beat on the closed shutters till his hands were raw. He prowled the streets, haunted the *cantinas,* the markets, the cinema, but there was no sign of them. Finally, a week later, Cándido got word that Teófilo Aguadulce was coming to Tepoztlán to see his ailing grandfather, and when he crossed the plaza at twelve noon, Cándido was waiting for him. With half the village looking on, Cándido called him out, and he would have had his revenge too, and his honor, if the son of a bitch hadn't got the better of him with a perfidious wrestling move that left him stunned and bleeding in the dirt. No one said a word. No one reached down a hand to help him up. His friends and neighbors, the people he'd known all his life, simply turned their backs on him and walked away. Cándido got drunk. And when he sobered up he got drunk again. And again. He was too ashamed to go back to his aunt's and so he wandered the hills, sleeping where he fell, till his clothes turned to rags and he stank like a goat. Children pelted him with rocks and made up songs about him, rhymes to skip rope by, and the keening of their voices burned into him like a rawhide whip. He made for the border finally, to lose himself in the North, but the *coyote* was a fool and the U.S. Immigration caught him before he'd gone a hundred yards and pitched him back into the dark fastness of the Tijuana night.

He was broke, and he danced for people on the streets there, begged change from *turistas*, got himself a can of kerosene and became a *tragafuegos*, a streetcorner firebreather who sacrificed all sensation in his lips, tongue and palate for a few *centavos* and a few *centavos* more. What he made, he spent on drink. When his fall was complete, when he'd scraped every corner of himself raw, he came back to Tepoztlán and moved in with his aunt in the house he'd built for her. He made charcoal for a living. Climbed into the hills every morning, cut wood and slow-burned it for sale to housewives as fuel for their braziers and the stoves they'd made out of old Pemex barrels. He did nothing else. He saw no one. And then one day he ran across América in the street and everything changed. "Don't you know me?" she demanded, and he didn't know her, not at first. She was sixteen and she looked exactly like her sister, only better. He set down the bundle of sticks he was carrying and straightened out his back with an abbreviated twist. "You're América," he said, and then he gave it a minute as a car came up the road, scattering chickens and sending an explosion of pigeons into the air, "and I'm going to take you with me when I go North."

That was what he thought about as he lay there in the ravine, fragile as a peeled egg, that was what América meant to him—just his life, that was all—and that was why he was worried, edgy, afraid, deeply afraid for the first time in as long as he could remember. What if something should happen to her? What if the Immigration caught her? What if some *gabacho* hit *her* with his car? What if one of the *vagos* from the labor exchange . . . but he didn't like to think about them. They were too close to him. It was too much to hold in his aching head.

The sun had ridden up over the eastern ridge. The heat was coming on faster than it had during the past week, the mist burning off sooner—there would be winds in the afternoon and the canyon walls would hold the heat like the walls of an oven. He could feel the change of the weather in his hip, his elbow, the crushed side of his face. The sun crept across the sand and hit him in the crotch, the chest, his chin, lips and ravaged nose. He closed his eyes and let himself drift.

When he woke he was thirsty. Not just thirsty—consumed with thirst, maddened by it. His clothes were wet, the blanket beneath him damp with his sweat. With an effort, he pushed himself up and staggered into the shade where América kept their drinking water in two plastic milk jugs from which he'd cut the tops with his worn-out switchblade. He snatched up the near jug and lifted air to his lips: it was empty. So was the other one. His throat constricted.

He knew better than to drink the water straight from the stream—and he'd warned América about it too. Every drop had to be boiled first. It was a pain in the ass—gathering wood, stoking the fire, setting the blackened can on the coals—but it was necessary. América had balked at first—why go to the trouble? This was the U.S.A., plumbing capital of the world, the land of filtration plants and water purifiers and chlorine, and everyone knew of the *gringo* fascination with toilets: how could the water be unsafe? Here, of all places? But it was. He'd been here before, in this very spot, and he'd been sick from it. Could she even begin to imagine how many septic fields drained off of those mountains? he demanded. Or how many houses were packed up there all the way to the asshole of the canyon, and every one of them leaching waste out into the gullies and streams that fed into the creek?

He knew better than to drink the water, but he did. He was dying. He was dried out like the husk of something washed up at high tide and left for a month in the sun, dried out like a fig, a soda cracker. It was beyond him even to contemplate gathering up twigs, searching for a scrap of paper, the matches, waiting till the water boiled for five full minutes and then waiting for it to cool—way beyond him. Mad with thirst, crazed, demented, he threw himself down in the sand, plunged his face into the algal scum of the pool beneath him and drank, drank till he nearly drowned himself. Finally, his stomach swollen like a *bota* bag, he lay back, sated, and the afternoon went on and he dozed and worried and suffered his wounds only to wake and worry and suffer again.

It amazed him how quickly the shits came. When he'd drunk from the creek the sun had been just east of overhead and now had settled a degree or two to the west, but it was still high and still hot. What did that add up to—two hours? Three? But there it was—the stirring in his gut, the cramping, the desperate uncontainable rush that every man, woman and child knew so intimately in his country, a poor under-developed place in which sanitation was a luxury and gastrointestinal infection the leading cause of death. Cándido had just enough time to get across the stream and behind the cluster of great splintered boulders he and América used as a privy before it came. And when it came, it came in an explosion, a raging cataract of shit that left him drained in an instant, and then it hit him again and again till he lost the strength of his legs and collapsed in the sand like a puppet with the strings cut.

Lying there, coated in sweat and sand and worse, his trousers ballooning round his ankles, he heard the first sharp cries from above—*gabacho*-accented cries—and he knew it was over. They were coming for him. They'd got hold of América and she'd told them where he was. ¡Ay, caray! What a mess! How could he run? Half-crippled, be-strewn with shit—and even now he could feel his guts churning again. And América—where was América?

He mouthed a prayer to the *Virgen Sagrada* and became one with the rocks.

América sat in the shade of the wall-less shelter the *gringos* had built to keep the itinerant job-seekers out of the sun (and coincidentally off the street, out of the post office parking lot and out of sight) and brooded about Cándido. He was too stubborn to think she could help. Too much the boss, the man, the *patrón*. He treated her like a child, a know-nothing, someone who needed to be led by the hand and protected from all the evils of the world. Well, she had news for him: she was no longer a child. Did children bear children? In five months she'd be a mother, and then what? And while this new place terrified her—the whole country, the *gringos* with their superior ways and their almighty dollar and their new clothes and fancy hairdos, the strange customs, the language that was like the incessant braying of a four-legged beast—she was doing what she had to do and she could look out for herself. She could.

After sitting in the corner all day yesterday, afraid to talk to anyone, she'd screwed up her courage this morning and gone straight to the man in charge and told him her name and asked for work. Of course, if he'd been a *gringo* she never would have had the nerve to open her mouth—and he wouldn't have understood her anyway—but this man was a *campesino* from Oaxaca, in battered jeans and a molded straw hat like the men in Tepoztlán wore, and he used the familiar with her right away and even called her "daughter."

There must have been fifty or sixty men there at least, and they all stopped talking when she went up to the man from Oaxaca. No one seemed to take notice of her when she was off by herself, hunched beside a stump in the dawn, miserable like the rest of them, but now she felt as if she were onstage. The men were staring at her, every one of them, some openly, some furtively, their eyes ducking for cover beneath the brims of their *sombreros* and baseball caps whenever she looked up. Of all that mob, she was the only woman. And though she felt uneasy under their collective gaze—and nervous too to think that women must not get jobs here if she was the only one—she felt a strange sense of peace as she spoke to the headman in his battered jeans. She didn't know what it was at first, but then it hit her: all these faces were familiar. Not literally, of course, but they were the faces of her own people, her tribe, the faces she'd grown up with, and that was a comfort in itself.

The headman's name was Candelario Pérez. He looked to be in his forties and he was squat and work-hardened. He'd been informally elected by the others to keep order (making sure the men waited their turn instead of mobbing every pickup that pulled into the lot), clean up the trash and mediate between the workers and the *gringos* of the community who'd donated the land and the lumber for the sake of the hungry and homeless. "There's not much work for women here, daughter," he said, and she could see the tug of sympathy in his eyes. He didn't know her from anybody, and yet he cared, she could see that.

"Doesn't anyone in these big houses need a stove cleaned or a floor mopped? Doesn't that ever happen?"

All the men were watching her. Traffic—amazing traffic—whined past on the canyon road, forty, fifty miles an hour, bumper-to-bumper, with barely room to breathe in between. Candelario Pérez gave her a long look. "We'll see, daughter, we'll see," he said, and then he showed her where to sit, pointing to the corner she'd occupied now for three hours and more.

She was bored. She was frightened. What if she didn't get work—not today, not ever? What would they eat? What would her baby do for clothes, shelter, nourishment? And this place—wasn't it the perfect spot for *La Migra* to come in their puke-green trucks and tan shirts and demand documents, *la tarjeta verde,* a birth certificate, driver's license, social security card? What was stopping them? It would be like shooting fish in a barrel. As each car pulled into the lot and two or three men gathered round it, she held her breath in hope and fear, wanting work, desperately wanting it, yet mortally afraid of the bland white faces of the men staring out from behind the windshield. What, exactly, did they want? What were the rules? Were they from Immigration? Were they perverts, rapists, murderers? Or were they good people, decent rich people who needed help with a baby, with laundry, with the pots and pans and the ironing?

As it turned out, it didn't matter. She sat there from dawn till noon and she didn't get work. At eleven or so—she had no way of telling the time exactly—a big *gringa* with wild dead-metal hair and eyes the color of a Coke bottle came up the canyon road with a strange jerking gait, passed through the open-air building like a zombie and threw herself down in the dirt beside América. It was hot already—ninety, at least—and yet the woman was dressed in the heavy brocade you might find on a sofa in a house of easy virtue, and she wore a shawl of the same material around her shoulders. When she got close, América could see the thin wire loop that punctured her right nostril.

"How you doing?" the woman said. "I'm Mary. *Llama* Mary."

"*Me llamo América,*" América returned. "*¿Habla usted español?*"

Mary grinned. Her teeth were enormous, like cow's teeth, more yellow than white. "*Poco,*" she said. Little. "No work today, huh? You know, work, *trabaja.*"

Work. Was this woman offering her work? América's heart began to race, but then she caught herself. She didn't look like a housewife, this woman, not the kind América knew from the North American films and TV. She looked dirty, and she had the sad smell of poverty about her.

"I'm looking too," the woman said, and she punched a thumb into her own chest for emphasis. "Me. I work—*trabaja.* Clean house, paint, odd jobs—*comprendo?* Sometimes get, sometimes no. You *sabe?*"

América didn't *sabe.* Nor did she understand. Was this woman trying to tell her that she, a *gringa* in her own country, was looking for the same work as América? It couldn't be. It was a fantasy. Crazy.

But Mary persisted. She made wiping motions with her hands, cleaned an imaginary window, even making little squeaking sounds to imitate the pressure of the rag and the release of the ammonia, and she dipped her imaginary rag into an imaginary bucket until América got the idea: she was a *criada*, a maid, a cleaning lady, here in her own country, and as fantastic as it seemed, she was competing for the same nonexistent jobs América was.

Well, it was a shock—like seeing that *gabacho* with the long hair in Venice, begging on the streets. América felt all the hope crumple in her. And then the *gringa*—Mary—was digging around inside her clothes as if she were scratching fleas or something, actually squirming in the dirt. But it wasn't a flea she came up with, it was a bottle. Pint-size. She took a long swallow and laughed, then offered it to América. No, América gestured, shaking her head, and she was thinking: *Have I sunk to this, a good student and a good girl who always respected her parents and did as she was told, sitting here penniless in the dirt with a common drunk?* "Escuse, pleese," she said, and got up to seek out Candelario Pérez again to see if there was anything for her.

She couldn't find him. It was too late. By arrangement with the local citizens, the labor exchange closed down at noon—they might have been liberal and motivated by a spirit of common humanity and charity, but they didn't want a perpetual encampment of the unemployed, out of luck and foreign in their midst. Twelve o'clock came and you went home, unless you were lucky enough to have found a job for the day, and then you went home when the boss told you to go. They were very strict about camping in the ravine or in the brush along the road—not only the *gringos*, but men like Candelario Pérez, who knew that one encampment could ruin it for them all. There was nothing to stop the *gringos* from tearing down this building and calling in the cops and the hard-faced men from the INS. América knew nothing of this, and that was a small mercy. She did know that it was noon, and that the gathering was breaking up voluntarily.

She walked aimlessly round the lot. Cars went by on the canyon road, but fewer of them now, and at greater intervals. There was a gas station, a secondhand-clothing store; across the street, the post office, and then the little shopping center where the *paisano* from Italy had his store. The men were staring at her openly now, and their stares were harder, hungrier. Most of them were here alone, separated from their families—and their wives—for months at a time, sometimes years. They were starving, and she was fresh meat.

The image spooked her, and she started off down the road, conscious of their eyes drilling into her. All the warmth she'd felt earlier, the familiarity, the brother- and sisterhood, was gone suddenly, and all she could think of, looming nightmarishly, was the faces of those animals at the border—*Mexican* animals—the ones who'd come out of the night to attack her and Cándido as they crossed over. Mexicans. Her own people. And when the light hit them their faces showed nothing—no respect, no mercy, nothing.

América had been terrified to begin with—what she and Cándido were doing was illegal, and she'd never done anything illegal in her life. Crouching there beside the corrugated iron fence, her mouth dry and heart racing, she waited through the long night till the *coyote* gave the word, and then she and Cándido and half a dozen others were running for their lives on the hard-baked earth of another country. Two-thirds of their savings had gone to this man, this *coyote*, this emissary between the two worlds, and he was either incompetent or he betrayed them. One minute he was there, hustling them through a gap in the fence, and the next minute he was gone, leaving them in a clump of bushes at the bottom of a ravine in a darkness so absolute it was like being thrust into the bottom of a well.

And then the animals jumped them. Just like that. A gang of them, armed with knives, baseball bats, a pistol. And how did they know that she and Cándido would be there beneath that particular bush—and at the ungodly hour of four a.m.? There were six or seven of them. They pinned Cándido down and cut the pockets from his trousers, and then, in that hot subterranean darkness, they went for her. A knife was in her face, their hands were all over her, and they jerked the clothes from her as if they were skinning a rabbit. Cándido cried out and they clubbed him; she screamed, and they laughed. But then, just as the first one loosened his belt, taking his time, enjoying it, the helicopter came with its lights and suddenly it was bright day and the vermin were scattering and Cándido had her and the wash of the propellers threw the dirt against her bare skin like a thousand hot needles. "Run!" Cándido screamed. "Run!" And she ran, naked, her feet sliced by the rocks and the stabbing talons of the desert plants, but she couldn't outrun a helicopter.

That was the most humiliating night of her life. She was herded along with a hundred other people toward a line of Border Patrol jeeps and she stood there naked and bleeding, every eye on her, until someone gave her a blanket to cover herself. Twenty minutes later she was back on the other side of the fence.

Bitter reflections. She continued down the road, thinking to duck off onto one of the hilly side streets to her right, as she'd done yesterday. There were backyard gardens there, fruit trees, tomatoes and peppers and squash. She didn't mean to steal. She knew it was wrong. And she'd never stolen a thing in her life.

Until yesterday.

The voices echoed through the confined space of the ravine as if it were a public bath, high-pitched with excitement, almost squealing: "Hey, look—didn't I tell you?" "What—you find something?" "What the fuck you think that is—a fucking fireplace—and look, a fucking blanket!"

Cándido crouched there behind the rocks, afraid to breathe, trembling as uncontrollably as if he'd suddenly been plunged into an ice bath, and all he could think of was América. He'd been caught three times before—once in L.A., once in Arizona, and then with América just over the Tijuana fence—and the fear of that took his breath away and turned his stomach over yet again. It wasn't himself he was afraid for, it was her. For him it was nothing. A pain in the ass, sure, a bus ride to the border, his meager possessions scattered to the winds—but how would he get back to his wife? A hundred and eighty miles and no money, not a cent. There might be a beating. The *gabachos* could be brutal—big men with little blond mustaches and hate in their eyes—but usually they were just bored, just going through the motions. A beating he could take—even now, even with his face and his arm and the shit pouring out of him—but it was América he trembled for.

What would happen to her? How would he find her? If they'd caught her already—at the labor exchange, walking along the road—she could be on a bus even now. And worse: if they hadn't caught her and she came back here, back to nothing, what then? She'd think he'd deserted her, run off from his responsibilities like a cock on the loose, and what love could survive that? They should have made a contingency plan, figured out a place to meet in Tijuana, a signal of some kind . . . but they hadn't. He listened to the voices and gritted his teeth.

"Hey, dude, check this out—"

"What?"

"Look at this shit."

But wait a minute—these weren't the voices of INS agents, of the police, of grown men . . . no, there was something in the timbre, something harsh and callow in the way the words seemed to claw for air as if they were choking on them, something adolescent . . . Cándido stealthily pushed himself to a sitting position, pulled up his trousers and crept forward on hands and knees to a place where he could peer between the rocks without being detected. What he saw got him breathing again. Two figures, no uniforms. Baggy shorts, hi-top sneakers, big black billowing T-shirts, legs and arms pale in the slashing sun as they bent to his things, lifted them above their heads and flung them, one by one, into the creek. First the blanket, then the grill he'd salvaged from an abandoned refrigerator, then his rucksack with his comb and toothbrush and a change of clothes inside, and then América's things.

"Shit, man, one of them's a girl," the bigger one said, holding up América's everyday dress, blue cotton washed so many times it was almost white. In that moment Cándido confirmed what his ears had suspected: these weren't men; they were boys, overgrown boys. The one holding the dress out before him was six feet at least, towering, all limbs and feet and with a head shaved to the ears and *gabacho-*

colored hair gone long on top—*redheads,* did they all have to be red-heads?

"Fucking Beaners. Rip it up, man. Destroy it."

The other one was shorter, big in the shoulders and chest, and with the clear glassy cat's eyes so many of the *gringos* inherited from their mothers, the *gringas* from Sweden and Holland and places like that. He had a mean pinched face, the face of an insect under the magnifying glass—bland at a distance, lethal up close. The bigger one tore the dress in two, balled the halves and flung them at the other one, and they hooted and capered up and down the streambed like apes that had dropped from the trees. Before they were done they even bent to the rocks of the fireplace Cándido had built and heaved them into the stream too.

Cándido waited a long while before emerging. They'd been gone half an hour at least, their shrieks and obscenities riding on up the walls of the canyon till finally they blended with the distant hum of the traffic and faded away. His stomach heaved on him again, and he had to crouch down with the pain of it, but the spasm passed. After a moment he got up and waded into the stream to try to recover his things, and it was then that he noticed their parting gift, a message emblazoned on the rocks in paint that dripped like blood. The letters were crude and the words in English, but there was no mistaking the meaning:

BEANERS DIE

5

DELANEY COULDN'T FEEL BAD FOR LONG, NOT UP
here where the night hung close round him and the crickets thundered
and the air off the Pacific crept up the hills to drive back the lingering
heat of the day. There were even stars, a cluster here and there fighting
through the wash of light pollution that turned the eastern and southern borders of the night yellow, as if a whole part of the world had
gone rancid. To the north and east lay the San Fernando Valley, a
single endless plane of parallel boulevards, houses, mini-malls and
streetlights, and to the south lay the rest of Los Angeles, ad infinitum.
There were no streetlights in Arroyo Blanco—that was one of the at-
tractions, the rural feel, the sense that you were somehow separated
from the city and wedded to the mountains—and Delaney never felt
the lack of them. He didn't carry a flashlight either. He enjoyed making
his way through the dark streets, his eyes adjusting to the shapes and
shadows of the world as it really was, reveling in the way the night
defined itself in the absence of artificial light and the ubiquitous blast
of urban noise.

Though the walk had calmed him, he couldn't suppress a sudden
pounding in his chest as he passed the Dagolian place—heedless
people, slobs—and turned up Piñon Drive, conscious once again of
the burden in the pocket of his windbreaker. His house sat at the
end of Piñon, in a cul-de-sac that marked the last frontier of urban

development, and the chirring of the crickets seemed louder here, the darkness more complete. As if to prove the point, a great horned owl began to hoot softly from the trees behind him. Someone's sprinklers went on with a hiss. High overhead, a jet climbing out of LAX cut a tear in the sky. Delaney had just begun to relax again when a car suddenly turned into the street from Robles Drive, high beams obliterating the night. He glanced over his shoulder, squinted into the light and kept on walking.

The car was moving, but barely. Its exhaust rumbled menacingly, all that horsepower held in check, and from behind the rolled-up windows came the bottom-heavy thump of rap music—no words, no instrument, no melody discernible, just a thump. Delaney kept walking, annoyed all over again. Why couldn't they pass by already and let the night close back over him? Why couldn't he have a minute's peace even in his own neighborhood?

The car pulled slowly alongside him, and he could see that it was some sort of American car, older, a big boat of a thing with mag wheels and an elaborate metal-flake paint job. The windows were smoked and he couldn't see inside. What did they want—directions? No face was visible. No one asked. He cursed under his breath, then picked up his pace, but the car seemed to hover there beside him, the speakers sucking up all available sound and then pumping it back out again, *ka-thump, ka-thump, ka-thump.* The car stayed even with him for what seemed an eternity, then it gradually accelerated, made the end of the street, wheeled round and rolled slowly back down the block again—*ka-thump, ka-thump, ka-thump*—and this time the lights, still on bright, glared directly into Delaney's eyes. He kept going and the car crept past him again and finally faded to a pair of taillights swinging back onto Robles. It wasn't till Delaney was inside, and the door locked behind him, that he thought to be afraid.

Who would be up here at this hour in a car like that? He thought of the solemn fat man at the meeting and his litany of woes, the bringer of bad tidings, the Cassandra of Arroyo Blanco. Was it burglars, then? Muggers? Gangbangers? Is that what they were? As he crossed the kitchen and surreptitiously slipped Sacheverell's foreleg into the freezer beneath a bag of frozen peas—he'd bury it tomorrow, after Kyra went off to work—he couldn't help thinking about the gate. If there was a gate that car wouldn't have been there, and who knew what he'd just escaped—a beating, robbery, murder? He poured himself a glass of orange juice, took a bite of the macaroni and cheese Jordan had left on his plate at dinner. And then he saw the light in the bedroom: Kyra was waiting up for him.

He felt a stirring in his groin. It was nearly eleven, and normally she was in bed by nine-thirty. That meant one thing: she was propped up against the pillows in one of the sheer silk teddies he'd bought her at Christmas for just such an occasion as this, reading Anaïs Nin's erotica or paging through one of the illustrated sex manuals she kept in a box under the bed—waiting, and eager. There was something about the little tragedies of life, the opening of the floodgates of emotion, that seemed to unleash her libido. For Kyra, sex was therapeutic, a release from sorrow, tension, worry, and she plunged into it in moments of emotional distress as others might have sunk themselves in alcohol or drugs—and who was Delaney to argue? She'd been especially passionate around the time her mother was hospitalized for her gallbladder operation, and he could remember never wanting to leave the motel room they'd rented across the street from the hospital—it was the next best thing to a second honeymoon. Smaller sorrows aroused her too—having a neighbor list her house with a rival company, discovering a dent in the door of her Lexus, seeing Jordan laid low with the flu or swollen up with the stigmata of poison oak. Delaney could only imagine what the death of a dog would do to her.

He came into the room with his shirt unbuttoned to the waist, ready for anything. She was there, just as he'd pictured her, the pillows fluffed, the silk clinging to her breasts, her eyes moist with desire as she lifted them from the page. "How was the meeting?" she whispered.

He watched, transfixed, as she swung her smooth tanned legs over the side of the bed, set her book down on the night table and snapped off the reading light, leaving only the sensual flicker of a scented candle to guide them. "The meeting?" he echoed, and he was whispering too, he couldn't help himself. "It was nothing. The usual."

And now she was on her feet, her arms encircling his shoulders, her body straining against his. "I thought"—her voice cracked and tiny— "I thought they were . . . debating the . . . gate and all?"

Her mouth was warm. He pressed himself to her like a teenager at a dance, oblivious of gates, coyotes, dogs and Mexicans. She moved against him, and then she pulled away to perch again at the edge of the bed, her fingers busy at his zipper. After a long pause, he whispered, "That's right . . . and you know how I feel about it, but—" And though his pants were down around his ankles and they were kissing again and he was caressing her through the black liquid silk, he couldn't help thinking about that car and the low rumbling menace of it and how that modified his views vis-à-vis gated communities, public spaces and democratic access . . . He lifted the silk from her thighs. "I guess I'm not sure anymore—"

She was wet. He sank into her. The candle sent distorted shadows floating up and down the walls. "Poor Sacheverell," she breathed, and then suddenly she froze. Her eyes, inches from his, flashed open. "He's dead, isn't he?"

There'd been movement, warmth, a slow delicious friction, but now all movement ceased. What could he say? He tried to kiss her, but she fought his mouth away. He let out a sigh. "Yes."

"For sure?"

"For sure."

"You found him, didn't you? Tell me. Quick."

She was clutching him still, but there was no passion in it—at least not the sort of passion he'd anticipated. Another sigh. "A piece of him. His foreleg, actually. The left."

She drew in a sudden sharp breath—it was as if she'd burned herself or been pricked with a pin—and then she pushed him aside and rolled out from under him. Before he knew what was happening she was on her feet, rigid with anger. "I knew it! You lied to me!"

"I didn't lie, I just—"

"Where is it?"

The question took him by surprise. "What do you mean?"

"The"—her voice broke—"what's left of him."

He'd done all he could. He would have had to tell her in the morning anyway. "In the freezer," he said.

And then he was standing naked in the kitchen, watching his wife peer into the palely glowing depths of the freezer, her negligee derealized in the light of a single frigid bulb. He tried to nuzzle up against her but she pushed him impatiently away. "Where?" she demanded. "I don't see anything."

Miserable, his voice pitched low: "Third shelf down, behind the peas. It's wrapped up in a Baggie."

He watched her poke tentatively through the bright plastic sacks of vegetables until she found it, a nondescript lump of hair, bone, gristle and meat wrapped like a chicken leg in its transparent shroud. She held it in the palm of her hand, her eyes swollen with emotion, the heavy breath of the freezer swirling ghostlike round her bare legs. Delaney didn't know what to say. He felt guilty somehow, culpable, as if he'd killed the dog himself, as if the whole thing were bound up in venality, lust, the shirking of responsibility and duty, and yet at the same time the scene was irresistibly erotic. Despite himself, he began to stiffen. But then, as Kyra stood there in a daze and the freezer breathed in and out and the pale wedge of light from the open door pressed their trembling shadows to the wall, there came a clacking of canine nails on the polished floorboards, and Osbert, the survivor, poked his head in the door, looking hopeful.

It was apparently too much for Kyra. The relic disappeared into the depths of the freezer amid the peas and niblet corn and potato puffs, and the door slammed shut, taking all the light with it.

You didn't move property with a long face and you didn't put deals together if you could barely drag yourself out of bed in the morning—especially in this market. Nobody had to tell Kyra. She was the consummate closer—psychic, cheerleader, seductress and psychoan-alyst all rolled in one—and she never let her enthusiasm flag no matter how small the transaction or how many times she'd been through the same tired motions. Somehow, though, she just couldn't seem to mus-ter the energy. Not today. Not after what had happened to Sacheverell. It was only eleven in the morning and she felt as worn and depleted as she'd ever been in her life. All she could think about was that grisly paw in the freezer, and she wished now that she'd let Delaney go ahead with his deception. He would have buried the evidence in the morning and she'd never have been the wiser—but no, she had to see for her-self, and that little foreleg with its perfectly aligned little toenails was a shock that kept her up half the night.

When she did finally manage to drift off, her dreams were haunted by wolfish shapes and images of the hunt, by bared fangs and flashing limbs and the circle of canny snouts raised to the sky in primordial triumph. She awoke to the whimpering of Osbert, and the first emotion that seized her was anger. Anger at her loss, at the vicissitudes of nature, at the Department of Fish and Game or Animal Control or whatever they were called, at the grinning stupid potbellied clown who'd put up the fence for them—why stop at six feet? Why not eight? Ten? When the anger had passed, she lay there in the washed-out light of dawn and stroked the soft familiar fluff behind the dog's ears and let the hurt overwhelm her, and it was cleansing, cathartic, a moment of release that would strengthen and sustain her. Or so she thought.

At eleven-fifteen she pulled up in front of the house she was showing—the Matzoob place, big and airy, with a marble entrance hall, six bedrooms, pool, maid's room and guesthouse, worth one-point-one two years ago and listed at eight now and lucky to move for six and a half—and the first thing she noticed was the puddle of water on the front porch. Puddle? It was a pond, a lake, and the depth of it showed all too plainly how uneven the tiles were. She silently cursed the gar-dener. There had to be a broken sprinkler head somewhere in the shrubbery—yes, there it was—and when the automatic timer switched on, it must have been like Niagara out here. Well, she'd have to dig

around in the garage and see if she could find a broom somewhere—
she couldn't very well have the buyers wading through a pond to get
in the house, not to mention noticing that the tiles were coming up
and the porch listing into the shrubbery. And then she'd call the gardener. What was his name—she had it in her book somewhere, not
the service she usually used, some independent the Matzoobs had
been big on before they moved to San Bernardino—Gutiérrez? Gon-
zález? Something like that.

Kyra had no patience with incompetence, and here it was, staring
her in the face. How the gardener could come back week after week
and not notice something as obvious as an inch and a half of water on
the front porch was beyond her, and the pure immediate unalloyed
aggravation of it allowed her to forget Sacheverell for the moment and
focus on the matter at hand, on business, on the moving of property.
Nothing escaped her. Not a crack in the plaster, a spot of mold on
the wall behind the potted palm or an odor that wasn't exactly what it
was supposed to be.

Odors were the key. You could tell three-quarters of everything
about a house by the way it smelled—condition, upkeep, what kind
of people owned it, whether the roof leaked or the basement flooded.
What you didn't want was that dead tomblike smell of a shut-up house,
as if it were a funeral parlor, or anything that smelled of dry rot or
chemicals or even paint. Cooking odors were anathema. Ditto the stink
of animals. She'd listed one house—one of her few failures—in which
an old lady had died surrounded by thirty-two cats that had pissed,
crapped and sprayed on every surface available, including the ceilings.
The only hope for that place was to burn it down.

Now, stepping into the Matzoobs', the first thing Kyra did was close
the door behind her and take a good long lingering sniff. Then she
exhaled and tried it again, alert to every nuance, her nose as keen as
any connoisseur's. Not bad. Not bad at all. There was maybe the
faintest whiff of cooking oil from some long-forgotten meal, a trace of
dog or cat, mothballs maybe, but she couldn't be sure. It helped that
the place was empty—when it first went on the market eight months

ago the Matzoobs were still here, the halls, closets and bathrooms steeping in their own peculiar odor. And to call the odor "peculiar" wasn't being judgmental, not at all—it was merely descriptive. Every family, every house, had its own aroma, as unique and individual as a thumbprint.

The Matzoobs' was a rich ferment of smell, ranging from the perfume of the fresh-cut flowers Sheray Matzoob favored to the pungent stab of garlic and coriander Joe Matzoob had learned to use in his gourmet cooking classes and the festering sweat socks of Matzoob Jr., the basketball star. It was a homey smell, but too complicated to do anybody any good. And the furniture was a nightmare. Big cumbersome pieces finished in an almost ebony stain that seemed to drink up what little light penetrated the thick blanket-like curtains Sheray Matzoob had inherited from her mother. And the portraits—they were something else altogether. Big, crude, cheesy things that made the Matzoobs look like ghouls, with gold-tinted frames and paint so thick it might have been applied with a butter knife.

But now the place was empty, and that suited Kyra just fine. Once in a while you'd get a place that was so exquisitely furnished you'd ask the sellers to leave their things in place until the house was in escrow, but that was rare. Most people had no taste. No dream of it. Not a clue. And yet they all thought they had it—were smug about it even—and they'd walk right out the door because of an unfortunate lamp or a deep plush carpet in a shade they couldn't fathom. All things considered, Kyra preferred it this way—a neutral environment, stripped to the essentials: walls, floors, ceilings and appliances. A vacant house became hers in a way—it had been abandoned, deserted, left in her hands and hers alone, and sometimes the sellers were off in another state or country even—and she couldn't help feeling proprietorial about it. Sometimes, making the rounds of her houses—she had forty-six current listings, more than half of them unoccupied—she felt like the queen of some fanciful country, a land of high archways, open rooms and swimming pools that would have made an inland sea if stretched end-to-end across her domain.

There was a broom in the garage—practically the only thing left there, if you discounted the two trash cans and a box of heavy-duty garbage bags. Kyra swept the water from the front porch and then went into the bathroom in the master suite to freshen up her face before Sally Lieberman from Sunrise arrived with her buyers. The bathroom was dated, unfortunately, by its garish ceramic tiles, each with the miniature yellow, blue and green figure of a bird emblazoned on it, and by the tarnished faux-brass fixtures and cut-glass towel racks that gave the place the feel of the ladies' room in a Mexican restaurant. Ah, well, each to her taste, Kyra was thinking, and then she caught a good look at herself in the mirror.

It was a shock. She looked awful. Haggard, frowsy, desperate, like some stressed-out Tupperware hostess or something. The problem was her nose. Or, actually, it was Sacheverell and the night she'd spent, but all the grief and shock and exhaustion of the ordeal was right there, consolidated in her nose. The tip of it was red—bright red, flaming— and when the tip of her nose was red it seemed to pull her whole face in on itself like some freakish vortex, The Amazing Lady with the Shrinking Face. Ever since she'd had her nose modified when she was fourteen, it had a tendency to embarrass her in times of stress. Whatever the doctor had done to it—remove a sliver of bone, snip a bit here and there—it was always just a shade paler than her cheeks, chin and brow, and it took on color more quickly. It always seemed to be sunburned, for one thing. And when she had a cold or flu or felt agitated or depressed or overwrought it blazed out from the center of her face like something you'd expect to find at the top of a Christmas tree.

You couldn't move property with a nose like that. But why dwell on it? She took out her compact and went to work.

Just as she was putting the finishing touches to her face she heard Sally Lieberman chiming from the front door, "We're here!"

Sally was mid-forties, dressed like she owned the store, worked out at the gym, a real professional. Kyra had closed six properties with her over the course of the past two years and she valued her input. The buyers, though, left something to be desired. They hung back at the door, looking sulky and hard-to-please. Sally introduced them as the Paulymans, Gerald and Sue. He was frazzle-haired and unshaven, in a pair of blue jeans gone pale with use, and she had pink and black beads braided into her hair. Kyra knew from experience not to judge from first appearances—she'd once had a woman in her seventies who dressed like a bag lady but wound up writing a check for a two-point-seven-mil estate in Cold Canyon—but they didn't look auspicious. Maybe they were musicians or TV writers, she thought, hoping for the best. They had to have something going for them or Sally wouldn't have brought them around.

"So what's with the wet spot on the porch?" the husband wanted to know, confronting her eyes, his voice nagging and hoarse.

You couldn't be evasive—evasive didn't work. Even the most complacent buyer would think you were trying to put something over on them, and a buyer like this would eat you alive. Kyra put on her smile. "A broken sprinkler head. I've already called the gardener about it."

"That porch has a real pitch to it."

"We offer a one-year buyer-protection policy on every house we list, gratis."

"I can't believe this carpet," the wife said.

"And look at this," the husband whined, pushing past Kyra and into the living room, where he went down on his hands and knees to wet a finger and run it along the baseboard, "the paint is flaking."

Kyra knew the type. They were looky-loos of the first stripe, abusive, angry, despicable people who'd make you show them two hundred houses and then go out and buy a trailer. Kyra gave them her spiel—deal of the century, room to spare, old-world craftsmanship, barely been lived in—handed them each a brochure with a glossy color photo of the house reproduced on the front and left them to wander at will.

By two, she had a headache. Nothing was moving, anywhere, there were no messages on her machine and only six people had showed up for the realtors' open house she'd catered herself on a new listing in

West Hills—all that Chardonnay, Brie and Danish soda bread gone to waste, not to mention half a platter of California roll, *ebi* and salmon sushi. She spent the rest of the afternoon at the office, doing busywork, writing up ad copy and making phone calls, endless phone calls. Three extra-strength Excedrin couldn't begin to quell the throbbing in her temples, and every time she lifted a document from her desk she saw Sacheverell as a puppy chasing a wadded-up ball of paper as if it were a part of him that had gotten away. She called Delaney at five to see how Jordan was taking it—he was fine, Delaney told her, so absorbed in his Nintendo he wouldn't have known a dog from a chicken—and then she left work early to close up her houses and head home.

The parking attendant gave her her keys with a smile full of teeth and a mock bow that took him almost to the ground. He was a young Latino with slicked-back hair and dancing eyes and he always made her feel good, and though it was a little thing and she knew it was his job to make the ladies feel good, she couldn't help smiling back at him. Then she was in her car and the rest of the world wasn't. She switched off the car phone, fed one of her relaxation tapes into the slot in the console—waves breaking on a beach, with the odd keening cry of a seagull thrown in for variety—and eased out into the traffic snarled on the boulevard in front of the office.

Traffic was traffic, and it didn't faze her a bit. She moved with it, sat in it, ran with its unfathomable flow. The car was her sanctuary, and with the phone switched off and the waves rolling from the front speakers to the rear and back again, nothing could touch her. Just sitting there, locked in, the exhaust rising about her, she began to feel better.

She was responsible for closing up five houses every night, seven days a week, and opening them again in the morning so her fellow realtors could show them. These were the houses she was keying on, and though they had lockboxes, she needed to make sure they were secure at night—she couldn't count the times a careless realtor had left a window or even a door open—and to collect the cards of any of her colleagues who might have been through with a client. It added a good hour or more to her day, but it kept the sellers happy and she could go home and network with those cards while Delaney put up dinner and Jordan did his homework. And five houses was nothing, really—she'd had as many as twelve or thirteen during the boom years.

She went through the first four houses on automatic pilot—in the door, douse the lights, check on the automatic timers, punch in the alarm code and lock up, key in the lockbox—but with the last house, the Da Ros place, she took her time. This was a house you could get lost in, a house that made her other listings look like bungalows. Of all the places she'd ever shown, this was the one that really spoke to her, the sort of house she would have when she was forty and kissed Mike Bender goodbye and opened her own office. It sat high on a bluff above the canyon at the end of a private drive, with an unobstructed view of the Pacific on one side and the long green-brown spine of the Santa Monica Mountains on the other. Way below it, like some sort of fungus attached to the flank of the mountain, lay the massed orange tile rooftops of Arroyo Blanco.

There were twenty rooms, each arranged to take advantage of the views, a library, billiard room, servants' quarters, formal gardens and fishpond. In all, the house comprised eleven thousand square feet of living space, done up in the style of an English manor house, with towering chimneys, fieldstone walls and a roof stained russet and green to counterfeit age and venerability, though it only dated back to 1988. It was on the market because of a suicide. Kyra was representing the widow, who'd gone to live in Italy after the funeral.

Her headache was gone now, but it had been replaced by a fatigue that went deeper than any physical exhaustion, a funk, a malaise she couldn't seem to shake. All this over a dog? It was ridiculous, she knew it. There were people out there going through Dumpsters for a scrap to eat, people lined up on the streets begging for work, people who'd lost their homes, their children, their spouses, people with real problems, real grief. What was wrong with her?

Maybe it was her priorities, maybe that was it. What was she doing with her life? Cutting deals? Making Mike Bender richer? Seeing that Mr. and Mrs. Whoever found or sold or leased or rented their dream house while the world was falling to shit around her and dogs were dying and she got to spend an hour and a half a day with her son if she was lucky? She looked round her and it was as if she were waking from a dream, the sky on fire, the towers blazing above her. It was then, for just a moment, standing there in the tiled drive of Patricia Da Ros's huge wheeling ark of a house, that she caught a glimpse of her own end, laid to rest in short skirt, heels and tailored jacket, a sheaf of escrow papers clutched in her hand.

She tried to shrug it off. Tried to tell herself that what she did was important, vital, altruistic even—after food and love, what was more important than shelter?—but the cloud wouldn't lift and she felt numb from the balls of her feet to the crown of her head. She found herself drifting through the gardens, checking to see that everything was in order—she couldn't help herself—and there was no carelessness here because the gardener was her own and he knew just what was expected of him. All was quiet. The koi lay deep in their pools and the lawns glistened under a soft uniform mist from the sprinklers.

It was quarter past six and still warm—uncomfortably warm—but there was an offshore breeze and Kyra could see a skein of fog unraveling across the water below. The evening would be cool. She thought of her own house then, of Delaney going round opening the windows and turning on the big slow ceiling fans to gather in the breeze while the salad chilled and the pasta steamed and Jordan kicked a ball against the garage door. If she hurried, she could be home by seven.

But she didn't hurry. The more she thought of her own house, of her son, her husband, her solitary dog, the more enervated she felt. She lingered on the doorstep, wandered through the cavernous rooms like a ghost, ran her hand over the felt of the billiard table as if she were caressing the short stiff nap at the base of Jordan's neck. She was just checking to see that everything was in order, that was all, but in a way, a growing way, a way that almost overwhelmed her, she didn't want to leave, not ever again.

Late morning, the house silent, light muted, telephone off the hook. Delaney sat in his office, a converted bedroom fitted out with desk, couch and filing cabinets, leaning into a pool of artificial light while the sun cut precise slashes between the slats of the drawn blinds. He'd been out earlier with shovel and pickax, the heavy clay soil like asphalt, to dispose of the dog's remains, putting an end to that chapter. Mercifully. And now he was back at work, severed limbs, distraught wives, frightened children and public meetings behind him, putting the finishing touches to his latest column:

PILGRIM AT TOPANGA CREEK

Who am I, manzanita stick in hand and nylon pack clinging to my shoulders like a furled set of wings, out abroad in the wide world? Who am I, striding into the buttery glaze of evening sun amidst stands of bright blooming mustard that reach to my elbows and beyond? I'm a pilgrim, that's all, a seer, a worshiper at the shrine. No different from you, really: housebound half the day, a slave to the computer, a man who needs his daily fix of electricity as badly as any junkie needs his numinous drug. But different too, because I have these mountains to roam and these legs to carry me. Tonight—this evening—I am off on an adventure, a jaunt, a peregrination beneath the thin skin of the visible to breathe in the world around me as intensely as Wordsworth's leech-gatherer and his kin: I am climbing into the fastness of the Santa Monica Mountains, within sight and sound of the second-biggest city in the country (within the city limits, for that matter), to spend a solitary night.

I am excited. Bursting. Thrilling like a plucked string. For while I know these hills in the broad light of midday, and I know them in early morning and evening (and I've tasted them, as you might taste an exotic fruit) between the curtains of the night, this will be my first sojourn here under the stars. From the moment my wife drops me off at the Trippet Ranch trailhead with a kiss and a promise to come for me at nine the next morning, I feel a primeval sense of liberation, of release, and as I wend my way upward through the stands of undiscouraged shrubs, I can't help singing out their names in a sort of mantra—bush poppy, sumac, manzanita, ceanothus, chamise, redshanks—over and over again.

The mustard is an interloper here, by the way, an annual introduced by the Franciscan padres, who, so it is said, broadcast handfuls of seed along the Camino Real to mark the trail, but of course they had an ulterior motive too: this is the same mustard that winds up in a jar on our table. It blooms after the rains and transforms the hills, yellow flowers stretching to the horizon in pointillistic display, but by this time of the year it has already begun to fade. In a month there will be nothing left but shriveled leaves and dried-out stalks.

By contrast, the manzanita and toyon, with their lode of palatable berries, are on for the long haul, as are our two hardy members of the rose family, chamise (Adenostoma fasciculatum) and redshanks (Adenostoma sparsifolium). Tough customers, these. They deposit toxins in the soil to inhibit germination of competing plants and carry resins in their woody stems to feed the periodic brushfires that allow them to regenerate. They will see no rain—indeed, no moisture at all save for what little may drift in on the sea mist—till November or December. But there they are, holding the ground like an army keeping the sun at bay.

I will spend the night not at the prescribed campground (Musch Ranch), but in a more solitary place off the Santa Ynez Canyon Trail, with nothing more elaborate between me and terra firma than an old army blanket and a foam pad. Of course, unwelcome bedfellows are always a concern up here, with rattlesnakes heading the list, but certain oversized members of the Arachnida class—tarantulas and scorpions, specifically—can be equally disconcerting.

A friend once joked that the scorpion has evolved his pincers in order to seize the big toe of the unsuspecting Homo sapiens and gain purchase for the fine penetrating over-the-back sting. Look at a scorpion lying there in the aperture of his burrow or scuttling about in the beam of a flashlight, and you might almost think it true. But like everything else in this Creation, the scorpion is beautiful in his way and beautifully adapted to seizing, paralyzing and absorbing his insect prey. (I once kept two of them in a jar—a mustard jar, for that matter—and fed them on spiders. Though one was half again as large as the other, they seemed to coexist peacefully enough until I went away for a week and returned to see the larger drinking up the vital juices of the smaller, which at that point resembled nothing so much as a tiny scorpion-shaped balloon that someone had let the air out of.)

But that is why I am here instead of home in my armchair with a book in my lap: to savor not only the fixed joys and certitudes of Nature but the contingencies too. It's a heady feeling, the sort of feeling that makes you know you're alive and breathing and part of the whole grand scheme of things, drinking from the same fount as the red-tailed hawk, the mule deer, the centipede and the scorpion too.

Darkness is coming on as I spread my blanket on the earth at the head of a canyon near a trickling waterfall and settle in to watch the night deepen round me. My fare is humble: an apple, a handful of trail mix, a Swiss cheese sandwich and a long thirsty swallow of aqua pura from the bota bag. From somewhere deep in the hollow space below me comes the soft, almost delicate, hoot of the great horned owl—more a coo really—and it is answered a moment later by an equally diffident hoot off to the east. By now the night has taken over and the stars have begun to extricate themselves one by one from the haze. An hour passes. Two. I am waiting for something, I don't know what, but if I can filter out the glowing evidence of our omnipresent civilization (passenger jets, streaking high overhead on their incessant journeys, the light pollution that makes the eastern sky glow as if with the first trembling light of dawn), I feel that all this is mine to have and hold, for this night at least.

And then I hear it, a high tenuous glissade of sound that I might almost have mistaken for a siren if I didn't know better, and I realize that this is what I've been waiting for all along: the coyote chorus. The song of the survivor, the Trickster, the four-legged wonder who can find water where there is none and eat hearty among the rocks and the waste places. He is out there now, ringing-in the night, gathering in his powers and dominions, hunting, gamboling, stealing like a shadow through the scrub around me, and singing, singing for my benefit alone on this balmy seamless night. And I? I lie back and listen, as on another night I might listen to Mozart or Mendelssohn, lulled by the impassioned beauty of it. The waterfall trickles. The coyotes sing. I have a handful of raisins and a blanket: what more could I want? All the world knows I am content.

6

THE BEANS WERE GONE, THE *TORTILLAS*, THE LARD, the last few grains of rice. And what were they going to eat—grass? Like the cows? That was the question she put to Cándido when he tried to prevent her from going up the hill to the labor exchange for the fifth weary day in a row, and so what if it had a sting in it? What right did he have to tell her where she could go and what she could do? He wasn't helping any. He could barely get up and take a pee on his own—and what of the *gabacho* boys who'd ripped up her dress and flung their blanket into the creek, where was he then? She threw it all at him, angry, hurt, terrified; and then he rose up off the blanket and slapped her. Hard. Slapped her in the pale rocky dawn of the ravine till her head snapped back on her neck like one of those rubber balls attached to a paddle. "Don't you tell me," he growled through his teeth. "It's an insult. A kick in the ass when I'm down." He spat at her feet. "You're no better than your sister, no better than a whore."

But you couldn't eat grass, and for all his bluster, he must have realized that. He was healing, but he was still in no shape to climb up out of the canyon and throw himself back into *la lucha*, the struggle to find a job, to be the one man picked out of a crowd, and then to work like ten men to show the *patrón* you wanted to come back to-morrow and the next day and the day after that. She understood his frustration, his fear, and she loved him, she did, to the bottom of her heart. But it hurt to be the target of those hard and filthy words, hurt more than the blow itself. And when it was all over, when the birds had started in again and the stream made its noise against the rocks and the cars clawed at the road above, what had been accomplished? Bitterness, that was all. She turned her back on him and made her way up that crucible of a hill for the fifth useless time in as many useless days.

Somebody handed her a cup of coffee. A man she'd seen the last two mornings, a newcomer—he said he was from the South, that was all. He was tall—nearly six feet, she guessed—and he wore a baseball cap reversed on his head like one of the *gringos* in the supermarket. His skin was light, so light he could almost have passed for one of them, but it was his eyes that gave him away, hard burnished unblinking eyes the color of calf's liver. He'd been damaged somehow, she could see that, damaged in the way of a man who has to scrape and grovel and kiss the hind end of some irrecusable yankee boss, and his eyes showed it, jabbing out at the world like two weapons. He was Mexican, all right.

She had to turn away from those eyes, and she knew she shouldn't have accepted the coffee—steaming, with milk and so much sugar it was like a confection, in a styrofoam cup with a little plastic lid to keep the heat in—but she couldn't help herself. There was nothing in her stomach, nothing at all, and she was faint with the need of it. She was in her fourth month now, and the sickness was gone, but she was ravenous, mad with hunger, eating for two when there wasn't enough for one. She dreamed of food, of the *romeritos* stew her mother made on Holy Thursday, *tortillas* baked with chopped tomatoes, *chiles* and grated cheese, chicken heads fried in oil, shrimp and oysters and a *mole* sauce so rich and piquant with *serranos* it made the juices come to her mouth just to think about it. She stood there in the warm flowing flower-scented dawn and sipped the coffee, and it only made her hungrier.

By seven, three pickup trucks had already swung into the lot, Candelario Pérez had separated out three, four and three men again, and they were gone. The stranger from the South was not chosen, and there were still ten men who'd arrived before him. Out of the corner of her eye, América watched him contend with Candelario Pérez—she couldn't hear the words, but the man's violent gestures and the contortions of his scowling pale half-a-*gringo*'s face were enough to let her know that he wasn't happy waiting his turn, that he was a grumbler, a complainer, a sorehead. "Son of a bitch," she heard him say, and she averted her eyes. *Please,* she was praying, *don't let him come over to me.*

But he did come over. He'd given her a cup of coffee—she still had the evidence in her hand, styrofoam drained to the last sugary caffeinated drop—and she was his ally. She was sitting in her usual spot, her back pressed to the pillar nearest the entrance, ready to spring to her feet the minute some *gringo* or *gringa* pulled in needing a maid or a cook or a laundress, and the stranger eased down beside her. "Hello, pretty," he said, and his voice was a high hoarse gasp, as if he'd been poked in the throat, "—enjoy the coffee?"

She wouldn't look at him. Wouldn't speak.

"I saw you sitting here yesterday," he went on, the voice too high, too ragged, "and I said to myself, 'There's a woman that looks like she could use a cup of coffee, a woman that deserves a cup of coffee, a woman so pretty she should have the whole plantation,' and so I brought you one today. What do you think of that, eh, *linda?*" And he touched her chin with two grimy hard fingers, to turn her face toward him.

Miserable, guilty—she'd taken the coffee, hadn't she?—she didn't resist. The weird tan eyes stared into hers. "Thank you," she whispered.

He smiled then and she saw that there was something wrong with his teeth, something catastrophic, each visible tooth a maze of fracture lines like an old picture in a church. Dentures, he was wearing dentures, that was it, cheap dentures. And then he breathed out and she had to turn away again—there was something rotting inside of him. "*Me llamo José,*" he said, holding out a hand to shake, "*José Navidad. ¿Y tú? ¿Cómo te llamas,* pretty?"

This was bad. This man was bad. She thought of Cándido and bit her tongue.

"Come on," the man coaxed in his strange high choked tones, "come on, loosen up, baby. I don't bite. I'm a friendly guy—don't you like friendly guys?" And then his voice changed, dropping down suddenly to a growl. "You like coffee, though, don't you?"

"All right," she said, and she felt the anger come up in her as she stood to brush the litter from her dress, "I like coffee and I thank you, I thank you again, but I want you to know that I'm a married woman and it's not right to talk to me like that—"

He was sitting there on the ground, lanky, the knots of his fists thrust over his knees, the long blue-jean-clad shanks of his legs, and he just laughed, laughed till his eyes filled and she knew he was crazy, *loco*, demented, and she was already turning away to appeal to Candelario Pérez for protection when he grabbed her ankle—just grabbed it, and held on. "Married woman," he mocked, his voice gone high and ragged again. "Maybe so." He let go of her ankle. "But not for long, pretty, not for long."

Later, it must have been nine, nine-thirty, a new shiny expensive car pulled into the lot and a fat man—a giant of a fat man, a real *guatón*—stepped wheezing from its luxurious interior. Candelario Pérez said something to him in English and the man said something back, something long and complicated, and then—miracle of miracles!—Candelario Pérez looked to her and called out her name. Excited, timid, trembling, hungry, she started across the lot, feeling every eye on her, feeling the envy, the hate even—she had a job and they didn't. But then, at the moment she arrived there to stand in front of the big bearded *guatón* of a white man with no consciousness of how she'd gotten there, how her legs had worked and her feet negotiated the way, she heard a cry behind her.

"Hey, take me!" a voice cried out, a woman's voice, in English.

América turned her head and there she was, Mary, the big hippie *gringa* with the wire driven through her nose like some barnyard animal, and she was coming across the lot in double time, hitching at the seat of a pair of spreading and filthy sweatpants.

The fat man, the *gringo,* called out something to her, and in the next moment Mary was insinuating herself between América and the prospective employer, jabbering at him in English with her hands flailing and her big bloated eyes swelling out of her head. "Take me," she said, ignoring América, and though América didn't understand the words, she felt the thrust of their meaning just as surely as if the *gringa* had shoved a knife between her shoulder blades. "She doesn't speak any English—what do you want with her?"

"Quiero trabajar," América said, appealing to the fat man first and then, in response to the blank look on his face, to Candelario Pérez, "I want to work."

Candelario Pérez said something to the man—América was there before the *gringa,* first come, first served—and the man looked at her for a long lingering moment—too long—and she felt like squirming under that blue-eyed gaze, but she forced herself to return his stare. And then the man decided something—she could see it in the way his shoulders came forward and his jaw squared—and Candelario Pérez told her, "It's all right, six hours' work and he'll give you twenty-five dollars," and then she was in the car, the luxury of it, leather seats and a sweet new machine smell, before the door opened on the other side and Mary—big Mary, the drunk, the *gringa* maid who'd tried to cut her out—got in too.

Though he still felt like shit, like some experiment gone wrong in the subbasement of the *Laboratorio Médico* in Mexico City, Cándido did manage to rouse himself sufficiently to move their poor camp upstream, out of harm's way. Those boys—those teenage *gabachos*—had terrified him. They weren't *La Migra,* no, and they weren't the police, but the way they'd attacked his harmless little bundle of things had real teeth in it, real venom. They were dangerous and crazy and the parents who'd raised them must have been even worse—and what would have happened if they'd come in the night, when he and América were rolled up asleep in their blanket?

He'd fished the blanket out of the stream and hung it on a limb to dry, and he was able to find the grill and their cookpot too, but he'd lost a shirt and his only change of underwear, and of course América's dress was nothing but rags. He knew they had to move, but he was still too weak. Three days crawled by and he just lay there, gathering his strength, jumping at every sound, and there was precious little to eat and at night they slept in terror. And then this morning América awoke hungry, with bitter words on her lips, stings and accusations, and he slapped her and she turned her back on him and went up the hill to the labor exchange as if she weren't his wife at all, just somebody he'd met in the street.

All right, he thought, all right. Sucking in his breath against the pain in his hip, his left arm, the flayed hemisphere of his face, he bundled their things together and moved upstream, into the current, where the canyon walls steepened till they were like the walls of a room. He'd gone maybe half a mile when he came to a dead end—a pool, murky and of uncertain depth, stretched from one wall to the other. Beyond it, the wreck of a car lay beached on its back, the refuse of last winter's floods crammed into every crevice.

Cándido tried the water, the torn rucksack and mildewed blanket and everything else he could carry thrust up above his head in the grip of his one good hand—if he could make it to the far side and set up camp there, then no one could get to them, unless they were part fish. The water was tepid, stained the color of tea brewed through a twice-used bag. A thin yellowish film clung to the surface. There was hardly any current. Still, the moment he lifted the second foot from the bank he lost his balance, and only the quickness of his reaction and a thin friable stalk of cane prevented him from pitching face forward into the pool. He understood then that he would have to remove his *huaraches*—they had no grip at all, slick as the discarded tires from which the soles had been cut—and feel his way barefoot. It wasn't a prospect he relished. Who knew what could be down there—snakes, broken bottles, those ugly pale water beetles that could kill a frog and suck it dry till there was nothing left but skin? He backed out of the pool, sat heavily, and removed his sandals.

When he waded back in, clinging to the rough canyon wall for support, the *huaraches* were strung around his neck and the rucksack propped up on the crown of his head. The water reached his knees, his crotch, his waist, and finally it came right up to his armpits, which meant that América would have to swim. He thought of that as his toes felt their way through the muck, of América swimming, the hair spread wet on her shoulders, her dress balled up in one slim pretty hand and held high above her, and he began to feel horny, a sure sign that he was healing.

He found what he was looking for at the rear of the pool, just behind the wreckage of the car. There was a spit of sand there, a private beach just wide enough for a blanket and some sort of shelter—a lean-to, maybe—and then the canyon closed up like a fist. A sheer wall of stone, thirty feet or more in height, rose up out of a shallow pool to a cleft from which the stream splayed out into the air in a perpetual shower. The light was soft, filtered through the vegetation above, and what Cándido saw wasn't stone and leaf and grain of sand, but a sitting room with a big shaded lamp dangling from the ceiling, with sofas and chairs and a polished wooden floor that gleamed beneath a burden of wax. It was a revelation. A vision. The sort of thing that might have inspired a pilgrim to build a shrine.

Cándido set down his rucksack and rested in the warm sand till his clothes dried to a uniform dampness. Then he got up and began constructing a rude hearth, one rock at a time, one beside the other, and in his excitement, in the heat of the moment, he forgot his pain. When it was done, when the circle was complete and the battered refrigerator grill laid neatly atop it, he found he still had the strength to gather firewood—anything to keep moving—and he began to think about what América might bring home with her. If she'd found work, that is. And of course he'd have to wait at the old spot for her and they'd have to wade across with the groceries . . . but maybe she'd have some *tortillas* or a piece of meat and something to cook down into a stew, some vegetables and rice or a couple of potatoes . . .

There'd been no breakfast, nothing, not a twig to suck, and he was as hungry as he'd ever been in his life, but the hunger spurred him on and as the pile of water-bleached sticks began to grow an idea took hold of him: he would surprise her, that's what he would do. With a real camp. Something solid and substantial, a place they could call home—at least till he got back on his feet and found work and they could have their own apartment in a nice neighborhood with trees and sidewalks and a space for the car he was going to buy her, and he could see the outline of that space already, fresh blacktop, all neatly laid out and marked with crisp yellow paint . . .

He found some twine—or was it fishing line?—in a pile of water-run brush, and two black plastic bags that he was able to work into the thatch of the roof. His hip hurt him still, and his knee, and his ribs when he stretched, but he was a slave to the idea, and by the time the sun had passed over the lip of the canyon and left him in an artificial twilight, a sturdy lean-to of interlaced branches stood on the spit behind the rusted hulk of the car, work he could be proud of.

He dozed, exhausted from his efforts, and when he woke a weak patina of sunlight painted the eastern rim of the ledge above him. He looked up drowsily, full of a false sense of well-being, and then it hit him: *América. Where was she?* She wasn't here . . . but then, how could she be? This wasn't their old camp, this wasn't a place she knew. He got to his feet, the pain digging claws into his hip, and cursed himself. It must have been four, five o'clock. She'd be back there, downstream, looking for him, and how could she doubt that he'd run out on her for good?

Cursing still, cursing nonstop, he plunged into the pool and slashed through the murky water, heart hammering, and never mind his clothes. He hurried along the streambed as fast as his hip would allow, frantic now, in a panic—and then he rounded the bend that gave onto their old camp and she wasn't there. The leaves hung limp, the stream stood still. There was no trace of her, no note, no pile of stones or scribble in the sand. This was *muy gacho,* bad news. And fuck his stinking *pinche* life. Fuck it.

Then it was up the hill, each step a crucifixion, and what choice did he have?—up the hill for the first time since the accident. He hadn't gone a hundred feet before he had to stop and catch his breath. The clothes hung sodden from his frame—and he'd lost weight, he had, lying there in the stinking sand with nothing but scraps and vegetables to eat for the last nine days like some wasted old sack of bones in a nursing home. He spat in the dirt, gritted his teeth, and went on.

The sun was hot still, though it must have been six o'clock at least, higher and hotter than down below. Despite his wet clothes he began to sweat, and he had to use his hands—or his one good hand—to help him over the rough places. When he was halfway up, at a spot where the trail jogged to the right and dodged round a big reddish chipped tooth of a boulder, he had a surprise. A nasty surprise. Turning the corner and throwing a quick glance up the trail ahead, he saw that he wasn't alone. A man was coming down from above, a stranger, long strides caught up in the mechanics of a walk that threw his hips out as if they belonged to somebody else. Cándido's first reaction was to duck into the bushes, but it was too late: the man was on top of him already, leaning back against the pitch of the slope like an insect climbing down a blade of grass.

"Hey, 'mano," the man said, his voice as high and harsh as a hawk's call. "*¿Qué onda?* What's happening?" He'd stopped there in the middle of the trail that was no more than two feet wide, a tall pale man made taller by the slope, speaking the border Spanish of the back alleys and *cantinas* of Tijuana. He was wearing a baseball cap turned backwards on his head and his eyes were a color Cándido couldn't identify, somewhere between yellow and red, like twin bruises set in his skull. He was one of the *vagos* from the labor exchange, that's what he was. And he'd have a knife in his pocket or tucked into the back of his belt.

"*Buenas,*" Cándido murmured, keeping an eye on him, though God knew he had nothing worth stealing but the clothes on his back—and they'd been washed and mended so many times they wouldn't fetch more than a few *centavos* at a rag shop. But you could never tell: sometimes they'd steal your shirt just for pure meanness.

"What's it like down there, brother?" the man asked, indicating the ravine with a flick of his eyes. The sun glanced off his face. His skin was the color of a dirty bar of soap—not white, but not brown either. "Comfortable? Quiet? There's water, right?"

When the stranger swiveled his shoulders to scan the ravine, Cándido saw that he had a bedroll wound up tight and slung across his back with a length of twine. Cándido didn't want to give him any encouragement—if word got out, the whole labor exchange would be down there. "Not much," he said.

This was funny. The man let out a little bark of a laugh and grinned to show off a cheap set of fake teeth. "Judging from the look of you, *carnal*, there's enough to go swimming in, eh?"

Cándido held the man's eyes. He shrugged. "It's an unlucky place. I had a camp down there but they raided it three days ago. *Gabachos*. They painted things on the rocks with their spray cans. You won't catch me down there again."

Birds flitted from bush to bush. The sun stood still. The man was taking his time. "That what happened to your face? And that arm?"

"Yeah. Or no—not then." Cándido shrugged again, conscious of the tattered sling that cradled his left arm. The arm was better, a whole lot better, but that still gave him an arm and a half to the stranger's two—if it came to that. "It's a long story," he said.

The stranger seemed to be weighing the matter, arms folded across his chest, studying Cándido's ravaged face as if it were the key to a puzzle. He made no move to step aside and let Cándido pass—he was in control, and he knew it. "So where's your things?" he demanded, his voice riding up out of range. "I mean, if what you say is true. You got no bedroll, no cooking things, no money stashed away in a jar someplace maybe? Nothing in your pocket?"

"They took it all," Cándido lied. "*Pinche gabachos.* I hid in the bushes."

A long slow moment ticked by. Cándido eased his hand into his pocket and felt the weight of his own poor rusted switchblade there, the one he'd got after those punks had gone after América at the border. "Listen," he said, trying to take hold of the situation without provoking anything he would regret—he was no match for this guy, not in the shape he was in now—"it's been good talking to you, always good to talk to a *compañero*, but I've got to be moving along. I need to find a place to sleep tonight . . . you don't know of anything, do you? Someplace safe?"

No response. The stranger stared out over Cándido's head into the gaping nullity of the ravine, patting mechanically at his breast pocket before reaching into it and producing a single stick of gum in a dull aluminum wrapper. Slowly, casually, as if he had all the time in the world, he inserted the flat wedge of gum between the thin flaps of his lips and began chewing, crumpling the wrapper as if he were strangling something. Cándido watched it drop from his fingers into the fine white dust of the trail.

"I could really use something to eat too," Cándido prodded, giving him a pathetic look, the look of a dog, a beggar on the street. "You wouldn't have a little bite of something on you, would you?"

The man came back to him then, pinning him with those strange tan eyes: Cándido had turned the tables on him—he was the one asking the questions now. The stranger looked uncomfortable suddenly, his jaws working gingerly round the stick of gum, and Cándido thought of his grandfather, reduced to eating mush in his fifties, his dentures so cracked and ill-fitting they might have been designed by a Nazi torturer. The moment had passed. The menace was gone.

"Sorry, *'mano*," the man said, and then he brushed by Cándido and headed down the path. The last Cándido saw of him was the peak of his reversed cap vanishing round the bend, and he couldn't be sure whether the stranger was looking backwards or forwards.

Shaken, Cándido turned and started back up the trail. Now he had to worry about this stinking crack-toothed *pendejo* nosing around down in the canyon, as if he didn't have enough problems already. And what if he found their camp? What then? Cándido felt jealous suddenly, possessive: the son of a bitch. There was a whole range of mountains here, canyons all over the place—too many to count—and why did he have to pick this one? Anger spurred him on—and worry. He was breathing hard and his hip hurt, his knee, the throbbing crust of scab that masked the left side of his face. He kept going, forcing himself on, until a sudden screech of tires let him know that the road was just above him, and he stopped a moment to catch his breath.

And then he emerged from the bushes and he was out on the road, the traffic hurtling past him in a crazy *gringo* taillight-chasing rush— and what was the hurry, the constant hurry? Making a buck, that's what. Building their glass office towers and adding up the figures on their dark little TV screens, getting richer—that's what the hurry was. And that was why the *gabachos* had cars and clothes and money and the Mexicans didn't. He walked along the highway, feeling strange— this was just where he'd been hit, just here—and he felt the cold steel rush of a passing car at his back and someone leaned on the horn and he nearly jumped out of his skin. He watched the taillights and cursed under his breath.

He looked first in the parking lot at the Chinese store, but América wasn't there. There were no Mexicans around at this hour, not a one—you'd think they'd all vanished into the earth, like those toad-stools that spring up after a rainfall and disappear by sunset. The place was swarming with *norteamericanos* though, hordes of them, jumping in and out of their cars, hustling into the store and hustling back out again with their brown paper bags full of beer and wine and little sweet things to put in the mouth. They looked at Cándido like he was a leper.

On up the street, careful, careful, look both ways and cross. Nobody was coming down the canyon, but they were all going up, endlessly, relentlessly, enough cars to fill twenty big boats going back to Japan where they'd all come from in the first place. There was a little shop-ping plaza here, the one with the larger market and the *paisano* from Italy. This was where América would be if she'd missed him down below, or if—and the idea hit him with the sudden force of inspiration—if she was working. Maybe that was it. Maybe he'd been worrying for nothing. Maybe she would have money and they could buy food.

Food. His stomach clenched at the thought of it and he felt faint for just a moment—a moment, that was all, but it was enough to make him lurch into a big beefy *gabacho* with sideburns that ate up half his face and hair all piled up slick on his head like Elvis in one of those black velvet tapestries. The man shoved him away, a violent thrust of the arms, and said something harsh, something hateful, his face exploding with it. "Escuse, escuse," Cándido blurted, throwing up his hands and backing away, but they were all watching now, all the *gabachos* in the parking lot, and he would have run but his legs wouldn't carry him.

At six p.m., with the sun starting to slant down in the west and the shadows of the trees swelling against the windows like images out of a dream, América was working. Still working. Though the six hours were up and the fat man was nowhere to be found. Candelario Pérez had said six hours' work, twenty-five dollars, and this was eight hours now and she was wondering, did this mean the fat man would pay her more? Six divided into twenty-five was four dollars and sixteen cents an hour, and so, for two extra hours she should get, what—eight dollars and thirty-two cents more. She glowed with the thought of it. She was earning money, money for food, for Cándido and her baby—she, who'd never earned a *centavo* in her life. She'd worked in her father's house, of course, cooking and cleaning and running errands for her mother, and he gave her an allowance each week, but it was nothing like this, nothing like earning a wage from a stranger—and a *gringo*, no less. Cándido would be surprised. Of course he would have guessed by now that she was working, but wait till he saw her tonight, coming down that trail into the canyon with all the groceries she could carry, with meat and eggs and rice and a can of those big sardines, the ones in oil so rich you lick it from the tips of your fingers . . .

She thought of that, held the image in her brain till it was imprinted there, and her hands were quick and nimble even after eight hours, and the fumes hardly bothered her. They bothered Mary, though. Bothered her plenty. The big *gringa* with the ring through her nose hadn't shut up about it since the fat man had led them into this great long beautiful room of his house lined with windows and given them each a pair of yellow latex gloves and the plastic bottles of the corrosive. América didn't understand what the woman was saying, of course, and she tried to block her out too, but the drift of it was inescapable. Mary didn't like the work. Mary didn't need the work. Mary had a house with a roof and four walls and a refrigerator with food in it. She didn't like the fumes or the fat man or his beautiful house or life on this planet. She tipped back a pint of that liquor she had with her and as the day went on she got slower and slower till practically all she did at the end was sit there and complain.

The work was hard, no doubt about it. The man had hundreds of straw cases lining the walls of the room and stacked up to the ceiling in the back, and in each case was a stone figurine of the Buddha, gone black with mold and age. They were all the same: two feet high, heavier than lead, the bald head and pregnant gut and the stupid grin that was meant to be a look of wisdom but could as easily have been senility or constipation. And each Buddha had to be scrubbed with the corrosive to take the discoloration off the brow, under the eyelids and lips, in the crevices beneath the arms and the tiny blackened indentation of the navel. When it was cleaned, when the corrosive had devoured the mold and the wire brushes had dug their deepest, the Buddha took on a rosy sheen, and then it was time to affix the glossy gold strip of paper with the glue already on it that read JIM SHIRLEY IMPORTS.

América didn't care about the fumes or the tired nasal rant of the *gringa* or the stiffening in her fingers and the ache in her back from lifting statue after statue out of its cradle and setting it on the table before her—all she cared about was pleasing this healthy big bearded fat man who'd given her the chance to earn the money she needed to stay alive till things got better. She worked hard. Worked like two women. And she never stopped, not even to stretch her aching back or massage her cramping fingers, not even for a minute.

Finally, at quarter past seven by the bronze sunburst clock on the wall, the fat man slammed through the door, running sweat, and gave them a wild-eyed look. He was panting, and the big T-shirt he wore—Mickey Mouse poised on the steps of the Magic Kingdom—was wet under the arms. He barked out something in a roaring deep voice and Mary sprang to her feet, roaring something back at him. América had her head down, raking the wire brush across the belly of the nearest Buddha as if she were trying to saw it in two. She was tired and hungry and she had to pee, but at the same time she wanted to stay here forever in the big clean open room earning four dollars and sixteen cents for every hour the blood flowed through her veins and the air swelled her lungs. She scrubbed at the statue. Scrubbed furiously.

The *patrón* didn't seem to notice. His words were truncated, clipped off as if he couldn't spare the breath for them—"Okay, that's it, let's go"—and he clapped his hands twice, two short impatient bursts as abrupt as a cannonade. América didn't dare look up. Her fingers flew, the brush rasped. He was standing right over her now—"Come on, let's go, I'm in a hurry here"—and she felt a quick surge of panic. It was time to go, yes? Eight hours and more—of course it was. And yet she couldn't escape the feeling that he was criticizing her, urging her to work faster, harder, to ply the brush and pour the corrosive and make every Buddha in the room shine as if it had just emerged from the mold.

"Jesus," he said, letting the air hiss over his teeth, and she understood him now. She wanted to apologize—the words were on her lips—but she didn't have the chance. The next thing she knew he had her by the elbow and he was pulling her roughly from the seat—"Finish now, finish," he was saying—while Mary, a cigarette clamped between her lips, called out *"Vamos"* in a drunken slur and they were moving, all three of them, out the door, down the steps and into the rich new car with the airtight doors.

Mary sat up front with the *patrón*; América had the broad plane of the rear seat to herself, like a queen or a movie star. She sank back in the seat and let her eyes play over the blue-green lawns with their bursts of flowers—flowers everywhere, the very trees on the streets in bloom—and the tall angular houses that rose out of the hills behind them, every one striped and striped again with windows, as if they were expecting an invasion from the sea. She wondered what it would be like to live in one of those houses, gazing out the kitchen window at the sunstruck crags of the canyon while the machine for the dishes did your work for you and the radio played the soft sad music of violins and cellos. She studied the back of the fat man's neck for clues. It was unrevealing. Thick, pinkish, with little puckered mouths of flesh at the nape and a riot of hacked stiff hairs, it could have been anybody's neck. And then she wondered about his wife—what was she like? Was she fat too? Or was she one of those women you saw in the ads with a leotard clinging to her puffed-up breasts and her eyes staring out from the page like an animal's?

They went through a gate—two broad pastel-colored steel grids that swung back automatically as the car approached. The gate hadn't been there in the morning—América was sure of that. It had been ten-thirty or so when they came through and she was alive to everything, to every nuance, to the houses, the cars, the people in them, and she remembered seeing half a dozen of her own people there, with picks and shovels and a cement mixer—she thought she recognized one of the men from the labor exchange but the car went by too quickly to be sure. Two stone pillars had framed the road under a wrought-iron bonnet with a Spanish inscription—ARROYO BLANCO—and then a word in English she couldn't decipher, and there was a little booth there, like the ticket booth in the movies, but no one was inside and the fat man didn't stop. Now the gate was up. América looked over her shoulder and saw that the steel bars extended on the outside of the two main pillars to a series of smaller stone columns that were only half-built. She saw a wheelbarrow, three shovels lined up neatly, a pick, and then they were out on the canyon road and heading back down the hill to the labor exchange.

Mary was saying something to the *patrón*, waving her hands, pointing—directions, that was it—and he turned off onto a side street that wound through a stand of dusty oaks to a cluster of little cottages tucked under the arches of the trees. The cottages were in need of paint, but they were fine, charming even, with their wooden shingles, sturdy porches and beams gone gray with age. Pickup trucks and foreign sports cars sat out front of them. There were flowers in pots, cats all over the place, the smell of barbecue. This was where Mary lived, the *gringa* maid.

The fat man pulled to a stop in front of a redwood bungalow at the end of the lane, Mary said something, and he shifted in the seat to reach for his wallet. América couldn't see what he was paying her but from the way the big worthless cow of a drunken *gringa* was acting she was sure it was for the full eight hours and not just the twenty-five dollars she'd been promised—or had Mary been promised more? The thought stabbed at América as she sat there in the car and watched a boy of twelve or so burst into view on a dirt bike and vanish round the side of the bungalow in a mirage of exhaust. Candelario Pérez had said twenty-five dollars, but maybe Mary was getting thirty or thirty-five, plus the extra two hours, because she was white, because she spoke English and wore a ring through her nose. América was sure of it. She watched the two big heads, complicitous, watched the shoulders dip as the money changed hands, and then Mary was out of the car and the *patrón* was leaning over the seat saying something in his breathless cut-up incomprehensible garble of a language.

He wanted her to sit in front, that was it. The contortions of his face, the gestures of his swollen hands told her as much. All right. América got out and slid into the cupped seat beside him. The fat man backed around and shot up the road in an explosion of dust.

He turned on the radio. No violins, no cellos: guitars. She knew the song vaguely—*Hotel California* or something like that, *Welcome, welcome*—and she thought about the strangeness of it all, sitting here in this rich man's car, earning money, living in the North. She never dreamed it would actually happen. If someone had told her when she was a girl at school she wouldn't have believed them—it would have been a fairy tale like the one about the charmaid and the glass slipper. And when the fat man laid his hand casually across her thigh, even before he cheated her of the extra two hours and pushed her rudely from the car, she wanted to fling it away from her, hack it off with a machete and bury it in some *bruja*'s yard, but she didn't. She just let it lie there like a dead thing, though it moved and insinuated itself and she wanted to scream for the car to stop, for the door to open and for the hard dry brush of the ravine to hide her.

7

DELANEY WAS IN A HURRY. HE'D BEEN COOKING DOWN his marinara sauce since two and the mussels were already in the pot and steaming when he discovered that there was no pasta in the house. The table was set, the salad tossed, Kyra due home any minute, Jordan transfixed by his video game, the pasta water boiling. But no pasta. He decided to take a chance, ten minutes down the road, ten minutes back up: Jordan would be okay. "Jordan," he called, poking his head in the door of the boy's room, "I'm going down to Gitello's for some pasta. Your mother'll be here any minute. If there's an emergency, go next door to the Cherrystones'. Selda's home. I just talked to her. Okay?"

The back of the boy's head was reedy and pale, the seed pod of some exotic wildflower buffeted by the video winds, a twitch here, a shoulder shrug there, the forward dip of unbroken, inviolable concentration.

"Okay?" Delaney repeated. "Or do you want to come with me? You can come if you want."

"Okay."

"Okay what? Are you coming or staying?"

There was a pause during which Delaney adjusted to the room's dim artificial light, the light of a cell or dungeon, and felt the fierce unyielding grip of the little gray screen. The shades were down and the rapid-fire blasts and detonations of the game were the only sounds, relieved at intervals by a canned jingle. He thought then of the house burning down with Jordan in it, Jordan aflame and barely aware of it—ten minutes down the road, ten minutes back up—and realized he couldn't leave him even for a second, even with Selda right next door and the mussels getting tough and the water boiling and Kyra due home. The kid was six years old and the world was full of nasty surprises—look what had happened to the dog in their own backyard. What was he thinking?

Jordan never even turned his head. "Stay," he murmured.

"You can't stay."

"I don't want to go."

"You have to go."

"Mom'll be home in a minute."

"Get in the car."

No traffic coming down the hill at this hour—it was nearly six—and Delaney made it in eight minutes, despite having to sit behind two cars at the gate that had gone up this afternoon to keep the riffraff out of the Elysian Groves of Arroyo Blanco Estates. The parking lot was crowded though, commuters with strained looks shaking the stiffness out of their joints as they lurched from their cars and staggered through the door in search of the six-pack, the prechopped salad (just add the premixed dressing) and the quart of no-fat milk. Jordan sat in the front seat, securely belted in, bent over his Game Boy. "You coming in?" Delaney asked.

Zip, bang, zing-zing-zing. "Uh-uh."

And then Delaney was in full flight, springing up off his toes—and what else did they need: milk? bread? coffee?—his shoulders hunched defensively as he sought the gaps between the massed flesh and dilatory carts of his fellow shoppers. He had the pasta tucked under his arm—perciatelli, imported, in the blue-and-yellow box—and two baguettes, a wedge of Romano, a gallon of milk and a jar of roasted peppers clutched to his chest, when he ran into Jack Jardine. He'd been thinking about the horned lizard he'd seen on his afternoon hike (or horned toad, as most people erroneously called it) and its wonderful adaptation of ejecting blood from its eye sockets when threatened, and he was right on top of Jack before he noticed him.

It was an awkward moment. Not only because Delaney was practically jogging down the aisle and almost blundered into him, but because of what had happened at the meeting a week and a half ago. Looking back on it, Delaney had a nagging suspicion that he'd made a fool of himself. "Jack," he breathed, and he could feel his face going through all the permutations before settling on an exculpatory smile.

Jack was cocked back on one hip, his jacket buttoned, tie crisp, a plastic handbasket dangling from his fingertips. Two bottles of Merlot were laid neatly in the basket, their necks protruding from one end. He looked good, as usual, in a pale double-breasted suit that set off his tan and picked up the color of his tight blond beard. "Delaney," he said, leaning forward to reach for a jar of marinated artichoke hearts, his own smile lordly and bemused. He set the jar in his basket and straightened up. "You were pretty exercised the other night," he observed, showing his teeth now, the full rich jury-mesmerizing grin. "You even took me by surprise."

"I guess I got carried away."

"No, no: you were right. Absolutely. It's just that you know as well as I do what our neighbors are like—if you don't keep to the agenda you've got chaos, pure and simple. And the gate thing is important, probably the single most important agendum we've taken up in my two years as president."

For a moment Delaney saw the phantom car again, creeping down Piñon Drive with its speakers thumping like the pulse of some monstrous heart. He blinked to drive the image away. "You really think so? To me, I say it's unnecessary—and, I don't know, irresponsible somehow."

Jack gave him a quizzical look. "Irresponsible?"

Delaney shifted his burden, milk from the right hand to the left, baguettes under the arm, pasta to his chest. "I don't know. I lean more to the position that we live in a democracy, like the guy in the shorts said at the meeting . . . I mean, we all have a stake in things, and locking yourself away from the rest of society, how can you justify that?"

"Safety. Self-protection. Prudence. You lock your car, don't you? Your front door?" A cluck of the tongue, a shift from one hip to the other, blue eyes, solid as stone. "Delaney, believe me, I know how you feel. You heard Jack Cherrystone speak to the issue, and nobody's credentials can touch Jack's as far as being liberal is concerned, but this society isn't what it was—and it won't be until we get control of the borders."

The borders. Delaney took an involuntary step backwards, all those dark disordered faces rising up from the streetcorners and freeway on-ramps to mob his brain, all of them crying out their human wants through mouths full of rotten teeth. "That's racist, Jack, and you know it."

"Not in the least—it's a question of national sovereignty. Did you know that the U.S. accepted more immigrants last year than all the other countries of the world *combined*—and that half of them settled in California? And that's *legal* immigrants, people with skills, money, education. The ones coming in through the Tortilla Curtain down there, those are the ones that are killing us. They're peasants, my friend. No education, no resources, no skills—all they've got to offer is a strong back, and the irony is we need fewer and fewer strong backs every day because we've got robotics and computers and farm machinery that can do the labor of a hundred men at a fraction of the cost." He dropped his hand in dismissal. "It's old news."

Delaney set the milk down on the floor. He was in a hurry, dinner on the stove, Jordan in the car, Kyra about to walk in the door, but in the heat of the moment he forgot all about it. "I can't believe you," he said, and he couldn't seem to control his free arm, waving it in an expanding loop. "Do you realize what you're saying? Immigrants are the lifeblood of this country—we're a nation of immigrants—and neither of us would be standing here today if it wasn't."

"Clichés. There's a point of saturation. Besides which, the Jardines fought in the Revolutionary War—you could hardly call us immigrants."

"Everybody's an immigrant from somewhere. My grandfather came over from Bremen and my grandmother was Irish—does that make me any less a citizen than the Jardines?"

A woman with frosted hair and a face drawn tight as a drumskin ducked between them for a jar of olives. Jack worked a little grit into his voice: "That's not the point. Times have changed, my friend. Radically. Do you have any idea what these people are costing us, and not just in terms of crime, but in real tax dollars for social services? No? Well, you ought to. You must have seen that thing in the *Times* a couple weeks ago, about the San Diego study?"

Delaney shook his head. He felt his stomach sink, heard the thump of phantom speakers. Suddenly the horned lizard sprang back into the forefront of his consciousness: what good was squirting blood from your eyes? Wouldn't that just be gravy for whatever was about to clamp down on you?

"Look, Delaney," Jack went on, cool, reasonable, his voice in full song now, "it's a simple equation, so much in, so much out. The illegals in San Diego County contributed seventy million in tax revenues and at the same time they used up two hundred and forty million in services—welfare, emergency care, schooling and the like. You want to pay for that? And for the crime that comes with it? You want another crazy Mexican throwing himself under your wheels hoping for an insurance payoff? Or worse, you want one of *them* behind the wheel bearing down on you, no insurance, no brakes, no nothing?"

Delaney was trying to organize his thoughts. He wanted to tell Jack that he was wrong, that everyone deserved a chance in life and that the Mexicans would assimilate just like the Poles, Italians, Germans, Irish and Chinese and that besides which we'd stolen California from them in the first place, but he didn't get the chance. At that moment Jack Jr. appeared from behind the cranberry juice display, the great fluttering sail of his T-shirt in motion, his pants wide enough to bankrupt the factory. Two liters of Pepsi sprouted from his knuckles and he cradled a bag of nachos the size of a pillow under his arm. The bag had been torn raggedly open. Delaney could see flecks of MSG, food coloring and salt crystals caked in the corners of the boy's mouth. "Hey, Dad," Jack Jr. murmured, ducking his head to avoid a display banner and greeting Delaney with a dip of his eyes and an awkward croak of salutation. "Got to go, Dad," he prodded, his voice aflame with hormonal urgency. "Steffie's waiting."

And then they were moving in the direction of the cash registers— all three of them, as a group—and Jack, the conciliatory Jack, Jack the politician, Jack the soother of gripes, grievances and hurts real or imaginary, put an arm over Delaney's shoulder and warbled his sweetest notes: "Listen, Delaney, I know how you feel, and I agree with you. It's not easy for me either—it's nothing less than rethinking your whole life, who you are and what you believe in. And trust me: when we get control of the border again—*if* we get control of it—I'll be the first to advocate taking that gate down. But don't kid yourself: it's not going to happen anytime soon."

Though there were three checkers, people were lined up six deep at the registers. Delaney gave Jack a weak smile and got in line beside him. He gazed out over the mob of his fellow shoppers, past the checkout girl and the banners and baubles and slogans to the parking lot, where his Acura stood gleaming in the sun, and remembered that he was in a hurry—or had been. He could see the crown of Jordan's head bobbing and weaving just above the dashboard and pictured the electronic Armageddon raging in that confined space, the boy's nimble fingers sending intergalactic invaders to their doom even as the next ship landed.

Delaney opted for the paper bag—recycle, save the environment— and waited for the girl to ring up Jack and Jack Jr.'s purchases, the rack behind her bright with batteries, Slim Jims, toenail clippers and gum. He was thinking he could work that horned toad into his next column—it was symbolic somehow, deeply symbolic, though he wasn't sure of exactly what.

"Sorry for the lecture," Jack crooned in his ear. "You see my point though?"

Delaney turned to him as the checkout girl swept Jack Jr.'s Pepsi bottles over the scanner with a practiced flick of her wrist. "All right, Jack," he said finally, conceding the field, "I don't like the gate—I'll never like it—but I accept it. None of us want urban crime up here—that'd be crazy. And if I got a little carried away at the meeting it was because this feeding of the predator species has got to stop, I mean people have to realize—"

"You're right," Jack said, giving his elbow an affirmative squeeze. "Absolutely."

"And I tell you, Kyra was really heartbroken over that dog—and I was too. You live with a pet all that time . . ."

"I know exactly how you feel."

They moved toward the door, bags cradled in their arms, Jack Jr. looming over them like a distorted shadow. The door slid back and they were out in the lot, all three of them, the sun glancing off the windshields of the cars, the hills awash in light. Jack said he was sorry to hear about the dog and wondered if Delaney had ever thought about putting out a little newsletter for the community, the sort of thing that would alert them to the dangers of living on the edge of the wild and maybe even reprint one or two of his columns? People would love it. They would.

But Delaney wasn't listening. Across the short span of the lot, over by the gift shop, there was some sort of altercation going on—a fat-faced truck-driver type with an elaborate hairdo going ballistic over something . . . was it a fight? The three of them froze just behind Delaney's car as the trouble came toward them—*You wetback motherfucker, watch where the fuck you're going or I swear I'll kick your sorry ass from here to Algodones and back*—and Delaney got a look at the other man involved. He saw the sideways movement, the scuttling feet in their dirty tire-tread sandals, the skittish red-flecked eyes and graying mustache, and experienced a shock of recognition: here it was all over again.

He felt anger and shame at the same time—the man was a bum, that was all, hassling somebody else now, and yet the look of him, the wordless plea in his eyes and the arm in a sling and the side of his face layered with scab like old paint brought all Delaney's guilt back to the surface, a wound that refused to heal. His impulse was to intercede, to put an end to it, and yet in some perverse way he wanted to see this dark alien little man crushed and obliterated, out of his life forever. It was then, in the moment of Delaney's vacillation, that the big man lurched forward and gave the Mexican a shove that sent him staggering into the rear of Delaney's car. There was the dull reverberation of sheet metal, a soft cry from the Mexican, and the big man, his face inflamed, spat out a final curse and swung round on his heels.

Jack Jr. stood rooted to the spot by the black leather blocks of his hi-tops, clenching his fists. Unruffled, Jack Sr. had stepped neatly aside, the pleats of his pants like two plumb lines, his mouth pursed in distaste. Delaney was reaching for his keys when the altercation swept toward them, and now he stood poised over the trunk of his car, groceries pressed like a shield to his chest, keys dangling limply from his fingers, looking on numbly as the dark man got shakily to his feet, muttering apologies in his own dark language. The Mexican seemed dazed—or maybe deranged. He lifted his heavy eyes to focus blearily on Jack, then Jack Jr. and finally Delaney. Faintly, from inside the car, came the thin tinny sound effects of Jordan's electronic war. The man stood there a long moment, squinting into Delaney's eyes, the rag of a sling hanging from his arm, his face sunk in its helmet of bruises, and then he turned away and limped across the lot, hunched under a rain of imaginary blows.

"See what I mean?" Jack said.

"What would you do with all this space?" Kyra heard herself asking, and even before the question passed her lips she knew it was wrong. She should have exclaimed, *And look at all this space!* with the rising inflection of a cheerleader, but somehow she'd put a negative spin on it, the very question implying that the expanse of brilliantly buffed floors and high beamed ceilings was excessive, de trop, somehow too much, that the living room was the size of a basketball court and the master bedroom bigger than most people's houses—and who needed all that? Who but a monster of ego, a parvenu, a robber baron? It wasn't the sort of question a closer should ask.

Louisa Greutert gave her a curious look—nothing more than the briefest darting glance of surprise—but it was enough. Kyra knew what she was thinking.

Louisa's husband, Bill—thin, nervous, with a tonsure of silver hair and the face of an ascetic—was wandering through the immensity of the dining room, hands clasped behind his back. He was president of his own company, Pacific Rim Investments, and he'd lived in Bel Air for the past twenty years, the majority of that time with his first wife, who'd kept the house as part of the divorce settlement. Kyra pegged him for sixty-five or so, though he looked younger; Louisa was in her late forties.

"You know we know the Da Roses socially," Louisa murmured, running a jeweled hand over the surface of a built-in mahogany china cabinet, "or we did, that is, before Albert took his life . . . They made some bad investments, is what I hear . . ." This wasn't so much a statement of fact as a supposition, an opening: she wanted gossip. And gossip was a commodity Kyra readily served up, if it suited her purposes. This time, though, she merely said: "She's living in Italy."

"Italy?"

"Her family has an estate there. Near Turin. Didn't you know?" In fact, Kyra barely knew Patricia Da Ros—the referral had come to her from an associate at the Beverly Hills office, and aside from two long-distance calls, all the arrangements had been made via fax.

Louisa was silent a moment, lingering over some ceramic figurines displayed on a brightly painted Gothic Revival dresser; then she lifted her head like a hunting dog attuned to the faintest distant sound. It was four-thirty in the afternoon and the curtains of the big central room were aflame with light. "They were funny about this house. Did you know they never entertained. I mean never?"

Kyra let a small vaguely interrogatory noise escape her. This was her signal to talk the place up, rhapsodize over the views, the privacy, the value and exclusivity, but something held her back. She was reticent today, not herself at all, and as she watched this lithe busy woman stalk through the corridors and poke into the cupboards she had a revelation that took her by surprise—she realized that deep down she didn't want to sell the place. She wanted the listing, yes, and she was born to move property and the commission would put her over the top and ensure her of the sales crown for the fourth consecutive year, but she'd never felt this way about a house before. The more time she spent in it, cushioned from the hot, dry, hard-driving world, the more she began to feel it was hers—really hers, and not just in some metaphorical sense. How could these people even begin to appreciate it the way she did? How could anyone?

"Of course," the woman went on now, trying the lower drawer of a locked sideboard, "they were a bit out of the way up here . . . and yet it's a terrific location, I don't mean to say that, right on the edge of Malibu and only, what, twenty minutes from Santa Monica? Still, I wonder who'd want to schlepp all the way out here even if they were the type to entertain . . ."

Kyra had nothing to say to this, one way or the other. Bill Greutert had already confided to her that he and his wife were looking for something out of the way and had specifically asked about this house. *It's just so crowded down there,* he said, *you get this feeling of the city closing in on you, even in Bel Air. There's just so many*—he'd waved his hand in exasperation, searching for the judicious term—people, *you know what I mean?*

Kyra knew. Since the riots she'd met dozens of couples like the Greuterts. They all wanted something out of the way, something rustic, rural, safe—something removed from people of whatever class and color, but particularly from the hordes of immigrants pouring in from Mexico and Central America, from Dubai, Burundi and Lithuania, from Asia and India and everywhere else in the known world. Brown people. Colored people. People in saris, *serapes* and kaffiyehs. That was what Bill Greutert meant. He didn't have to say anything more.

An hour later, Louisa Greutert was still making the rounds of the house, poking through drawers like a detective at the scene of a crime, while her husband paced back and forth against the backdrop of the canyon, hands clasped rigidly behind his back. Kyra tried to remain attentive, tried her best to look sincere and helpful, but her heart wasn't in it. She stood to make a commission on both ends of the deal—there was no other realtor involved—but still she just couldn't seem to motivate herself. By the end of the second hour she'd settled into a leather wing chair in the library, gazing out into the hazy sun-struck distance, idly thumbing through one of Albert Da Ros's leather-bound volumes—poetry, as it turned out. Louisa Greutert had to come looking for her finally, her voice echoing through the vast empty space of the house, the sound of her heels like gunshots coming up the corridor. "Through already?" Kyra murmured, rising guiltily from the chair.

And there was that look again, the head tilted to one side, the cold hard eyes fixing her with a look of amusement and disdain. "We've been here nearly two and a half hours."

"Oh, well, I didn't mean—I didn't realize it had been that long." Kyra let her gaze wander over the shelves of books, the leather-backed chairs, the wainscoting, the lamps in their sconces, and it was as if she were seeing them for the first time. "It's just that the place is so restful—"

She was aware in that moment of the presence of the husband in the hallway behind her, a ghostly figure like some unsettled spirit of the place. He crossed the room to his wife, there was a brief whispered consultation, and then the wife's voice came back at her with the suddenness of a twig snapping underfoot: "I'm afraid it's not for us."

In the morning, Delaney sat at his keyboard, his face illuminated by the pale glow of the monitor. Over breakfast, he'd watched a pair of starlings crowding out the wrens and finches at the bird feeder, and an idea came to him: why not do a series of sketches on introduced species? The idea excited him—the whole thrust of the "Pilgrim" columns was that he himself was a recent transplant, seeing the flora and fauna of the Pacific Coast with the eye of a neophyte, and a series on creatures like the opossum, the escargot, the starling and the parakeet would be perfect. The only problem was, the words wouldn't come, or the images either. When he tried to envision the canyon, the white dust trails threaded through stands of mesquite and yucca till the very bones of the mountains lay exposed, or even the parking lot at the Woodland Hills McDonald's, swarming with one-legged blackbirds and rumpled, diseased-looking starlings, he saw only the Mexican. *His* Mexican. The man he had to forget all over again.

He'd wanted to shout out an indictment—"That's him! That's the one!"—but something held him back. What, exactly, he didn't know. Misplaced sympathy? Guilt? Pity? It was a wasted opportunity because Jack was there to see for himself how blameless Delaney was—the man was a nuisance, a bum, a panhandler. If anything, Delaney was the victim, his twenty dollars separated from him through a kind of extortion, an emotional sleight of hand that preyed on his good nature and fellow feeling. He'd read about beggars in India mutilating themselves and their children so as to present the horror of the empty sleeve, the dangling pantleg or the suppurating eye socket to the well-fed and guilt-racked tourist. Well, wasn't this Mexican cut from the same mold, throwing himself in front of a car for the thin hope of twenty bucks?

Of course, dinner had been ruined. By the time Delaney got over the shock, said his goodbyes to Jack and swept out into the rush-hour traffic and back up the hill to the new gate and the newly installed guard waiting there to grill him on the suitability of his entering his own community, the marinara sauce had been scorched to the bottom of the pan, and the mussels, though he'd turned off the flame beneath them, had taken on the consistency of Silly Putty. Jordan wasn't hungry. Kyra was dreamy and distant. Osbert mourned his lost sibling, crouching behind the sofa for the better part of the evening, and even the cat lapped halfheartedly at a can of Tuna & Liver Flavor Complete Feline Dinner. A gloom seemed to hang over the household, and they turned in early.

But now it was another day and the house was quiet and Delaney had nothing to occupy him but nature and the words to contain it, yet there he sat, staring into the screen. After several false starts, he poked halfheartedly through his natural-history collection and discovered that the starlings he saw in the McDonald's lot were descendants of a flock released in Central Park a hundred years ago by an amateur ornithologist and Shakespeare buff who felt that all the birds mentioned in the Bard's works should roost in North America, and that the snails ravaging his garden and flowerbeds were imported by a French chef who'd envisioned them roasting in their own shells with a sauce of garlic and butter. It was rich material, fascinating in its way—how could people be so blind?—and he could feel the germ of it growing in him, but ultimately he was too unsettled to work. Though it was barely half-past ten, he shut down the computer and went out early for his afternoon hike.

There was a year-round stream he'd been meaning to explore up off the main canyon, a sharp brushy ascent cut into the face of the rock, and the extra two and a half hours would enable him to do it. It would require parking along the canyon road, in an area of heavy morning and afternoon traffic and narrow shoulders, hiking down into the main canyon and following the creekbed until he hit the smaller, unnamed canyon, and finally making his way up it. The prospect invigorated him. He pulled on his shorts, T-shirt and hiking boots, and he added two cream-cheese-and-alfalfa-sprout sandwiches to the *bota* bag of water, snakebite kit, sunblock, map, compass, windbreaker and binoculars he always kept in his blue nylon daypack and unfailingly carried with him, no matter how short the hike. He didn't leave a note. He figured he'd be back in plenty of time to pick up Jordan from the summer activities program at the elementary school, after which he'd fix the boy a snack, and then when Kyra got home they'd go out to Emilio's. He just didn't feel like cooking. Not after last night.

It was clear and dry, the last day of June, the coastal fog that had lingered through the spring giving way to the high arching skies of summer. Delaney enjoyed the drive. The traffic was minimal at this hour and the Acura clung effortlessly to the road as he looped through the canyon, cutting cleanly through one curve only to accelerate into the next. He passed Gitello's, the lumberyard, the place where he'd hit the Mexican, and he didn't think twice about it—he was free of his desk and heading out into the wild and he felt blessed and unconquerable. He rolled down the window to catch the breeze in his face.

From here he could see where the previous year's firestorm had cut the canyon in two, the naked bones of the trees and bushes painted in black against the hillside, but even that cheered him. The canyon had already recovered, and he noted with satisfaction that the pyromaniac who'd set the blaze couldn't have conceived of the abundance of vegetation that would succeed it. Fertilized by ash, the grasses and wildflowers had put out a bumper crop, and the hills stood waist-deep in stiff golden grass, all part of the cycle, as undeniable as the swing of the earth over its axis.

After a while he began slowing to look for a safe place to pull over, but there were several cars behind him, including one of those pickups that sit about six feet off the ground and are invariably driven by some tailgating troglodyte—as this one was—and he had to go all the way down to the bottom of the canyon before swinging round in a gas station on the Coast Highway and starting back up. The ocean was there momentarily, filling the horizon, and then it was in his rearview mirror, reduced to a nine-by-three-inch strip. The first curve erased it.

There was a road crew up ahead on the right, just beyond the bridge where the road crossed the creek at the lower mouth of the canyon. He'd been slowed by them on his way down, and now, impulsively, he swung off the road just beyond the line of big yellow earthmovers. Why not start out here, he was thinking, where the banks were only twenty or thirty feet above the streambed? He'd have to work his way all the farther upstream, but he would save himself the long hike down from above. Of course, he didn't really like leaving the car at the side of the road, but there wasn't much choice. At least the road crew would slow traffic down some and hopefully keep the drunks and sideswipers at bay. He shouldered the pack, took a last admiring look at the car and the way its sleek white lines were set off against the chaparral, as if in one of those back-to-nature car commercials, then turned to plunge down the gravelly slope and into the cool dapple of the streambed.

The first thing he saw, within sixty seconds of reaching the stream and before he'd had a chance to admire the light in the sycamores or the water uncoiling over the rocks like an endless rope, was a pair of dirty sleeping bags laid out on the high sandy bank opposite. Sleeping bags. He was amazed. Not two hundred feet from the road, and here they were, brazen, thoughtless, camping under the very nose of the authorities. He climbed atop a rock for a better look and saw a blackened ring of stones to the immediate right of the sleeping bags and a moth-eaten khaki satchel hanging from the low branch of a tree. And refuse. Refuse everywhere. Cans, bottles, the shucked wrappers of ready-made sandwiches and *burritos,* toilet paper, magazines—all of it scattered across the ground as if dropped there by a dying wind. Delaney sucked in his breath. The first thing he felt wasn't surprise or even anger—it was embarrassment, as if he'd broken into some stranger's bedroom and gone snooping through the drawers. Invisible eyes locked on him. He looked over his shoulder, darted a quick glance up and down the streambed and then peered up into the branches of the trees.

For a long moment he stood there, frozen to the spot, fighting the impulse to cross the stream, bundle the whole mess up and haul it back to the nearest trash can—that'd send a message, all right. This was intolerable. A desecration. Worse than graffiti, worse than anything. Wasn't it enough that they'd degraded the better part of the planet, paved over the land and saturated the landfills till they'd created whole new cordilleras of garbage? There was plastic in the guts of

Arctic seals, methanol in the veins of the poisoned condor spread out like a collapsed parasol in the Sespe hills. There was no end to it.

He looked down at his hands and saw that they were shaking. He tried to calm himself. He was no vigilante. It wasn't his place to enforce the law, no matter how flagrant the abuse—that was what he paid taxes for, wasn't it? Why let a thing like this ruin his day? He'd take his hike, that's what he'd do, put miles between him and this sordid little camp, this shithouse in the woods, and then, when he got back home, he'd call the Sheriff's Department. Let them handle it. At night, preferably, when whoever had created this unholy mess was sunk to their elbows in it, nodding over their dope and their cheap wine. The image of his Mexican rose up yet again, but this time it was no more than a flicker, and he fought it down. Then he turned and moved off up the stream.

It was rough going, clambering over boulders and through battlements of winter-run brush, but the air was clean and cool and as the walls of the canyon grew higher around him the sound of the road faded away and the music of running water took over. Bushtits flickered in the trees, a flycatcher shot up the gap of the canyon, gilded in light. By the time he'd gone a hundred yards upstream, he'd forgotten all about the sleeping bags in the dirt and the sad tarnished state of the world. This was nature, pure and unalloyed. This was what he'd come for.

He was making his way through a stand of reeds, trying to keep his feet dry and watching for the tracks of raccoon, skunk and coyote in the mud, when the image of those sleeping bags came back to him with the force of a blow: *voices*, he heard voices up ahead. He froze, as alert suddenly as any stalking beast. He'd never encountered another human being down here, never, and the thought of seeing anyone was enough to spoil his pleasure in the day, but this was something else altogether, something desperate, dangerous even. The sleeping bags behind him, the voices ahead: these were transients, bums, criminals, and there was no law here.

Two voices, point/counterpoint. He couldn't make out the words, only the timbre. One was like the high rasp of a saw cutting through a log, on and on till the pieces dropped away, and then the second voice joined in, pitched low, abrupt and arrhythmic.

Some hikers carried guns. Delaney had heard of robberies on the Backbone Trail, of physical violence, assault, rape. The four-wheel-drive faction came up into the hills to shoot off their weapons, gang members annihilated rocks, bottles and trees with their assault rifles. The city was here, now, crouched in the ravine. Delaney didn't know what to do—slink away like some wounded animal and give up possession of the place forever? Or challenge them, assert his rights? But maybe he was making too much of it. Maybe they were hikers, day-trippers, maybe they were only teenagers skipping school.

And then he remembered the girl from the birding class he'd taken out of boredom. It was just after he'd got to California, before he met Kyra. He couldn't recall her name now, but he could see her, bent over the plates in Clarke's *An Introduction to Southern California Birds* or squinting into the glow of the slide projector in the darkened room. She was young, early twenties, with thin black hair parted in the middle and a pleasing kind of bulkiness to her, to the way she moved her shoulders and walked squarely from the anchors of her heels. And he remembered her cheeks—the cheeks of an Eskimo, of a baby, of Alfred Hitchcock staring dourly from the screen, cheeks that gave her face a freshness and naiveté that made her look even younger than she was. Delaney was thirty-nine. He asked her out for a sandwich after class and she told him why she never hiked alone, never, not ever again.

Up until the year before she'd been pretty blithe about it. The streets might have been unsafe, particularly at night, but the chaparral, the woods, the trails no one knew? She had a passion for hiking, for solitary rambles, for getting close enough to feel the massive shifting heartbeat of the world. She spent two months on the Appalachian Trail after graduating from high school, and she'd been over most of the Pacific Coast Trail from the Mexican border to San Francisco. One afternoon in May she went out for a short hike up one of the feeder streams of the Big Tujunga Creek, in the San Gabriels. She'd worked past two, waitressing for the lunch crowd at a grill in Pasadena, but she thought she'd get two or maybe three hours in before dinner. Less than a mile up there was a pool she knew at the base of a cliff that rose to a thin spray of water—she'd never been beyond the pool and planned to climb round the cliff and follow the stream to its source.

They were Mexicans, she thought. Or maybe Armenians. They spoke English. Young guys in baggy pants and shiny black boots. She surprised them at the pool, the light faded to gray, a faint chill in the air, their eyes glazed with the beer and the endless bullshit, stories about women and cars and drugs. There was an uncomfortable moment, all five of them drilling her with looks that automatically appraised the shape of her beneath the loose sweatshirt and jeans and calculated the distance to the road, how far a scream would carry. She was working her way around the cliff, unsteady on the loose rock, her back to them, when she felt the grip of the first hand, right there—she showed him—right there on her calf.

Delaney held his breath. The voices had stopped abruptly, replaced by a brooding silence that hung in the air for what seemed an eternity before they started up again, lazy now, contented, the buzz of a pair of flies settling down on the sidewalk. And then, through some auditory quirk of the canyon walls, the voices suddenly crystallized and every word came to him true and distinct. It took him a moment, and then he understood: Spanish, they were talking Spanish.

He was already angry with himself, angry even before he turned away and tried to slink out of the reeds like a voyeur, angry before the choice was made. The hike was over, the day ruined. There was no way he was just going to waltz out of the bushes and surprise these people, whoever they were, and the defile was too narrow to allow him to go round them undetected. He lifted one foot from the mud and then the other, parting the reeds with the delicacy of a man tucking a blanket under the chin of a sleeping child. The sound of the creek, which to this point had been a whisper, rose to a roar, and it seemed as if every bird in the canyon was suddenly screaming. He looked up into the face of a tall raw-boned Latino with eyes like sinkholes and a San Diego Padres cap reversed on his head.

The man was perched on a boulder just behind and above Delaney, no more than twenty feet away, and how he'd got there or whether he'd been there all along, Delaney had no idea. He wore a pair of tight new blue jeans tucked into the tops of his scuffed workboots, and he sat hunched against his knees, prying a stick of gum out of his shirt pocket with exaggerated care. He attempted a smile, spreading his lips in a show of bravado, but Delaney could see that the man was flustered, as confounded by Delaney's sudden appearance as Delaney was by his. "Hey, *amigo,* how's it going?" he said in a voice that didn't seem to fit him, a voice that was almost feminine but for the rasp of it. His English was flat and graceless.

Delaney barely nodded. He didn't return the smile and he didn't reply. He would have moved on right then, marching back to his car without a word, but something tugged at his pack and he saw that one of the reeds had caught in his shoulder strap. He bent to release it, his heart pounding, and the man on the rock sprawled out his legs as if he were sinking into a sofa, folded the stick of gum into his mouth and casually flicked the wrapper into the stream. "Hiking, huh?" the man said, and he was smiling still, smiling and chewing at the same time. "Me," he said, "I'm hiking too. Me and my friend." He jerked his head to indicate the friend, who appeared behind Delaney now, just beyond the reeds.

The friend regarded Delaney out of an expressionless face. His hair hung in coils to his shoulders and a thin wisp of beard trailed away from the base of his chin. He was wearing some sort of poncho or *serape,* jagged diamonds of color that leapt out against the quiet greens of the streambed. He had nothing to add to the first man's description. They were hiking, and that was it.

Delaney looked from the first man to his companion and back again. He wasn't alarmed, not exactly—he was too angry for that. All he could think of was the sheriff and getting these people and their garbage heap out of here, of hustling them right back to wherever they'd come from, slums, *favelas, barrios,* whatever they called them. They didn't belong here, that was for sure. He jerked the reed out of the ground and flung it away from him, adjusted his pack and began picking his way back down the streambed.

"Hey, *amigo*"—the man's voice came at him in a wild high whinny—"you have a nice day, huh?"

The walk to the road was nothing—it barely stretched his muscles. The anticipation had gone sour in his throat, and it rankled him—it wasn't even noon yet and the day was shot. He cursed as he passed by the sleeping bags again, and then he took the bank in five strides and he was out in the glare of the canyon road. He had a sudden impulse to continue on down the stream, under the bridge and around the bend, but dismissed it: this was where the creek fanned out into its floodplain before running into the ocean, and any idiot who could park a car and clamber down a three-foot embankment could roam it at will, as the successive layers of garbage spread out over the rocks gave testimony. There was no adventure here, no privacy, no experience of nature. It would be about as exciting as pulling into the McDonald's lot and counting the starlings.

He turned and walked back up the road, past the line of cars restrained by a man in a yellow hard hat with a portable sign that read STOP on one side and SLOW on the reverse. The trucks and bulldozers were quiet now—it was lunchtime, the workers sprawled in the shade of the big rippled tires with their sandwiches and *burritos,* the dust settling, birds bickering in the scrub, chamise and toyon blooming gracefully alongside the road with no help from anyone. Delaney felt the sun on his face, stepped over the ridges of detritus pushed into the shoulder by the blades of the earthmovers and let the long muscles of his legs work against the slope of the road. In one of his first "Pilgrim" columns he'd observed that the bulldozer served the same function here as the snowplow back East, though it was dirt rather than snow that had to be cleared from the streets. The canyon road had become a virtual streambed during the rainy season and Caltrans had been hard-pressed to keep it open, and now, in early summer, with no rain in sight for the next five months, they were just getting round to clearing out the residual rubble.

That was fine with Delaney, though he wished they'd chosen another day for it. Who wanted to hear the roar of engines and breathe diesel fuel down here—and on a day like this? He was actually muttering to himself as he passed the last of the big machines, his mood growing progressively blacker, and yet all the defeats and frustrations of the morning were nothing compared to what awaited him. For it was at that moment, just as he cleared the last of the Caltrans vehicles and cast a quick glance up the road, that he felt himself go numb: the car was gone.

Gone. Vanished.

But no, that wasn't where he'd parked it, against the guardrail there, was it? It must be around the next bend, sure it was, and he was moving more quickly now, almost jogging, the line of cars across the road from him creeping down toward the bridge and a second man in hard hat and bright orange vest flagging his SLOW sign. Every eye was on Delaney. He was the amusement, the sideshow, stiff-legging it up the road with the sweat stinging his eyes and slicking the frames of his glasses. And then he made the bend and saw the tight shoulderless curve beyond it and all the naked space of the canyon spread out to the horizon, and knew he was in trouble.

Dumbstruck, he swung reluctantly round on his heels and waded back down the road like a zombie, tramping back and forth over the spot where he'd parked the car and finally even going down on one knee in the dirt to trace the tire tracks with his unbelieving fingertips. His car was gone, all right. It was incontrovertible. He'd parked here half an hour ago, right on this spot, and now there was nothing here, no steel, no chrome, no radial tires or personalized license plates. No registration. No *Introduction to Southern California Birds* or *Trail Guide to the Santa Monica Mountains*.

The first thing that came into his head was the police. They'd towed it. Of course. That was it. There was probably some obscure regulation about parking within two hundred feet of a road crew or something—or they'd posted a sign he'd missed. He rose slowly to his feet, ignoring the faces in the cars across from him, and approached a group of men lounging in the shade of the nearest bulldozer. "Did anybody see what happened to my car?" he asked, conscious of the barely restrained note of hysteria in his voice. "Did they tow it or what?"

They looked up at him blankly. Six Hispanic men, in khaki shirts and baseball caps, arrested in the act of eating, sandwiches poised at their lips, thermoses tipped, the cans of soft drink sweating between their fingers. No one said a word.

"I parked right there." Delaney was pointing now and the six heads dutifully swiveled to regard the vacant shoulder and the scalloped rim of the guardrail set against the treetops and the greater vacancy of the canyon beyond it. "A half hour ago? It was an Acura—white, with aluminum wheels?"

The men seemed to stir. They looked uneasily from one to the other. Finally, the man on the end, who seemed by virtue of his white mustache to be the senior member of the group, set his sandwich carefully down on a scrap of waxed paper and rose to his feet. He regarded Delaney for a moment out of a pair of inexpressibly sad eyes. "No espick Ingliss," he said.

Fifteen minutes later Delaney was having his hike after all, though it wasn't exactly what he'd envisioned. After questioning the boss of the road crew—*We haven't towed nothin' here, not to my knowledge*—he started back up the canyon road on foot. It was three miles or so to the near grocery and the telephones out front, but it was all uphill and the road wasn't designed for pedestrians. Horns blared, tires screeched, some jerk threw a beer can at him. For fear of his life he had to hop the guardrail and plow through the brush, but it was slow going and the burrs and seedheads caught in his socks and tore at his naked legs, and all the while his head was pounding and his throat gone dry over the essential question of the day: what had happened to the car?

He called the police from the pay phone and they gave him the number of the towing service and he called the towing service and they told him they didn't have his car—and no, there was no mistake: they didn't have it. Then he called Kyra. He got her secretary and had to sit on the curb in front of the pay phone in a litter of Doritos bags and candy wrappers for ten agonizing minutes till she rang him back. "Hello?" she demanded. "Delaney?"

He was bewildered, immobilized. People pulled into the lot and climbed casually out of their cars. Doors slammed. Engines revved. "Yes, it's me."

"What is it? What's the matter? Where are you?" She was wound tight already.

"I'm at Li's Market."

He could hear her breathing into the receiver, and he counted the beats it took her to absorb this information, puzzle over its significance and throw it back at him. "Listen, Delaney, I'm in the middle of—"

"They stole my car."

"What? What are you talking about? Who stole it?"

He tried to dredge up all he'd heard and read about car thieves, about chop shops, counterfeit serial numbers and theft to order, and he tried to picture the perpetrators out there in broad daylight with hundreds of people driving obliviously by, but all he could see was the bruised face and blunted eyes of his Mexican, the wheel clutched between his hands and the bumper gobbling up the fragments of the broken yellow line as if the whole thing were one of those pulse-thumping games in the arcade. "You better call Jack," he said.

8

IT WAS LIKE BEING HAUNTED BY DEVILS, RED-
haired devils and *rubios* in eighty-dollar running shoes and sunglasses
that cost more than a laboring man could make in a week. What had
he done to deserve such a fate? Cándido was a sinner like any other
man, sure, but no worse. And here he was, half-starved and crippled
by their infernal machines, bounced from one to another of them like
a pinball, first the big jerk with the Elvis hair and then the *pelirrojo*
who'd run him down in the road, the very one, and his gangling tall
awkward *pendejo* of a son who'd hiked all the way down into the canyon
to violate a poor man's few pitiful possessions. It was too much. He
needed to go to confession, do penance, shrive himself somehow. Even
Job would have broken down under an assault like this.

For the next hour he hid himself in a clump of shrubbery at the far
end of the parking lot, watching the door of the *supermercado* for América. This was where she'd look for him—it was the only place she
knew besides the Chinese store, and she must have known he wouldn't
hang around there any longer than he had to. So he waited in the
bushes, out of sight, and though his concealment made him feel
better—at least now no one was going to push him around—he was
still in a fever of worry. What if he'd missed her and she was down
below in the canyon, staring numbly at the bleak pile of rocks where
their camp used to be? What if the *patrón* of the job he hoped she'd

gotten forced her to do something with him? What if she was lost, hurt or worse?

The traffic was thinning on the road now and fewer cars were pulling in and out of the lot. His tormentors—the *gabachos* young and old— had shoved into their cars and driven off without so much as a backward glance for him. He was about to give it up and cross the road to the labor exchange and look hopelessly round the empty lot there and then maybe head back down the road to where the path cut into the brush and shout out her name for every living thing in the canyon to hear, when a Mercedes sedan pulled up in front of the grocery and América stepped out of it.

He watched her slim legs emerge first, then her bare arms and empty hands, the pale flowered dress, the screen of her hair, and he was elated and devastated at the same time: she'd got work, but he hadn't. They would have money to eat, but he hadn't earned it. No: a seventeen-year-old village girl had earned it, and at what price? And what did that make him? He crouched there in the bushes and tried to read her face, but it was locked up like a strongbox, and the man with her, the *rico,* was like some exotic animal dimly viewed through the dark integument of the windshield. She slammed the door, looked about her indecisively for a moment as the car wheeled away in a little blossom of exhaust, and then she squared her shoulders, crossed the lot and disappeared into the market.

Cándido brushed down his clothes, made good and certain that no one was looking his way, and ambled out of the bushes as if he'd just come back from a stroll around the block. He kept his head down, avoiding eye contact with the *gringos* he passed as he crossed the lot and ducked into the grocery. After a week and a half of living on so little that his stomach had shrunk and his pants were down around his hips, the effect of all that abundance was devastating. There was no smell of food here, no hint of the rich stew of odors you'd find in a Mexican market—these people sanitized their groceries just as they sanitized their kitchens and toilets and drove the life from everything, imprisoning their produce in jars and cans and plastic pouches, wrapping their meat and even their fish in cellophane—and yet still the sight and proximity of all those comestibles made his knees go weak again.

Candy, there was a rack of candy right by the door, something sweet and immediate to feed the hunger. Little cakes and things, Twinkies and Ho-Ho's. And there, there were the fruits and vegetables lit up as on an altar, the fat ripeness of tomatoes, mangoes, watermelon, corn in its husk, roasting ears that would sweeten on the grill. He swallowed involuntarily. Looked right and then left. He didn't see América. She must be down one of the aisles pushing a basket. He tried to look nonchalant as he passed by the checkers and entered the vast cornucopia of the place.

Food in sacks for pets, for dogs and cats and parakeets, seltzer water in clear bottles, cans of vegetables and fruit: God in Heaven, he was hungry. He found América poised in front of one of the refrigerated displays, her back to him, and he felt shy suddenly, mortified, the unwanted guest sitting down at the starving man's table. She was selecting a carton of eggs—*huevos con chorizo, huevos rancheros, huevos hervidos con pan tostado*—flicking the hair out of her face with an unconscious gesture as she pried open the box to check for fractured shells. He loved her in that moment more than he ever had, and he forgot the Mercedes and the rich man and the *gabachos* in the parking lot assailing him like a pack of dogs, and he thought of stew and *tortillas* and the way he would surprise her with their new camp and the firewood all stacked and ready. Things would work out, they would. "América," he croaked.

The face she turned to him was joyful, proud, radiant—she'd earned money, her first money ever, and they were going to eat on it, stuff themselves, feast till their stomachs swelled and their tongues went thick in their throats—but her eyes, her eyes dodged away from his, and he saw the traces there of some shame or sorrow that screamed out at him in warning. "What's the matter?" he demanded, and the shadowy form of that rich man in the Mercedes rose up before him. "Are you all right?"

She bowed her head. Then she reached into her pocket and pulled out three clean fresh newly minted bills, two tens and a five, and her smile came back. "I worked all day," she said, "and there's more work tomorrow, scrubbing Buddhas."

"What? Scrubbing what?"

The *gabachos* were watching them now, from every corner of the market, darting glances at them as they hustled by with their quick strides and dry-cleaned clothes, little baskets clutched to their chests, staring at a poor man and his wife as if they were diseased, as if they were assassins plotting a murder. América didn't answer him. She laid the eggs in the cart, on the little wire rack some *gabacho* genius had designed for them, and looked up at him with widening eyes. "But you're here," she said. "I mean, you're walking. You made it up out of the canyon."

He shrugged. Felt his face tighten in its twisted mask. "I was worried."

Her smile bloomed and she fell into his arms and he hugged her tight and to hell with every *gringo* in the world, he thought. And then they shopped—the discount *tortillas,* the pound of *hamburguesa* meat, the eggs, the sacks of rice and beans, the coffee and the powdered milk, and before long they were walking back down the road in the hush of the falling night, the shared sweetness of a chocolate bar with almonds seeping into the secret recesses of their mouths.

The light held for them till they reached the bottom of the trail, and then it thickened into darkness. Cándido clutched his wife's hand as they groped along the streambed, a plastic sack of groceries dangling from the crook of his bad arm. He was breathing hard, aching all over, but he felt buoyant and hopeful for the first time since the accident. He was mending and he would go up the hill to the labor exchange in the morning, América had earned money today and she would earn more tomorrow, they would fill their stomachs and lie on the blanket in their hut and make love hidden away from the world. They would eat the sardines with the white bread first, while the fire settled and the *hamburguesa* meat snapped and hissed in the bottom of the pot, and then they would dip into the hot grease with their *tortillas* to take the edge off their hunger, and the meat would form the foundation of the stew till at eleven or maybe even twelve midnight they would pour steaming cups of it from the pot. All that.

He was able to find his way with his fingers, the night like pitch, moonless and with that ugly yellow urban sky clamped like a lid over their heads. The stream soughed through the rocks, something pounded its wings in the dark and flapped through the trees. He suppressed his fear of rattlesnakes and went on, trying to erase the memory of the thick coiled whiplash of a thing he'd encountered somewhere along here last month and the *mala suerte* that hung over the killing, skinning and roasting of it. And where was its mate? Its mother? Its mother's mother? He tried not to think about it.

When they came to the pool he told América she was going to have to take her clothes off and she giggled and leaned into him, brushing her lips against his cheek. He could just make out the pale hovering presence of her face against the absence of her hair and clothes. The water was black, the trees were black, the walls of the canyon black as some deep place inside a man or woman, beneath the skin and bones and all the rest. He felt strangely excited. The crickets chirred. The trees whispered.

Cándido stripped, balled up his clothes and stuffed them in the plastic sack with the eggs. His wife was there, right there against him, and he helped her off with her dress in the dark and then he pulled her to him and tasted the chocolate on her lips. "Take your shoes off too," he warned, running a hand down her leg to her ankle and back up again. "It's not deep, but the bottom's slippery."

The water was warm, heated by the sun as it trickled down through the canyon, traveling all those tortuous miles to get here, to this pool, and the air on their wet skin was cool and gentle. Cándido felt his way, step by step, and América followed him, the water lapping at her breasts—she was so short, so skinny, such a *flaca*—the groceries and her bundled dress held up high above her head. He stumbled only once, midway across. It was almost as if a human hand had jerked his foot out from under him, but it must have been a branch, slick with algae and waving languidly in the current, some trick of the bottom— still, it caused him to fling out his arm in reaction and when he did the bag of eggs slammed against the rock wall like a lesson in fragility. "Are you all right?" América whispered. And then: "The eggs? Are they broken?"

But they weren't—except for two, that is, and he and América lapped them from the shells for strength even as he bent to light the fire and show off the fastness of the place and the hut he'd built with its stick-frame entrance and thatched roof. The fire caught and swelled. He knelt in the sand, feeding sticks into the grasping greedy fingers of flame, the smell of woodsmoke pricking his memory through the nostalgia of a thousand mornings at home, and he saw his mother burning a handful of twigs to get the stove going, corn gruel and toast and hot coffee smothered in sugar, and then he turned his head from the fire and watched his wife's limbs and hips and breasts fill with light. She was squatting, so busy with the meat, the pot, the onions and *chiles* and rice that she had no consciousness of her nudity, and he saw now, for the first time, that her pregnancy was a reality, as solid and tangible a thing as dough rising in a pan. She glanced up, saw him looking, and reached automatically for her dress. "No," he said, "no, you don't need it. Not here, not with me."

A long slow look, the hair hanging wet on the ends, and then she smiled again to show off her big square honest teeth. The dress stayed where it was.

They cooked the meat, the knots in their stomachs pulled tighter and tighter by the smell of it, the *hamburguesa* meat working with the onions and *chiles* to enrich the poor neutral breath of the canyon. They sat side by side in the sand, warmed by the fire, and shared the tin of sardines and ate half the loaf of store bread, North American bread baked in a factory and puffed up light as air. She held the last sardine out for him and he put his hands on her breasts and let her feed it into his mouth, the fire snapping, the night wrapped round them like a blanket, all his senses on alert. He took the sardine between his lips, between his teeth, and he licked the golden oil from her fingers.

In the morning, just before first light, they squatted over the pot and dipped *tortillas* into the lukewarm stew. They drank their coffee cold, took a package of saltines and a slice of cheese each for lunch, and went naked into the pool. The water felt chilly at this hour and it was a trial to slosh through it like penitents in the penitential dawn, cursed by birds and harassed by insects. Their clothes felt clammy and damp and they looked away from each other's nudity as they hurriedly dressed on the cold shore. Still, as América followed Cándido's familiar compact form up the narrow dirt trail, she felt a surge of hope: the worst of it was behind them now. She would work, no matter what the fat man demanded of her, and Cándido would work too, and they'd take out just what they needed for food and necessities and the rest would go under a stone in the ground. In a month, maybe two, they could go up the canyon and into the city she barely knew. There was an apartment waiting there for them, nothing fancy, not for now—a single room with a hot shower and a toilet, some trees on the street and a market, someplace she could buy a dress, some lipstick, a brush for her hair.

Cándido was limping and he had to stop three times to catch his breath, but he was improving, getting better by the day, and that was an answer to her prayers too. They waited till there was a break in the traffic before emerging from the bushes and they kept their heads down and their feet moving as they hurried up the shoulder of the road. The cars terrified her. There was a chain of them, always a chain—ten, twenty, thirty—and they sucked the air with them, tore it from her lungs, and left a stink of exhaust behind. The tires hissed. The faces stared.

It was early, very early, and they were the first ones at the labor exchange, there even before Candelario Pérez. Most of the men took buses or hitched rides to get there, some coming from twenty and thirty miles away. And why go so far? Because they were country people and they hated the city streets, hated lining up on *las esquinas*, the street corners, where there were gangs and dirt and filthy things written on the walls. América didn't blame them. She remembered her trip to Venice, the terror and disconnectedness of it, and as she settled into her customary spot against the pillar, drawing her legs up under her, she looked out into the heavy ribs of the trees and felt glad to be there.

Cándido sat heavily beside her, the good half of his face turned toward her in soft focus. He was fidgeting with his hands, snatching twigs from the dirt, snapping them in two and flicking the pieces away from him, over and over again. He'd removed the sling from his arm, but he still carried it awkwardly, and some of the crust had fallen away from the wound on his face, pale splotches of flesh like paint flecks showing through. He was quiet, moody, all the high spirits of the previous night dissolved in a look of silent fury that reminded her of her father, bent at night over the fine print of the newspaper, his back aching and his feet twisted from the confinement of the shoes they made him wear in the restaurant. Cándido was brooding, she could see that, afraid no one would choose him for work because of his face and the limp he couldn't disguise—even though he was first in line and would work his heart out. And though he hadn't said a word, neither of apology nor of thanks, she knew it hurt him to have a woman earning his keep. She made small talk to distract him—It was going to be warm, wasn't it? The stew had turned out well, hadn't it? Would he be sure to remind her to pick up a little soap powder so she could wash their clothes tonight?—but no matter what she said he responded only with a grunt.

Candelario Pérez arrived ten minutes later in a battered white pickup with six other men, and then the lot began to fill. Men came singly and in groups of two or three, appearing out of nowhere, loose-jointed and hopeful, men of all ages, their hands empty, their clothes simple and clean. A few of them stood apart, gathering across the road at the intersection of one of the side streets, or milling around in clumps of two or three in the post office parking lot, taking their chances with the *gringos,* but most shuffled across the expanse of gravel, dust and weed to report to Candelario Pérez.

And then the contractors began to arrive, the white men with their big bleached faces and soulless eyes, enthroned in their trucks. They wanted two men or three, they wanted four or five, no questions asked, no wage stipulated, no conditions or terms of employment. A man could be pouring concrete one day, spraying pesticide the next—or swabbing out urinals, spreading manure, painting, weeding, hauling, laying brick or setting tile. You didn't ask questions. You got in the back of the truck and you went where they took you. And the bosses, the ones who did the hiring, sat up front, as motionless as if they were carved of wood. América wondered if they were somehow grafted to their trucks, if their mothers had given birth to them right there on the seat of the cab and they'd sprouted up behind the windshield like some sort of unnatural growth. All she ever saw of them was elbows and faces. She sat there quietly, waiting for someone who might need a floor mopped or an oven cleaned and the trucks pulled up, the tinted windows sank noiselessly into the gleaming door panels and the elbows appeared, followed by the sharp pointed noses and oversized ears, the flat hard calculating eyes wrapped in sunglasses.

Ten trucks must have pulled into the labor exchange that morning— and another half dozen into the lot by the post office—and forty men got work. Cándido was the first in line each time and each time he scrambled up out of the dirt for nothing. She watched him with a sinking feeling, his look of eagerness and hope as he disguised the hitch in his walk and tried to hold the bad arm rigid at his side, and then the face of rage and despair and the ravaging limp as he came back to her.

At nine-thirty or so the fat man wheeled into the lot in his rich long car. América had been chattering away about Tepoztlán to take Cándido's mind off the situation—she was remembering an incident from her childhood, a day when a September storm swept over the village and the hail fell like stones amid the standing corn and all the men rushed out into the streets firing their pistols and shotguns at the sky—but she stopped in midsentence when she heard the crunch of gravel and looked up into the lean shoulders and predatory snout of the *patrón's* car. She felt the living weight of the big man's hand in her lap all over again and something seized up inside her: nothing like that had ever happened to her before, not in her own country, not in Tepoztlán, not even in the dump in Tijuana. She was seventeen years old, the youngest of eight, and her parents had loved her and she'd gone to school all the way through and done everything that was expected of her. There were no strange men, no hands in her lap, there was no living in the woods like a wild animal. But here it was. She rose to her feet.

América crossed the lot in a kind of daze, picturing the bright expanse of that big room with the Buddhas and the windows that laid all the world at her feet, and the money too, twenty-five dollars, twenty-five more than nothing. The window of the car threw her reflection back at her for a moment, then it ceremonially descended to reveal the face of the *patrón*. He didn't get out of the car, but there he was, expressionless, the beard clipped close round his mouth to frame his colorless lips. Candelario Pérez came up to him, managing to look officious and subservient at the same time—*A sus órdenes,* let me bow and scrape for you—but the big man ignored him. He motioned with his head for América to go round the car and get in the front seat beside him, and then he glanced up at Candelario Pérez and said something in English, a question. Did he want Mary too, was that it?

Mary was nowhere in sight. Probably drunk in her little redwood house sitting in front of a refrigerator stocked with hams. América turned to look for Cándido, and he was right there, right in back of her, and they exchanged a look before she dropped her eyes, hurried round the car and got in. The *patrón* gave her the faintest nod of acknowledgment as she shut the door and settled herself as far away from him as possible, and then he turned back to Candelario Pérez, who was touting the virtues of Cándido and the next two men in line—anybody could scrape the crud from a stone Buddha—but the fat man shook his head. He wanted only women.

And then they were out of the lot and wheeling up the canyon road, the trees rushing past them, the car leaning gracefully into the turns, turn after turn after turn, all the way up to the gate and the men working there with their picks and shovels. The radio was silent. The *patrón* said nothing, didn't even look at her. He seemed pensive—or tired maybe. His lips were pursed, his eyes fixed on the road. And his hands—fleshy and white, swollen up like sponges—stayed where they belonged, on the wheel.

She had the big room to herself. She lifted the Buddhas from the cartons, dipped them in the corrosive, scrubbed them with the brush, affixed the labels and packed them back up again. It wasn't long before her eyes had begun to water and she found herself dabbing at them with the sleeves of her dress—which was awkward, because they were short sleeves and she had to keep lifting one shoulder or the other to her eyes. And her nose and throat felt strange too—the passages seemed raw and abraded, as if she had a cold. Was the solution stronger than what they'd been using yesterday? Mary, the big *gringa,* had complained all through the day without remit like some insect in the grass, but América didn't remember its being as bad as this. Still, she kept at it, the Buddhas floating through a scrim of tears, until her fingers began to bother her. They weren't stiffening as they had yesterday, not yet, but there was a sharp stinging sensation round the cuticles of her nails, as if she were squeezing lemon into a cut, and she realized with a jolt that the big man had neglected to give her the plastic gloves. She held her hands up to the light then and saw that the skin had begun to crack and peel and that all the color had gone out of the flesh. These weren't her hands—they were the hands of a corpse.

She was alarmed. If she didn't have those gloves there would be nothing left of her fingers by the end of the day—only bones, as if in some horrible costume for the Day of the Dead—but she was too timid to go look for them. The *patrón* might be watching even now, watching to see if she was scrubbing hard enough, ready to burst in and abuse her in his harsh superior language, to send her home, fire her, lay his big bloated paw in her lap. Her fingers were burning. Her throat was a cinder. She couldn't see the Buddhas for the water in her eyes. Finally, she stole a look over her shoulder.

No one was watching her. Both doors that gave onto the room were shut and the house was silent. The near door, the one she'd come in through, led to the garage and the stairway to the second floor, and the other must have been to the bathroom, judging from the amount of time Mary had spent behind it yesterday. For her part, América had been afraid to get up from her seat—who knew when the *patrón* would come to check on them?—and that was a trial, because she felt like she always had to pee lately and she'd had to hold it all day (it was the baby crowding her organs, she knew that, and she wished she could talk to her mother about it, even for a minute). But that was over. That was yesterday. The second she and Cándido got off the road and into the cover at the head of the trail, she'd squatted in the bushes and the problem was solved. This was different. This was dangerous—and it wasn't her fault. The *patrón* should have given her the gloves, he should have remembered.

It was eleven-fifteen by the sunburst clock. The mountains pressed at the windows. Her fingertips burned. The statue before her loomed and receded and her head felt light. Finally she got up from the chair and hurried across the room—she had to rinse her hands at least, to take the sting away, no one would deny her that . . .

There was a bathroom behind the door, as she'd surmised, pink and white tile, a little shower stall, fluffy pink mats and wallpaper decorated with dewy-eyed little rabbits, and she couldn't help admiring it—this was just what she wanted, so pretty and efficient, so clean. She ran the cold water over her hands, and then, not wanting to risk dirtying the plush white towels, she dried them on her dress. That was when she caught a glimpse of herself in the mirror, her hair all ragged and wild—she looked like a madwoman, a gypsy, a beggar in the street—but she suppressed the image, eased back the lid of the toilet and sat down quickly, thinking to relieve herself now and get everything over with at once.

Sequestered there in that pink bathroom with the bunnies on the walls and the pristine towels and the lilac soap in a little ceramic dish, she felt at peace for the first time since she'd stepped away from Cándido and slipped into the big man's car. She studied the architecture of the shower, marveling at all that pretty tile, and thought how nice it would be to have hot water whenever you wanted it, a dab of shampoo, soap, a bristle toothbrush instead of a stalk of dry grass. And then she thought about the fat man, all lathered up with soap, and his pink ridiculous flesh and fat white feet. Maybe he'd go away to China to buy more Buddhas for his store and she could stay here and sleep in the big room at night and use the bathroom ten times a day if she wanted . . .

She was thinking about that, daydreaming—just for a second—when a sudden noise from above brought her back to herself. There was a dull thump, as if someone had just pushed a chair back from a table, followed by the sound of footsteps. América jumped up from the toilet, afraid to flush it for fear of giving herself away, and in her extremity forgot what she'd come for. The footsteps were directly overhead now, and for a moment she froze, unable to think, unable to move. *The gloves,* that was it. She tore open the cabinet under the sink, rifled the drawers beside it—one, two, three, four—but there were no gloves and the footsteps seemed to be coming closer, coming down the stairs. She hit the chair on the run and snatched up her brush in a panic.

The footsteps ceased. There was no one on the stairs, no one overhead. The Buddha on the table gave her his look of inscrutable wisdom.

Three Buddhas later, she had to give it up. She couldn't take it a second longer—no one could. She rinsed her hands again and the relief flooded over her. Then, steeling herself, she went to the door, eased it open and peered up the stairs to where a larger, more formal-looking door gave onto the floor above. She hesitated a moment, gazing into the penumbral depths of the garage. The car was there, the car that cost more than her entire village could make in a year, and there was a refrigerator too, a washer and dryer, all sorts of things. Tennis rackets. Sticks for that game they play on the ice. Birdcages, bicycles, chairs, beds, tables, a pair of sawhorses, cardboard boxes of every shape and size, tools, old clothes and stacks of newspapers, all of it amassed on the garage floor like the treasure of some ancient potentate.

She mounted the stairs on silent feet, her heart pounding. How would she ask for gloves? In pantomime? What if the big man got dirty with her? Wasn't she asking for it by coming into his house all alone? She hesitated again, on the landing at the top of the stairs, and then she forced herself to knock. Her knock was soft, apologetic, barely a whisper of the knuckles against the wood. No one answered it. She knocked again, a bit more forcefully. Still nothing. She didn't know what to do—she couldn't work without those gloves. She'd cripple herself, dissolve the skin from her bones . . .

She tried the doorknob.

It was open. "Alo?" she called, her face pressed to the crack of the door. "¿Alguien está aquí?" But what was it they said in those old movies on television that used to crack up all the girls in the village? *Yoo-hoo,* wasn't that it? She gave it a try. "Yoo-hoo!" she called, and it sounded as ridiculous on her lips as on any actress's.

She waited a moment and tried it again. "Alo? Yoo-hoo?"

There was the sound of movement, heavy footsteps on the floor, and the fat man shuffled into view. He was wearing a pair of wire-rim spectacles that seemed to pinch his face, and house slippers on his feet. He looked puzzled—or irritated. The white lips glared out from the nest of his beard.

"Escuse, pleese," América said, half-shielded by the door. She was on the landing still, not daring to enter the house. She held up her hands. "*Guantes.* Pleese. *Para las manos.*"

The *patrón* had stopped ten paces from the door. He looked bewildered, as if he'd never seen her before. He said something in English, something with the lift of a question to it, but his tone wasn't friendly, not at all.

She tried again, in dumb show this time, rubbing her hands together and making the motions of pulling on a pair of imaginary gloves.

Then he understood. Or seemed to. He came forward in two propulsive strides, took hold of her right wrist and examined her hand as if it were something he'd found stuck to the bottom of his shoe. Then he dropped it with a curse—flung it way from him—turned his back on her and stalked out of the room.

She stood there waiting, her eyes on the floor. Had he understood? Did he care? Had he gone to get her the gloves or was he ignoring her—after all, what should he care if the flesh rotted off her bones? He'd laid his big presumptuous paw in her lap and she'd shrunk from it—what use did he have for her? She wanted to turn and dash back down the stairs, wanted to hide herself among the Buddhas—or better yet, in the bathroom—but she stood her ground. When it came down to it, she'd rather starve than dip her hands in that solution for even one second more, she would.

But then she heard the heavy footfall again, the vase on the little table by the door trembling with the solidity of it, and the *patrón* came round the corner, moving quickly, top-heavy and tottering on his feet. The little glasses were gone. In his hand, a pair of yellow plastic gloves. He thrust them at her impatiently, said something in his cacophonous blast of a voice—thank you, goodbye, I'm sorry; she couldn't tell what—and then he slammed the door shut on her.

The day sank into her veins like an elixir and she worked in a delirium of fumes, scrubbing statue after statue, her aching hands sealed away from the corrosive in the slim plastic envelope of the gloves. Her eyes watered, her throat was raw, but she concentrated on her work and the substantiality of the twenty-five dollars the *patrón* would give her, trying not to think about the ride back and what it would be like sitting next to him in the car. She pictured the *cocido* she and Cándido had made from yesterday's profits, visualizing each chunk of meat, the *chiles,* the beans, the onions—and the *tortillas* and cheese and hard-cooked eggs that went with it—all of it carefully wrapped in the plastic bags from the store and secreted beneath a rock in a cool spot she'd dug out in the wet sand of the streambed. But what if an animal got to it? What did they have here in the North? *El mapache,* the short-nosed cousin of the coatimundi, a furtive, resourceful animal. Still, the stone was heavy and she'd wrapped the food as tightly as she could. No: it was more likely that the ants would discover it—they could get into anything, insidious, like so many moving grains of sand—and she saw a line of them as thick as her wrist pouring in and out of the pot as she scrubbed one of a thousand blackened Buddhas. The vision made her hungry and she removed the gloves a moment to devour the dry crackers and slivers of cheese she'd brought along, and then she dashed across the room to wet her mouth under the faucet and relieve herself, flushing quickly this time and darting back to the table before the roar of the rushing water had subsided.

She worked hard, worked without stint for the rest of the day, fighting back tears and lightheadedness to prove her worth, to show the *patrón* that all by herself she could transform as many Buddhas as both she and Mary had been able to the day before. He would notice and he would thank her and ask her back the next day and the next, and he would know that she was worth more than the kind of girl who would have lifted his hand from her lap and pressed it to her breasts. But when he finally reappeared—at six by the sunburst clock on the wall—he didn't seem to notice. He just nodded his head impatiently and turned to trundle heavily to the car while the garage door rose beyond him as if by levitation.

He didn't put his hand in her lap. He didn't turn on the radio. When they swung into the lot at the market, he pulled out his wallet, shifting his weight with a grunt, extracted a twenty and a five and turned his blue-eyed gaze to the horizon as she fumbled with the door handle and let herself out. The door slammed, the engine gave a growl, and he was gone.

She didn't see Cándido anywhere. The parking lot was full of white people hurrying in and out of the market with brown plastic bags tucked under their arms, and the labor exchange across the street was deserted. She felt a sharp letdown—this was where they'd agreed to meet—and for a long moment she just stood there in the middle of the lot, looking round her numbly. And then it occurred to her that Cándido must have gotten work. Of course. Where else would he be? A feeling like joy took hold of her, but it wasn't joy exactly or joy without limit—she wouldn't feel that until she had a roof over her head. But if Cándido had work they'd have enough money to eat for a week, two weeks maybe, and if they could both find a job—even every second day—they could start saving for an apartment.

For now, though, there was nothing to do but wait. She crossed the lot, clutching the bills in her hand, and found an inconspicuous perch on a tree stump at the corner of the building. From here she could watch the lot for Cándido and stay out of the way—all those *gringos* made her nervous. Every time a car swung into the lot she felt her heart seize. She couldn't help thinking of *La Migra* and those tense silent men in the tan uniforms who'd ministered over the worst night of her life, the night she'd been stripped naked in front of all those people, though Cándido assured her they wouldn't find her here. The chances were small. Minuscule. But she didn't like chances, any chances, and she shrank into the vegetation and waited.

An hour went by. She was bored, scared, beginning to imagine all sorts of calamities: Cándido had been picked up by the police, he'd gone back to the canyon and stepped into a nest of rattlesnakes, another car had hit him and he lay bleeding in the bushes. From there her mind took her to their camp—maybe he was down there now, starting the fire, warming the stew—and then to the stew itself, and her stomach turned inside out and gnawed at her. She was hungry. Ravenous. And though the store intimidated her, the hunger drove her through the doors with her money and she bought another tin of sardines and a loaf of the sweet white bread that was puffed up like edible clouds and a Twix bar for Cándido. She was afraid someone would speak to her, ask a question, challenge her, but the girl at the checkout stand stared right through her and the price—$2.73—showed in red above the cash register, sparing her the complication of having to interpret the unfathomable numbers as they dropped from the girl's lips. Outside, back on her stump, she folded the sardines into slices of bread and before she knew it she'd eaten the whole tin. Her poor bleached fingers were stained yellow with the evidence.

And then the sun fell behind the ridge and the shadows deepened. Where was Cándido? She didn't know. But she couldn't stay here all night. She began to think about their camp again, the lean-to, the stewpot, the blanket stretched out in the sand, the way the night seemed to settle in by degrees down there, wrapping itself round her till she felt safe, hidden, protected from all the prying eyes and sharp edges of the world. That was where she wanted to be. She was tired, enervated, giddy from breathing fumes all day. She rose to her feet, took a final glance around and started off down the road with her bread, the Twix bar and her twenty-two dollars and twenty-seven cents all wrapped up in the brown plastic bag dangling from her wrist.

At this hour, the traffic had slowed considerably. The frenetic stream of cars had been reduced to the odd vehicle here and there, a rush of air, a hiss of tires, and then the silence of the canyon taking hold of the night, birds singing, the fragment of a moon glowing white in a cobalt sky. She looked carefully before crossing, thinking of Cándido, and kept to the edge of the shoulder, her head down, walking as fast as she could without drawing attention to herself. By the time she reached the entrance of the path she was breathing hard, anxious to get off the road and hide herself, but she continued past it, slowing her pace to a nonchalant stroll: a car was coming. She kept her head down, her footsteps dragging, and let it pass. As soon as it had disappeared round the bend by the lumberyard, she retraced her steps, but then another car swung round the curve coming toward her and she had to walk past the trailhead again. Finally there was a respite—no one coming either way—and she ducked into the bushes.

The first thing she did was relieve herself, just like last night. She lifted her dress, squatted over her heels and listened to the fierce impatient hiss of the urine as the light settled toward dusk and the smell of the earth rose to her nostrils. A moment ago she'd been out there on the road, exposed and vulnerable—frightened, always frightened—and now she was safe. But the thought of that frightened her too: what kind of life was it when you felt safe in the bushes, crouching to piss in the dirt like a dog? Was that what she'd left Tepoztlán for?

But that was no way to think. She was tired, that was all. Her shoulders ached and her fingers burned where the skin was peeling back from her nails. And she was hungry, always hungry. If she'd stayed in Tepoztlán through all the gray days of her life she would have had enough to eat, as long as her father was alive and she jumped like a slave every time he snapped his fingers, but she would never have had anything more, not even a husband, because all the men in the village, all the decent ones, went North nine months a year. Or ten months. Or permanently. To succeed, to make the leap, you had to suffer. And her suffering was nothing compared to the tribulations of the saints or the people living in the streets of Mexico City and Tijuana, crippled and abandoned by God and man alike. So what if she had to live in a hut in the woods? It wouldn't be for long. She had Cándido and she'd earned her first money and now Cándido was able to work again and the nightmare of the past weeks was over. They'd have a place by the time the rains came in the fall, he'd promised her, and then they'd look back on all this as an adventure, a funny story, something to tell their grandchildren. *Cándido,* she would say, *do you remember the time the car hit you, the time we camped out like Indians and cooked over the open fire, remember?* Maybe they'd have a picnic here someday, with their son and maybe a daughter too.

She was holding that picture in her head, the picnic basket, one of those portable radios playing, a little boy in short pants and a girl with ribbons in her hair, as she worked her way down the trail with her brown plastic bag. Pebbles jumped away from her feet and trickled down the path ahead of her like water down a streambed. There was a clean sharp smell of sage and mesquite and some pale indefinable essence that might have been agave. There were certainly enough agave plants scattered across the slopes, their huge flowering stalks like spears thrown from the sky. Did they have a scent? she wondered. They had to, didn't they, to attract the bees and hummingbirds? She'd have to get up close and smell one sometime.

She had almost reached the place where the big rounded spike of rock stuck out of the ground when a sudden noise in the undergrowth startled her. Her eyes darted to the path in front of her and she caught her breath. She had a fear of snakes, especially when the light began to fail and they came out to prowl, their coarse thick evil-eyed bodies laid alongside the trail like sticks of wood, like shadows. But this was no snake, and she had to laugh at herself even as the first of the quail, slate heads bobbing, scuttered across the path with a rasp of dead leaves. Cándido was forever trying to snare the little birds but they were too quick, folding themselves into the brush or crying out like scared children as they spread their wings and shot up over the bushes and down the canyon to safety. She stopped a moment to let them pass, the chicks at their heels, and then she stepped into the deep purple shadow cast by the rock.

He was waiting there for her, with his hoarse high voice and his skin that was like too much milk in a pan of coffee, with his hat turned backwards on his head like a *gringo* and the raw meat of his eyes. There was another man with him, an Indian, burnt like a piece of toast. They were sitting there, perched on blunt stools of sandstone, long silver cans of beer dangling from their fingertips. "Well, well," he said, and his face was expressionless in the smothered light, *"buenas noches, señorita?*—or should I say *señora?* Yes? Right?" And he threw it back at her: "Married woman."

There was no time for revision, no time for remonstrance or plea. She turned and ran, uphill, toward the road she'd just escaped—they wouldn't touch her there, they couldn't. She was young and in good shape from climbing up and down out of the canyon twice a day for the last six weeks and she was fast too, the blood singing in her ears, but they were right there, right behind her, and they were grown healthy men with long leaping houndlike strides and the sinews gone tight in their throats with the pulse of the chase. They caught up with her before she'd gone a hundred feet, the tall one, the one from the South, slamming into her like some irresistible force, like the car that had slammed into Cándido.

A bush raked her face, something jerked the bag from her wrist, and they fell together in the dust that was exactly like flour spread over the trail by some mad baker. He was on top of her, sitting on her buttocks, his iron hand forcing her face into the floury dust. She cried out, tried to lift her head, but he slammed his fist into the back of her neck once, twice, three times, cursing to underscore each blow. "Shut up," he snarled. "Shut the fuck up."

The other one stood behind him, waiting. She could hear the rasp of their breathing, anything possible now, and she recoiled from the stinking graveyard breath of the one atop her. He hit her again, suddenly, once at the base of the skull and then in the small of the back. Then he eased up from her, leaning all his weight on the hand that pinned her face to the ground, and with the other hand he took hold of the collar of her dress, her only dress, and tore it down the length of her till the cool evening air pricked at her naked skin. In a frenzy, in a rage, the curses foaming on his lips, he shredded her panties and rammed his fingers into her.

It was as if a tree had fallen on her, as if she were the victim of some random accident, powerless, unable to move. She breathed the dust. Her neck hurt. His fingers moved inside her, in her private places, and it was like he was squirting acid into her. She squirmed in the dirt and he shoved back at her, hard and unrelenting. Then he lifted his hand from the back of her neck, breathing spasmodically, and she could hear him fumbling in his pocket for something and her heart froze—he was going to murder her, rape and murder her, and what had she done? But it wasn't that, it wasn't that at all—it was something in a wrapper, silver foil, the rustle of silver foil. Was it one of those things, one of those—no, a stick of gum. There, in the quickening night, with his dirty fingers inside her as if they belonged there and the Indian waiting his turn, he stopped to put a stick of gum in his mouth and casually drop the wrapper on the exposed skin of her back, no more concerned than if he were sitting on a stool in a bar.

She clenched her eyes shut, gritted her teeth. His hand went away and she could feel him shift his weight as he balanced himself to work down his pants. She stiffened against the pounding of her blood and the moment hung there forever, like the eternal torment of the damned. And then, finally, his voice came at her, probing like a knife. "Married woman," he whispered, leaning close. "You better call your husband."

PART TWO

El Tenksgeevee

1

"HAPPENS ALL THE TIME," KENNY GRISSOM AS-
sured him, and from the undisguised joy in his voice you would have
thought he'd stolen the car himself to drum up business. This was the
moment he lived for, his moment of grace and illumination: Delaney
was without a car and he had a lot full of them. "You'd be surprised,"
he added. "But look what it says about your car and its desirability—
it's a class car all the way; people want it. No offense, but probably
some judge or police chief down in Baja is driving it right now. They
contract out. They do. Señor So-and-So says get me a Mercedes or a
Jag or an Acura Vigor GS, white with tan interior, all the options, and
the dude down there calls his buddies in Canoga Park and they cruise
the streets till they find one. Three hours later it's in Mexico." He
paused to shift his shoulders, tug at his tie. "Happens all the time."

Small comfort to Delaney. It happened all the time, but why did it
have to happen to him? "I still can't understand it," he muttered, sign-
ing the papers as Kenny Grissom handed them across the desk. "It
was broad daylight, hundreds of people going by—and what about the
alarm?"

The salesman blew a quick sharp puff of air between his teeth. "
That's for amateurs, joyriders, kids. The people that got your car are
pros. You know that tool the cops have for when somebody locks their
keys in the car, flat piece of metal about this long? They call it a Slim

Jim?" He held his index fingers apart to demonstrate. "Well, they slip that down inside the glass and flip the lock, then they ease open the door so it doesn't trip the alarm, pop the hood, flip the cable off the battery to disarm the thing, hot-wire the ignition, and bye-bye. A pro can do it in sixty seconds."

Delaney was clutching the pen like a weapon. He felt violated, taken, ripped off—and nobody batted an eyelash, happens all the time. His stomach clamped down on nothing and the sense of futility and powerlessness he'd felt when he came up the road and saw that empty space on the shoulder flooded over him again. It was going to cost him four and a half thousand on top of the insurance to replace the car with the current year's model, and that was bad enough, not to mention the dead certainty that his insurance premiums would go up, but the way people seemed to just accept the whole thing as if they were talking about the weather was what really got him. Own a car, it will be stolen. Simple as that. It was like a tax, like winter floods and mudslides.

The police had taken the report with all the enthusiasm of the walking dead—he might as well have been reporting a missing paper clip for all the interest they mustered—and Jack had used the occasion to deliver a sermon. "What do you expect," he'd said, "when all you bleeding hearts want to invite the whole world in here to feed at our trough without a thought as to who's going to pay for it, as if the American taxpayer was like Jesus Christ with his loaves and fishes. You've seen them lined up on the streets scrambling all over one another every time a car slows at the corner, ready to kill for the chance to make three bucks an hour. Well, did you ever stop to think what happens when they don't get that half-day job spreading manure or stripping shingles off a roof? Where do you think they sleep? What do you think they eat? What would you do in their place?" Jack, ever calm, ever prepared, ever cynical, drew himself up and pointed an admonishing finger. "Don't act surprised, because this is only the beginning. We're under siege here—and there's going to be a backlash. People are fed up with it. Even you. You're fed up with it too, admit it."

And now Kenny Grissom. Business as usual. A shoulder shrug, a wink of commiseration, the naked joy of moving product. From the minute Kyra had dropped Delaney off at the lot—he was determined to replace his car, exact model, color, everything—Kenny Grissom had regaled him with stories of carjackings, chop shops, criminality as pervasive as death. "Don't get me wrong—I'm not blaming it all on the Mexicans," Kenny said, handing him yet another page of the sales agreement, "it's everybody—Salvadorians, I-ranians, Russians, Vietnamese. There was this one woman came in here, she's from Guatemala I think it was, wrapped up in a shawl, bad teeth, her hair in a braid, couldn't have been more than four and a half feet tall. She'd heard about credit—'we don't refuse credit' and that sort of thing, you know?—and even though she didn't have any money or collateral or any credit history whatever, she just wondered if she could sign up for a new car and maybe drive it down to Guatemala—"

The broad face cracked open, the salesman's laugh rang out, and Delaney imagined how thoroughly sick of that laugh the other salesmen must have been, not to mention the secretaries, the service manager and Kenny Grissom's wife, if he had one. He was sick of it himself. But he signed the papers and he got his car and after Kenny handed him the keys, slapped him on the back and told him the story of the woman who'd wrecked two brand-new cars just driving out of the lot, Delaney sat there for a long while, getting used to the seats and new-car smell and the subtle difference between this model and the one he was familiar with. Little things, but they annoyed him out of all proportion. He sat there, running sweat, grimly reading through the owner's manual, though he was late for his lunch date with Kyra. Finally, he put the car in gear and eased it out onto the road, taking surface streets all the way, careful to vary speeds and keep it under fifty, as the manual advised.

He drove twice round the block past the Indian restaurant in Woodland Hills, where they'd agreed to meet, but there was no parking at this hour: lunch was big business. The valet parking attendant was Mexican, of course—Hispanic, Latino, whatever—and Delaney sat there in his new car with thirty-eight miles on the odometer, seat belt fastened, hand on the wheel, until the driver behind him hit his horn and the attendant—he was a kid, eighteen, nineteen, black shining anxious eyes—said, "Sir?" And then Delaney was standing there in the sun, his shirt soaked through, another morning wasted, and the tires chirped and his new car shot round the corner of the building and out of sight. There were no personalized license plates this time, just a random configuration of letters and numbers. He didn't even know his own plate number. He was losing control. A beer, he thought, stepping into the dark coolness of the restaurant through the rear door, just one. To celebrate.

The place was crowded, businesspeople perched over plates of *tandoori* chicken, housewives gossiping over delicate cups of Darjeeling tea and coffee, waiters in a flurry, voices riding up and down the scale. Kyra was sitting at a table near the front window, her back to him, her hair massed over the crown of her head like pale white feathers. A Perrier stood on the table before her, a flap of *nan* bread, a crystal dish of lime pickle and mango chutney. She was bent over a sheaf of papers, working.

"What kept you?" she said as he slid into the chair across from her. "Any problems?"

"No," he murmured, trying to catch the waiter's attention. "I just had to drive slow, that's all—you know, till it's broken in."

"You did get the price we agreed on? They didn't try anything cute at the last minute—?" She looked up from her papers, fixing him with an intent stare. A band of sunlight cut across her face, driving the color from her eyes till they were nearly translucent.

He shook his head. "No surprises. Everything's okay."

"Well, where is it? Can I see it?" She glanced at her watch. "I have to run at one-thirty. I'm closing that place in Arroyo Blanco—on Dolorosa?—and then, since I'll be so close, I want to stop in and see that there're no screwups with the fence company . . ."

They'd got a variance from the Arroyo Blanco Zoning Committee on the fence height in their backyard, as a direct result of what had befallen poor Sacheverell, and they were adding two feet to the chain-link fence. Kyra hadn't let Osbert out of her sight since the attack, insisting on walking him herself before and after work, and the cat had been strictly confined to the house. Once the fence was completed, things could go back to normal. Or so they hoped.

"I left the car out back," he said, "with the parking attendant." He shrugged his shoulders. "Maybe after lunch, if you still . . ." He trailed off. What he wanted to tell her was how angry he was, how he hadn't wanted a new car—the old one barely had twenty thousand miles on it—how he felt depressed, disheartened, as if his luck had turned bad and he was sinking into an imperceptible hole that deepened centimeter by centimeter each hour of each day. There'd been a moment there, handing over the keys to the young Latino, when he felt a deep shameful stab of racist resentment—did they *all* have to be Mexican?—that went against everything he'd believed in all his life. He wanted to tell her about that, that above all else, but he couldn't.

"I'm out front," she said, and they both looked out the window to where Kyra's midnight-blue Lexus sat secure at the curb.

The waiter appeared then, a pudgy balding man who spoke in the chirping singsong accent of the Subcontinent. Delaney ordered a beer—"To celebrate my new car," he explained sourly to Kyra's lifted eyebrows—and asked for a menu.

"Certainly, sir," the waiter barked, and his eyes seemed to jump round in their sockets, "but the lady has—"

"I've already ordered," Kyra said, cutting him off and laying a hand on Delaney's arm. "You were late and I've got to run. I just got us a veggie curry and a bite of salad, and some *samosas* to start."

That was fine, but Delaney felt irritated. It wasn't lunch—at this point he didn't care what he ate—it was the occasion. He wasn't materialistic, not really, and he never bought anything on impulse, but when he did make a major purchase he felt good about it, good about himself, the future of the country and the state of the world. That was the American way. Buy something. Feel good. But he didn't feel good, not at all. He felt like a victim.

Kyra hurried him through the meal and he drank the beer—one of those oversized Indian beers—too quickly, so that he felt a little woozy with the blast of the sun in the parking lot. He handed the ticket to one of the slim young sprinting Mexicans in shiny red vests and glanced up at the roof of the restaurant, where a string of starlings stared hopefully back at him. "I'll just take a quick look," Kyra said, pinching her purse under one arm and leaning forward to leaf through the papers in her briefcase, "and then I've got to run."

It was then that they heard the dog barking, a muffled hoarse percussive sound that seemed to be emanating from everywhere and nowhere at once. Barking. It was a curiosity. Delaney idly scanned the windows of the apartment building that rose up squarely just beyond the line of parked cars, expecting to see a dog up there somewhere, and then he glanced behind him at an empty strip of pavement, begonias in pots, a couple emerging from the rear of the restaurant. A car went noisily up the street. Kyra looked up from her briefcase, cocked her head, listening. "Do you hear a dog somewhere?"

"Aw, the poor thing," a woman's voice breathed behind them and Kyra turned long enough to see where the woman was pointing: two-thirds of the way down the line of cars was a green Jeep Cherokee, the window barely cracked and the black snout of an Afghan pressed to the opening. They could see the jaws fitfully working, the paw raised to the window. Two more percussive barks trailed off into a whine. It was all Kyra needed.

Purse and briefcase dropped like stones and she was off across the lot, hammering at the pavement with the spikes of her heels, her stride fierce with outrage and self-righteousness. Delaney watched numbly as she stalked up to the Jeep's door and tried the handle. He could see the frustration in the set of her shoulders as she tugged savagely at it, once, twice, and then whirled round and came marching back across the lot, a dangerous look on her face.

"It's a crime," the woman behind him said and Delaney felt compelled to give her a quick look of acknowledgment. The man beside her—natty dresser, a wide painted tie standing out at an angle from his throat—looked impatiently round for one of the attendants, the parking stub clutched in his hand.

Delaney's car and Kyra arrived at the same instant, and as the attendant jumped out to collect his tip, Kyra took hold of his arm. "Whose car is that?" she demanded, indicating the green Jeep. "The one with the dog in it."

The attendant's face drew in on itself; his eyes flashed on the Jeep and then came back to Kyra. "Doan know," he said. "This," pointing from the Acura to Delaney, "him." He held up the ticket stub to show her.

"I know that," Kyra said, raising her voice in exasperation. "What I want to know is whose car is that"—pointing again—"because they're breaking the law locking a dog in like that. The animal could die of heat exhaustion, you understand?"

He didn't understand. "Doan know," he repeated, and broke away from her to snatch the stub from the man in the painted tie and dash across the lot.

"Hey!" Kyra shouted, the furrow Delaney knew so well cut like a scar between her furious eyes. "Come back here! I'm talking to you!"

Three men emerged from the restaurant in a burst of laughter, fumbling for their sunglasses; a fourth man stood in the doorway behind them, patting down his pockets for the parking stub. "Honey, Kyra," Delaney coaxed, catching at her arm, "calm down, we'll ask in the restaurant—" But she was already on her way, brushing past the knot of men with her shoulders held rigid, purse and briefcase forgotten, while the new Acura softly purred at the curb, door flung open wide, keys in the ignition. It took him a moment to reach in for the keys, scoop up her purse and briefcase and dodge back into the restaurant.

Kyra was standing in the front room, sizzling in the light through the window, the smell of curry hanging like a pall over the place, clapping her hands like an athletic coach. "Excuse me," she called out, "excuse me!" Conversations died. Waiters froze. The maître d' looked up miserably from his stand behind the potted palm at the front door, ready for anything. "Does anybody here own a green Jeep? License plate number 8VJ237X?"

No one responded. The waiters began to move. The maître d' relaxed.

"Well somebody must own it," Kyra insisted, appealing to the crowd. "It's parked in the lot out back with a dog locked in it—an Afghan." People had turned away from her; conversations resumed. She clapped her hands again. "Are you listening to me?" she demanded, and Delaney saw the maître d's face change all over again. "An Afghan? Does anybody here own an Afghan?"

Delaney was at her side now. "Kyra," he said softly, "come on. It must be somebody else. We'll ask outside again."

She came, reluctantly, muttering under her breath—"I can't believe these people, can you imagine somebody being so stupid, so unaware?"—and for a moment Delaney forgot about the miserable morning, the new car, the theft and the Mexican and his growing sense of confusion and vulnerability: she was glorious in her outrage, a saint, a crusader. This was what mattered. Principles. Right and wrong, an issue as clear-cut as the on/off switch on the TV. In that instant, the cloud was dispelled, and he felt a kind of elation that floated on the wings of the beer and made him feel that everything would ultimately work out for the best.

As soon as they passed back through the door and into the glare of the lot, the feeling was gone, killed in the cradle: the green Jeep was there, at the door, and the man who'd been patting down his pockets for the ticket stub was handing the attendant a folded-up bill. Kyra was on him like a bird of prey.

"Are you the one?" she cried, snatching at the door handle.

The man was of medium height, a little bit of a paunch, long blondish hair swept back in a graying ponytail, blue metallic discs for sunglasses. He wore a tiny diamond stud in his left ear. "Excuse me?" he said, and Delaney could see the dog panting behind him in the passenger's seat.

"Do you know you locked that poor animal in the car, in this heat—?"

The man stood there, looking from Kyra to Delaney and back again. The attendant had vanished from sight. "So what of it?" the man said.

"What of it?" Kyra threw the words back at him in astonishment. "Don't you know you could've killed the poor animal? Don't you care?"

"Kyra," Delaney said.

She threw him a furious look and turned back on the man with the ponytail. "They could take the dog away from you, are you aware of that? Animal Control, by law, can break into any vehicle with a pet locked in it and—"

Something happened to the man's face beneath the dead blue discs of his glasses. His jaw set. His lip curled. "Why don't you just fuck off, lady," he said finally, and he stood there rigid as a statue, holding his ground.

"Now wait a minute," Delaney said, stepping forward, the purse and briefcase still clutched in his arms.

The man regarded him calmly. The dog had begun to whine. "Fuck you too, Jack," the man said, and then he very slowly, very deliberately, eased himself into the car, shut the door and rolled up the window. The locks clicked. Delaney pulled Kyra aside and the Jeep was gone, a belligerent cloud of exhaust left hanging in its place.

Kyra was trembling. So was Delaney. He hadn't been in a fight since high school, and for good reason—he'd lost that one, badly, and the humiliation of it still stung him. "I can't believe—" Kyra said.

"Me either."

"They should lock people like that up."

"I don't know why everybody has to be so, so"—he was searching for the right word—"so *nasty* all the time."

"Urban life," Kyra said, and there was a depth of bitterness to the pronouncement that surprised him. He wanted to say something more, wanted to pursue it, have another beer, a cup of coffee, anything, but she glanced at her watch and gave out a gasp. "My god," she said, snatching the purse and briefcase back from him, "I've got to run." He watched her hurry up the sidewalk and disappear round the corner at the front of the building, and all the gloom and anger came up on him again.

What next? he thought, sinking wearily into the car seat. He hadn't sat there half a second before some moron was honking behind him, and he jerked the car angrily out into the street, ignoring the manufacturer's warnings, and roared up Ventura Boulevard for the canyon road.

He was in a rage, and he tried to calm himself. It seemed he was always in a rage lately—he, Delaney Mossbacher, the Pilgrim of Topanga Creek—he who led the least stressful existence of anybody on earth besides maybe a handful of Tibetan lamas. He had a loving wife, a great stepson, his parents had left him enough money so he didn't have any worries there, and he spent most of his time doing what he really wanted to do: write and think and experience nature. So what was the problem? What had gone wrong? Nothing, he told himself, accelerating round a car trying to make an illegal U-turn, nothing at all. And then it came to him: the day was shot anyway, so why not go straight out into the hills? If that didn't calm him, nothing would.

It was barely two. He could go out to Stunt Road and hike up in the hills above the ocean—he wouldn't have to be back until five for Jordan, and they could go out to eat. He turned west on Mulholland and followed it to where the houses began to fall away and the stark naked hills rose up out of the chaparral, and he cranked down the windows to let the heat and fragrance of the countryside wash over him. For once, he'd have to do without his daypack—he always carried a smaller satchel with sunscreen and bottled water no matter where he went, even if it was only to the supermarket or the Acura dealer, and he glanced over at it on the slick new spotless seat beside him. If he went home for his things he'd have to deal with the fence people—somebody new, somebody Kyra had got through the office—and he just wasn't in the mood for any more hassles today.

When he got there, to the place where the trail crossed the road and a narrow dirt parking strip loomed up on the left, he cut across the blacktop and eased the car in: no sense in scratching it the first day. There were no other cars—that was a good sign: he'd have the trail to himself—and he stepped out into the grip of the heat that radiated off the hills with all the intensity of a good stacked split-log fire. The heat didn't bother him, not today. It was good just to be away from all that smog, confusion and sheer—he came back to the word—nastiness. The way the guy had just said "fuck you" to his wife, when he was in the wrong and anybody could see it. And Kenny Grissom. The hordes of the poor and downtrodden. Jack. The theft.

It was then that he stood back and looked at the car for the first time, really looked at it. Brand new. Not a scratch on it. Not a dent or ding. He thought: Maybe I should go down into Tarzana to the car wash and have it waxed, to protect it, just in case. And then he thought: No, I'm here, I'll hike. He smeared his face with sunblock, tucked the bottle of mineral water down his shirt and started off up the trail.

He didn't get far. He kept thinking about that new car—forty miles on it and four and a half thousand dollars on top of the insurance—and how vulnerable it was sitting there beside the road. Sure, this wasn't as busy as the canyon road, but if they'd got the first car, what was to stop them from getting this one too? The fact that it was quieter out here just played into their hands, didn't it? Fewer people to see the crime, as if anybody would do anything about it anyway. And any car parked here guaranteed that the owner would be away from it for hours.

Suddenly, without thinking, he sank into the brush no more than a hundred yards from the road. He could see the car glittering in the sunlight through the stalks and branches of the vegetation that lined the trail. He was being paranoiac, that was all—you couldn't hold on to everything, could you? He knew that, but for the moment he didn't care. He was just going to sit here, sit here through the afternoon, hidden in the bushes, sit here and watch.

The waves washed over her, back and forth through the speakers, wearing the corners smooth, buffing her like a shell, mother-of-pearl, and by the time the seagulls chimed in with their eerie faraway cries, she'd forgotten all about the green Jeep, the jerk with the ponytail and his poor pathetic dog. She was going to have to stop in at the office for a minute, and then it was up the hill to Arroyo Blanco to congratulate the Kaufmans on their new home and hand-deliver her little housewarming present—a fifty-dollar gift certificate for two at Emilio's and a pair of tickets to the Los Angeles Philharmonic. Most realtors wouldn't have bothered, but that was what set Kyra apart, and she knew it. The little things, the courtesies and reminders, the birthday cards and the inexpensive but tasteful gifts meant more than a hundred open houses. Goodwill, that's what counted. She'd tried to explain it time and again to Delaney, but he had no head for business, and that was just as well—no reason to have two marketing geniuses in the house. But she knew that people in her area changed their place of residence once every 3.7 years, and that they had cousins, children, parents and old college roommates who needed housing too. And when the time came to list their property, they would go to Kyra Menaker-Mossbacher, the empress of goodwill.

She was in and out of the office, and then she realized she was going to need gas to get up the canyon and then cross back over the hill to the place she was showing at four in Monte Nido. The station she liked, where they still had old-fashioned service and only charged you thirty-five cents a gallon more for it, was at the corner of Ventura and Fallbrook, so she'd have to backtrack past the restaurant—but she still had plenty of time. The Kaufmans weren't expecting her till two-forty-five, and that would still leave her fifteen minutes or so to stop home and check up on the fence people.

She was right on schedule, but she was destined to be late, though

she didn't yet realize it, as she pulled out of the gas station, heading
east. For Kyra, this stretch of Ventura Boulevard was among the most
familiar stretches of road in the world, and because it was her business
she kept a sharp eye out for change—restaurants closing, stores opening, condos going up—but it was still capable of surprising her. As it
did now. Two blocks up, at Shoup, she noticed a group of men gathered round the 7-Eleven parking lot. They were Mexicans, looking for
work. They'd started appearing along here about two years back, but
there'd never been more than a handful of them. Now there must have
been fifty or more, clustered in groups just off the parking lot and
stretched in a ragged line all the way back to where the road snaked
under the freeway overpass. This was a new development, which war-
ranted checking up on, and she swung impulsively into the parking lot,
nearly running down a pair of short dark men stationed at the entrance.
The men didn't look alarmed, only hopeful.

This was not a good situation. There were too many of them here
and that was the sort of thing that scared buyers away from the area.
Not that this stretch of the boulevard—single- and double-story older
commercial buildings—was exactly her cup of tea, but there were
homes five blocks from here that would go for four and five hundred
thousand even now. She pulled into a space in front of the store and
found an excuse to go in—she could use a package of gum, a Diet
Coke maybe. None of the men dared approach her in the lot—the
7-Eleven manager would have seen to that—but they all watched her
as she stepped out of the car, and their eyes were wistful, proud,
indifferent. They'd take on another look if she crossed the lot.

There were two women behind the counter, both Asian, both young.
They smiled at Kyra when she came in the door, kept smiling as she
went back to the cooler, selected her Diet Coke and made her way
back to the counter. They smiled as she selected her gum. "Find everything?" the shorter of the two asked.

"Yes," Kyra said. "Thank you." And this gave her her opening. "There
seem to be a lot of men out there on the sidewalk—more than
usual, no?"

The shorter girl—she seemed to be in charge—shrugged. "No more, no less."

"Bad for business, no?" Kyra said, falling into the rhythm of the girl's fractured English.

Another shrug. "Not bad, not good."

Kyra thanked her and stepped back out into the heat. She was about to slip into the air-conditioned envelope of the car and be on her way, when she suddenly swung round and crossed the lot to where the men were gathered. Now the looks were different—all the men stared at her, some boldly, some furtively. If this were Tijuana they'd be grabbing for her, making lewd comments, jeering and whistling, but here they didn't dare, here they wanted to be conspicuous only to the right people, the people who needed cheap labor for the day, the afternoon, the hour. She imagined them trading apocryphal stories of the beautiful *gringa* who selected the best-built man for a special kind of work, and tried to keep a neutral look on her face.

She passed by the first group, and then turned onto the sidewalk, her gaze fixed on the row of cheap apartments that backed up onto the commercial strip of the boulevard and faced out on the dense growth of pepper trees that screened the freeway from view. The apartments were seedy and getting seedier, she could see that from here—open doors, dark men identical to those crowding the sidewalk peering out at her, the antediluvian swimming pool gone dry, paint blistered and pissed over with graffiti. She stopped in the middle of the block, overwhelmed with anger and disgust and a kind of sinking despair. She didn't see things the way Delaney did—he was from the East Coast, he didn't understand, he hadn't lived with it all his life. Somebody had to do something about these people—they were ubiquitous, prolific as rabbits, and they were death for business.

She was on her way back to the car, thinking she'd drive Mike Bender by here tomorrow and see if he couldn't exert some pressure in the right places, call the INS out here, get the police to crack down, something, anything. In an ironic way, the invasion from the South had been good for business to this point because it had driven the entire white middle class out of Los Angeles proper and into the areas she specialized in: Calabasas, Topanga, Arroyo Blanco. She still sold houses in Woodland Hills—that's where the offices were, after all, and it was still considered a very desirable upper-middle-class neighborhood—but all the smart buyers had already retreated beyond the city limits. Schools, that's what it was all about. They didn't bus in the county, only in the city.

Still, this congregation was disturbing. There had to be a limit, a boundary, a cap, or they'd be in Calabasas next and then Thousand Oaks and on and on up the coast till there was no real estate left. That's what she was thinking, not in any heartless or calculating way—everybody had a right to live—but in terms of simple business sense, when she became aware that one of the men hadn't stepped aside as she crossed back into the parking lot. There was a lamppost on her left, a car parked to the right, and she had to pull up short to avoid walking right into him.

He looked up at her, sought out her eyes and smiled. He couldn't have been more than eighteen, his hair long and frozen to his scalp with oil, pants neatly pressed, shirt buttoned up to the collar though it must have been ninety-five degrees or more. "You want work, Miss?" he said.

"No," she said, "no thank you," and stepped around him.

"Cheap," he said at her back, and then he was right there again at her elbow, like something that had stuck to the fabric of her jacket. "Pleese," he said. "I do anything." And then he added, again, as she inserted the key in the door of the car, swung it open and escaped into the cool familiar embrace of the leather interior: "Cheap."

The Kaufmans were pleased, though she was a few minutes late, and the fence people knew exactly what they were doing. She pulled into her driveway and Al Lopez's truck was there, in Delaney's spot. She'd worked with Al before, through the office, hiring him to do everything from replacing cracked kitchen tiles to plumbing and electrical and patching stucco on the houses she had in escrow. Anytime there was a dispute, she could bring Al in and do a quick cosmetic job on whatever the buyers got hung up on. He'd seemed a natural for the fence, especially since she wouldn't consider going back to the idiot who'd put up the original fence and assured her that nothing could get over six feet of chain link.

Since she still had time before her four o'clock, she took Osbert out on the leash for ten minutes and chatted with Al while his men poured concrete and set new eight-foot posts into the holes where the old posts had stood. He'd told her at the outset that he could simply extend the existing poles at half the price, but she didn't want anything tacky-looking, and above all, she told him, she wanted strength and impregnability. "I don't want anything getting in here ever again," she'd said.

Now, as she stood there with Osbert, making small talk about traffic, smog, the heat and the housing market, Al said casually, almost slyly, "Of course, there's not much you can do about snakes—"

Snakes. An image rose up in her head, cold and primordial, the coil and shuffle, the wicked glittering reptilian eyes: she hated snakes. Worse than coyotes, worse than anything. She'd never given a thought to coyotes when they moved in—it was Delaney who'd insisted on the fence—but no one had to warn her about the snakes. Selda Cherrystone had discovered one coiled up in her dryer and its mate beneath the washing machine, and half the people on the block had found rattlesnakes in their garages at one time or another. "Can't you run something along the base of the fence?" she asked, thinking of a miniature trap or net or maybe a weak electric current.

Al looked away, his eyes squinted into the globes of his cheeks. He was heavyset, in his fifties, with white hair and skin the color and texture of an old medicine ball. "We've got a product," he said, still fixing his gaze on the distant tree-studded crotch of the canyon, and then he turned back to her. "Plastic strips, a real tight weave in the mesh of the fence—we go about three feet and down under the ground maybe six inches. That takes care of your snakes."

"How much?" Kyra asked, gazing off into the distance herself now.

"Two-fifty."

"Two hundred," she said, and it was a reflex.

"Two-twenty-five."

"I don't know, Al," she said, "we've never had a snake here yet."

He bent strategically to stroke Osbert's ears. "Rattlers," he sighed, "they get in under the fence, nothing to stop 'em really, and they bite a little dog like this. I've seen it happen. Up here especially." He straightened up and forced out a deep moaning trail of breath with the effort. "I'll give it to you for two-ten, just say the word."

She nodded yes and he shouted something in Spanish to one of the men bent over the cement mixer, and that was when she noticed him for the first time, the man with the limp and the graying mustache, his face bruised and swollen like bad fruit. He went right by her on his way to the truck and she sucked in her breath as if she'd burned herself. This was the man, the very man—it had to be. She watched him slide the long plastic strips from the back of the truck and balance them on one shoulder, and she felt a space open up inside her, a great sad empty space that made her feel as if she'd given birth to something weak and unformed. And as he passed by her again, jaunty on his bad leg, the space opened so wide it could have sucked in the whole universe. He was whistling, whistling under his breath.

Later, after she'd shown the Monte Nido house to a crabbed old couple with penurious noses and swollen checkbooks who added up to a strong maybe, she went round shutting up her houses as briskly and efficiently as she could, hoping to be home by six. Everything was in order at the first four places, but as she punched in the code at the Da Roses' gate, something caught her eye in the brush along the gully on the right-hand side of the road, just inside the gate. Something shiny, throwing light back at the hard hot cauldron of the evening sun. She hit the command key, let the gate swing back, and walked up the road to investigate.

It was a shopping cart, flung on its side in the ditch and all but buried in the vegetation. The red plastic flap on the baby seat bore the name of a local supermarket—Von's—but the nearest Von's was miles from here. For that matter, there wasn't a store of any kind within miles. Kyra bent to examine the thing, her skirt pulled tight against her haunches, heels sinking into the friable dirt, as if it would give a clue as to how it had gotten here. But there was no clue. The cart seemed new, bright in its coat of corruscating metal, barely used. She went back to the car, which she'd left running, to get a pen and her memo book so she could jot down the store's number and have someone come out and pick the thing up. After dragging it out of the ditch and wheeling it beyond the gate so they could get to it, she slid back into the car and wound her way up the road to the house, puzzled still, and suspicious, her eyes fastening on every detail.

The house rose up before her, its windows solid with light, commanding the hilltop like a fortress looking out on the coast of Brittany instead of the deep blue pit of the Pacific. She pulled up in front of the big wooden doors of the garage and killed the engine. For a long moment she just sat there, windows down, breathing in the air and listening. Then she got out of the car and walked round the house twice, checking each door and window at ground level. At the same time she scanned the upper windows, looking for signs of entry or vandalism, but nothing seemed out of the ordinary. Finally, with a glance over her shoulder, she went inside.

The interior was cool and quiet and it smelled faintly of almonds. That was a good smell for a house to have, a clean patrician smell, and Kyra realized it must have come from the furniture polish the maid used. Or could it have been an air freshener? She stood for a moment by the alarm panel, which she'd shut down this morning so Claudia Insty from Red House could show the place, and now she punched in the code to see if any of the twenty-three zones had been tampered with. They hadn't. The place was secure. She made a quick tour of the rooms, out of habit, all the while trying to imagine possible scenarios to explain away the shopping cart: the gardener had been using it and left it behind by mistake, teenagers had stolen it as a prank and flung it from their car, yes, sure, that had to be it. And yet how had it gotten inside the gate? Why would they go to the effort of lifting it to that height—why would anyone? Unless, of course, they'd gone round the gate through the scrub and valley oaks—but that didn't answer the why part of the question.

She'd locked up and was standing at the door of the car, the air alive with birds and insects, when it hit her: transients used those carts. Bums. The homeless and displaced. Crazies. Mexicans. Winos. But no, that was a city problem, the sort of thing she'd expect to find out back of the 7-Eleven, in Canoga Park, Hollywood, downtown L.A. This was just too remote. Wasn't it?

She'd swung open the door of the car, and now she shut it again. If someone was camping here, squatting, living out in the bushes . . . Delaney had told her they were camping in the canyon, miles from anything. If they could camp there, why not here? Suddenly the image of a village she'd seen on a tour of the Yucatán ruins came back to her in all its immediacy: naked children, pigs, cookfires, wattle huts—she couldn't have that. Not here. Not on the Da Ros property. How could you explain something like that to a prospective buyer?

But maybe she was jumping to conclusions—all she'd seen was a shopping cart, and a new one at that, empty and innocuous. Still, she thought, she'd better take a tour of the grounds, just in case, and though she wanted to get home early she left the car where it stood and struck off to the south, in heels and stockings, to trace the perimeter of the property. It was a mistake. The lawn gave out less than a hundred feet from the back of the garage and a ten-foot-tall hedge of red oleander camouflaged the fact that the property sloped down into the scrub from there. She ruined a good pair of stockings pushing through the oleanders and hadn't gone five steps beyond that before she twisted her ankle in a gopher hole and damned near snapped the heel off her shoe. She saw the fence line in the distance, chain link buried in scrub so thick it was almost invisible, a meandering border that roughly followed what must have been a dry streambed and then plunged precipitously over the cliff the house commanded. Kyra leaned into a tree to remove her shoes, then turned to wade back through the oleanders to the lawn.

That was when she noticed something moving at the base of the main lawn, sunk down out of sight of the front of the house. Buff-colored. A deer, she thought. A coyote. But the movement didn't halt or hesitate in the way of an animal, and in the next instant she watched the head and shoulders of a man appear over the rim of the slope, followed by his torso, hips and striding legs, and then a second man, close at his heels. They were Mexicans, she was sure of it, even at this distance, and the origin of the shopping cart suddenly became clear to her. She didn't think to be afraid. In her suit, the sweat beading her makeup, stockings torn and heels in her hand, she stalked across the lawn to confront them.

When she came round the corner of the garage, they were no more than thirty feet away, arrested by the sight of the car. The taller one—he wore a baseball cap reversed on his head and had a bedroll thrust over one shoulder—had stopped short, hunched inside himself, and he'd turned to say something to the other. The second man spotted her first and she could see him flinch in recognition and mouth a warning to his companion as she turned the corner and came toward them. "What do you think you're doing here?" she cried, her voice shrill with authority. "This is private property."

The tall man turned his head to look at her then and she stopped where she was. There was something in his look that warned her off—this was no confrontation over a dog in a restaurant parking lot. His eyes flashed at her and she saw the hate and contempt in them, the potential for cruelty, the knowledge and certainty of it. He was chewing something. He turned his head to spit casually in the grass. She was ten feet from them and ten feet at least from the car. "I'm sorry," she said, and her voice quavered, she could hear it herself, gone lame and flat, "but you can't be here. You're, you're trespassing."

She saw the look the two exchanged, flickering, electric, a look of instant and absolute accord. The nearest house was a quarter mile down the ridge, out of sight, out of hearing. She was afraid suddenly, struck deep in the root of her with the primitive intimate shock of it.

"You own these place, lady?" the tall one said, fixing her with his steady unblinking gaze.

She looked at him, then at the other man. He was darker, shorter, with hair to his shoulders and a silky peltlike streak of hair on his chin. "Yes," she lied, addressing them both, trying to maintain eye contact, trying to sell them. "My husband and I do. And my brother." She gestured toward the house. "They're in there now, making drinks for dinner."

The tall one looked dubiously toward the house, the great broad artifact of stone, lumber and glass that cut across the horizon like a monument to the ruling tribe, and then said something in Spanish to his companion, a quick sudden spurt of language. She wanted to break for the car, fling open the door and hit the automatic locks before they could get to her; then she could start it up with a roar and swing round in a vicious circle, jam the wheel, hit the accelerator—

"We are sorry too much," the tall one said, and he ducked his head, false and obsequious at the same time, then came back to her with a smile. She saw false teeth, yellowed gums. His eyes bored right through her. "Me and my friend? We don't know these place, you know? We hike, that's all. Just hike."

She had nothing to say to this, but she forced herself to stand firm, watching for sudden movement.

The man turned his head, spat out something to his companion, and for the first time she noticed the strange high breathy quality of his voice. "Sorry," he repeated, coming back to her eyes. "A mistake, that's all. No problem, huh?"

The blood pounded in her temples. She could hardly breathe. "No problem," she heard herself say.

"Okay," the man said, and his voice boomed out as he tugged at his bedroll and turned to leave, the decision made, the moment expended, "okay, no problem." She watched them head back the way they came, and she'd begun, almost involuntarily, to drift toward the car, when the tall one suddenly stopped short, as if he'd forgotten something, and turned back to level his smile on her. "You have a nice day, huh?" he said, "—you and your husband. And your brother too."

2

CÁNDIDO HAD BEEN LUCKY. DESPITE HIS FACE AND his limp and the fact that it was half an hour after the labor exchange closed down for the day and everyone had gone home, he got work, good work, setting fence posts for five dollars an hour, and then later painting the inside of a house till past dark. The boss was a Mexican-American who could speak English like a *gringo* but still had command of his native tongue. Cándido had been sitting there in the dirt by the closed-down labor exchange, feeling hopeless and angry, feeling sorry for himself—his wife had got work, a seventeen-year-old village girl who didn't know the first thing about anything, and he hadn't, though he could do any job you asked him, from finish carpentry to machine work to roofing—when Al Lopez pulled into the lot. He had an Indian from Chiapas in the back of the truck and the Indian called out to him, "*¿Quieres trabajar?*" And then Al Lopez had stuck his head out the window and said, "*Cinco dólares,*" because his regular man, another Indian, had got sick on the job, too sick to work.

It was nearly one o'clock by the time they got to the place, a big house in a development of big houses locked away behind a brand-new set of gates. Cándido knew what those gates were for and who they were meant to keep out, but that didn't bother him. He wasn't resentful. He wasn't envious. He didn't need a million dollars—he wasn't born for that, and if he was he would have won the lottery. No, all he needed was work, steady work, and this was a beginning. He mixed concrete, dug holes, hustled as best he could with the hollow metal posts and the plastic strips, all the while amazed at the houses that had sprouted up here, proud and substantial, big *gringo* houses, where before there'd been nothing. Six years ago, the first time Cándido had laid eyes on this canyon, there had been nothing here but hills of golden grass, humped like the back of some immemorial animal, and the dusty green canopies of the canyon oaks.

He'd been working up in Idaho, in the potatoes, sending all his money home to Resurrección, and when the potatoes ran out he made his way south to Los Angeles because his friend Hilario had a cousin in Canoga Park and there was plenty of work there. It was October and he'd wanted to go home to his wife and his aunt Lupe, who'd practically raised him after his mother died and his father remarried, and the timing was right too because most of the men in the village were just then leaving to work in the citrus and he'd be cock of the walk till spring. But Hilario convinced him: You're here already, he'd argued, so why run the risk of another crossing, and besides, you'll make more in two months in Los Angeles than you did in the past four in Idaho, believe me. And Cándido had asked: What kind of work? Gardening, Hilario told him. Gardening? He was dubious. You know, Hilario said, for the rich people with their big lawns and their flower-beds and the trees full of fruit they never eat.

And so they pooled their money with four other men and bought a rusted-out 1971 Buick Electra with a balky transmission and four bald-as-an-egg tires for three hundred and seventy-five dollars, and started south in the middle of the season's first snowstorm. None of them except Cándido had ever seen snow before, let alone experienced or even contemplated the peculiar problems of driving in it. With its bald tires on the slick surface, the Buick fishtailed all over the road while huge howling semitrailers roared past them like Death flapping its wings over the deepest pit. Cándido had driven before—but not much, having learned on an old Peugeot in a citrus grove outside of Bakersfield on his first trip North—and he was elected to do the bulk of the driving, especially in an emergency, like this one. For sixteen hours he gripped the wheel with paralyzed hands, helpless to keep the car from skittering like a hockey puck every time he turned the wheel or hit the brakes. Finally the snow gave out, but so did the transmission, and they'd only made it as far as Wagontire, Oregon, where six *indocumentados* piling out of the smoking wreck of a rust-eaten 1971 Buick Electra were something less than inconspicuous.

They hadn't had the hood up ten minutes, with Hilario leaning into the engine compartment in a vain attempt to fathom what had gone wrong with a machine that had already drunk up half a case of transmission oil, when the state police cruiser nosed in behind them on the shoulder of the road. The effect was to send everybody scrambling up the bank and into the woods in full flight, except for Hilario, who was still bent over the motor the last time Cándido laid eyes on him. The police officers—pale, big-shouldered men in sunglasses and wide-brimmed hats—shouted incomprehensible threats and fired off a warning shot, but Cándido and two of the other men kept on running. Cándido ran till his lungs were on fire, a mile at least, and then he collapsed in a gully outside of a farmhouse. His friends were nowhere in sight. He was terrified and he was lost. It began to rain.

He couldn't have been more at a loss if he'd been dropped down on another planet. He had money—nearly four hundred dollars sewed into the cuff of his trousers—and the first thing he thought of was the bus. But where was the bus? Where was the station and how could he hope to find it? There was no one in the entire state of Oregon who spoke Spanish. And worse: he wasn't even sure, in terms of geography, where exactly Oregon was and what relation it bore to California, Baja and the rest of Mexico. He crouched down in the ditch, looking wistfully across the field to the farmhouse, as the day closed into night and the rain turned to sleet. He had a strip of jerky in his pocket to chew on, and as he tore into the leathery flavorless meat with quivering jaws and aching teeth, he remembered a bit of advice his father had once given him. In times of extremity, his father said, when you're lost or hungry or in danger, *ponte pared,* make like a wall.

That is, you present a solid unbreachable surface, you show nothing, neither fear nor despair, and you protect the inner fortress of yourself from all comers. That night, cold, wet, hungry and afraid, Cándido followed his father's advice and made himself like a wall.

It did no good. He froze just the same, and his stomach shrank regardless. At daybreak, he heard dogs barking somewhere off in the distance, and at seven or so he saw the farmer's wife emerge from the back door of the house with three pale little children, climb into one of the four cars that stood beside the barn, and make her way down a long winding drive toward the main road. The ground was covered with a pebbly gray snow, an inch deep. He watched the car—it was red, a Ford—crawl through that Arctic vista like the pointer on the bland white field of a game of chance at a village *fiesta*. Awhile later he watched a girl of twenty or so emerge from the house, climb into one of the other cars and wind her way down the drive to the distant road. Finally, and it was only minutes later, the farmer himself appeared, a *güero* in his forties, preternaturally tall, with the loping, patient, over-worked gait of farmers everywhere. He slammed the kitchen door with an audible crack, crossed the yard and vanished through the door to the barn.

Cándido was a wall, but the wall was crumbling. He wasn't used to the North, had snow only twice before in his life, both times with the potatoes in Idaho, and he hated it. His jacket was thin. He was freezing to death. And so, he became a moving wall, lurching up out of the ditch, crossing under a barbed-wire fence and making his way in *huaraches* and wet socks across the field to the barn, where he stopped, his heart turning over in his chest, and knocked at the broad plane of painted wood that formed one-half of the door through which the farmer had disappeared. He was shivering, his arms wrapped round his shoulders. He didn't care whether they deported him or not, didn't care whether they put him in prison or stretched him on the rack, just so long as he got warm.

And then the farmer was standing there, towering over him, a man of huge hocks and beefy arms with a head the size of a prize calabash and great sinewy thick-fingered hands, a man who could easily have earned his living touring Mexico as the thyroid giant in a traveling circus. The man—the giant—looked stunned, shocked, as surprised as if this actually were another planet and Cándido a strange new species of being. "Pleese," Cándido said through jackhammering teeth, and realizing that he'd already used up the full range of his English, he merely repeated himself: "Pleese."

The next thing he knew he was wrapped in a blanket, sitting in a big gleaming American kitchen, appliances humming, a steaming cup of coffee clutched in his hands. The farmer moved about the kitchen on feet the size of snowshoes. All the broad geometry of his back was in motion as he fussed over his appliances, six slices of toast in the shining silver toaster, eggs and a slab of ham in the little black oven that congealed the yolks and set the meat sizzling in two minutes flat, and then he was standing there, offering the plate and trying to work his face into a smile. Cándido took the plate from the huge callused hands with a dip of his head and a murmur of *"Muchísimas gracias,"* and the big man lumbered across the kitchen to a white telephone hanging on the wall and began to dial. The eggs went cold in Cándido's mouth: this was it, this was the end. The farmer was turning him in. Cándido crouched over the plate and made like a wall.

There are always surprises. Life may be inverately grim and the surprises disproportionately unpleasant, but it would be hardly worth living if there were no exceptions, no sunny days, no acts of random kindness. The farmer motioned him to the phone, and on the other end of the line there was an angelic voice, the sweet lilting gently lisping voice of Graciela Herrera, a *chicana* from a town five miles away, talking to him in the language of their ancestors. Graciela picked him up in her bright yellow Volkswagen and dropped him off at the bus station, where she translated for the ticket agent so he could purchase his ticket. Cándido wanted to raise a shrine to her. He kissed her fingertips and gave her the only thing he had to give: the laminated picture card of the Virgin of Guadalupe he carried for luck.

In Canoga Park, Cándido was able to find Hilario's cousin with no problem—the town was like a Mexican village writ large—and he got work right away, with an English-speaking boss who managed half a dozen gardening crews of three men each. The cousin's name was Arturo and he showed Cándido what to do—it was nothing: pull the cord on the mower, walk behind the airblast of the blower, cultivate the flowerbeds and trim the shrubs—while they both awaited news of Hilario. Weeks went by. Cándido shared a place off Shoup in Woodland Hills with six other men and the close quarters and the dirt and the foul smells reminded him of his first stay in Los Angeles, in the filth of Echo Park. He sent money home and wired Resurrección that he'd be home by Christmas. News came finally that Hilario was back in Guerrero, deported from Oregon and stripped of everything he owned by the Federal Judicial Police the minute he reentered Mexico.

Things were good for a while. Cándido was making a hundred and sixty dollars a week, spending two hundred a month on rent, another hundred on food, beer, the occasional movie, and sending the rest home. Arturo became a good friend. The work was like play compared to struggling through the mud of the potato fields like a human *burro* or picking lemons in hundred-and-twenty-degree heat. He began to relax. Began to feel at home. Wagontire, Oregon, was a distant memory.

And then the roof fell in. Someone tipped off *La Migra* and they made a sweep of the entire area, six o'clock in the morning, snatching people off the street, from in front of the 7-Eleven and the bus stop. A hundred men and women were lined up on the sidewalk, even a few children, staring at their feet while the puke-green buses from the Immigration pulled up to the curb to take them one-way to Tijuana, the doors locked, the windows barred, all their poor possessions—the eternally rolling TVs, the mattresses on the floor, their clothes and cooking things—left behind in their apartments for the scavengers and the garbagemen.

Six a.m. Cándido was among the throng, dressed for work, a hundred and ten dollars in his string bag under the sink in the apartment behind him, the darkness broken only by the ugly yellow light of the streetlamps and the harsh glowing eyes of the buses. It was cold. A woman was crying softly beside him; a man argued with one of the Spanish-speaking Immigration agents, a hard high nagging whine: "My things," he said, over and over, "what about my things?" Cándido had just left his apartment to wait out front for Arturo to swing by for him in the boss's pickup when *La Migra* nailed him, and now he stood in line with all the hopeless others. Eight Immigration agents, two of them female, worked their way down the line of Mexicans, one by one, and the Mexicans, as if they were shackled together, joined at the elbow, rooted to the pavement, never thought to run or flex a muscle or even move. It was the Mexican way: acquiesce, accept. Things would change, sure they would, but only if God willed it.

Cándido was listening to the woman cry softly beside him and thinking about that fatalism, that acquiescence, the inability of his people to act in the face of authority, right or wrong, good or bad, when a voice cried out in his head: *Run! Run now, while the fat-faced overfed* pendejo *from the Immigration is still five people up the line with his flashlight and his pen and his clipboard and the green-eyed bitch behind him. Run!*

He broke for the line of pepper trees across the street, and seeing him run, two other men broke from the line and fled with him, the whole *macho* corps of the Immigration crying out in unison and flowing toward them in a wave. "Stop!" they shouted. "You're under arrest!"—things like that, the words of English every Mexican knew—but Cándido and the two men who had broken with him didn't stop. They went across the road and into the trees, struggling up the refuse-choked bank to the freeway fence, and then, with *La Migra* right behind them, they went up and over the fence and onto the shoulder of the freeway.

The cars streamed by in a rush, even at this hour. Four lanes in each direction, the torrent of headlights, sixty-five and seventy miles an hour: suicide. Cándido shot a glance at the two men beside him—both young and scared—and then he began to jog up the shoulder, against the traffic, looking to make it to the next exit and disappear in the bushes, no thought but that. The two men—they were boys really, teenagers—followed his lead and the three of them ran half a mile or more, two hard-nosed men from the Immigration flinging themselves up the shoulder behind them, the traffic raging, thundering in their ears, and when they came in sight of the exit they saw that *La Migra* had anticipated them and stationed a green van on the shoulder ahead. The boys were frantic, their breathing as harsh as the ragged roaring whine of the engines as the headlights picked them out and the first of the police sirens tore at the air. Was it worth dying for this? Half the people on those buses would be back in a day, back in forty-eight hours, a week. It wasn't worth it. It wasn't.

Cándido would never forgive himself for what happened next. He was the one, he should have known, and they were only boys, scared and directionless. It wasn't worth it, but when the agents came panting up to them, their faces contorted and ugly with their shouts and threats, something uncoiled inside of him and he sprang out into the traffic like a cornered rabbit leaping from a cliff to avoid the dogs. The boys followed him, both of them, and they gave up their lives. All he could remember was the shrieking of the brakes and the blare of the horns and then the sound of all the glass in the world shattering. Pulp, that's what those boys were—they were nothing forever—and they could have been back in forty-eight hours. The first boy went down like a piston, torn off his legs at the hip, down and gone, and the second made it nearly to Cándido in the third lane over when he was flung into the air in one whole pounded piece. The fourth lane was free and Cándido was across it while the apocalypse of twisted metal and skating cars blasted the world around him till even the traffic across the divider was stopped dead in horror. He climbed the divider, walked to the far side on melting legs, vaulted the fence and became one with the shadows.

And after that? After that the trauma drove him from yard to yard, from green strip to green strip, and finally up over the dry Valley-side swell of Topanga Canyon and into the cleft of the creekbed. He bought food and two pints of brandy with the money in his pockets and he lay by the trickling creek for seven days, turning the horror over in his mind. He watched the trees move in the wind. He watched the ground squirrels, the birds, watched light shine through the thin transparent wings of the butterflies, and he thought: Why can't the world be like this? Then he picked himself up and went home to Resurrección.

That was the first time he'd seen the canyon, and now he was here again, feeling good, working, protecting América from all that was out there. His accident had been bad, nearly fatal, but *si Dios quiere* he would be whole again, or nearly whole, and he understood that a man who had crossed eight lanes of freeway was like the Lord who walked on the waters, and that no man could expect that kind of grace to descend on him more than once in a lifetime. And so he worked for Al Lopez and painted till nearly ten at night and then Al Lopez dropped him off at the darkened labor exchange, fifty dollars richer.

América would have missed him, he knew that, and the stores were closed at this hour, everything shut down. At seven, Al Lopez had bought Pepsis and *burritos* in silver foil for him and the Indian, and so he didn't need to eat, but still he felt a flare of hunger after all those days of enforced fasting. As he limped down the dark road, flinching at the headlights of the cars, he wondered if América had kept the fire going under the stew.

It was late, very late, by the time he bundled up his clothes and waded the pool to their camp. He was glad to see the fire, coals glowing red through the dark scrim of leaves, and he caught a keen exciting whiff of the stew as he shrugged into his clothes and called out softly to América so as not to startle her. "América," he whispered. "It's me, Cándido—I'm back." She didn't answer. And that was strange, because as he came round the black hump of the ruined car, he saw her there, crouched by the fire in her underthings, her back to him, the dress in her lap. She was sewing, that was it, working with needle and thread on the material she kept lifting to her face and then canting toward the unsteady light of the fire, the wings of her poor thin shoulder blades swelling and receding with the busy movement of her wrists and hands. The sight of her overwhelmed him with sadness and guilt: he had to give her more, he had to. He'd buy her a new dress tomorrow, he told himself, thinking of the thrift shop near the labor exchange. There were no bargains in that shop, he knew that without looking—it was for *gringos,* commuters and property owners and people on their way to the beach—but without transportation, what choice did he have? He fingered the bills in his pocket and promised himself he'd surprise her tomorrow.

Then he came up and put a hand on her shoulder and said, "Hey, *mi vida,* I'm back," and he was going to tell her about the job and Al Lopez and the fifty dollars in his pocket, but she jerked away from him as if he'd struck her, and turned the face of a stranger to him. There was something in her eyes that hadn't been there before, something worse, far worse, than what he'd glimpsed the night before when she left the rich man in his car. "What is it?" he said. "What's the matter?"

Her face went blank. Her eyes dropped away from his and her hands curled rigid in her lap till they were like the hands of a cripple.

He knelt beside her then and talked in an urgent apologetic whisper: "I made money, good money, and I'm going to buy you a dress, a new dress, first thing tomorrow, as soon as—once I'm done with work— and I know I'm going to get work, I know it, every day. You won't have to wear that thing anymore, or mend it either. Just give me a week or two, that's all I ask, and we'll be out of here, we'll have that apartment, and you'll have ten dresses, twenty, a whole closetful . . ."

But she wasn't responding—she just sat there, hanging her head, her face hidden behind the curtain of her hair. It was then that he noticed the welts at the base of her neck, where the hair parted to fall forward across her shoulders. Three raised red welts that glared at him like angry eyes, unmistakable, irrefutable. "What happened?" he demanded, masking the damage with a trembling hand. "Was it that *rico*? Did he try anything with you, the son of a bitch—I swear I'll kill him, I will—"

Her voice was tiny, choked, the faintest intrusion on the sphere of the audible: "They took my money."

And now he was rough, though he didn't mean to be. He jerked at her shoulders and forced her to look him in the face. "Who took your money—what are you talking about?" And then he knew, knew it all, knew as certainly as if he'd been there: "Those *vagos*? It was the one with the hat, wasn't it? The half-a-*gringo*?"

She nodded. He forgot his hunger, forgot the pot on the coals, the night, the woodsmoke, the soil beneath his knees, oblivious to everything but her face and her eyes. She began to cry, a soft kittenish mewling that only infuriated him more. He clutched at her shoulders, shook her again. "Who else?"

"I don't know. An Indian."

"Where?" he shouted. "Where?"

"On the trail."

On the trail. His heart froze around those three words. If they'd robbed her in the parking lot, on the road, at the labor exchange, it was one thing, but *on the trail* . . . "What else? What else did they take? Quick, tell me. They didn't, they didn't try to—?"

"No," she said. "No."

"You're lying. Don't lie to me. Don't you dare lie to me."

She broke his grip and stared into the fire, rubbed a wrist across her eyes. "They took my money."

Cándido was ready to kill, ready to hack through every bush in the mountains till he found their camp and crushed their skulls while they lay sleeping. The image infested his brain: the tan dog's eyes, the stirring limbs and the rock coming down, again and again. "Is that all?" he hissed, fighting against the knowledge. "Is that all they took?" He gripped her arm again. "Are you sure?"

"Yes," she whispered, turning to level her gaze on him, "I'm sure."

It hurt, that's all she knew. Burned. Burned like acid in an open wound, like the corrosive at the fat man's house when it got down into the split skin at the quick of her nails. Every time she peed it was like fire passing through her. She didn't know what it was—some lingering effect of what they'd done to her that night, her insides scored and dirty, rubbed raw like a skinned knee . . . or was it just a new and unexpected phase of her pregnancy? Was this normal? Was this the way it was supposed to be in the beginning of the fifth month, flaming pee? Her mother would know. Her aunts, her older sisters, the village midwives. If she were home she could even have asked Señora Serrano, the neighbor lady who'd given birth to sixteen children, the oldest grown up and with children of their own, the youngest in diapers still. But here? Here there was no one, and that frightened her—frightened her now and for when her time came.

América waited there in the hut behind the wrecked car for Cándido, day after day, bored and aching—he wouldn't let her go to the labor exchange, never again—her breasts tender, her stomach queasy, needing her mother, needing to ask the questions a daughter never asks, not till she's married. But then, she and Cándido never were married, not officially, not in the church. In the eyes of the Church, Cándido was already married, forever married, to Resurrección. And América and Cándido had gone off in the night, silent as thieves, and only a note left for her mother, not a word to her face, and even then América was pregnant, though she didn't know it. She wanted to call her mother now, on the telephone, one of those outdoor phones with the little plastic bonnets lined up in a row by the Chinese store and hear her voice and tell her she was all right and ask her why it burned so when she peed. Was that the way it was supposed to be? Did all women go through that? But then, even if she had the money, all lined up on the plastic shelf in all the silver denominations, she'd have to call the village pharmacy because her parents had no phone, and how was she to do that? She didn't know the number. Didn't know how to dial Mexico even.

And so she waited there in her little nook in the woods like some princess in a fairy story, protected by a moat and the sharp twisted talons of a wrecked car, only this princess had been violated and her pee burned and she jumped at every sound. Cándido had got her some old magazines in English—he'd found them in the trash at the supermarket—and six greasy dog-eared *novelas*, picture romances about *El Norte* and how poor village girls and boys made their fortunes and kissed each other passionately in the gleaming kitchens of their gleaming *gringo* houses. She read them over and over again and she tried not to think of the man with the cap and the Indian and their filthy writhing bodies and the stinking breath in her face, tried not to think of her nausea and lightheadedness, of her mother, of the future, tried not to think of anything. She explored the creekbed out of boredom. She bathed in the pool. Collected firewood. Repaired her old dress and saved the new one, the one Cándido had brought home one afternoon, for when they had an apartment and she needed something nice to get work. A week passed. Then another. It got hot. Her pee burned. And then, gradually, the pain faded and she began to forget what had happened to her here in the paradise of the North, began to forget for whole minutes at a time.

It was during one of those forgetful periods, when she was lying on her back in the sand, staring up into the shifting patchwork of the leaves above her, so still and so empty she might have been comatose, that she became aware of the faintest stirring behind her. The day was high and hot, the birds silent, the distant traffic a drowsy hum. There was another sentient creature there with her in the hollow place at the base of the intermittent falls, another breathing, seeing, sensing thing. She wasn't alarmed. Though she couldn't see it, she could hear it, feel it, and it was no man, no snake, no thing that would do her harm. Very gradually, millimeter by millimeter, like a plant turning to the sun, she shifted her head in the sand until she could see behind her.

At first, she was disappointed, but she was patient, infinitely patient, rooted to the ground by the boredom of the days, and then she saw movement and the thing materialized all at once, as in one of those trick-of-the-eye drawings where you can look and look forever and see nothing until you turn your head the magic way. It was a coyote. Bristle fur, tanned the precise shade of the dried hill grasses, one paw lifted, ears high. It held there, sensing something amiss, and looked right through her with eyes of yellow glass, and she saw that it had dugs and whiskers and a black slotted nose and that it was small, small as the dog she'd had as a girl, and still it didn't move. She looked at that coyote so long and so hard that she began to hallucinate, to imagine herself inside those eyes looking out, to know that men were her enemies—men in uniform, men with their hats reversed, men with fat bloated hands and fat bloated necks, men with traps and guns and poisoned bait—and she saw the den full of pups and the hills shrunk to nothing under the hot quick quadrupedal gait. She never moved. Never blinked. But finally, no matter how hard she stared, she realized the animal was no longer there.

The fire snapped and fanned itself with a roar. Sparks and white flecks of ash shot straight up into the funnel of the ravine, trailing away into the night until the dark drank them up. The night was warm, the stars were cold. And Cándido, feeding the fire with one hand while skewering a sausage with the other and cradling a gallon jug of Cribari red between his thighs, was drunk. Not so drunk that he'd lost all caution—he'd observed the canyon from above, on the trail, with the fire going strong, and reassured himself that not even the faintest glimmer escaped the deep hidden nook where they'd made their camp. The smoke was visible, yes, but only in daylight, and in daylight he made sure the fire was out, or at least reduced to coals. But now it was dark and who could detect a few threads of smoke against the dark curtain of the sky?

Anyway, he was drunk. Drunk and feeding the fire, for the thin cheer of it, for the child's game of watching the flames crawl up a stick, and for the good and practical purpose of cooking sausages. A whole package, eight hot Italian sausages, not as good as *chorizo* maybe, but good nonetheless. One after another, roasting them till they split, using a *tortilla* like a glove to squeeze them off the stick and feed them into his mouth, bite by sizzling bite. And the wine, of course. Lifting the jug, heavy at first but getting lighter now, the wine hot in his gut and leaking from the corners of his mouth, and then setting the jug down again, between his legs, in the sand. That was the process, the plan, the sum of his efforts. Stick, sausage, wine.

América, grown modest in proportion to the way the baby was changing her shape, stood off in the shadows, by the hut, trying on the clothes he'd brought back for her from the Goodwill in Canoga Park. They'd been working up the street, repairing stucco on an apartment building that was changing hands, and Rigoberto—the Indian who worked for Al Lopez—told him about the store. It was cheap. And he found maternity clothes—big flower-print shorts with an expanding waistline, dresses like sacks, corduroy pants that could have fit a clown. He'd selected one shapeless dress with an elastic waistband—pink, with green flowers all over it—and a pair of shorts. She'd asked for blue jeans, something durable to wear around the camp and save her two dresses, but there was no sense in buying her jeans that wouldn't fit for another three or four months, and so he'd settled on the shorts as a compromise. She could always take them in later.

All that was fine, but he was drunk. Drunk for a purpose, for a reason. Drunk because he was fed up with the whole yankee *gringo* dog-eat-dog world where a poor man had to fight like a conquering hero just to keep from starving to death, drunk because after three weeks of on-again, off-again work and the promise of something better, Al Lopez had let him go. Rigoberto's brother, the one who'd been ill, was back from his sickbed and ready to work. A hernia, that's what he had, and he'd gone to the *gringo* doctors to sew it up, and that was all right, because he had papers, *la tarjeta verde,* and he was legal. Cándido was not. "Haven't I done good work?" he asked Al Lopez. "Haven't I run after everything you told me to do like a human *burro,* haven't I busted my balls?" "Yes, sure," Al Lopez had said, "but that's not the problem. You don't have papers and Ignacio does. I could get in trouble. Big trouble." And so Cándido had bought the sausages and the wine and come home drunk with the dress and the shorts in a paper bag, and he was drunk now and getting drunker.

In three weeks, he'd made nearly three hundred dollars, minus some for food and the first dress he'd bought América, the pretty one, from the *gringo* store. That left him just over two hundred and fifty dollars, which was half what he'd need for a car and a quarter what he'd need for a decent apartment, because they all—even the Mexican landlords—wanted first and last months' rent and a deposit too. The money was buried in a plastic peanut butter jar under a rock behind the wrecked car and he didn't know how he was going to be able to add to it. He'd only got work once when Al Lopez hadn't come for him, and that was just half a day at three dollars an hour, hauling rock for a wall some old lady was building around her property. It was the end of July. The dry weather would hold for four months more, and by then América would have had her baby—his son—and they would have to have a roof over their heads. The thought darkened his mood and when América stepped into the firelight to show off the big shorts with her jaguar's smile, he snapped at her.

"Those *vagos*," he said, and the tongue was so thick in his throat he might have swallowed a snake, "they took more than just your money, didn't they? Didn't they?"

Her face went numb. "You go to hell," she said. "*Borracho*. I told you, I told you a thousand times," and she turned away and hid herself in the hut.

He didn't blame her. But he was drunk and angry and he wanted to hurt her, wanted to hurt himself, twisting the knowledge round and round his brain like a rotten tooth rotated in its socket. How could he pretend not to know what had happened? How could he allow himself to be fooled? She hadn't let him touch her in three weeks, and why was that? The baby, she claimed. She felt sick. She had a headache. Her digestion wasn't right, no, Cándido, no . . . well, maybe it was true. But if he ever found that son of a bitch with the raw eyes and that stupid *pinche* baseball cap . . . and he looked for him too, everywhere, every time Al's truck took a turn and there was somebody there beside the road, a pair of shoulders, a cap, blue jeans and a stranger's face . . . Cándido knew what he would do when he found him, his fist pounding on the window till the truck stopped, the *vago* loping up to the truck for a ride, his lucky day, and the first thing Cándido could lay his hands on, the big sledge for driving stakes, the machete for clearing brush, and if he went to prison for a hundred years it would be sweet compared to this . . .

If she was lying to him it was to spare him, he knew that, and his heart turned over for her in his drunkenness. Seventeen years old, and she was the one who'd found work when he couldn't, she was the one who'd had them sniffing after her like dogs, she was the one whose husband made her live in a hut of sticks and then called her a liar, a whore and worse. But as he lay there watching the sparks climb into the sky, the wine infesting his veins, he knew how it was going to be, how it had to be, knew he would follow her into that hut and slap his own pain out of her, and that was so sick and so bad he wanted nothing more in that moment than to die.

But then dead men didn't work either, did they?

3

Smoke rose from the barbecue in fragrant ginger-smelling tufts as Delaney basted the tofu kebabs with his special honey-ginger marinade and Jordan chased a ball round the yard with Osbert yapping at his heels. Kyra was stretched out by the pool, having finished up her jog with forty laps of the crawl and her weekly glass of Chardonnay, and though her briefcase stood at her side, she seemed for the moment to be content with contemplating the underside of her eyelids. It was a Sunday in mid-August, seven in the evening, the sun fixed in the sky like a Japanese lantern. There was music playing somewhere, a slow moody piano piece moving from one lingering faintly heard note to the next, and when Delaney looked up from turning the kebabs he watched a California gnatcatcher—that rare and magical gray-bodied little bird—settle on the topmost wire of the fence. It was one of those special moments when all the mad chittering whirl of things suddenly quits, like a freeze-frame in a film, and Delaney held on to it, savored it, even as the fragrance of ginger faded into the air, the piano faltered and the bird shot away into nothingness. Things had been tough there for a while, what with the accident, the loss of Sacheverell, the theft of his car, but now life had settled back onto an easy even keel, a mundanity that allowed the little things to reveal themselves, and he was grateful for it.

"Is it ready yet?" Kyra called in a smoky languorous voice. "Do you want me to put the dressing on the salad?"

"Yes, sure, that would be great," he said, and he felt blissful, rapturous even, as he watched his wife swing her legs over the side of the chair, adjust the straps of her swimsuit and stride gracefully across the patio and into the rear of the house.

At dinner, which Delaney served on the glass-topped table by the pool, Kyra filled her glass with Perrier and announced, with a self-deprecating giggle, that she'd "cleaned up Shoup." Jordan was toying with his tofu, separating it from the mushrooms, the mushrooms from the tomatoes and the tomatoes from the onions. Osbert was under the table, gnawing at a rawhide bone. "What?" Delaney said. "What do you mean?"

Kyra looked down at her plate as if uncertain how to go on. "Remember I told you about all those people gathering there on the streetcorners—day laborers?"

"Mexicans," Delaney said, and there was no hesitation anymore, no reluctance to identify people by their ethnicity, no overlay of liberal-humanist guilt. Mexicans, there were Mexicans everywhere.

"Mexicans," Kyra confirmed with a nod. Beside her, Jordan stuffed a forkful of white rice in his mouth, chewed thoughtfully a moment and extruded a glistening white paste back onto the tines of his fork. "I don't know," Kyra went on, "it was a couple of weeks ago, remember? By the 7-Eleven there?"

Delaney nodded, dimly remembering.

"Well I got on Mike's case about it because when it gets to be a certain number—ten maybe, ten is okay, but any more than that and you can see the buyers flinch when you drive by. That's the sort of thing they're moving out here to get away from, and you know me, I'll go out of my way, the most circuitous route, to give people a good impression of the neighborhood, but sometimes you just have to take the boulevard, it's unavoidable. Anyway, I don't know what happened, but one day I suddenly realize there's like fifty or sixty of them out there, all stretched out up and down the block, sitting on the sidewalk, leaning up against the walls, so I said to Mike, 'We've got to do something,' and he got on the phone to Sid Wasserman and I don't know what Wasserman did but that streetcorner is deserted now, I mean deserted."

Delaney didn't know what to say. He was wrestling with his feelings, trying to reconcile the theoretical and the actual. Those people had every right to gather on that streetcorner—it was their inalienable right, guaranteed by the Constitution. But whose constitution—Mexico's? Did Mexico even have a constitution? But that was cynical too and he corrected himself: he was assuming they were illegals, but even illegals had rights under the Constitution, and what if they were legal, citizens of the U.S.A., what then?

"I mean," Kyra was saying, lifting a morsel of tofu and oyster mushroom to her lips, "I'm not proud of it or anything—and I know how you feel and I agree that everybody's got a right to work and have a decent standard of living, but there's just so many of them, they've overwhelmed us, the schools, welfare, the prisons and now the streets . . ." She chewed thoughtfully. Took a sip of water. "Oh, by the way, did I tell you Cynthia Sinclair got engaged? At the office?" She laughed, a little trill, and set her fork down. "I don't know what made me think of it—prisons?" She laughed again and Delaney couldn't help joining in. "Sure. Prisons. That was it."

And then she began to fill him in on Cynthia Sinclair and her fiancé and all the small details of her education, work habits and aspirations, but Delaney wasn't listening. What she'd said about cleaning up the streetcorner had struck a chord, and it brought him back to the meeting he'd attended with Jack two nights ago. Or it wasn't a meeting actually, but a social gathering—"A few guys getting together for a drink," as Jack put it.

Jack had come in the door just after seven, in a pair of shorts—white, and perfectly pressed, of course—and an Izod shirt, and he and Delaney walked down the block and up two streets to Via Mariposa in the golden glow of evening. Jack hadn't told him where they were going—"Just over to a neighbor's house, a friend, a guy I've been wanting you to meet"—and as they strolled past the familiar sprawling Spanish-style homes, the walk took on the aspect of an adventure for Delaney. He and Jack were talking about everything under the sun— the Dodgers, lawn care, the situation in South Africa, the great horned owl that had taken a kitten off the Corbissons' roof—and yet Delaney couldn't help wondering what the whole thing was about. What friend? What neighbor? While he barely knew half the people in the community, he was fairly confident he knew everybody in Jack's circle, the ones in Arroyo Blanco, anyway.

But then they came to a house at the very end of Via Mariposa, where the road gave out and the hills rose in a wedge above the roofline, and Delaney realized he had no idea who lived here. He'd been by the place a hundred times, walking the dog, taking the air, and had never really paid much attention to it one way or the other: it was just a house. Same model as his own place, only the garage was reversed, and instead of Rancho White with Navajo trim, the owner had reversed the colors too, going with the lighter shade for the trim and the darker for the stucco. The landscaping was unremarkable, no different from any of the other places on the block: two tongues of lawn on either side of a crushed stone path, shrubs that weren't as drought-tolerant as they should be, a flagpole draped with a limp flag and a single fat starling perched atop it like a clot of something wiped on a sleeve.

"Whose place is this?" he asked Jack as they came up the walk.

"Dominick Flood's."

Delaney shot him a glance. "Don't think I know him."

"You should," Jack said over his shoulder, and that was all.

A maid showed them in. She was small, neat, with an untraceable accent and a tight black uniform with white trim and a little white apron Delaney found excessive: who would dress a servant up like somebody's idea of a servant, like something out of a movie? What was the point? They followed her down a corridor of genuine hand-troweled plaster, spare and bright, past a pair of rooms furnished in a Southwestern motif, Navajo blankets on the walls, heavy bleached-pine furniture, big clay pots of cactus and succulents, floors of unglazed tile. At the rear of the house, in the room Delaney used for his study, was a den with a wet bar, and eight men were gathered round it, drinks in hand. They were noisy and grew noisier when Jack stepped into the room, turning to him as one with shouts of greeting. Delaney recognized Jack Cherrystone and the bearded fat man from the meeting—Jim Shirley—and two or three others, though he couldn't place their names.

"Jack!" a voice cried out behind them and Delaney turned to see the man he presumed to be their host coming up the hallway. Flood looked to be about sixty, tanned and hard as a walnut, with close-set eyes and a tight artificial weave of white hair swept back from his brow. He was barefooted, in a pair of shorts and an oversized Hawaiian-print shirt, and it was impossible not to notice the device on his ankle. It was a black plastic box, two inches square, and it clung tight to the flesh like some sort of high-tech parasite. A thick elastic strap held it in place.

"Dom," Jack sang, shaking the older man's hand, and then he turned to introduce Delaney.

"The naturalist," Flood said without irony, and fixed him with a narrow look. "Jack's told me all about you. And of course I follow your column in *Wide Open Spaces*, terrific stuff, terrific."

Delaney made a noise of demurral. "I didn't think anybody really paid that much attention—"

"I subscribe to them all," Flood said, "—*Nature*, *High Sierra*, *The Tule Times*, even some of the more radical newsletters. To me, there's nothing more important than the environment—hey, where would we be without it, floating in space?"

Delaney laughed.

"Besides, I have a lot of time on my hands"—at this, they both glanced down at the box on his ankle and Delaney had his first intimation of just what its function might be—"and reading sustains me, on all issues. But come on in and have a drink," he was saying, already in motion, and a moment later they were standing at the bar with the others while a man in a blue satin jacket and bow tie fixed their drinks—Scotch, no ice, for Jack, and a glass of sauvignon blanc for Delaney.

It was a convivial evening, a social gathering and nothing more—at least for the first hour—and Delaney had begun to enjoy himself, set at ease immediately by his host's praise and the easy familiarity of the others—they were his neighbors, after all—when the smaller conversations began to be subsumed in a larger one, and the theme of the evening gradually began to reveal itself. Jim Shirley, sweating and huge in a Disneyland T-shirt, was leaning forward on the sofa with a drink in his hand, addressing Bill Vogel and Charlie Tillerman, the two men Delaney had recognized on entering, and the room fell silent to pick up his words. "Go unlisted, that's what I say. And I'm going to raise the issue at the next community meeting, just to warn everybody—"

"I don't think I'm following you, Jim," Jack Cherrystone rumbled from the bar, the seismic blast of his everyday voice setting the glass ashtrays in motion on the coffee table. "What do you mean, go unlisted? What difference would that make?"

Jim Shirley was a querulous fat man, bringer of bad tidings, a paranoiac, and Delaney didn't like him. But the moment belonged to Jim Shirley, and he seized it. "I'm talking the latest rash of burglaries? The three houses on Esperanza that got hit two weeks back? Well, the gate helps, no doubt about it, but these characters came in in a pickup truck, ratty old clothes, a couple rakes and a mower in back, and said they were doing the Levines' place, 37 Via Esperanza. The guard waves them through. But the thing is, they got the address out of the phone book, called the Levines to make sure they were out, and hit the place. And while they were at it, they got the Farrells and the Cochrans too. So my advice is, go unlisted. And I mean everybody in the development."

It had gotten dark, and Delaney looked through his reflection to the shadowy lawn out back, half-expecting to see criminals disguised as gardeners tiptoeing past with rolled-up Karastan rugs and CD players. Was nobody safe—anywhere, ever?

"I like the advice, Jim," Jack Jardine said. He was sitting at the bar still, nursing his second Scotch. A single thick strand of hair had fallen across his forehead, giving him the look of an earnest high-school debater. "And I think you should bring it up at the next meeting, but what we should really be looking at is the larger issue of how these people are getting into our community to begin with and the fact that the gate is just a stopgap—hell, anybody can just park out on the canyon road and walk in from the south or take any one of half a dozen off-the-road tracks and be out back of the development in five minutes. We're all vulnerable to that. And what Jim didn't tell you—or hasn't told you yet—is what happened to Sunny DiMandia."

There was a portentousness to Jack's tone that put Delaney off— he was manipulating the room the way he manipulated a courtroom, and Delaney resented him for it. Was this what Jack had brought him for—to get him on his team? Jim Shirley, who seemed to be the official trader in horror stories, was about to lay bare the Sunny DiMandia episode in all its lurid detail, when Delaney heard his own voice plunging into the gap: "So what do you mean, Jack? Isn't the gate enough? Next thing you'll want to wall the whole place in like a medieval city or something—"

Delaney had expected laughter, a murmur or two of assent, anything to confirm the absurdity of the proposition, but he was met by silence. Everyone was watching him. He felt uneasy suddenly, all the spirit of camaraderie dissolved in that instant. Wall the place in. That was exactly what they intended to do. That was what they were here for. That was the purpose of the gathering.

"We're all praying for Sunny," Jim Shirley said then, "and the latest prognosis is for a full and speedy recovery, but the man—or men, the police aren't sure yet—who got in there last week did a lot of damage, and I don't mean just physical damage, because I don't know if a woman ever really recovers from something like this . . ." He paused to heave a deep alveolar sigh. A hand went to his face, moist and doughy, and he pressed his drink to his brow like a wet cloth. "You all know Sunny, don't you?" he said finally, lifting his head to survey the room. "Fabulous woman, one of the best. Sixty-two years old and as active in this community as anybody." Another sigh, a rigid compression of the jowls. "She left the back door open, that was her mistake. Thinking it was safe up here—what an irony, huh?"

"It was our first violent crime," Jack put in. "The first, and let's make damn sure it's the last."

"Amen," Jim Shirley said, and then he went into the grisly details, step by step, moment by moment, sparing them nothing.

Delaney filtered him out. He was watching his host, who was curled up now in the corner of a pastel couch, his bare legs propped on the coffee table, idly scratching his calf. As they'd sat together earlier at the bar, Jack had given him an abbreviated explanation of the device on Flood's ankle. He was a client of Jack's, a good guy, ambitious, and his bank—there'd been three local branches and he personally oversaw them all—had got entangled in some unwise investments, as Jack put it. The device was on loan from the Los Angeles County Electronic Monitoring Service house-arrest program, and he would be wearing it, night and day, for the next three years. Delaney had been stunned. " Three years?" he'd whispered, glancing in awe at the black plastic manacle on Flood's ankle. "You mean he can't leave this house for three years?" Jack had nodded curtly. "Better than prison, wouldn't you say?"

Now, as Jim Shirley droned on, practically slavering over the nasty little details of the assault on Sunny DiMandia (who'd begun to take on a mythical dimension since Delaney didn't know her from Queen Ida or Hillary Clinton), Delaney couldn't help studying Dominick Flood out of the corner of his eye. Three years without a walk in the woods, dinner out, even a stroll down the supermarket aisles: it was unthinkable. And yet there it was: if he left the one-hundred-and-fifty-foot radius they'd given him, a buzzer would go off and the police would come and lock him away in a place with a lot fewer amenities

than this one. No wonder he liked to read about the great outdoors—
he wasn't going to see anything beyond the backyard fence for a long
time to come.

The conversation had focused for a while on Sunny DiMandia—
expressions of concern, outrage, fear and loathing—and now the maid
reappeared with coffee and a tray of cakes and brioches. The distraction was welcome, and as the eleven men settled down to the quotidian
tasks of stirring the hot liquid, measuring out sugar and Sweet'n Low,
plying knife and fork, chewing, swallowing, belching softly to themselves, a peace fell over the room, dispelling the news of rapes and
break-ins and the general decline and disintegration of the world
around them. Someone mentioned baseball and the conversation
chased off after the subject with a sense of genuine relief. From the
hills behind the house came the distant breathless barking yelp of a
coyote, answered almost immediately by another, somewhere off to the
north.

"The natives are getting restless," Jack Cherrystone rumbled, and
everyone laughed.

"You think they want to come in and join us?" Bill Vogel said. He
was a tall, wraithlike man bowed under the weight of a sickle nose. "
They probably get a little tired of raw rat or whatever they're eating
out there—if I was a coyote I'll bet a bit of this cheesecake would
really hit the spot."

Jack Cherrystone, diminutive, his head too big for his frame, his
eyes too big for his head, turned to Delaney. "I don't think Delaney
would approve, Bill," he said, his voice carving canyons beneath their
feet. "Would you, Delaney?"

Delaney reddened. How many of these men had been present at
the meeting the night he'd made such an ass of himself? "No," he said,
and he tried to smile, "no, I'm afraid I wouldn't."

"What about that labor-exchange business, Dom?" Jack Jardine said
out of nowhere, and the grinning faces turned from Delaney to him,
and then to their host.

Flood was standing now, dipping his chin delicately to take a sip of coffee from the cup he held over the saucer in his hand. He gave Jack a wink, moved across the floor to lay an arm over his shoulder, and addressed the room in general. "That little matter's been taken care of. And it was no big deal, believe me—just a matter of a few phone calls to the right people. Joe Nardone of the Topanga Homeowners' Association told me the people down there were good and sick of the whole business anyway—it was an experiment that didn't work."

"Good." Jack Cherrystone was perched on a barstool, his legs barely reaching the bottom rung. "I mean, I'm as sympathetic as the next guy and I feel bad about it—and I can see where the Topanga property owners really wanted to do something for these people, but the whole thing was wrongheaded from the start."

"I'll say," Bill Vogel put in with real vehemence, "the more you give them the more they want, and the more of them there are," but the professional boom of Jack Cherrystone's voice absorbed and flattened his words, and Jack went on without missing a beat.

"Why should we be providing jobs for these people when we're looking at a ten percent unemployment rate right here in California—and that's for *citizens*. Furthermore, I'm willing to bet you'll see a big reduction in the crime rate once the thing's closed down. And if that isn't enough of a reason, I'm sorry, but quite frankly I resent having to wade through them all every time I go to the post office. No offense, but it's beginning to look like fucking Guadalajara or something down there."

Dominick Flood was beaming. He was the host, the man of the house, the man of the hour. He shrugged his shoulders in deprecation—what he'd done was nothing, the least thing, a little favor, that was all, and they should all rest easy. "By this time next week," he announced, "the labor exchange is history."

Delaney was thinking about that as Kyra came to the end of her dissertation on Cynthia Sinclair: Kyra had cleaned up the corner of Shoup and Ventura, and Dominick Flood had cleaned up the labor exchange. All right. But where were these people supposed to go? Back to Mexico? Delaney doubted it, knowing what he did about migratory animal species and how one population responded to being displaced by another. It made for war, for violence and killing, until one group had decimated the other and reestablished its claim to the prime hunting, breeding or grazing grounds. It was a sad fact, but true.

He tried to shrug it off—the evening was perfect, his life on track again, his hikes as stimulating as ever and his powers of observation and description growing sharper as he relaxed into the environment. Why dwell on the negative, the paranoiac, the wall-builders and excluders? He was part of it now, complicit by his very presence here, and he might as well enjoy it. Looking up from his food, he said: "Want to take in a movie tonight?"

"Yes!" Jordan shouted, raising his clenched fists in triumph. "Can we?"

Kyra carefully set down her glass. "Paperwork," she said. "I couldn't dream of it. Really, I couldn't."

Jordan emitted little batlike squeals of disappointment and protest. His features flattened, his eyebrows sank into his head. His hair was so light it was almost invisible. He might have been a shrunken baldheaded old man who's just been told his prescription can't be refilled.

"Come on," Delaney coaxed, "it's only a movie. Two hours. You can spare two hours, hon, can't you?"

"*Please,*" Jordan squealed.

Kyra wouldn't hear of it. Her face was neutral, but Delaney could see that her mind was made up. "You know it's my second-busiest time of the year, all these buyers with children popping up out of nowhere to try and get in before school starts . . . You know it is. And Jordan, honey"—turning to her son—"you know how busy Mama is right now, don't you? Once the summer's over I'll take you to any movie you want—and you can bring a friend along too, anybody you want."

Delaney watched as she helped herself to the salad and squirted a little tube of no-fat dressing over her portion. "And we'll get treats too," she was saying, "bonbons and Coke and any kind of candy you want to pick out." And then, to Delaney: "What movie?"

He was about to say that he hadn't really decided, but there were two foreign films in Santa Monica, one at eight-forty-five and one at nine-oh-five, but of course that would exclude Jordan, and he was wondering if they could get the Solomon girl in to babysit on such short notice, when he saw the transformation in Kyra's face. She was looking past him, out beyond the pool and the deep lush fescue lawn she'd insisted on, though Delaney thought it was wasteful, and her eyes suddenly locked. He saw surprise first, then recognition, shock, and finally horror. When he whipped round in his seat, he saw the coyote.

It was inside the fence, pressed to the ground, a fearful calculation in its eyes as it stalked the grass to where Osbert lay sprawled in the shade of a potted palm, obliviously gnawing at the rawhide bone. Wings, he was thinking as he leapt from the chair with a shout, the damned thing must have wings to get over eight feet of chain link, and then, though he was in motion and though he wanted nothing more in the world than to prevent the sequel, he watched in absolute stupefaction as the animal swept across the grass in five quick strides, snatched the dog up by the back of the neck and hit the fence on the fly.

He wouldn't have believed it if he hadn't seen it. Despite his headlong rush, despite the quickness of his feet and the hard-honed sinewy strength of his legs, despite his rage and determination and the chorus of howls from his wife and son, he was impotent. The coyote scaled the fence, rung by rung, as if it were a ladder, and flew from the eight-foot bar at the top like a big dun wingless bird, and then it was gone, melted into the brush with its prey. And the fence? Delaney clung to it, just a heartbeat later—at the very spot—but he had to go all the way round the house and through the side gate to get out.

By then, of course—and no one had to explain this to Kyra, or even to Jordan—it was too late.

4

AND THEN HE GOT WORK FIVE DAYS IN A ROW. BRUSH clearance. Hard hot dirty work, breathing dust and little pale flecks of crushed weed till you choked, and the sun beating at the back of your neck like a scourge and the seeds of all those incorrigible desert plants like needles, like fisherman's hooks stabbing through your clothes and into your flesh every time you moved, and all you did was move. Three dollars and twenty-five cents an hour and he wasn't complaining. A *gabacho* boss had pulled into the labor exchange lot in a truck with high wooden sides, picked Cándido and another man and pantomimed what he wanted. They got in the back·of his truck, five mornings in a row, and he took them to a canyon with eight new houses in it and they cleared brush from the hillside and raked it up and loaded it into the truck. Each afternoon he paid them in cash and each morning he was there again, seven a.m., regular as clockwork. On the fifth day, when work was finished, he didn't show them any money, but with gestures and a few garbled Spanish phrases he let them know that he was short and would pay them when he came to pick them up in the morning. Cándido wondered about that, especially since they'd scraped the hillside bare, right down to the dirt, but then maybe there was another canyon and another hillside. There wasn't. At least not for Cándido. He never saw the man again.

All right. He'd been cheated before—it wasn't the first time. He would survive it. But then he didn't get work, not that day or the next or the day after that, and he came dragging back into camp at one each afternoon, dejected and heartsick with worry, and he let América fuss over him in her big maternity shorts while the worry trailed off into boredom and the boredom into rage. But he controlled himself. América was innocent. She was everything to him. He had no one to rage at but himself and he raged internally till he had to get up and move, use his hands, do something, anything. He devised make-work projects for himself: damming the far edge of the pool to keep the water level up as the creek slowed to a trickle, adding a cut-willow veranda to the lean-to, hunting birds and lizards and anything else he could find to stretch their supplies and avoid dipping into the apartment fund in the jar beneath the rock. They had three hundred and twenty dollars in that jar and he needed to triple it at least if they were going to have a roof over their heads by the time his son was born.

One afternoon, coming back defeated from the labor exchange with a few chilies, onions and a sack of dried pinto beans, he found a scrap of clear plastic mesh by the side of the road and stuffed it into his back pocket. He was thinking he might be able to cut a long green switch, bend the tip into a loop and sew the mesh to it so he'd have a net to snare some of the birds that were constantly flitting in and out of the chaparral. Using a length of discarded fishing line and América's two-inch sewing needle, Cándido bent to the task. In less than an hour he'd fashioned a sturdy professional-looking net while América looked on in stony silence—her sympathies lay clearly with the birds. Then he climbed back up the trail, watched where the birds plunged into the scrub to the fortresses of their nests, and waited. The first day he got nothing, but he sharpened his technique, lying motionless in the bone-white dust and flicking his wrist to snap the net like a tennis player working on his backhand.

No one hired him the following day either, and while América soaked the beans and reread her *novelas* for the hundredth time, he went back to try his luck. Within an hour he'd caught four tiny gray-bodied little birds, no longer than his thumb, pinching their heads to stifle them, and then he got lucky and stunned a scrub jay that hopped off into the undergrowth with a disarranged wing until he could run it down. He plucked the birds and rinsed them in the stream—they weren't much, particularly the little gray ones—and then he built up the fire and fried them in lard, heads and all. América wouldn't touch them. But Cándido ran each miniature bone through his teeth, sucking it dry, and there was a satisfaction in that, the satisfaction of the hunter, the man who could live off the land, but he didn't dwell on it. How could he? The very taste on his lips was the taste of desperation.

The next morning he was up at first light, as usual, blowing into his coffee while América fried eggs, chilies and *tortillas* over a smokeless fire, and then he made his way up the hill to the labor exchange, feeling optimistic, lucky even, the wings of the little birds soaring in his veins. The limp was gone now—or almost gone—and though his face would never look quite the same again, at least the crust of scab had fallen away, giving back some of the flesh beneath. He wasn't planning on entering any beauty contests anyway, but at least now the *patrones* in the trucks wouldn't automatically look past him to the next man. The sky swelled with light. He began to whistle through his teeth.

Out of habit he kept his head down as he walked along the side of the road, not wanting to risk making eye contact with any of the *gringos* or *gringas* on their way to work in their unblemished new Japanese cars. To them he was invisible, and that was the way he wanted to keep it, showing himself only in the lot at the labor exchange, where they could see what he was and what he had to offer. He barely glanced up at the tumult in the lot at the Chinese grocery—the sweet buns, coffee in styrofoam cups, frantic cigarettes—and he didn't really lift his head until he felt the gravel of the labor exchange lot under his feet. He was wondering idly if he'd be first in line, thinking of the day ahead, whistling a radio tune he hadn't heard in years, when he looked up and it hit him: *there was nothing there*. No pillars, no roof, no *campesinos* in khaki shirts and straw hats. Nothing. It was as if a hurricane wind had come up in the night, a tornado, and sucked the whole thing up into the sky. Cándido stood there, dumbstruck, and looked round him twice to get his bearings. Was he dreaming? Was that it?

But no. He saw the chain then—two chains—and the signs. Posts had been driven into the ground at each of the two entrances, and they were linked by chains thick enough to anchor a boat. The signs were nailed to the posts. PRIVATE, they screamed in blazing red letters, ALL PERSONS WARNED AGAINST TRESPASS, and though Cándido couldn't read English, he got the drift. What was going on? he asked himself. What was the problem? But even as he asked he knew the answer: the *gringos* had gotten tired of seeing so many poor people in their midst, so many Mexicans and Hondurans and Salvadoreños. There was no more work here. Not now, not ever.

Across the street, in front of the post office, three men slunk around the butts of their cigarettes like whipped dogs. Cándido saw their eyes snatch at him as he watched for a break in the traffic and jogged across the road to them. They looked down at the ground as he greeted them. "*Buenos días,*" he said, and then, "What's going on?"

"*Buenos,*" the men mumbled, and then one of them, a man Cándido recognized from the exchange, spoke up. "We don't know. It was like that"—a jerk of the head—"when we got here."

"Looks closed," the man beside him put in.

"Yeah," the first man said, and his voice was lifeless, "looks like the *gabachos* don't want us here anymore." He dropped the stub of his cigarette in the street, shoved his hands in his pockets. "I don't give a shit," he said. "I'm going to stand right here till somebody hires me—it's a free country, isn't it?"

"Sure," Cándido said, and the way he was feeling he couldn't hold back the sarcasm, "—as long as you're a *gringo*. But us, we better look out."

It was then that Candelario Pérez's familiar white pickup separated itself from the chain of commuter cars and nosed into the post office parking lot, wheeling up so close to them they had to take an involuntary step back to avoid the inconvenience of having their toes crushed. He was alone, and his face was so heavy he couldn't seem to lift it out of the car. All four of them crowded round the driver's window. "What's going on?" the first man demanded, and they all joined in, Cándido too.

"It's closed, over, *terminado*." Candelario Pérez spoke with an exhausted voice, and it was apparent he'd been overusing it, wasting it on deaf ears, on useless argument and pointless remonstrance. He waited a moment before going on, the *whoosh-whoosh-whoosh* of the commuters' cars as steady as the beat of the waves on a beach. "It was the man that donated the property. He took it back. They don't want us here, that's the long and short of it. And I'll tell you something, a word of advice"—another pause—"if you don't have a green card you better make yourself scarce. *La Migra*'s going to make a sweep here this morning. And tomorrow morning too." The dead black eyes sank in on themselves like the eyes of an iguana and he lifted a thumbnail to his front teeth to dislodge a bit of food stuck there. He shrugged. "And probably the day after that."

Cándido felt his jaws clench. What were they going to do now? If there was no work here anymore and *La Migra* to make sure of it, he and América would have to leave—either that or starve to death. That meant they'd have to go into the city, down to Santa Monica or Venice, or up over the canyon and into the Valley. That meant living on the streets, exposing América to the obscenity of the handout, the filth, the dumpsters out back of the supermarkets. And they were so close —another couple weeks of steady work and they could have had their apartment, could have established themselves, could have looked for work like human beings, riding the bus in freshly laundered clothes, seeking out the back rooms and sweatshops where nobody cared if you had documents or not. From there, in a year or two, they could have applied for their green cards—or maybe there would be another amnesty, who could tell? But now it was over. Now there was no more safe haven, no more camp in the woods. Now it was the streets.

In a daze, Cándido drifted away from the group gathered round the pickup, the weight of the news like a stone crushing his chest. Why not kill himself now and get it over with? He couldn't go back to Mexico, a country with forty percent unemployment and a million people a year entering the labor force, a country that was corrupt and bankrupt and so pinched by inflation that the farmers were burning their crops and nobody but the rich had enough to eat. He couldn't go back to his aunt, couldn't live off her again, butt of the entire village, couldn't face América's parents when he gave her back to them like some precious heirloom he'd borrowed and sullied. And he had a son coming, *un hijo,* the son he'd been yearning for since the day he'd met Resurrección, and what legacy did he have to leave him? Three hundred and twenty dollars in a peanut butter jar? A house of sticks even the prehistoric Indians would have rejected? A broken-down father who couldn't feed himself, let alone his family?

He staggered past the post office, his feet like lead, past the storefronts, the bright windows, the cars lined up like ciphers of the wealth that bloomed all around him, unattainable as the moon. And what was it all about? Work, that was all. The right to work, to have a job, earn your daily bread and a roof over your head. He was a criminal for daring to want it, daring to risk everything for the basic human necessities, and now even those were to be denied him. It stank. It did. These people, these *norteamericanos:* what gave them the right to all the riches of the world? He looked round him at the bustle in the lot of the Italian market, white faces, high heels, business suits, the greedy eyes and ravenous mouths. They lived in their glass palaces, with their gates and fences and security systems, they left half-eaten lobsters and beefsteaks on their plates when the rest of the world was starving, spent enough to feed and clothe a whole country on their exercise equipment, their swimming pools and tennis courts and jogging shoes, and all of them, even the poorest, had two cars. Where was the justice in that?

Angry, frustrated, his face twisted into an expression that would have terrified him if he'd caught sight of himself in one of the windows he passed, Cándido shambled aimlessly through the lot. What should he do? Buy a sack of food and hole up in the canyon for a week until the Immigration lost interest and moved on? Risk hitchhiking the ten miles up into the Valley and stand on a streetcorner in the faint hope of work? Or should he just die on the spot and save the *gringos* the embarrassment of having to look at him? He was on his second circuit of the lot, drifting past the ranks of cars without purpose or direction, muttering to himself and refusing to look away from the startled eyes that swooped at him in alarm, when he came upon the blue-black Lexus sitting at the curb with the windows rolled down.

He was moving still, moving past it, but he couldn't help noticing the lady's purse on the passenger seat and the black leather briefcase wedged in beside it. What was in that purse—checks, cash, house keys, a little wallet with pictures and more cash? Hundreds of dollars maybe. Hundreds. Enough to take him and América right out of the woods and into an apartment in Canoga Park, enough to solve all his problems in a single stroke. And the briefcase? He imagined it crammed full of bills like in the movies, neat stacks of them bound with little strips of bank paper. To the owner of a car like that a few hundred dollars was nothing, like pennies to an ordinary person. They could just go to the bank and get more, call their insurance company, flash a credit card. But to Cándido it was the world, and in that moment he figured the world owed him something.

No one was watching him. He glanced right, left, swung round on his heels and strolled past the car again. The blood was like fire in his veins. He thought his head would explode with the pressure in his temples. *There it is, you idiot,* he told himself, *take it. Take it now. Quick!*

And he might have, suspended in the moment between conception and action, all his glands discharging their complicated loads, but for the woman with the pale blond hair and see-through eyes making straight for him with a styrofoam cup clutched in her white, white hand. He froze. Stood there paralyzed in front of her car while she hid her eyes behind a pair of sunglasses, her heels clicking on the pavement, her skirt as tight as any whore's. She came right for him, and before he could move aside, before he could protest his innocence or fade back into invisibility, he felt the touch of her hand and his fingers closing involuntarily on the coins.

Her touch annihilated him. He'd never been more ashamed in his life, not when he was a drunk in the streets, not when Teófilo Agua-dulce took his wife from him and threw him down in the square with the whole village looking on. He hung his head. Let his arms drop to his sides. He stood rooted to the spot for what seemed like hours after she'd ducked into the car, backed out of the lot and vanished, and only then did he open his hand on the two quarters and the dime that clung there as if they'd been seared into the flesh.

When she heard the news—"They closed down the labor exchange," Cándido told her, his eyes defiant, spoiling for a fight—América had to struggle to keep a neutral face. She felt relief, joy, a surge of hope like nothing she'd experienced since the night she lay in bed at her father's house waiting for Cándido to tap at the window and take her away to the North. Finally, she thought, letting the breath escape her in a long ex-halation that Cándido would have taken for grief. She kept her features rigid, let the hair fall across her face. Cándido was bitter, angry, ready to erupt. He was worried too, she could see that, and for a moment she felt the uncertainty take hold of her and she was scared. But then it came back to her: there was no choice now, no doubt but that they were going to have to leave this prison of trees, this dirt heap where she'd been robbed and hurt and brutalized, where the days crept by like the eternal years. She had no love for this place. Insects bit her. The ground was hard. Every time she wanted a cup of coffee she had to gather twigs and start a fire. What kind of life was that? She'd have been better off in Morelos, in her father's house, waiting on him like a servant till she was an old maid dried up like a fig.

"We'll have to leave," she murmured, and the city she knew—alien, terrifying, a place where blacks roamed the streets and *gabachos* sat on the sidewalk and begged—gave way to the city she dreamed of. There would be shops, streets lined with trees, running water, toilets, a shower. They had three hundred and twenty dollars—maybe they could share a place with another couple, somebody like themselves, Tepoztecos or Cuernavacans, pool their resources, live like a big family. No matter how small the place, no matter how dirty it was, with rats and cockroaches and gunshots outside the windows, it had to be better than this. All this time Cándido had been stalling because he was afraid—they couldn't go yet, they needed more money, have patience, *mi vida*, have patience—but now he could stall no longer.

"Not yet," he said.

Not yet? She wanted to jump up and shout in his face, pummel him with her fists. Was he crazy? Did he intend to live down here like a caveman for the rest of his life? She controlled herself, sat there in the sand hunched over the *novela* she'd read so many times she could recite it from memory, and waited. He was like her father, just like him: immovable, stubborn, the big boss. There was no use in arguing.

Cándido sat at the edge of the pool in his undershorts, his skin glistening with beads of water. He'd just come back from above, just stepped out of the pool and thrown himself down beside her with his momentous announcement. It was the hottest hour of the day. Everything was still. América could feel the sweat under her arms and down below, where she itched, itched constantly, though at least her pee no longer burned. "Tomorrow morning I'm going to walk up the canyon," he said, "early, while it's still dark, before *La Migra* comes nosing around the post office and the labor exchange. I'm going to keep my eyes open—I was thinking of Canoga Park maybe—and see if I can find anything."

"An apartment?"

"Apartment? What's the matter with you?" His voice jumped up the register. "You know we can't afford an apartment—how many times do I have to tell you?" He turned to look at her. His eyes were dangerous. "Sometimes I just can't believe you," he said.

"Maybe a motel," she said, "—just for a night. We could take a shower, ten showers, shower all night. This water's dirty, filthy, full of scum and bugs. It stinks. My hair smells like an old dog."

Cándido looked away. He said nothing.

"And a bed to sleep in, a real bed. God, what I wouldn't give for a bed—just for one night."

"You're not going with me."

"Yes I am."

"You're not."

"You can't stop me—what are you going to do, hit me again? Huh? Big man? I don't hear you?"

"If that's what it takes."

She saw the bed, the shower, a *taquería* maybe. "You can't leave me here, not anymore. Those men . . . What if they come back?"

There was a long silence, and she knew they were both thinking about that inadmissible day and what she couldn't tell him and how he knew it in his heart and how it shamed him. If they lived together a hundred years she could never bring that up to him, never go further than she just had. Still, how could he argue with the fact of that? This was no safe haven, this was the wild woods.

"*Indita,*" he said, "you've got to understand—it's ten miles each way, and I'll be on the streets, maybe getting work, maybe finding someplace for us, someplace to camp closer in to the city. You're safe here. Nobody would come up this far." He'd been looking her in the face, but now he dropped his eyes and turned away again. "It's the trail that's dangerous," he murmured, "just stay off the trail."

Indita. She hated it when he called her that: his little Indian. He passed it off as an endearment, but it was a subtle dig at her, a criticism of her looks, her Indian blood, and it made her feel small and insignificant, though she knew she was one of the beauties of Tepoztlán, celebrated for her figure, her shining hair, her deep luminous eyes and her smile that all the boys said was like some rich dessert they could eat with a spoon, bite by bite. But his skin was lighter and he had the little hook in his nose that his family had inherited from the *conquistadores,* though his stepmother was black as a cane cutter and his father didn't seem to mind. *Indita.* She sprang up suddenly and flung the *novela* into the water, *splash,* and he was wet again. "I won't stay here," she said, and her voice rose in her throat till it shattered, "not one more day."

In the morning—it was early, three a.m. maybe, she couldn't tell— she folded bean paste, *chiles* and slivers of cheese into corn *tortillas* and wrapped them up in newspaper for the trip out of the canyon. They'd agreed to leave their things behind, just in case and because they'd attract less attention without them, and to try their luck over- night at least. Cándido had even promised they'd find a room for the night, with a shower and maybe even a TV, if it wasn't too dear. Amér- ica worked by the glow of the coals and the tinfoil light of the moon that hung like an ornament just over the lip of the gorge. She was giddy with excitement, like a girl waking early on her saint's day. Things would work out. Their luck was bound to improve. And even if it didn't, she was ready for a change, any change.

Cándido unearthed the peanut butter jar, removed twenty dollars and shoved it deep into his pocket; then he flared up the fire with a handful of kindling and had her sew the remaining three hundred dollars into the cuff of his trousers. She pulled on her maternity dress—the pink one with the big green flowers that Cándido had bought her—tucked the *burritos* into her string purse and made them coffee and salted *tortillas* for breakfast. Then they started up the hill.

There was almost no traffic at all at this hour, and that was a pleas- ant surprise. Darkness clung to the hills, and yet it was mild and the air smelled of the jasmine that trailed from the retaining walls out front of the houses along the road. They walked in silence for an hour, the occasional car stunning them with its headlights before the night crept back in. Things rustled in the brush at the side of the road—mice, she supposed—and twice they heard coyotes howling off in the hills. The moon got bigger as it dipped behind them and América never let the weight of the baby bother her, or its kicks either. She was out of the canyon, away from the spit of sand and that ugly wrecked hulk of a car, and that was all that mattered.

When they reached the top and the San Fernando Valley opened up beneath them like an enormous glittering fan, she had to stop and catch her breath. "Come on," Cándido urged, leaning over her as she sat there in a patch of stiff grass, "there's no time to rest." But she'd overestimated herself, and now she felt it: a pregnant woman grown soft in that prison by the stream. Her feet were swollen. She could smell her own sweat. The baby was like a dead weight strapped to the front of her. "*Un momento,*" she whispered, gazing out on the grounded constellations of the Valley floor, grid upon grid of lights, and every one a house, an apartment, a walk-up or flat, every one the promise of a life that would never again be this hard.

Cándido crouched beside her. "Are you okay?" he whispered, and he bent forward to hold her, press her head to his shoulder the way her father used to do when she was little and his favorite and she skinned her knee or woke with a nightmare. "It's not much farther," he said, his breath warm on her cheek, "just down there," and she made him point to a place beyond where the office buildings rose up like stony monoliths to a double band of lights running perpendicular to the great long vertical avenues that stretched on into the darkness of the mountains on the far side of the Valley. "That's it," he said. "That string of lights there—see it? Sherman Way."

Sherman Way. She held the words in her head like a talisman, *Sherman Way,* and then they were moving again, along the black swatch of the road that chased its own tail down the side of the hill. Cándido knew the shortcuts, steep narrow trails that plunged through the brush to pinch off the switchbacks at the neck, and he held her hand and helped her through the worst places. Her feet were like stone, clumsy suddenly. Needlegrass stabbed through her dress and things caught at her hair. And now, every time they made the pavement again, there were the cars. It wasn't yet light and already they were there, the first sporadic awakening of that endless stream, roaring up the road opposite them, and there was no joy in that. América kept her head down and skipped along as fast as she could go, eaten up with the fear of *La Migra* and the common accidents of the road.

By the time the sun was up, the ordeal was behind them. They were walking hand in hand up a broad street overhung with trees, a sidewalk beneath their feet, pretty houses with pretty yards stretching as far as they could see. América was exhilarated, on fire with excitement. All the fatigue of the past hours dropped magically away from her. Clinging to Cándido's arm, she peered in at the windows, examined the cars in the driveways and the children's things in the yards with the eye of an appraiser, gave a running commentary on each house as they passed it by. The houses were adorable, *linda, simpática,* cute. That color was striking, didn't he think so? And the bougainvillea—she'd never seen bougainvillea so lush. Cándido was mute. His eyes darted everywhere and he looked troubled—he *was* troubled, worried sick, she knew it, but she couldn't help herself. Oh, look at that one! And that!

They turned next onto a commercial boulevard, the main one in this part of the city, Cándido explained, and this was even better. There were shops, wall-to-wall shops, restaurants—was that a Chinese, was that what that writing was?—a supermarket that sprawled out over a lot the size of a *fútbol* stadium with thirty shops more clustered round it. After Tepoztlán, Cuernavaca even, after the Tijuana dump and Venice and the leafy dolorous hell of the canyon, this was a vision of paradise. And when she came to the furniture store—the couches and settees and rugs and elegant lamps all laid out like in the Hollywood movies—Cándido couldn't budge her. "Come on, it's getting late, you can look at this junk some other time, come on," he said, tugging at her arm, but she wouldn't move. Not for ten whole minutes. It was almost as if she were in a trance and she didn't care. If she could have done it, she would have moved right into the store and slept on a different couch every night and it wouldn't have bothered her a whit if the whole world was looking in at the window..

Canoga Park was different.

It was pinched and meaner, a lot of secondhand shops and auto-parts stores, dirty restaurants and *cantinas* with bars on the windows, but there were people just like her all over the streets and that made her feel better, made her feel for the first time that she too could live here, that it could be done, that it had been done by thousands before her. She heard Spanish spoken on the streets, nothing but Spanish.

Children shot by on skateboards and bicycles. A street vendor was selling roasted ears of corn out of a barrel. América felt as if she'd come home.

Then Cándido took her into a restaurant, a little hole in the wall with five stools at the counter and a couple of Formica tables stuck in a corner, and she could have wept for joy. She fussed with her hair before they went in—she should have braided it—and tried to smooth down her dress and pick the fluff out of it. "You never told me," she said. "I must look like a mess."

"You look fine," he said, but she didn't believe him. How could she? She'd been camping in the woods without so much as a compact mirror for as long as she could remember.

The waiter was Mexican. The chef behind the grill was Mexican. The dishwasher was Mexican and the man who mopped the floor and the big swollen mother with her two *niñitos* and the five men sitting on the five stools blowing into their cups of coffee. The menu was printed in Spanish. "Order anything you want, *mi vida*," Cándido said, and he tried to smile, but the look of worry never left his face.

She ordered *huevos con chorizo* and toast, real toast, the first she'd had since she left home. Butter melted into the toast, sweet yellow pools of it, the *salsa* on the table was better than her mother had ever made and the coffee was black and strong. The sugar came in little packets and she poured so much of it into her coffee the spoon stood up straight when she tried to stir it. Cándido ordered two eggs and toast and he ate like an untamed beast let out of its cage, then went up to the counter and talked to the men there while she used the bathroom, which was dirty and cramped but a luxury of luxuries for all that. She looked at herself in the mirror through a scrim of triangular markings and slogans scratched into the glass and saw that she was pretty still, flushed and healthy-looking. She lingered on the toilet. Stripped to the waist and washed the top half of her body with the yellow liquid soap and let the water run in the basin long after she'd finished with it, just let it run to hear it.

Later, Cándido stood on the streetcorner with two hundred other men while she shrank by his side. The talk was grim. There was a recession. There was no work. Too many had come up from the South, and if there was work for them all six years ago, now there were twenty men for every job and the bosses knew it and cut the wage by half. Men were starving. Their wives and children were starving. They'd do anything for work, any kind of work, and they'd take what the boss was paying and get down on their knees and thank him for it.

The men slouched against buildings, sat on the curb, smoked and chatted in small groups. América watched them as she'd watched the men at the labor exchange and what she saw made her stomach sink with fear: they were hopeless, they were dead, as bent and whipped and defeated as branches torn from a tree. She and Cándido stood there for an hour, not so much in the hope of work—it was ridiculous even to think of it with two hundred men there—but to talk and probe and try to get the lay of the land. Where could they stay? Where was the cheapest place to eat? Was there a better streetcorner? Were they hiring at the building supply? In all that time, a full hour at least, she saw only two pickups pull in at the curb and only six men of all that mob climb in.

And then they started walking. They walked all day, up and down the streets, through the back alleys, down the boulevards and back again, Cándido gruff and short-tempered, his eyes wild. By suppertime nothing had been settled, except that they were hungry again and their feet hurt more than ever. They were sitting on a low wall out in front of a blocky government building—the post office?—when a man in baggy pants and with his long hair held in place by a black hairnet sat down beside them. He looked to be about thirty and he wore a bold-check flannel shirt buttoned at the neck though the air was like a furnace. He offered Cándido a cigarette. "You look lost, *compadre*," he said, and his Spanish had a North American twang to it.

Cándido said nothing, just pulled on the cigarette, staring off into space.

"You looking for a place to stay? I know a place," the man said, leaning forward now to look into América's face. "Cheap. And clean. Real clean."

"How much?" Cándido asked.

"Ten bucks." The man breathed smoke out his nostrils. América saw that he had a tattoo circling his neck like a collar, little blue numbers or letters, she couldn't tell which. "Apiece."

Cándido said nothing.

"It's my aunt's place," the man said, something nasal creeping into his voice, and América could hear the appeal there. "It's real clean. Fifteen bucks for the two of you." There was a pause. Traffic crawled by. The air was heavy and brown, thick as smoke. "Hey," he said, "*compadre*, what's the problem? You need a place to stay, right? You can't let this pretty little thing sleep on the street. It's dangerous. It's no good. You need a place. I'll give you two nights for twenty bucks—I mean, it's no big deal. It's just around the corner."

América watched Cándido's face. She didn't dare enter into the negotiations, no matter how tired and fed up she was. That wasn't right. This was between the two men. They were feeling each other out, that was all, bargaining the way you bargained at the market. The baby moved then, a sharp kick deep inside her. She felt nauseated. She closed her eyes.

When she opened them Cándido was on his feet. So was the other man. Their eyes told her nothing. "You wait here," Cándido said, and she watched him limp up the street with the stranger in the hairnet and baggy trousers, one block, two, the stranger a head taller, his stride quick and anxious. Then they turned the corner and they were gone.

5

PILGRIM AT TOPANGA CREEK

As I sit here today at the close of summer, at the hour when the very earth crackles for the breath of moisture denied it through all these long months of preordained drought, I gaze round my study at the artifacts I've collected during my diurnal wanderings—the tail feathers of the Cooper's hawk, the trilobite preserved in stone since the time the ground beneath my feet was the bed of an ancient sea, the owl pellets, skeletons of mouse and kangaroo rat, the sloughed skin of the gopher snake—and my eye comes to rest finally on the specimen jar of coyote scat. There it is, on the shelf over my desk, wedged between the Mexican red-kneed tarantula and the pallid bat pickled in formalin, an innocuous jar of desiccated ropes of hair the casual observer might take for shed fur rather than the leavings of our cleverest and most resourceful large predator, the creature the Indians apotheosized as the Trickster. And why today do my eyes linger here and not on some more spectacular manifestation of nature's plethora of wonders? Suffice it to say that lately the coyote has been much on my mind.

Here is an animal ideally suited to its environment, able to go without water for stretches at a time, deriving the lion's share of its moisture from its prey, and yet equally happy to take advantage of urban swimming pools and sprinkler systems. One coyote, who makes his living on the fringes of my community high in the hills above Topanga Creek and the San Fernando Valley, has learned to simply chew his way through the plastic irrigation pipes whenever he wants a drink. Once a week, sometimes even more frequently, the hapless maintenance man will be confronted by a geyser of water spewing out of the xerophytic ground cover the community has planted as a firebreak. When he comes to me bewildered with three gnawed lengths of PVC pipe, I loan him a pair of Bausch & Lomb 9×35 field glasses and instruct him to keep watch at dusk along the rear perimeter of the development. Sure enough, within the week he's caught the culprit in the act, and at my suggestion, he paints the entire length of the irrigation system with a noxious paste made of ground serrano chilies. And it works. At least until the unforgiving blast of the sun defuses the chilies' potency. And then, no doubt to the very day, the coyote will be back.

Of course, a simpler solution (the one most homeowners resort to when one of these "brush wolves" invades the sanctum sanctorum of their fenced-in yard) is to call in the Los Angeles County Animal Control Department, which traps and euthanizes about 100 coyotes a year. This solution, to one who wishes fervently to live in harmony with the natural world, has always been anathema (after all, the coyote roamed these hills long before Homo sapiens made his first shaggy appearance on this continent), and yet, increasingly, this author has begun to feel that some sort of control must be applied if we continue to insist on encroaching on the coyote's territory with our relentless urban and suburban development. If we invade his territory, then why indeed should we be surprised when he invades ours?

For Canis latrans is, above all, adaptable. The creature that gives birth to four or fewer pups and attains a mature weight of twenty-five pounds or less in the sere pinched environment in which it evolved has spread its range as far as Alaska in the north and Costa Rica in the south, and throughout all the states of the continental

U.S. Nineteen subspecies are now recognized, and many of them, largely because of the abundant food sources we've inadvertently made available to them (dogs, cats, the neat plastic bowls of kibble set just outside the kitchen door, the legions of rats and mice our wasteful habits support), have grown considerably larger and more formidable than the original model, the average size of their litters growing in proportion. And the march of adaptability goes on. Werner Schnitter, the renowned UCLA biologist, has shown in his radio-collaring studies that the coyotes of the Los Angeles basin demonstrate a marked decline in activity during periods coinciding with the morning and evening rush hour. This is nothing less than astonishing: you would think the coyotes were studying us.

The problem, of course, lies at our own doorstep. In our blindness, our species-specific arrogance, we create a niche, and animals like the raccoon, the opossum, the starling and a host of other indigenous and introduced species will rush in to fill it. The urban coyote is larger than his wild cousin, he is more aggressive and less afraid of the humans who coddle and encourage him, who are so blissfully unaware of the workings of nature that they actually donate their kitchen scraps to his well-being. The disastrous results can be seen in the high mortality among small pets in the foothills and even the as yet rare but increasingly inevitable attacks on humans.

I had the infinitely sad task last year of interviewing the parents of Jennifer Tillman, the six-month-old infant taken from her crib on the patio of the Tillmans' home in the hills of Monte Nido, directly over the ridge from my own place of residence. The coyote involved, a healthy four-year-old female with a litter of pups, had been a regular daytime visitor to the area, lured by misguided residents who routinely left tidbits for her on the edge of their lawns.

But forgive me: I don't mean to lecture. After all, my pilgrimage is for the attainment of wonder, of involving myself in the infinite, and not for the purpose of limiting or attempting to control the uncontrollable, the unknowable and the hidden. Who can say what revolutionary purpose the coyote has in mind? Or the horned lizard, for that matter, or any creature? Or why we should presume or even desire to preserve the status quo? And yet something must be done, clearly, if we are to have any hope of coexisting harmoniously with this supple suburban raider. Trapping is utterly useless—even if traps were to be set in every backyard in the county—as countless studies have shown. The population will simply breed up to fill in the gap, the bitches having litters of seven, eight or even more pups, as they do in times of abundance—and with our interference, those times must seem limitless to the coyote.

Sadly, the backlash is brewing. And it is not just the ranchers' and hunters' lobbies and the like pushing for legislation to remove protections on this animal, but the average homeowner who has lost a pet, humane and informed people, like the readers of this periodical, devoted to conservation and preservation. Once classified as a "varmint," the coyote had a price on his head, governmental bounties paid out in cash for each skin or set of ears, and in response he retreated to the fastnesses of the hills and deserts. But we now occupy those fastnesses, with our ready water sources (even a birdbath is a boon to a coyote), our miniature pets and open trash cans, our feeble link to the wild world around us. We cannot eradicate the coyote, nor can we fence him out, not even with eight feet of chain link, as this sad but wiser pilgrim can attest. Respect him as the wild predator he is, keep your children and pets inside, leave no food source, however negligible, where he can access it.

Little Jennifer's neck was broken as neatly as a rabbit's: that is the coyote's way. But do not attempt to impose human standards on the world of nature, the world that has generated a parasite or predator for every species in existence, including our own. The coyote is not to blame—he is only trying to survive, to make a living, to take advantage of the opportunities available to him. I sit here in the comfort of my air-conditioned office staring at a jar of scat and thinking of all the benefit this animal does us, of the hordes of rats and mice and ground squirrels he culls and the thrill of the wild he gives us all, and yet I can't help thinking too of the missing pets, the trail of suspicion, the next baby left unattended on the patio.

The coyotes keep coming, breeding up to fill in the gaps, moving in where the living is easy. They are cunning, versatile, hungry and unstoppable.

6

THE DA ROS PLACE WAS A WHITE ELEPHANT. THERE was no way it was going to move in this market, unless at a significantly reduced price, and though the house had cast a spell over Kyra, she was beginning to wonder if it would ever cast the same kind of spell over a qualified buyer. No one had even looked at the place in the past two weeks and the maintenance issue was becoming one big emotional drain. She'd called Westec about the two men she'd encountered on the property and Delaney had insisted on putting in a report with the Sheriff's Department too, but nothing came of it. The Westec people had poked around and found no evidence that the men had been back. They didn't think anyone had been camping there either, at least not recently, though they did find a ring of blackened stone in the scrub at the northwest corner of the property. "But what you got to realize is that could've been there for years," the security officer explained to her over the phone, "there's just no way of telling."

Kyra wasn't satisfied. She warned the gardener to keep an eye out for anything unusual, and of course she was there herself twice a day, opening the place up in the morning and closing it down again at night. Which had become a real chore. She wasn't frightened exactly, not anymore, but every time she turned up the drive her stomach sank—

almost as if someone had knocked the wind out of her—and she had to bend forward to the air-conditioning vent and take little gulps of air till her breathing went back to normal. The encounter with those men—those drifters or bums or whatever they were—had shaken her more than she would admit, a whole lot more. She'd always been in command of her life, used to getting her way, trading on her looks and her brains and the kind of preparation that would have prostrated anybody else, man or woman, and she felt the equal of any situation, but that night she saw how empty all of that was.

She'd been scared. As scared as she'd ever been. If it hadn't been for her quick thinking—the lie about her husband, the fictitious brother, cocktails for god's sake—who knew what might have happened? Of course, it could have been innocent—maybe they were just hikers, as they claimed—but that wasn't the feeling she got. She looked into that man's eyes—the tall one, the one with the hat—and knew that anything could happen.

She was thinking about that as she wound her way up the road to the Da Ros place, hurrying, a little annoyed at the thought of the burden she'd taken on when she'd jumped at the listing. Now it almost seemed like it was more trouble than it was worth. And tonight of all nights. It was almost seven, she hadn't been home yet, and she'd agreed to help Erna Jardine and Selda Cherrystone canvas the community on the wall issue at eight.

That was Jack's doing. He'd called her two days after Osbert had been killed, and she was still in a state of shock. To see her puppy taken like that, right before her eyes, and on top of everything else . . . it had been too much, one of the worst experiences of her life, maybe *the* worst. And Jordan—he was just a baby and he had to see that? Dr. Reineger had prescribed a sedative and she'd wound up missing a day at the office, and Jordan had gone to his grandmother's for a few days—she just wouldn't let him stay in that house, she couldn't. She was sitting at her desk the next day, feeling woozy, as if her mind and body had been packed away in two separate drawers for the summer, when the phone rang.

It was Jack. "I heard about your little dog," he said, "and I'm sorry."

She felt herself choking up, the whole scene playing before her eyes for the thousandth time, that slinking vicious thing, the useless fence, and Osbert, poor Osbert, but she fought it back and managed to croak out a reply. "Thanks" was all she could say.

"It's a shame," Jack said, "I know how you must feel," and he went on in that ritualistic vein for a minute or two before he came to the point. "Listen, Kyra," he said, "I know nothing's going to bring your dog back and I know you're hurting right now, but there is something you can do about it." And then he'd gone into the wall business. He and Jack Cherrystone, Jim Shirley, Dom Flood and a few others had begun to see the wisdom in putting up a wall round the perimeter of the community, not only to prevent things like this and keep out the snakes and gophers and whatnot, but with an eye to the crime rate and the burglaries that had been hitting the community with some regularity now, and had she heard about Sunny DiMandia?

Kyra had cut in to say, "How high's the wall going to be, Jack? Fifteen feet? Twenty? The Great Wall of China? Because if eight feet of chain link won't keep them out, you're just wasting your time."

"We're talking seven feet, Kyra," he said, "all considerations of security, aesthetics and economics taken into account." She could hear the hum of office machinery in the background, the ringing of a distant phone. His voice came back at her: "Cinder block, with a stucco finish in Navajo White. I know Delaney's opposed on principle—without even thinking the matter through—but it so happens I talked with the coyote expert at UCLA the other day—Werner Schnitter?—and he says stucco will do the trick. You see, and I don't want to make this any more painful for you than it already is, but if they can't actually see the dog or cat or whatever, there'd be no reason for them to try scaling the wall, you follow me?"

She did. And though she'd never have another dog again, never, she wanted those hateful sneaking puppy-killing things kept off her property no matter what it took. She still had a cat. And a son. What if they started attacking people next?

"Sure, Jack," she said finally. "I'll help. Just tell me what to do."

She started with Delaney that night after work. He'd fixed a salade niçoise for dinner, really put some effort into it, with chunks of fresh-seared tuna and artichoke hearts he'd marinated himself, but all she could do was pick at it. Without Jordan and Osbert around, the house was like a tomb. The late sun painted the wall over the table in a color that reminded her of nothing so much as chicken liver—chicken-liver pink—and she saw that the flowers in the vase on the counter had wilted. Beyond the windows, birds called cheerlessly to one another. She pushed her plate away and interrupted Delaney in the middle of a monologue on some little bird he'd seen on the fence, a monologue transparently intended to take her mind off Osbert, coyotes and the grimmer realities of nature. "Jack asked me to work on the wall thing," she said.

Delaney was caught by surprise. He was in the middle of cutting a slice of the baguette he'd picked up at the French bakery in Woodland Hills, and the bread knife just stuck there in the crust like a saw caught in a tree. "What 'wall thing'?" he said, though she could see he knew perfectly well.

She watched the knife start up again and waited for the loaf to separate before she answered. "Jack wants to put a wall around the whole place, all of Arroyo Blanco. Seven feet tall, stucco over cinder block. To keep burglars out." She paused and held his eyes, just as she did with a reluctant seller when she was bringing in a low bid. "And coyotes."

"But that's crazy." Delaney's eyes flared behind his lenses. His voice was high with excitement. "If chain link won't keep them out, how in god's name do you expect—?"

"They can't hunt what they can't see." She threw her napkin down beside the plate. Tears started in her eyes. "That thing *stalked* Osbert, right through the mesh, as if it wasn't even there, and don't you try to tell me it didn't."

Delaney was waving the slice of bread like a flag of surrender. "I'm not. I won't. And I'm sure there's some truth in that." He drew in a breath. "Look, I'm as upset about this as you are, but let's be reasonable for a minute. The whole point of this place is to be close to nature, that's why we bought in here, that's why we picked the last house on the block, at the end of the cul-de-sac—"

Her voice was cold, metallic with anger. "Close to nature," she spat back at him. "Look what good it did us. And for your information, we bought in here because it was a deal. Do you have any idea how much this house has appreciated since we bought it—even in this market?"

"All I'm saying is what's the sense of living up here if you can't see fifty feet beyond the windows—we might as well be living in a condo or something. I need to be able to just walk out the door and be in the hills, in the wild—I don't know if you noticed, but it's what I do, it's how I make my living. Christ, the damn fence is bad enough—and that fucking gate on Arroyo Blanco, you know I hate that, you know it."

He set the bread down on his plate, untouched. "This isn't about coyotes, don't kid yourself. It's about Mexicans, it's about blacks. It's about exclusion, division, hate. You think Jack gives a damn about coyotes?"

She couldn't help herself. She was leaning forward now, belligerent, angry, channeling it all into this feckless naive unrealistic impossible man sitting across the table from her—he was the one, he was guilty, he was the big protector of the coyotes and the snakes and weasels and tarantulas and whatever in christ's name else was out there, and now he was trying to hide behind politics. "I don't ever," she shouted, "want one of those things on my property again. I'd move first, that's what I'd do. Bulldoze the hills. Pave it over. The hell with nature. And politics too."

"You're crazy," he said, and his face was ugly.

"Me? That's a laugh. What do you think this is—some kind of nature preserve? This is a community, for your information, a place to raise kids and grow old—in an exclusive private highly desirable location. And what do you think's going to happen to property values if your filthy coyotes start attacking children—that's next, isn't it? Well, isn't it?"

He put on his exasperated look. "Kyra, honey, you know that's not going to happen—that incident in Monte Nido, that was an aberration, a one-in-a-million chance, and it was only because the people were *feeding* the animals—"

"Tell that to the parents. Tell it to Osbert. And Sacheverell, don't forget Sacheverell."

Dinner didn't go well. Nor the rest of the evening either. Delaney forbade her to work on the wall committee. She defied him. Then she took over the living room, put on her relaxation tapes and buried herself in her work. That night she slept in Jordan's room, and the next night too.

All that was on her mind as she punched in the code, waited for the gate to swing back, and turned into the long, familiar Da Ros drive. The gate closed automatically behind her and she felt the flutter in her stomach, but it wasn't as bad as usual—she was in too much of a hurry to dwell on it and she was preoccupied with Delaney and the wall and too many other things to count. She did take what had now become the standard precaution of dialing Darlene, the receptionist at the office, to tell her she'd just entered the Da Ros property. They'd agreed on a fifteen-minute time limit—no lingering anymore, no daydreaming, no letting the house cast its spell. If Kyra didn't get back to Darlene at the end of those fifteen minutes to say she was leaving, Darlene would dial 911. Still, as Kyra cruised slowly up the drive, she was intensely aware of everything around her—it had been almost three weeks now, but she couldn't shake the feeling that had come over her that night when she understood just how vulnerable she was out here in the middle of nowhere. And in a way, she didn't want to shake it. Get complacent, and you become a statistic.

The house emerged through the trees, the front windows struck with light. She softened when she saw it. The place was something, after all, one of a kind, the fairy-tale castle you see on the underside of your eyelids when you close your eyes and dream. And it was hers in a way no other had ever been, white elephant or not. She'd seen it happen a thousand times with her buyers, that look in their eyes, that click of recognition. Well, this was her click of recognition, the place she would have bought if she was in the market. And yes, Delaney, she thought, I'd wall it in with seven feet of cinder block and stucco, that's the first thing I'd do.

Kyra swung round in the driveway, the car facing the way she'd just come, and before she switched off the engine she took a good long penetrating look out across the lawns and into the trees at the edge of the property. Then she lowered the window and listened. All was still. There was no breeze, no sound anywhere. The shrubs and trees hung against the backdrop of the mountains as if they'd been painted in place, flat and two-dimensional, and the mountains themselves seemed as lifeless as the mountains of the moon. Kyra stepped out of the car, leaving the door open behind her as a precaution.

Nothing's going to happen, she told herself as she strode up the walk. They were hikers, that was all. And if they weren't, well, they were gone now and wouldn't be back. She concentrated on the little things: the way the grass had been hand-clipped between the flagstones, the care with which the flowerbeds had been mulched and the shrubs trimmed. She saw that the oleander and crape myrtle were in bloom, and the bed of clivia beneath the library windows. Everything was as it should be, nothing amiss, nothing forgotten. She'd have to remember to compliment the gardener.

Inside too: everything looked fine. None of the zones had been tampered with and the timed lights had already switched on in the kitchen and the dining room. There were no realtors' cards on the table in the foyer, and that was a disappointment, a continuing disappointment, but then it would take the right buyer to appreciate the place, and it was bound to move, it was, sure it was—especially if she could convince Patricia Da Ros to drop the price. She checked her watch: five minutes gone. She made a quick circuit of the house—no need to kill herself since nobody had shown the place—then returned to the entrance hall, punched in the alarm code and stepped back out on the porch. One trip round the back and she'd be on her way.

Kyra always took long strides, even in heels—it was her natural gait. Delaney told her he found it sexy because it made her sway over her hips in an exaggerated way, but she'd never thought a thing about it—she'd always been athletic, a tomboy really, and she couldn't remember a time when she wasn't in a hurry. She went round the north side of the house first, striding over the flagstone path as if she were almost running, her head swiveling back and forth to take in every least detail. It wasn't till she turned the corner to the back of the house that she saw it, and even then she thought it was some trick of the light.

She stopped as if she'd been jerked on a leash. She was bewildered at first, then outraged, and finally just plain frightened. There, scrawled across the side of the house in six-foot-high spray-painted letters, was a message for her. Black paint, slick with the falling light, ten looping letters in Spanish:

PINCHE PUTA

The sun was distant, a molten speck in the sky, but hot for all that. Delaney was out back of the community center, where he'd been working on his paddleball game, one-on-one with the wall. He was sitting on the back steps, a sweat-beaded Diet Coke in hand, when he became aware of the murmur of voices coming from somewhere inside the room behind him. The shades were drawn, but the window was open a crack, and as the sun flared out from the windows and the inevitable turkey vulture rode the unflagging currents high overhead, the murmur became two distinct and discrete voices, and he realized he was listening to Jack Jr. and an unknown companion engage in the deep philosophic reflections of a torpid late-summer adolescent afternoon.

"Cal State, huh?" Jack Jr. said.

"Yup. Best I could do—with my grades." A snigger. A double snigger.

"Think you can handle Northridge? I mean, I hear it's like Little Mexico or something."

"Yup. That's right. Fuckin' Little Mexico all the way. But you know what the bright side is?"

"What?"

"Mexican chicks."

"Get out of here."

A pause. Slurping sounds. A suppressed belch.

"No shit, man—they give killer head."

"Get out of here."

Another pause, long, reflective. "Only one thing you got to worry about—"

"What's that?"

"The ten-pounds-a-year rule."

A tentative laugh, uncertain of itself, but game. "Yeah?"

"At sixteen"—slurp, pause—"they're killers, but from then on, every year they gain ten pounds till they wind up looking like the Pillsbury Dough Boy with a suntan—and who wants to stick your dick in something like that, even their mouth?"

Delaney stood. This was the punch line and it was accompanied by a virtuosic duet of sniggers. Jesus, he thought, and his legs felt heavy suddenly. This was Jack's kid. A kid who should know better, a kid with all the advantages, raised right here in Arroyo Blanco. Delaney was moving now, shaking the starch out of his legs, slapping the paddle aimlessly against his thigh. But then, maybe that was the problem, and his next thought was for Jordan: was that the way he was going to turn out? He knew the answer before he'd formulated the question. Of course it was, and there was nothing Kyra or Delaney or anybody else could do about it. That's what he'd tried to tell Kyra over this wall business—it might keep *them* out, but look what it keeps in. It was poisonous. The whole place was poisonous, the whole state. He wished he'd stayed in New York.

He felt depressed and out of sorts as he made his way through the familiar streets, the *Vias* and *Calles* and *Avenidas* of this, his exclusive private community in the hills, composed entirely of Spanish Mission-style homes with orange tile roofs, where the children grew into bigots, the incomes swelled and the property values rose disproportionately. It was four in the afternoon and he didn't know what to do with himself. Jordan was at his grandmother's still and Kyra had called to say she'd be home late, after which she'd be going over to Erna Jardine's to get on the phone and sell her neighbors a wall, so Delaney would be on his own. But Delaney didn't want to be on his own. That's why he'd got married again; that's why he'd been eager to take Jordan on, and the dogs, and all the joys and responsibilities of domestic life. He'd been on his own for eight years after he divorced his first wife, and that had been enough for him. What he really wanted, and he'd been after Kyra about it for the past year at least, was for her to have a baby, but she wouldn't hear of it—there was always another house to show, another listing, another deal to close. Yes. Sure. And here he was, on his own.

He'd just turned onto Robles, head down, oblivious to the heat, reflecting bitterly that he wouldn't even have the dogs to keep him company, when he became aware that someone was calling out his name. He swung round to see a tall, vigorous and vaguely familiar-looking man striding up the pavement toward him. "Delaney Moss-bacher?" the man said, holding out his hand.

Delaney took the hand. But for the two of them, the street was deserted, held in the grip of that distant molten sun.

"We haven't met," the man said, "—I'm Todd Sweet?—but I saw you at the meeting—the one over the gate thing awhile back?—and I thought I'd introduce myself. I hear you do a column for one of the nature magazines."

Delaney tried to work his face into a smile. The meeting? And then it hit him: this was the athlete with the willowy wife, the man who'd spoken out with such conviction against the gate. "Oh yes, sure," he said vaguely, mortified to be in the presence of anyone who'd seen him waving that bloody dog's appendage, and then, realizing that this wasn't exactly an appropriate response, he added, *"Wide Open Spaces."*

The man was grinning, beaming at him as if they'd just signed the contract for a deal that would make them both rich. He was wearing a silk sport shirt in a tiger-stripe pattern, pressed slacks and sandals, and though it was a hundred and two degrees, he showed no trace of discomfort, not even a bead of sweat at his temples. He looked both earnest and hip, a jazz musician crossed with a Bible salesman. "Listen, Delaney," he said, dropping his voice confidentially though there was no one within a hundred yards of them, no one visible at all, in fact, not in the sun-blistered expanse of the front yards or behind the drawn shades of the darkened windows, "I'm sure you're aware of what our friend Jack Jardine has in store for us—"

Our friend. Delaney couldn't help but catch the ironic emphasis. But yes, Jack was his friend, though they didn't always see eye-to-eye on the issues, and he felt defensive suddenly.

"Well, I just thought, being a naturalist—and a writer, a fine, persuasive one, I'm sure—that you might oppose what's going on here. It's coming down to a vote at next Wednesday's meeting, and I'm going house-to-house to try to talk people out of it—me and my wife, that is, we're both going around. I mean, isn't the gate bad enough? Isn't this supposed to be a democracy we're living in, with public spaces and public access?"

"I agree," Delaney said quickly. "Couldn't agree more. The idea of a wall is completely and utterly offensive and it's not going to be cheap, that's for sure."

"No—and that's what I'm emphasizing with these people. Nobody wants to see their assessment go up, right?" If he'd been beaming a moment ago, Todd Sweet looked positively reverential now. It was a look Delaney knew well, a California look, composed in equal parts of candor, awe and dazzlement, and it usually presaged the asking of a small favor or a tiny little loan. "Look," Todd Sweet said finally, "I wonder if I might stop by your place tonight and maybe we could write something up, together, I mean—I hate to say it, but I'm no writer—"

And then something came over Delaney—right there in the street, under the sun—a slow wash of shame and fear, a bitter stinging chemical seepage that carried with it the recollection of the Mexican in the bushes, the stolen car, Sunny DiMandia, Jim Shirley, the Metro section and all the rest. He had a vision then of all the starving hordes lined up at the border, of the criminals and gangbangers in their ghettos, of the whole world a ghetto and no end to it, and he felt the pendulum swing back at him. There would be war in his living room if he actively opposed this wall, war with his wife and with Jack and his triumvirate of Cherrystone, Shirley and Flood. Was he willing to risk that? Did the wall really matter all that much?

Todd Sweet was studying his face, the eyes harder now, more penetrating, the mask slipping. "If it's too much trouble," he said, "I mean, if you want to live in a walled city like something out of 'The Masque of the Red Death,' that's your prerogative, but I just assumed . . ." He trailed off, a thin petulant edge to his voice.

"No, no, that's not the problem," Delaney said, and why shouldn't he defy Kyra and Jack and stand up for what he believed in? But then he saw that phantom car again, the one with the rumbling speakers and impenetrable windows, and he hesitated. "Look," he said, "I'll call you," and turned to walk away.

"Seven-one-three, two-two-eight-zero," Todd Sweet called at his back, but he wasn't listening, his mind gone numb with ambivalence. He went on up the block, barely registering the world spread out before him, glum, dogless, on his own. Nothing was moving. The sun was everything. And then he turned into his own street, Piñon Drive, and saw that life existed after all: another figure was drifting across that static landscape in the blast of late-summer heat. He couldn't be sure, but it seemed to be the bipedal figure of a man, slipping through the heat haze like an illusion, legs scissoring the light. The man had a white cloth shoulder bag slung over one arm, Delaney saw as he came closer, and he was crossing the Cherrystones' lawn with the lingering insouciant stride of the trespasser—which is what he must have been, since Delaney knew for a fact that the Cherrystones had gone to Santa Monica and wouldn't be back till seven. And then Delaney came closer still, and noticed something else, something that struck him with the force of a blow: the man was Mexican. "Hey," Delaney called out, quickening his stride now, "can I help you?"

The man looked startled, looked guilty—caught in the act—and he just stood there on the lawn and let Delaney come up to him. And now the second surprise: Delaney knew him, he was sure he did. It took him a minute, something missing from the composite, but then, even without the baseball cap, Delaney recognized him: this was the hiker, the illegal camper, the man who'd soured the first half of one of the worst days of Delaney's life. And even then, even in that moment of recognition, the net widened suddenly: didn't Kyra say that the man who'd threatened her at the Da Ros place was wearing a Padres cap turned backwards? The man just stood there, guarding his satchel. He didn't look away from Delaney's gaze, and he didn't respond.

"I said, can I help you?"

"Help me?" he echoed, and his face broke into a grin. He winked an eye. "Sure," he said, "sure, *hombre,* you can help me." And then: "What's happening, man?"

Delaney was hot. He was uncomfortable. He was aggravated. The man stood a good three or four inches taller than he did and he was letting Delaney know just how unimpressed he was—he was mocking him, bearding Delaney right there in his own community, right there on his own street. Camping in the state park was one thing, but this was something else altogether. And what was in the satchel and why had he been crossing the Cherrystones' lawn when the Cherrystones weren't at home?

"I want to know what you think you're doing here," Delaney demanded, eyeing the satchel and imagining the Cherrystones' silverware in there, their VCR, Selda's jewelry. "This is private property. You don't belong here."

The man looked right through him. He was bored. Delaney was nothing, a minor annoyance, a gnat buzzing round his face.

"I'm talking to you," Delaney said, and before he could think, he had hold of the man's forearm, just above the wrist.

The tan eyes looked down at Delaney's hand, then up into his face. There was nothing in those eyes but contempt. With a sudden violent jerk, the man whipped his arm free, gathered himself up and spat scornfully between Delaney's feet. "I got these flies," he said, and he was almost shouting it.

Delaney was riding the crest of the moment, trembling, angry, ready for anything. The man was a thief, a liar, the stinking occupant of a stinking sleeping bag in the state forest, a trespasser, a polluter, a Mexican. "Don't give me that shit!" Delaney roared. "I'm calling the police. I know what you're doing up here, I know who you are, you're not fooling anybody." Delaney looked round him for support, for a car, a child on a bike, Todd Sweet, anyone, but the street was deserted.

The Mexican's expression had changed. The mocking grin was gone now, replaced by something harder, infinitely harder. He's got a knife, Delaney thought, a gun, and he went cold all over when the man reached into the satchel, so keyed up he was ready to spring at him, tackle him, fight to the death . . . but then he was staring into a flat white sheet of Xerox paper crawling with print. "Flies," the man spat at him. "I deliver these flies."

Delaney took a step back, so devastated he couldn't speak—what was happening to him, what was he becoming?—and the man shoved the flier into his hand and stalked away across the lawn. He watched, stupefied, as the Mexican headed up the street, carrying his shoulders with rage and indignation, watched as he strode up to Delaney's own house and inserted a flier in the slit between the screen door and the white wooden doorframe. Then, finally, Delaney looked down at the sheet of paper in his hand. A SPECIAL MESSAGE FROM THE PRESIDENT OF THE ARROYO BLANCO ESTATES PROPERTY OWNERS' ASSOCIATION, it read in block letters across the top. And then, beneath it: "I urge all of you to attend Wednesday's meeting on an issue vital to the security and well-being of us all . . ."

7

THE FIRST FIFTEEN MINUTES WERE NOTHING. AMÉRica never asked herself what she was doing sitting on that concrete wall out front of the post office building in Canoga Park, never gave it a thought. She was exhausted, her feet ached, she felt hot and sleepy and a little nauseous, and she just sat there in a kind of trance and let the rich stew of the city simmer around her. It was amazing, all this life. The sidewalks weren't crowded, not in the way she'd expected, not like in the market in Cuernavaca or even Tepoztlán, but there was a steady flow of people going about their business as if it were the most natural thing in the world to live here. People were walking dogs, riding bicycles, pushing babies in strollers, carrying groceries in big paper sacks cradled to their chests; they were smoking, chatting, laughing, tilting back their heads to drink from red-white-and-blue cans of Pepsi that said "Uh-huh!" on the label.

As tired as she was, as tentative and unsettled, she couldn't help being fascinated by the spectacle—and by the women especially. She watched them covertly, women her own age and maybe a little older, dressed like *gringas* in high heels and stockings, watched to see what they were wearing and how they did their hair and makeup. There were older women too, in *rebozos* and colorless dresses, *niños* hurtling by on skateboards, workingmen ambling past in groups of three or four, their eyes fixed on some distant unattainable vision way out ahead of them in the haze of the endless boulevard. And the traffic—it wasn't like the traffic on the canyon road at all. Here it moved in a stately slow procession from light to light, every kind of car imaginable, from low-riders to Jaguars to battered old Fords and Chevies and VW buses and tiny silver cars that flashed by like fishes schooling in the sea. After all those weeks of deprivation, those weeks when she had nothing to look at but leaves and more leaves, the city was like a movie playing before her eyes.

The second fifteen minutes were no problem either, though there was more of an edge to them, a hard hot little prick of anxiety that underscored the passing of each separate sixty-second interval. *Where is Cándido?* was a thought that began to intrude on her consciousness, and its variant, *What's keeping him?* Still, she was glad to be there sitting on that wall, glad to be out of that nightmare of leaves, and she was content, or nearly content. The people were amusing. The cars were brilliant. If she wasn't feeling nauseous and if her feet weren't blistered and if she knew where she was going to sleep tonight and if she had something to chew on—anything, a slice of bread, a cold *tortilla*—this waiting would be nothing, nothing at all.

There was a clock in the window of the appliance-repair shop across the way, and as the big illuminated pointer began to intrude on the third quarter of the hour, she realized that her nausea had begun to feature the brief powerful constrictions of hunger. She looked down at her feet and saw that they were swollen against the straps of her sandals (which she'd loosened twice already), and suddenly she felt so tired she wanted to lie back on the hard concrete wall and close her eyes, just for a minute. But she couldn't do that, of course—that's what bums did, street people, *vagos, mendigos*. Still, the thought of it, of lying back for just a minute, made her see the bed then, the promissory bed at the *chicano*'s aunt's house, and that made her think of Cándido, and where was he?

During the final quarter hour a man in stained clothes appeared out of nowhere and sat beside her on the wall. He was old, with a goat's beard and eyes that jumped out at her from behind a pair of glasses held together with a piece of frayed black tape. She smelled him before she turned round and saw him there, not twelve inches from her. She'd been watching two girls in jeans and heels, with black lingerie tops and hair starched up high with spray, and suddenly the wind shifted and she thought she was back in the dump at Tijuana. The old man reeked of urine, vomit, his own shit, and his clothes—three or four shirts and a long coat and what looked to be at least two pairs of pants—were as saturated in natural oils as a plantain in a frying pan. He didn't look at her, didn't speak to her, though he was holding a conversation with someone only he could see, his voice falling away to nothing and then cresting like a wave, his Spanish so twisted and his dialect so odd she could only pick up snatches of a phrase here and there. He seemed to be talking to his mother—to the memory of his mother, the ghost, the faint outline of her pressed into the eidetic plate of his brain—and there was a real urgency in the garbled message he had for her. His voice went on and on. América edged away. By the time the illuminated pointer touched the hour, he was gone.

Then it was the second hour and she was lost and abandoned. The sun was setting, the sky streaked with dying light, the storefronts trembling with a watery silver glow like puddles stood on end all up and down the street. There were fewer people on the sidewalks now, and América no longer found them amusing or even interesting. She wanted Cándido to come back, that was all, and what if he'd had an accident? What if he was hurt? What if *La Migra* had snatched him? For the first time since she'd sat herself down on that wall, the reality of her situation hit her: she had no money, knew no one, couldn't even find her way back to that miserable pile of sticks in the canyon. What if Cándido never came back, what if he'd died of a heart attack or got hit by another car? What then?

After an hour and a half had gone by and there was still no sign of him, América pushed herself up from the wall and started down the street in the direction he'd taken with the *chicano*, turning to look over her shoulder every few steps to see if by some miracle he might have come back to the wall from another direction. She passed antique stores, gloomy depthless places full of old gloomy furniture; a store that sold fish in every color swimming in water so pure it was like air; a closed and shuttered luncheonette; an auto-parts store that was a hub of activity. It was here, just past the auto-parts store, that she turned left, following Cándido's lead, and found herself on a side street, but a busy one, cars hurtling by against a yellow light, springs rattling, tires squealing. She saw groups of men in the lot out back of the auto-parts store, *gringos* and *Latinos* alike, the sprawl of their cars, hoods up, engines running, the music pounding from their stereos till the pavement shook with it. They hardly gave her a glance, and she was too timid, too afraid to ask them if they'd seen Cándido, her husband, her lost husband, and that other man. Then there was a bookstore, a few more storefronts, and the street turned residential.

It was getting dark. Streetlights blinked on. The windows of the houses had begun to glow softly against the shadowy shrubs, the flowers drained of color, the bougainvillea and wisteria gone gray in the fading light. She didn't see Cándido anywhere. Not a trace of him. The baby moved inside her and her stomach dipped and fluttered. All she wanted was to belong in one of those houses, any of them, even for a night. The people who lived in those houses had beds to stretch out on, they had toilets that flushed and hot and cold running water, and most important of all, they were home, in their own private space, safe from the world. And where was Cándido? Where was the room he'd promised her, the bed, the shower? This was shitty, really shitty. Worse than her father's house, a hundred times worse. She was a fool to have left, a fool to have listened to the stories, watched the movies, read the *novelas*, and more of a fool to ever for a second have envied the married girls in Tepoztlán whose husbands gave them so much when they came home from the North. Clothes, jewelry, a new TV— that wasn't what you got. You got this. You got streets and bums and burning pee.

Finally, after she'd searched even the side streets off of the side street, she went back to the wall in front of the post office. She didn't know what had happened to Cándido—she was afraid even to think about it—but this was where he would look for her, and she would just have to sit here and be patient, that was all. But now it was fully dark, now it was night, and the foot traffic had begun to pick up again—teenagers in groups, men in their twenties and thirties, out on the prowl. There was no one to protect her, no one to care. All she could see was the image of those animals at the border, the half-a-*gringo* and his evil eyes and filthy insinuating fingers, the fat white man with his fat white hands, and she withdrew into herself, dwelled there deep inside where nobody could touch her. "Hey, baby," they called when they saw her there trying to melt into the darkness, "hey, *ruca*, hey, sexy, ¿*quieres joder conmigo?*"

It was nearly midnight and she'd nodded off—she couldn't help it, couldn't keep her eyes open a second longer—when she felt a touch at her shoulder. She woke with a start—nearly jumped out of her skin—and there he was, Cándido. Even in the bleak half-light of the streetlamps she could see the blood on his face, slick and black and without color. It could have been oil, molasses, could have been coal tar or makeup for some fright-house play in the theater, but it wasn't and she knew it the minute she saw him. "They hit me with something," he said, his voice so pinched and hoarse she thought at first he'd been strangled. "A baseball bat, I think. Right here." He lifted a hand to his hairline and touched the place where the blood was blackest. "They got everything. Every penny."

And now she saw that his shirt was torn and the cuffs of his trousers hacked away till it looked as if some animal had been chewing its way up his legs. *They got everything*. She looked into his eyes in the dim subterranean glow of the streetlamp and let the words sink in. There would be no bed, no shower, no dinner even. And in the future: no apartment, no shops, no restaurants, no toys and blankets and diapers for her baby. Her mind raced ahead and back again, and then she thought of the woods, of the canyon, of that shitpile of sticks, and she wanted to die.

His head ached, but that was nothing new. For a while there, his eyes had been playing tricks on him, everything doubled and doubled again, two walls, two windows, two streetlamps, then four and eight and sixteen, till he had to clamp his lids shut and start all over again. The world was back to a single image at least, and that was all right, but his shoulder throbbed where he must have fallen on it, and what next? It was like getting hit by that car all over again, except that this time he had no one to blame but himself. How could he have been so stupid? That *chingón* had no aunt. He was as bad as any *vago* at the labor exchange, worse. "This way," he kept saying, "it's just up here, my aunt's house, you'll like it, man, you'll like it." He didn't have any aunt. But there were two more just like him waiting in the alley, and how many *mojados* had they clipped in their time? They knew just where to look—every dumb hick must have sewed his bankroll into his cuffs. Where else would it be? At the Bank of America? Under his pillow at the Ritz? It was his stinking bad luck, that was all, and now his head ached and he had nothing left in the world, not even a decent pair of pants, and América was looking at him as if he were the lowest form of life on the earth, no sympathy in her eyes, not a trace.

The first thing to do was find a gas station and have América ask to use the rest room so he could slip in and wash the blood off his face. It wasn't bad, a little headache, that was all—a headache and a whole lot of blood. He didn't give a damn for the blood, but if the police spotted him looking like this it would be the end of him. First the rest room, then something to eat. He hated to do this to her, to América, because this was just what he'd tried to protect her from, but they were going to have to go out back of one of the fast-food places— Kentucky Fried or Taco Bell or McDonald's—and go through the trash. After that they'd need a place to sleep, some business with shrubs around it and a little patch of lawn, someplace quiet where nobody would notice them, least of all the sons of bitches roaming the streets for blood, and now he had two of them to kill, *hijo de la chingada* and fuck the whole world.

"Okay," he said, and América wouldn't look at him, "okay now, listen to me . . ."

And she listened. Scared, angry, defeated, full of pity and hate, her heart in her mouth, no bed, no shower, no nothing. The nearest service station was five blocks up the street, up Sherman Way, and nobody said a word to her with Cándido at her side, his face a flag of blood, his pantlegs flapping like ragged banners. The attendant was Nicaraguan and he looked at her like she was dirt when she asked for the key to the rest room without buying anything, but she smiled and used her smallest voice and he relented. She took advantage of the opportunity to use the commode and cushion the back strap of her sandals with toilet paper, while Cándido washed the blood from his face and patted the mouth of the wound dry with paper towels. His face was pale and bristling with a vagrant's short stiff whiskers, but his hair hid the black slash of the contusion and when he'd finished he looked almost presentable, but for his torn shirt and the frayed ends of his trousers and the pit under his left eye that was part of him forever now.

He walked two steps ahead of her and he had nothing to say, his shoulders squared up like a fighting cock's, his eyes eating up the street. The few people out at this hour—drunks, mainly—gave him a wide berth. Though she was tired and shot through with despair, though her feet hurt and her stomach clenched on nothing, América didn't dare ask him where they were going or what the plan was or where they would sleep, eat, wash, live. She just followed along, numbed and vacant, and all the acid odors of the street assaulted her as if they'd been distilled just for her, for her and her alone. They walked for blocks and blocks, heading west, then turned onto a bright big boulevard to the south and followed it eternally, past shuttered restaurants, record shops and great hulking dimly lit malls floating like factory ships in black seas of macadam. It was very late. The leaves of the trees hung limp. There were hardly any cars at all on the streets.

Finally, just as she thought she was going to collapse, they came to another broad boulevard that looked familiar somehow, painfully familiar, though it was different now in the muted light, the sidewalks deserted, traffic dormant, every decent person home in bed. She'd never been very good with directions—Cándido joked that she could get lost just going from the kitchen to the bathroom—but she knew this place, didn't she? They were crossing against the light, no cars coming in either direction, when it came to her: they were back on the canyon road, right back where they'd started, where the shade trees overhung all those pretty little unattainable houses and the yards that were thick with swing sets and tricycles. She felt her heart sink. What were they doing here? He wasn't going to make her walk all the way back up the road and down into that miserable hole tonight, was he? He couldn't. He was crazy. Insane. She'd throw herself down right here on the sidewalk and die first.

She was about to say something, when he stopped suddenly just outside a restaurant she remembered from the morning, a little place set apart on its own paved lot, with plate-glass windows, a candy-striped roof and a big illuminated red-and-white bucket revolving round a pole atop it. The place was closed, dark inside, but the lot on either side of it was lit up like brightest day. "You hungry?" Cándido whispered, and they hadn't spoken in so long her voice sounded strange in her own ears when she said yes, yes she was. "Okay," he said, shooting a nervous glance up and down the street, "follow me and be quick about it—and keep your voice down."

She wasn't thinking. She was too tired to think, too depressed. There must have been some vague wonder in the back of her brain, some sort of puzzlement—did he know someone who worked here or was he going to lift something, supplies they delivered late at night?—but it never came to the surface and she just followed him stupidly into the harsh flood of the lights. They were in the back lot now, hidden from the street, fenced in on three sides. A big gray metal bin stood there, just outside the rear door, and it gave off an odor that told her immediately what it was.

Cándido astonished her. He strode right up to the thing and threw back the lid and he never noticed the dark quick shadow that shot out from beneath the bin and disappeared between the slats of the fence. All at once she understood: garbage, they were going to eat garbage. Sift through it like the *basureros* at the dump, take somebody else's filthy leavings, full of spit and maggots and ants. Was he crazy? Had he gone mad with the knock on his head? Even at their lowest, even in Tijuana in the dump they'd been able to scrape together a few *centavos* to buy steamed corn and *caldo* from the street vendors. She stood there frozen at the edge of the lot, watched in shock and disbelief as Cándido leaned into the bin till his legs came up off the ground and he began to kick for balance. She could feel the outrage burning in her, fueled by all the cruel disappointments of the day, a rising white-hot blaze of it that pushed her forward to sink her nails into his leg. "What are you doing?" she demanded in a whisper she could barely contain. "What in the name of Jesus do you think you're doing?"

His legs kicked. She heard him grunt from deep inside the bin. Somewhere out on the street an engine roared to life and she flinched and let go of him. What if someone caught them? She'd die of shame. "I'm not touching that, that shit," she hissed at the flailing legs, at his fat floundering rear. "I'd rather starve." She moved a step closer, outraged, and the smell hit her again, mold, rot, decay, filth. She wanted to shove him into the bin and slam the lid down on him, she wanted to break things, pound her fists against the walls. "Maybe you can live like this, but not me," she said, fighting to keep her voice down. "My family's respectable, miles above the likes of you and your aunt, and my father, my father—" She couldn't go on. She was breathless and weak and she thought she was going to cry.

There was a prolonged grunt from the depths of the bin, and then Cándido resurfaced, feeling his way with his feet, backing out of the mouth of the dumpster like a hermit crab emerging from its shell. He turned to her with his face ironed gray under the blast of the floodlights and she saw that his arms were spilling over with red-and-white-striped cardboard boxes, little things, like candy or cigar boxes. Grease, she smelled grease. Cooking grease. Cooking grease gone cold. "Your father," he said, holding out one of the boxes to her, "is a thousand miles away."

He looked round him quickly, that worried look on his face, tensed a moment, then relaxed. His voice softened. "Eat, *mi vida*," he said. "You're going to need it to keep up your strength."

8

IN THE EAST, FALL CAME IN ON A GUST OF CANADIAN air, invigorating and decisive. The leaves changed. The rain fell in cold gray splinters and the puddles developed a second skin overnight. The world was closing down, getting snug in dens and burrows, and the equinox was no casual thing. But here, in the bleached hills above Los Angeles, fall was just another aspect of the eternal summer, hotter, drier, hurled through the canyons on the breath of winds that leached all the moisture from the chaparral and brought combustible oils to the surface of every branch and twig. This was the season Delaney had the most trouble with. What was there to recommend in hundred-degree temperatures, zero-percent humidity and winds that forced fine grains of degraded sandstone up your nostrils every time you stepped out the door? Where was the charm in that? Other writers could celebrate the autumnal rituals of New England or the Great Smoky Mountains—watching the birds flock overhead, cutting wood for the stove, cranking up the cider press or stalking somnolent bears through the leafless woods with the first wet scent of snow in the air—but what could Delaney do to color the dismal reality of the season here? Sure, he educated his audience about fire-dependent germination, solvent extractives in manzanita and chamise, the release of nutrients in wood ash, but what could you do with a season that anticipated not the first soft magical transforming blanket of snow but the hellish raging infernos that vaporized everything in their path and shot roiling columns of atramental smoke twenty thousand feet into the air?

The winds blew, and Delaney sat at his desk and tried to make sense of them. He was still collecting material for a column on introduced species and population conflict, but the seasonal phenomena had to take precedence. How did the ground squirrels react to the drop in humidity? he wondered. Or the lizards? Maybe he could do something with the lizards, and not just the horned lizard, but all of them—the fence lizard, the western skink, the side-splotched lizard, the banded gecko. Did the winds change their behavior? Did the moisture content of their prey go down? Did they spend more time in their burrows during the heat of the day? He should have been out observing them, but the weather was getting him down. A high-pressure system had been stalled over the Great Basin for weeks now and every day was a replica of the day before: hot, cloudless, wind like a rope burn. He'd been out on the trails yesterday and spent most of his time applying Chap Stick and chasing his hat. Dust blew in his eyes. The scrub was whipped flat as if by the force of some great invisible hand. He cut his hike short and went home to sit in the air-conditioned living room, shades drawn, watching a joyless football contest between panting fat men who looked as if they'd rather be elsewhere.

Still, the lizard idea was a good one, definitely worth exploring, and he got up from his desk to sift through his nature library, picking up tidbits about the six-lined racer (eats the eggs of small ground-nesting birds by crushing them with its jaws and lapping up the contents), the chuckwalla (strictly vegetarian) and the gila monster (stores fat in its tail). But then, unaccountably, he thought of vultures—they must do pretty well under these conditions. No one had written much about the turkey vulture—too pedestrian—and that might make for an unusual column. And this was their season, no doubt about it. Water sources were drying up. Things were dying.

He was sitting there, lost in lizard lore and statistical analyses of disgorgement rates in nesting vultures, when the doorbell rang, a dull metallic passing of gas that hissed through the nether regions of the house like air leaking out of a balloon. He debated whether or not to answer it. This was his private time, his writing time, and he guarded it jealously. But who could it be at this hour? The mailman? Fed Ex? Curiosity got the better of him and he went to the door.

A man in a dirty T-shirt was standing there on the doormat, a cement mixer and two flatbed trucks piled high with cinder blocks looming behind him at the curb. He was wearing a hard hat and his arms were bruised with tattoos. Behind him, milling around the trucks, was a crew of Mexicans. "I just wanted to tell you we'll be coming through here today," he said, "and it would be a help if you could leave the side gate open."

Coming through? Delaney wasn't focusing, his head swarming with lizards and vultures.

The man in the T-shirt was watching him closely. "The wall," he said. "My people are going to need access."

The wall. Of course. He should have guessed. Ninety percent of the community was already walled in, tireless dark men out there applying stucco under conditions that would have killed anybody else, and now the last link was coming to Delaney, to his own dogless yard, hemming him in, obliterating his view—protecting him despite himself. And he'd done nothing to protest it, nothing at all. He hadn't answered Todd Sweet's increasingly frantic telephone messages, hadn't even gone to the decisive meeting to cast his vote. But Kyra—she'd made the wall her mission, putting all her closer's zeal into selling the thing, stuffing envelopes, making phone calls, working cheek by jowl with Jack and Erna to ensure that the sanctity of the community was preserved and that no terrestrial thing, whether it came on two legs or four, could get in without an invitation.

"Sure," Delaney said. "Yeah, sure," and he walked the man around the side of the house, unlatched the gate and propped it open with a stone he kept there for that purpose. The wind lashed the trees and a pair of tumbleweeds (Russian thistle, actually, another unfortunate introduction) leapt across the yard and got hung up on the useless fence. A sudden gust threw a handful of dirt in Delaney's face and he could feel the grit between his teeth. "Just be sure you shut it when you're done," he said, making a vague gesture in the direction of the pool. "We wouldn't want any of the neighborhood kids wandering in."

The man gave him a cursory nod and then turned and shouted something in Spanish that set his crew in motion. Men clambered up into the trucks, ropes flew from the load, wheelbarrows appeared from nowhere. Delaney didn't know what to do. For a while he stood there at the gate as if welcoming them, as if he were hosting a pool party or cookout, and a procession of dark sober men marched past him shouldering picks, shovels, trowels, sacks of stucco and concrete, their eyes fixed on the ground. But then he began to feel self-conscious, out of place, as if he were trespassing on his own property, and he turned and went back into the house, down the hallway and through the door to his office, where he sat back down at his desk and stared at full-color photographs of turkey vultures till they began to move on the page.

He tried to concentrate, but he couldn't. There was a constant undercurrent of noise—unintelligible shouts, revving engines, the clank of tools and the grinding ceaseless scrape of the cement mixer, all of it riding on the thin giddy bounce and thump of a boombox tuned to a Mexican station. He felt as if he were under siege. Ten minutes after he'd sat down he was at the window, watching the transformation of his backyard. The wall was complete as far as the Cherrystones' next door on the right; on the other side, they were still three houses down, at Rudy Hernandez's place, but the noose was tightening. They'd run a string along the property line weeks ago and now the workers were digging footings right up against the eight-foot chain-link fence, which was going to have to go, he could see that. The thing was useless anyway, and every time he looked at it he thought of Osbert. And Sacheverell.

He and Kyra would just have to pay to tear it down—yet another expense—but that wasn't what bothered him. What really hurt, what rankled him so much he would have gone out and campaigned against the wall no matter what Jack or Kyra said, was that there was going to be no access to the hills at all—not even a gate, nothing. The Property Owners' Association had felt the wall would be more secure if there were no breaches in it, and besides, gates cost money. But where did that leave Delaney? If he wanted to go for a stroll in the chaparral, if he wanted to investigate those lizards or the gnatcatcher or even the coyotes, he was either going to have to scale the wall or hike all the way out to the front gate and double back again. Which would tend to cut down on spontaneity, that was for sure.

He sat back down at his desk, got up again, sat down. Wind rattled the panes, workers shouted, *ranchera* music danced through the interstices with a manic tinny glee. Work was impossible. By noon the footings were in and the first eight-inch-high band of concrete block had begun to creep across the property line. How could he work? How could he even think of it? He was being walled in, buried alive, and there wasn't a thing he could do about it.

By the time Kyra came for him to go out and help her close up the Da Ros place for the night, he was like a caged beast. He resented having to escort her out there seven nights a week anyway, but the graffiti incident left him little choice. (And here he thought of that son of a bitch with his "flies" and it just stoked his mood.) "I hope you're happy," he said, sliding into the seat beside her.

She was all business, bright and chirpy, dressed in her property-moving best, the Lexus a massive property-moving tool ready to leap to life beneath her fingertips. It was dark. The wind beat at the windows. "What?" she said, all innocence. "What's that face for? Did I do something?"

He looked out the window, fuming, as she put the car in gear and wheeled out the driveway and down Piñon. "The wall," he said. "It's in. Or most of it, anyway. It's about a hundredth of an inch from the chain link."

They were on Arroyo Blanco now, Kyra giving a little wave to the moron at the front gate. This was their ritual, six o'clock every night, while dinner waited on the stove and an already fed Jordan sat before Selda Cherrystone's TV set: out the gate, up the hill and down the winding drive to the Da Ros place, out of the car, into the house, a quick look round the yard and back again. He hated it. Resented it. It was a waste of his time, and how could she expect him to put a decent dinner together if he was up here every night looking for phantoms? She should drop the listing, that's what she should do, get rid of it, let somebody else worry about the flowers and the fish and the Mexicans in the bushes.

"All right," she said, shrugging, her eyes on the road, "we'll have Al Lopez take the fence down; it's not like we need it anymore"—and here was the sting of guilt, the counterattack—"if we ever did."

"I can't walk out of my own yard," he said.

She was smiling, serene. The wind blew. Bits of chaff and the odd tumbleweed shot through the thin luminous stream of the headlights. "In the backseat," she said. "A present. For you."

He turned to look. A car came up behind them and lighted his face. There was a stepladder in the backseat, a little three-foot aluminum one, the sort of thing you might use for hanging curtains or changing the lightbulb in the front hallway. It was nestled against the leather seat and there was a red satin bow taped to the front of it.

"There's your solution," she said. "Anytime you want. Just hoist yourself over."

"Yeah, sure. And what about the ramparts and the boiling oil?"

She ignored the sarcasm. She stared out at the road, her face serene and composed.

Of course, she was right. If the wall had to be there, and through the tyranny of the majority it did, 127 votes for, 87 against, then he'd have to get used to it—and this was a simple expedient. He had a sudden ephemeral vision of himself perched atop the wall with his daypack, and it came to him then that the wall might not be as bad as he'd thought, if he could get over the bruise to his self-esteem. Not only would it keep burglars, rapists, graffiti artists and coyotes out of the development, it would keep people like the Dagolians out of the

hills. He couldn't really see Jack and Selda Cherrystone hoisting themselves over the wall for an evening stroll, or Doris Obst or even Jack
Jardine. Delaney would have the hills to himself, his own private nature
preserve. The idea took hold of him, exhilarated him, but he couldn't
admit it. Not to Kyra, not yet. "I don't want to do any hoisting," he
said finally, injecting as much venom into the participle as he could,
"I just want to walk. You know, like on my feet?"

There was no one at the Da Ros place, no muggers, no bogeymen,
no realtors or buyers. Kyra walked him through the house, as she did
every third or fourth night, extolling its virtues as if she were trying to
sell it to him, and he asked her point-blank if she shouldn't consider
dropping the listing. "It's been, what," he said, "nine months now without so much as a nibble?"

They were in the library, the leather-bound spines of six thousand
books carefully selected by a suicide glowing softly in the light of the
wall sconces, and Kyra swung round to tell him he didn't know a thing
about business, especially the real-estate business. "People would kill
for a listing like this," she said. "Literally kill for it. And with a property
this unique, you sometimes have to just sit on it till the right buyer
comes along—and they will, believe me. I know it. I know they will."

"You sound like you're trying to convince yourself."

A gust rattled the panes. The Santa Anas were in full force and the
koi pools would be clogged with litter. Kyra gave him her widest
smile—nothing could dampen her mood tonight—and she took hold
of both his hands and lifted them as if they were at the very start of
an elaborate dance. "Maybe I am," she said, and he let it drop.

On the way home they stopped in at Gitello's to pick up a few
things—odds and ends—for the feast they were planning on Thursday,
for Thanksgiving. They were having the Cherrystones and the Jardines
over, as well as Kyra's sister and brother-in-law, with their three children, and Kyra's mother, who was flying in from San Francisco. They'd
already spent two hundred and eighty dollars at the Von's in Woodland
Hills, where nearly everything was cheaper, but the list of odds and
ends had grown to daunting proportions. Kyra was doing the cooking,

with Delaney as sous chef and the maid, Orbalina, on cleanup detail, and she was planning a traditional dinner: roast turkey with chestnut dressing and giblet gravy, mashed potatoes and turnips, a cranberry compote, steamed asparagus, three California wines and two French, baked winter squash soup and a salad of mixed field greens to start, a cheese course, a home-blended *granité* of grapefruit and nectarine, and a hazelnut-risotto pudding and crème brûlée for dessert with espresso, Viennese coffee and Armagnac on the side.

Delaney retrieved the preliminary list from the folds of his wallet as Kyra strode brusquely through the door and selected a cart. The list was formidable. They needed whipping cream, baby carrots, heavy syrup, ground mace, five pounds of confectioners' sugar, balsamic vinegar, celery sticks and capers, among other things, as well as an assortment of cold cuts, marinated artichoke hearts, Greek olives and caponata for an antipasto platter she'd only just now decided on. As he followed her down the familiar aisles, watching her as she stood there examining the label on a can of smoked baby oysters or button mushrooms in their own juice, Delaney began to feel his mood lifting. There was nothing wrong, nothing at all. She was beautiful. She was his wife. He loved her. Why mope, why brood, why spend another angry night on the couch? The wall was there, a physical presence, undeniable, and it worked two ways, both for and against him, and if he was clever he could use it to his own advantage. It was Thanksgiving, and he should be thankful.

He stood at Kyra's side, touching her, offering suggestions and advice, inhaling the rich complex odor of her hair and body as she piled the cart high with bright irresistible packages, things they needed, things they'd run out of, things they might need or never need. Here it was, cornucopian, superabundant, all the fruits of the earth gathered and packaged and displayed for their benefit, for them and them alone. He felt better just being here, so much better he could barely contain himself. How could he have let such a petty thing come between them? He watched her select a jar of piccalilli relish and bend to set it in the cart, and a wave of tenderness swept over him. Suddenly he had his hands on her hips and he was pulling her to him and kissing her right there beneath the Diet Pepsi banner, under the full gaze of the lights and all the other shoppers with their carts and children and bland self-absorbed faces. And she kissed him back, with enthusiasm, and the promise of more to come.

And then, at the checkout, he was amazed all over again.

"You want your turkey?" the girl asked after she'd rung up the purchases—a hundred and six dollars and thirty-nine cents, and why not? The girl was dark-eyed, with a wild pouf of sprayed-up hair and penciled-in eyebrows, like a worldly waif in the silent films. She was snapping gum, animated, bathing in the endless shower of all this abundance.

"Turkey?" Delaney said. "What turkey?" Their turkey was home in the refrigerator, eighteen pounds, four ounces, range-fed and fresh-killed.

"It's a special offer, just this week only," the girl said, her voice a breathless trill playing over the wad of pink gum Delaney could just catch a glimpse of when she opened her mouth to say "special." "If your order totals over fifty dollars you get a free twelve-pound turkey, one to a customer."

"But we already—" Delaney began, and Kyra cut him off. "Yes," she said, looking up from her compact, "thank you."

"Carlos!" the girl sang out, shouting toward the distant fluorescent glare of the meat department at the back of the store. "Bring me another turkey, will you?"

For his part, Cándido Rincón didn't exactly welcome the season either. That it was hot, that the winds blew and the sweat dried from your skin almost before it had a chance to spill from the pores, was fine and good, ideal even—if only it could be sustained indefinitely, if only the sun would grace him for another two or three months. But he knew that the winds would soon blow themselves out and the sky would blacken and rot far out over the ocean and then come ashore to die. He couldn't smell the rains yet, but he knew they were coming. The days were truncated. The nights were cold. And where was his son going to be born—in a bed with a doctor looking on or in a hut with the rain driving down and nobody there but Cándido with a pot of water and his rusty knife?

None of this sat easy with him as he trudged up the rutted trail to the market. América was down below, in a funk—she wouldn't leave the lean-to, no matter how much he might beg or plead. She was like a deranged person, sitting there over her swollen belly, rocking back and forth and chanting to herself. She scared him. No matter what he did, no matter what he brought her—magazines, clothes, things to eat, a rattle and a pair of booties for the baby—she'd just give him the same numbed look, as if she didn't recognize him—or didn't want to recognize him.

It was this place, he knew it. The defeat of having to come back here, of having to live like *vagos* after the promise of that day in Canoga Park, after the luncheonette and the flush toilet and all those rich things and the houses with the cars out front and the peace and security inside. She'd had a breakdown then, like nothing he'd ever seen—even on the streets of Tijuana, even in the worst and lowest places. He'd seen women in hysterics before, but this was something else altogether, this was like a fit, a spell, as if somebody had put a curse on her. She wouldn't stand up. Wouldn't walk. Wouldn't eat the chicken he'd found for her, perfectly good pieces of Kentucky Fried Chicken the *gabachos* had thrown away untouched, and he'd had to drag her back down to their camp, fighting her all the way. Yes, they were desperate. Yes, they'd lost everything. Yes, he was a fool and a liar and he'd failed her yet again. But still they had to make the best of it, had to survive, didn't she see that?

She didn't. For the first few days she just sat there, immobilized, catatonic. He'd leave to go out scrounging for food, for work, for the cans he found along the roadway and turned in for a handful of nickels and pennies, and when he came back, whether it was two hours later or six or eight, there she'd be, just as he'd left her, sometimes in the same pose even. She wouldn't talk to him. She refused to cook. She stopped washing her hair and her body and within the week she stank like one of the homeless, like a wild thing, like a corpse. Her eyes gored him. He began to think he hated her.

Then he met Señor Willis. It was serendipity, good luck instead of bad. He'd got work a few times over the course of the first two weeks after the Canoga Park idiocy, standing out front of the post office with a knot of other men, not so many now, and keeping a sharp eye out for the INS or some vigilante *gabacho*, defying them, yes, but what choice did he have? The labor exchange was gone. Someone had come in and planted some pepper trees, little sticks six or eight feet high with a puff of foliage at the top, black plastic hose running from tree to tree like a lifeline. That was the labor exchange now: saplings in the ground and the dead blasted earth. So he stood there outside the post office and took his chances, breathing hard every time a car slowed— was it a job or a bust?—and he was there late one howling hot dry-as-a-bone day, two o'clock probably, and a sledgehammered old Corvair pulled into the lot like some arthritic bird, and there, sitting at the wheel, was a man in the same shape as the car, an old white man with a sunken chest and turtle-meat arms, white hairs growing out of his nose and ears. He just sat there, looking at Cándido out of watery old gray-blue eyes that were distended by the lenses of his glasses till they didn't look like eyes at all, till they looked like mouths, grasping crazy wide-open gray-blue mouths. He was drunk. You could see that from twenty feet away. "Hey, *muchacho*," he called out of the passenger's-side window, which still had the sparse teeth of broken glass sprouting from the frame, the rest a vacancy. *"¿Quieres trabajar?"*

It was a joke. It had to be. They let the old *gabachos* out of the nursing home and sent them down here to taunt honest men, that's what it was, Cándido was sure of it, and he felt his jaws clench with hate and anger. He didn't move a muscle. Just stood there rigid.

"Muchacho," the old man said after a minute, and the wind, the tireless Santa Ana, pinched his voice till it was barely there, *"¿qué pasa? ¿Eres sordo?* Are you deaf? I said, do you want to work?"

The car rumbled and farted through its crippled exhaust. The wind blew. The mouths of the old man's eyes beckoned. What the hell, Cándido said to himself, what have I got to lose? and he made his way round the car to the driver's-side window and leaned in. "What work?" he asked in Spanish.

There was a bottle on the seat next to the old man—two bottles, one of vodka, with a red label and clear liquid, the other with the same label but filled with a yellowish fluid, which Cándido later learned was urine. The old man didn't smell good. When he opened his mouth to smile there were only three teeth visible, two on the bottom and one on the top. "Building," the old man said, "construction. You got a strong back, you work for me, no pissing around, eight bucks an hour."

Eight bucks? Was he kidding? It was a joke. It had to be.

"Get in the car," the old man said, and Cándido went back round to the passenger's side, nothing to lose, jerked open the door—it was battered shut—and slid into the seat beside the two capped bottles, the clear and the tinted.

That was Señor Willis, and Señor Willis proved to be a surprise, a big surprise, the best surprise Cándido had had since he left Tepoztlán with his seventeen-year-old bride. The Corvair took the canyon road at about thirty miles an hour, the front end ratcheting and swaying, the tires gasping, black smoke pouring so thickly from the exhaust that Cándido was afraid the thing was on fire, but it made the crest and wound down into Woodland Hills, where Señor Willis pulled up in front of a house that was the size of three houses, and the bald nervous-looking *gringo* who owned it came out and shook his hand. That was Señor Willis.

Cándido worked past dark, doing what Señor Willis told him, lifting this, pulling that, fetching a wrench, a hammer, the screw gun and two boxes of tile from the trunk of the car. Señor Willis was remodeling one of the six bathrooms in this grand hushed house that was like a hotel with its potted plants and rich Persian carpets and leather chairs, and Señor Willis was a genius. An old genius. A drunken genius. A worn-out, battered and decrepit genius. But a genius all the same. He'd built hundreds of houses in his day, built whole developments, and not only in California, but in Panama too, where he'd picked up his Spanish that was so bad it made Cándido feel the way he had as a kid when the teacher would scratch her nails on the blackboard to get the attention of the class.

Cándido worked a full week with Señor Willis and then the job was done and the old man disappeared, drunk for a week more. But Cándido had money now, and he bought América things to try to cheer her, little delicacies from the grocery, white bread and sardines in oil, and the apartment fund began to grow again in the little plastic peanut butter jar. Two weeks went by. There was no work. *La Migra*, rumor had it, had snatched six men from in front of the post office, and the agents were in an unmarked car, black, plain black, and not the puke-green you could see a mile away. Cándido stayed away for a while. He dipped into the money he'd made. América was like a stranger and she was getting bigger by the day, so big he was afraid she'd burst, and she ate everything he could bring her and kept wanting more.

He climbed the hill. Stood out front of the post office and sweated the police. And where was Señor Willis? He'd died, that must have been it. Sleeping in his car because his wife hounded him so much he couldn't take it, drinking out of the one bottle and pissing in the other, seventy-six years old with bad hips and an irregular heart and who could survive that? He was dead. Sure he was. But then, one hopeless hot wind-tortured afternoon, there came the Corvair, drifting down the road like a mirage, and there was Señor Willis with one eye bruised purple and swollen shut like some artificial thing grafted to his face, a rubber joke you'd find in a novelty shop. "Hey, *muchacho*," he said, "we got work. Get in."

Three days this time. Installing new gates with gravity feed on an old iron fence around a swimming pool, then replacing the coping. And then Señor Willis was drunk, and then there was more work, and now, now that they had nearly five hundred dollars in the jar, there was a month's worth of work coming up, a whole big job of work, putting an addition on a young couple's living room in Tarzana, and what was wrong with that? América should jump for joy. They'd be out of here any day now, out of here and into an apartment where Señor Willis could come by and knock at the door and Cándido could come out and just get into the Corvair and not have to worry about *La Migra* snatching him off the street. But América wasn't jumping for joy. She wasn't jumping at all. She wasn't even moving. She was just sitting there by the moribund stream and the dwindling pool, bloated and fat and inanimate.

Cándido went up the hill. He was worried, always worried, but then life had its ups and downs and this time they were on the upswing, no doubt about it. He was making plans in his head and when he passed the big stubbed-toe rock where he'd encountered that son of a bitch of a half-a-*gringo* with the hat turned backwards on his head, he refused even to think about him. There was no work today or tomorrow either. It was a holiday, Señor Willis had told him, a four-day weekend, and they would start in on the new project, the big job, on Monday. But what holiday was it? Thanksgiving, Señor Willis had said, *El Día de las Gracias, El Tenksgeevee.*

Well that was all right. Cándido would rather be working, he'd rather be putting his first and last months' rent down on an apartment, any apartment, anywhere, and bringing his wife up out of the hole she was in, but it could wait another week at sixty-four dollars a day—or at least he hoped and prayed it could. América was due soon—she looked like an unpoked sausage swelling on the grill. But he had no control over that—sure, he'd stood out there by the post office this morning, but nobody came by, nobody, it was like the whole canyon was suddenly deserted—and now he was coming back up the hill, three o'clock in the afternoon, to buy rice, stewed tomatoes in the can, a two-quart cardboard container of milk for his wife and maybe a beer or two, Budweiser or Pabst Blue Ribbon, in the tall brown one-liter bottle, for *El Tenksgeevee.*

He kept his head up on the road. *La Migra* wouldn't be working today, not on *El Tenksgeevee*, the lazy overfed fat-assed bastards, but you could never tell: it would be just like them to pick you up when you least expected it. There wasn't a lot of traffic—more than in the morning, but still it was nothing compared to a working day. Cándido crossed the road—careful, careful—made his way through the maze of shopping carts and haphazardly parked vehicles in the lot, and entered the *paisano*'s market, stooping to pick up a red plastic handbasket just inside the door.

The place was the same as always, changeless, as familiar to him now as the market in his own village, and still there wasn't a scent of food, not even a stray odor, as if the smell of a beefsteak or a cheese or even good fresh sawdust was somehow obscene. The light was dead. The shoppers were the same as always, the same changeless bleached-out faces, and they gave him the same naked stares of contempt and disgust. Or no, they weren't the same, not exactly: today they were all dressed up in their finery for *El Tenksgeevee*. Cándido made his way down the canned-vegetable aisle, thinking to save the beer cooler for last, so as to keep the beer cold to the last possible moment—and he would reach way in back too, to get the maximally chilled ones. He smelled plastic wrap, Pine-Sol, deodorant.

He lingered over the beer, standing in front of the fogged-over door, comparing prices, the amber bottles backlit so that they glowed invitingly, and he was thinking: One? Or two? América wouldn't drink any, it was bad for the baby, and if she drank beer she might forget how implacably and eternally angry she was and maybe even let a stray smile fall on him. No, she wouldn't drink any, and one would make him feel loose at the edges, little fingers crepitating in his brain and massaging the bad side of his face, but two would be glorious, two would be thanksgiving. He opened the case and let the cool air play over his face a moment, then reached into the back and selected two big one-liter bottles of Budweiser, the King of Beers.

He was thinking nothing at the checkout, his face a mask, his mind back in Tepoztlán, the rocky *cerros* rising above the village in a glistening curtain of rain, the plants lush with it, fields high with corn and the winter dry season just setting in, the best time in all the year, and he didn't pay any attention to the *gringos* in line ahead of him, the loud ones, two men already celebrating the holiday, their garish shirts open at the neck, jackets tight in the shoulders. "Turkey?" one of them shouted in his own language, and his voice was rich with amusement, with mockery, and now Cándido looked up, wondering what it was all about. "What the hell do we want with a turkey?"

The man who'd been speaking was in his twenties, cocky, long-haired, rings leaping out of his knuckles. The other one, his companion, had six little hoops punched through his earlobe. "Take it, man," the second one said. "Come on, Jules, it's a goof. Take it, man. It's a turkey. A fucking turkey."

They were holding up the line. Heads had begun to turn. Cándido, who was right behind them, studied his feet.

"You gonna cook it?" the first man said.

"Cook it? You think it'll fit in a microwave?"

"That's what I'm saying: what the fuck do we want with a fucking turkey?"

And then time seemed to slow down, crystallize, hold everything suspended in that long three o'clock Thanksgiving moment under the dead light of the store and the sharp cat-eyed glances of the *gringos*. "What about this dude here? He looks like he could use a turkey. Hey, man"—and now Cándido felt a finger poke at his shoulder and he looked up and saw it all, the two sharp dressers, the plastic sack of groceries, the exasperated checkout girl with the pouf of sprayed-up hair and the big frozen bird, the *pavo* in its sheet of white skin, lying there frozen like a brick on the black conveyor belt—"you want a turkey?"

Something was happening. They were asking him something, point-ing at the turkey and asking him—what? What did they want from him? Cándido glanced round in a growing panic: everyone in the line was watching him. "No espick Ingliss," he said.

The one nearest him, the one with the hoops in his ear, burst out laughing, and then the other one, the first one, joined in. "Oh, man," the first one said, "oh, man," and the laughter twisted in Cándido like a knife. Why did they always have to do this? he thought, and his face went dark.

Now the checkout girl chimed in: "I don't think we can do that, sir," she said. "It's for the customer who made the purchase. If he"—and she indicated Cándido with a flick of her enameled fingers—"rings up fifty dollars he gets his turkey, just like you. But if you don't want one—"

"God, a turkey," the first one said, and he was giggling so hard he could barely get the words out, "what a concept."

"Hey, come on, move it, will you?" a tall black man with a knitted brow crowed from the back of the line.

The man with the rings shook out his long hair, looked back at the black man and gave him the richest smile in the world. "Yeah," he said finally, turning back to the checker, "yeah, I want my turkey," and Cándido looked away from his eyes and his leering smile and the turkey found its way into a plastic bag. But the men didn't leave, not yet. They stood just off to the side of the checker and watched her ring up Cándido's purchases with two frozen grins on their faces, and then, as Cándido tried to ease past them—he didn't want any trouble, he didn't, not now, not ever—the first man hefted the big frozen twelve-pound turkey and dropped it into Cándido's arms and Cándido had no choice but to grab the dead weight of it, rock-hard and cold through to the bone, and he almost dropped his bottles of beer, his precious beer, and still he didn't understand.

"Happy Thanksgiving, dude," the one with the rings said, and then the two of them were out the door, their long *gringo* legs scissoring the light, and the hot wind rushed in.

Cándido was dazed, and he just stood there looking at all those white faces looking at him, trying to work out the permutations of what had just happened. Then he knew and accepted it in the way he would have swallowed a piece of meat without cutting it up, gulping it down because it was there on the tines of the fork. He cradled the lump of the frozen bird under one arm and hurried out the door and across the lot before someone came and took it away from him. But what luck, he thought, skittering down the road, what joy, what a coup! This would put a smile on América's face, this would do it, the skin crusted and basted in its own juices, and he would build up the coals first, make an inferno and let it settle into a bed of coals, and then he would roast the *pavo* on a spit, slow-roast it, sitting right there and turning the spit till it was brown all over and not a blackened spot on it.

He hurried down the trail, and nothing bothered him now, not his hip or his cheekbone or the wind in his face, thinking of the beer and the turkey and América. "Gobble, gobble," he called, sloshing across the pool to where she sat like a statue in the sand, "gobble, gobble, gobble, and guess what *papacito*'s got for you!"

And she smiled. She actually smiled at the sight of the thing, stripped of its head and its feet and its feathers, rolled up into one big ball of meat, turkey meat, a feast for two. She took a sip of beer when he offered it to her and she pressed his bicep with her hand as he told her the insuperable tale of the turkey, and already the flames were rising, the wind sucking them higher as it tore through the canyon, and should he get up from the sand and the beer and América and all the birds in the trees and the frogs croaking at the side of the pool and feed it some more?

He got to his feet. The wind snatched at the fire and the fire roared. He went up and down the streambed in search of wood, rapping the bigger branches against the trunks of the trees to break them down, and every time he came back to feed the fire América was sitting there cradling the pale white bird as if she'd given birth to it, kneading the cold flesh and fighting to work the thick green spit through the back end of it. Yes, he told her, yes, that's the way, and he was happy, as happy as he'd ever been, right up to the moment when the wind plucked the fire out of its bed of coals and with a roar as loud as all the furnaces of hell set it dancing in the treetops.

PART THREE
Socorro

1

"BUT IT'S ONLY A COUPLE OF BLOCKS," DELANEY WAS saying to the steamed-over bathroom mirror while Kyra moved behind him in the bedroom, trying on clothes. He'd towel-dried his hair and now he was shaving. Even with the hallway door closed he could smell the turkey, the entire house alive with the aroma of roasting bird, an aroma that took him back to his childhood and his grandparents' sprawling apartment in Yonkers, the medley of smells that would hit him in the stairwell and grow increasingly potent with each step of the three flights up until it exploded when the door swung open to reveal his grandmother standing there in her apron. Nothing had ever smelled so good—no French bakery in the first hour of light, no restaurant, no barbecue or clambake. "It seems ridiculous to take the car."

Kyra appeared in the bathroom doorway. She was in a black slip and she'd put her hair up. "Hurry, can't you," she said, "I need the mirror. And yes, we're taking the car, of course we're taking the car—with this wind? My hair would be all over the place."

Jordan was in the living room, occupied with the tape-delayed version of the Macy's parade, Orbalina was scrambling to set the table and clean up the culinary detritus in the kitchen, and Kyra's mother—Kit—was in the guest room, freshening up. Delaney cracked the blinds. The day was clear, hot, wind-driven. "You've got a point," he conceded.

Back then, he'd always worn a suit, tie and overcoat, even when he was five or six, as the yellowed black-and-white photos testified. But those were more formal times. Plus it was cold. There'd be ice on the lakes now and the wind off the Hudson would have a real bite to it. But what to wear today—to Dominick Flood's cocktail party? Delaney sank his face into the towel, padded into the bedroom on bare feet and pushed through the things in his closet. This was California, after all—you could wear hip boots and a top hat and nobody would blink twice. He settled finally on a pair of baggy white cotton trousers and a short-sleeve sport shirt Kyra had bought him. The shirt carved alternate patches of white and burgundy across his chest and over his shoulders, and in each burgundy patch the multiplied figures of tiny white jockeys leapt, genuflected and gamboled their way through a series of obscure warm-up exercises. It was California all the way.

There must have been a hundred people at Dominick Flood's, two o'clock in the afternoon, umbrellas flapping over the tables set up in the backyard. A string quartet was stationed under the awning that shaded the den, and the awning was flapping too. Most of the guests were packed in near the bar, where two men in tuxedos and red ties were manipulating bottles with professional ease. To the left of the bar, along the interior wall and running the length of the room, was a table laden with enough food for six Thanksgiving feasts, including a whole roast suckling pig with a mango in its mouth and fresh-steamed lobsters surrounded by multicolored platters of sashimi and sushi. Dominick himself, resplendent in a white linen suit that flared at the ankle to hide the little black box on loan from the Los Angeles County Electronic Monitoring Service, stood just inside the door, greeting guests, a long-stemmed glass in his hand. Delaney maneuvered Kyra and her mother through the crowd to introduce them.

"Ahh, Delaney," Dominick cried, taking his hand theatrically even as he shifted his attention to Kyra and her mother. "And this must be Mrs. Mossbacher? And—?"

"Kit," Kyra's mother put in, taking Flood's hand, "Kit Menaker. I'm visiting from San Francisco."

The string quartet started up then, sawing harshly into something jangling and modern, their faces strained against the rush of wind and the indifferent clamor of the party, and Delaney tuned out the conversation. Kyra's mother, fifty-five, blond and divorced, with Kyra's nose and legs and an exaggerated self-presence, was the single most coquettish woman Delaney had ever known. She would tangle herself like a vine round Dominick Flood, whose incipient bachelorhood she could smell out in some uncanny extrasensory way, and she would almost certainly invite him to their little dinner party, only to be disappointed and maybe even a bit shocked by the black manacle on his ankle. And that, of course, would only whet her appetite. "Yes," he heard Kyra say, "but I was just a little girl then," and Kit chimed in with a high breathless giggle that was like a warcry.

Delaney excused himself and drifted off toward the food, picking at a few things here and there—he never could resist a bite of *ahi* tuna or a spicy scallop roll if it was good, and this was very good, the best—but pacing himself for the feast to come. He smiled at a stranger or two, murmured an apology when he jostled a woman over the carcass of the pig, exchanged sound bites about the weather and watched the bartender pour him a beer, but all the while he was fretting. He kept envisioning the turkey going up in flames, the potatoes congealing into something like wet concrete, Jordan sinking into boredom and distracting Orbalina with incessant demands for chocolate milk, pudding, Cup O' Noodles, a drink of juice. And their guests. He hadn't yet seen the Jardines or the Cherrystones (though he could hear Jack Cherrystone's booming basso profundo from somewhere out on the back lawn), but he was sure they'd fill up here and push their plates away at dinner. Delaney wasn't very good at enjoying himself, not in a situation like this, and he stood there in the middle of the crush for a moment, took a deep breath, let his shoulders go slack and swung his head from side to side to clear it.

He was feeling lost and edgy and maybe even a bit guilty to

be imbibing so early in the afternoon, even on a day dedicated to self-indulgence like this one, when he felt a pressure at his elbow and turned to see Jack, Erna and Jack Jr. arrayed in smiling wonder behind him. "Delaney," Jack sang out, holding on to the last syllable as if he couldn't let it go, "you look lost."

Jack was dressed. Three-piece suit, crisp white button-down shirt, knotted tie. His wife, a catlike bosomy woman who always insisted on the two-cheek, continental style of greeting and would clutch your shoulders with tiny fists until she'd been accomodated, as she did now, was dressed. Delaney saw that she was wearing a shroudlike evening gown, black satin, and at least sixty percent of her jewelry collection. Even Jack Jr., with his hi-tops, earrings and ridiculous haircut, was dressed, in a sport coat that accented the new spread of his shoulders and a tie he must have inherited from his father.

"I *am* lost," Delaney admitted. He hefted the beer and grinned. "It's too early in the afternoon for me to be drinking—you know me and alcohol, Jack—and I've got a six-course dinner to worry about. Which you're going to love, by the way. Old New England right here in California. Or old New York, anyway."

"Relax, Delaney," Erna purred, "it's Thanksgiving. Enjoy the party."

Jack Jr. gave him a sick grin. He stood a head taller than anyone else in the room. His voice cracked when he excused himself and drifted toward the suckling pig like some incubus of the food chain.

"I see from the letters this month you've been taking some heat on that coyote column," Jack said, and a glass of wine seemed to materialize magically in his hand. Erna grinned at Delaney, waved at someone over his shoulder.

Leave it to Jack to bore right in. Delaney shrugged. "Yeah, I guess so. There've been something like thirty letters, most of them critical, but not all. But that's something. I must have pushed some buttons."

Actually, the response had surprised him. He'd never generated— provoked?—more than half a dozen letters before, all from literal-minded biologists taking issue with his characterization of the dusky-footed wood rat or his use of the common name of some plant in

THE TORTILLA CURTAIN • 265

preference to the scientific. The readers, die-hard preservationists to the last man, woman and child, had seemed to feel he was advocating some sort of control on coyote populations, and though he'd been upset over Osbert when he wrote the piece, he didn't see the column as being at all environmentally incorrect. After the tenth letter had come in, he'd sat down and reread the column. Twice. And there was nothing there. They just weren't getting it—they weren't reading it in the spirit it was intended. He wasn't pushing for population controls—controls were futile and the historical record proved it. As he'd indicated. He was just elucidating the problem, opening up the issue to debate. Certainly it wasn't the coyotes that were to blame, it was us—hadn't he made that clear?

Jack was grinning, his lips ever so slightly drawn back to reveal a strategic flash of enamel. Delaney recognized the expression. It was skeptical, faintly ironic, meant to convey to judges, jurors and district attorneys alike that the issue had yet to be decided. "So what is it, Delaney—should we bring back the traps and quotas or not? You've lost two dogs, and how many others here have lost pets too?" He made a sweeping gesture to take in the room, the house, the community at large.

"That's right," Kyra said, slipping up behind Delaney and taking hold of his arm, "and that's where we had our falling-out over the wall—or actually, it was war, full-on, no-holds-barred."

Jack laughed. Erna laughed. Delaney managed a rueful smile as greetings went round and the string quartet built to a frenzy in the *con fuoco*. "But really," Kyra said, unwilling to let it go, "don't you feel safer now, all of you—Jack, Erna, Delaney? Don't you?" she said, turning her face to him. "Admit it."

Delaney reddened. Shrugged again. The beer glass in his hand was heavy as a cannonball. "I know when I'm licked," he was saying, but Erna Jardine had already leapt in to answer for him. "Of course we do," she said. "We all do. The wall's barely been completed and yet I'm breathing easier to know there'll never be another rattlesnake in my garage. Or another break-in." She gave them a pious look. "Oh, I know that doesn't mean we can let our guard down, but still, it's one more barrier, isn't it?" she said, and then she leaned into Kyra and lowered her voice confidentially. "Did you hear about Shelly Schourek? It was a follow-home. Right down the hill in Calabasas."

The party went on. Delaney fretted. Had a second beer. Jack Cherrystone joined them and gave a farcical synopsis of a movie he'd just done the trailer for, yet another apocalyptic futuro cyberpunk vision of Los Angeles in the twenty-first century. People gathered round when he shifted from the merely thunderous tones of his everyday voice to the mountain-toppling hysteria of the one he wielded professionally. "They brokered babies!" he roared, "ate their young, made love an irredeemable sin!" Jack's eyes bugged out. He shook his jowls and waved his hands as if he'd dipped them in oil. It was a real performance, all of that voice pouring out of so small a vessel, and Delaney found himself laughing, laughing till he felt something uncoil inside him, overcooked turkeys, mucilaginous potatoes and other culinary disasters notwithstanding. He finished the second beer and wondered if he should have a third.

That must have been about four in the afternoon—Delaney couldn't place the time exactly in the frantic sequence of events that followed, but he remembered looking at his watch about then and thinking he had to excuse himself soon if there was any hope of serving dinner by six. And then the sirens went off and the first of the helicopters sliced overhead and someone jumped up on one of the tables in the backyard and shouted, "Fire! Fire in the canyon!"

Kyra had been enjoying herself. Delaney might have looked constipated, wearing what she liked to think of as his night-before-the-exams face, sweating the little details of their dinner party—the firmness of the turkey, the condition of the silverware and god knew what else— but she was kicking back, not a care in the world. Everything's under control, she kept telling him, don't worry. She'd had everything organized for days, right down to the last detail—all it would take was to reheat a few things in the microwave and uncork the wines. She'd already finished her run for the day and swum forty laps too (in anticipation of taking on a few superfluous calories), the flowers were cut and arranged, the turkey was in the oven, and Orbalina was more than capable of handling any little emergency that might arise. And while she could have been out showing houses—holidays were always hot, even Thanksgiving, though among holidays it ranked next to last, just ahead of Christmas—she figured she deserved a break. When you worked ten and twelve hours a day, six days a week, and sat by the telephone on the seventh and hadn't taken a real vacation in five years, not even for your honeymoon, you had to give something back to your family—and yourself. Her mother was here, her sister was on the way. She was giving a dinner party. It was time to relax.

Besides, she'd always been curious about Dominick Flood. Erna was forever dropping his name, and there was always something hushed and secretive about the whole business—his conviction, the anklet he had to wear, his wife leaving him—and though he was known to entertain frequently (what else could he do?) Kyra had never met him till now or been inside the house either. She had to admit she was favorably impressed. The house was tasteful, nothing splashy or showy, quintessentially Southwestern, with a few really fine details like the Talavera tiles in the kitchen set off by a pair of ancient *retablos* depicting a saint at prayer, and it was interesting to see what he'd done with a floor plan identical to theirs. And the man himself had proven to be no disappointment either. Oozing charm. And with something dangerous in his eyes, the way he glanced at you, the easy crackle of his voice. He'd made one convert, at least—her mother hadn't left his side since they got there. It was a pity he couldn't come to dinner.

Kyra found herself drifting easily from group to group, almost as much at home as if it were her own party. She knew at least half the people here, and was curious about the ones she didn't know—Dominick's friends from outside Arroyo Blanco—in the same way she was curious about him. If she'd expected gangster types or little Milkens or whatever, she was disappointed. There wasn't a crack in the façade.

She talked to a couple from Brentwood about cacti, nineteenth-century Japanese prints, property values and yachts, and to a muddled, bespectacled man in his thirties who seemed to be some sort of scholar devoted to plowing through ancient manuscripts at the Vatican, though to what purpose she never determined. And then there was the group of three—two sisters and the husband of the chunkier of the two (or was it the slimmer?)—who kept urging her to refill her wineglass, though one was her limit, and with whom she discussed tennis, Nahuatlan figurines, property values and the North American Free Trade Agreement. There wasn't a *capo* or *consigliere* in sight.

She'd refilled her glass with Evian and was huddled over the canapés with Erna and Selda Cherrystone, her own little party beginning to splinter off, though her mother was still across the room monopolizing their host, and she was feeling good, really good, for the first time in a long while. Real estate was off her mind for the day at least—though the rest of the weekend would be full-bore, the last really big weekend of the season, people trying to get in on a thirty-day escrow before Christmas—and the Da Ros place was locked and shuttered and secured for the holiday. She hadn't told anybody yet—Delaney or Jordan, that is—but now that the wall was up and their troubles behind them, she was thinking—just thinking—of another dog, a sheltie maybe, for Jordan's birthday. That would bring things full circle. That would start the healing.

She looked out the window and the sun was a golden, beneficent thing, the rich green shining leaves of the camellias steeped in it, and she saw in a moment of clarity that it was a thing to reverence and enjoy, the realtor's greatest ally, and she forgot the winds, the late heat, the mad parched thirsty air rushing through the canyon for the sea, forgot all about it, until someone got up on a table and shouted "Fire!" and the day fell to pieces around her.

Delaney was no alarmist, but with the first blast of the sirens, he couldn't help but think of Jordan, alone, back at the house. He found himself out on the lawn at Dominick Flood's with all the rest of the partygoers, staring into the twisting column of black smoke that rose ominously from the canyon below. There was no need for panic. Not yet. Brushfires broke out routinely up here and half the time the fire department had them squelched in a matter of hours, and yet the brush was ready to explode and everyone knew it—no one better than Delaney. He looked round him at the anxious faces of his neighbors, their necks craning, mouths drawn tight, a cold vestigial glint of fear frozen in the depths of their eyes. They'd survived last year's firestorms and the quake too—and the mudslides, for that matter—and no one wanted to get hysterical, no one wanted to risk looking foolish, not yet. Not yet.

Still, Delaney found himself edging back through the crowd—"Sorry, excuse me please, sorry"—until he found Kyra and took hold of her arm. "Honey, we better go—I mean, just in case," he said, and already you could smell the smoke, metallic and bitter, and her eyes widened and she breathed a single word: "Jordan."

They'd just got in the car when the wind shifted and the muscular black column of smoke stood up straight in the sky and closed a fist over the sun. Kit was in the backseat, miffed, dismayed and thoroughly ruffled, the Menaker groove etched deeply into the flesh between her eyebrows. Delaney had actually had to pry her hand away from the crook of Dominick Flood's arm. "I can't really see what all the fuss is about," she said petulantly. "We have brushfires all the time in the Bay Area and they just come in with those planes and snuff them right out." As if on cue, the first of the bombers roared overhead and dropped its pink cloud of flame retardant into the cauldron below. Delaney said nothing. They'd almost been evacuated last fall, were right on the verge of it, but the main arm of the firestorm had passed two or three miles behind them, on the far side of the ridge, and the secondary fire had burned its way up the canyon on a collision course with Arroyo Blanco until the winds shifted and it fell back into the wasteland it had just created. Eighteen thousand acres had burned and three hundred and fifty homes were lost. Three people died.

By the time Delaney reached the driveway, the sun was gone. He backed the car in and left it there, ready for a quick escape if it came to that. The turkey smell hit him as he entered the house, but all the nostalgia it had dredged up earlier was gone now, and he told himself to stay calm, it was probably nothing, as Jordan came wheeling down the hall hollering, "Mommy, Delaney, there's a fire!" and Orbalina appeared from the kitchen to give them all a quick anxious look. Kyra bent to hug her son while her own mother looked on bewildered, as if she'd just washed her hands and couldn't find a towel to dry them. No one seemed to know what to do. Was the party on or off? Was the fire just a little thing, a minor inconvenience that would add piquancy to the day and provide a few after-dinner jokes, or were their lives in danger, their home, everything they owned? Kyra lifted her eyes to Delaney and he was aware in that moment that they were all watching him, his wife, her mother, the maid and Jordan, looking for signals, waiting for him to act, seize the moment, take the bull by the horns. That was when he crossed the room and flicked on the TV, and there it was, the fire, roiling in bright orange beauty, mesmerizing, seductive, the smoke unraveling round the edges as if whole empires were aflame.

They all stood there in silence while the camera pulled back to show the bombers diving on the flames and the helicopters hovering with a tinny televised clatter that mocked the booming vibrations overhead, and a voice that couldn't suppress a secret thrill said, "Driven by Santa Ana winds, the blaze, which officials now think began along the bed of Topanga Creek just below Fernwood less than an hour ago, was at first headed toward the Pacific Coast Highway, and all residents of the lower canyon are being evacuated. But as you can see from our dramatic helicopter footage, the winds have just now shifted and the main body of the fire seems to be climbing toward the populated areas around Topanga Village . . ."

That was all Kyra needed to hear. "Load up the cars!" she cried, and though she was still standing in place her movements were frantic, as if she were a conductor urging the full orchestra to a crescendo. "I want the photo albums, if nothing else—and Jordan, you pack clothes, hear me, clothes first, and then you can take video games."

"All right," Delaney heard himself say, and his voice was a desperate gulp for air, "and what should I take? The electronics, I guess. The computer. My books."

Kit sank heavily into the armchair, her gaze fixed on the TV and the glorious billowing orange-red seduction of the flames. She glanced up at Delaney, at Kyra, at the grim uncomprehending face of the maid. She was dressed in a champagne suit with a frilly mauve blouse and matching heels, her hair perfectly coiffed, makeup flawless. "Is it really that serious?"

No one had moved. Not yet, not yet. They all turned back to the TV, hoping for a reprieve, hoping that they'd been watching old footage, color-enhanced pictures of the Dresden bombing, anything but the real and actual. But there it was, the fire, in living color, and there the familiar studio set and the anchorpersons so familiar they might have been family. The anchorpersons were clucking and grieving and admonishing, straining their prototypic features to hear the dramatic eyewitness testimony of a reporter standing on the canyon road with his windblown hair and handheld mike: oh, yes, ladies and gentlemen, this was the real thing, oh, yes, indeed.

Kyra looked as if she were about to lift off and shoot through the ceiling. Orbalina, whose English was limited to a response to the six or seven most common scullery commands, stared at the screen in disbelief, no doubt thinking about her apartment in Pacoima and how she was going to get there if the buses weren't running—and this meant the buses wouldn't be running, didn't it? Jordan clung to his mother's leg. He was staring fascinated at the televised flames, his mother's admonition to pack already forgotten. And Kit, though she sank ever more deeply into the folds of the chair, still didn't seem to understand. "But they haven't told *us* to evacuate," she protested weakly. "I mean, no one said a word about the upper canyon. Did they?"

"We better shut off the turkey," Delaney said, and that seemed to lift the spell. "Just in case."

2

SO SHE SAT THERE, AS MISERABLE AS SHE'D EVER been in her life, and closed her mind down till the world went from a movie screen to a peephole, and still she wanted to close the peephole too. She was going mad, dancing round the edges of the abyss, and she didn't care. The baby grew and it pressed on her organs and made her skin flush with a stipple of red like a rash. Cándido gave her food and she ate it. But she wouldn't sleep with him. Wouldn't talk to him. It was all his fault, everything, from the stale air in the bus on the ride from Cuernavaca to Tijuana and the smell of the dump to this place, this vacancy of leaves and insects and hot naked air where men did dirty things to her and made her pee burn like fire. She looked through her peephole at the gray leaves of the gray trees and thought of Soledad Ordóñez, the stooped old shapeless woman from the San Miguel *barrio* who didn't speak to her husband for twenty-two years because he sold their pig in San Andrés and was drunk for a week on the proceeds. He was dying, stretched out on his deathbed with the priest and their three sons and four daughters there and all their seventeen grandchildren and his brother too, and he could barely croak out the words, "Soledad, talk to me," and her face was stone and the priest and the brother and all the grandchildren held their breath, and she said one word, "Drunkard," and he died.

América missed her mother with a pain of longing so intense it was as if some part of her body had been removed. She missed her sisters and her bed in the corner of the back room with the posters of rock stars and *las reinas del cine* above it and Gloria Iglesias and Remedios Esparza and the other girls she used to go around with. She missed human voices, laughter, the smells of the street and marketplace, the radio, TV, dances and shops and restaurants. And who had deprived her of all this? Cándido. And she hated him for it. She couldn't help herself.

But then one day, lying there by the desolate stream like some dead thing, América heard a bird calling, three high-pitched notes and then a quavering sustained low-throated whistle that broke her heart with the sadness of it, over and over, that sad beautiful bird calling for her mate, her love, her husband, and América felt the sun touch her face like the hand of God, and the peephole snapped open like the shutter of a camera. It wasn't much, just a fraction, the tiniest opening, but from that day on she began to recover. Her baby was coming. Cándido loved her. She made coffee the next morning, cooked him a meal. When he was gone she dug out the peanut butter jar and counted the limp gray bills there, the silver hoard of change, and she thought: Soon, soon. She wouldn't talk to him yet. She wouldn't smile at him. She hurt with a disappointment so yawning and wide she couldn't help spilling him into it, holding his head down in the black bitter waters, and that was true and unchanging and ongoing, but each day now the gulf inside her began to close even as the peephole widened.

And now, today, when he came back with the turkey that had dropped down out of heaven, the *Tenksgeevee* turkey, she couldn't make him suffer anymore. She was no Señora Ordóñez, she couldn't live a life of accusation and hatred, serving the coffee in a funereal dress, throwing down the plate of eggs and beans as if it were a weapon, always biting her lip and cursing in her head. She laughed to see him there, wet to the waist, the clink of the beer bottles, the big naked bird and gobble, gobble, gobble. He clowned for her, danced round the sandspit with the bird atop his head, doing a silly jogging *brinco* step like a man strapped to a jackhammer. The leaves were green again, the sky blue. She got up and held him.

And the fire, when it leapt to the trees like the coming of the Apocalypse, didn't affect her, not at first, not for a minute anyway. She was so intent on driving the sharp green stake of oak through the frozen carcass of the bird, so fixated on the image of crackling brown skin and rice with drippings, so happy to be alive again, that the roar didn't register. Not until she looked up and saw Cándido's face and every living leaf and branch and bole wrapped in a vesture of flame. That was half a second before the panic set in, half a second before the numbing crazy bone-bruising flight up the hill, but half a second in which she wished with all her heart that she'd been strong enough to let the peephole close down forever.

For Cándido, it was a moment of pure gut-clenching terror, the moment of the fatal mistake and the reaping of the consequences. What would he liken it to? Nothing, nothing he'd ever seen, except maybe the time in Arizona when the man they called Sleepy burned to death under the tractor when his cigarette ignited a spill of gasoline from the tank. Cándido had been up his ladder in a lemon tree, picking, and he heard the muted cry, saw the flames leap up and then the bright exploding ball of them. But now he was on the ground and the flames were in the trees, swooping through the canyon with a mechanical roar that stopped his heart.

There was no heat like this, no furnace, no bomb, no reactor. Every visible thing danced in the flames. América was going to die. He was going to die. Not in a rocking chair on the porch of his little house surrounded by his grandchildren, but here and now, in the pit of this unforgiving canyon. Ahead of them, down the only trail he knew, the flames rose up in a forty-foot curtain; behind them was the sheer rock wall of their cul-de-sac. He was no mountain goat and América was so big around she could barely waddle, but what did it matter? He sprang at her, jerked her up from the sand and the white frozen carcass of the bird—and it would cook now, all right—and pulled her across the spit to the rock wall and the trickle of mist that fell intermittently from above. "Climb!" he screamed, shoving her up ahead of him, pushing at her bottom and the big swollen ball of her belly, fighting for finger- and toeholds, and they were climbing, both of them, scaling the sheer face of the rock as if it were a jungle gym.

The heat seared his skin through the fabric of his shirt, stung the exposed flesh of his hands and face. There was no air, not a breath, all the oxygen sucked up to feed the inferno, and with each step the rock went rotten beneath their feet. He didn't think they were going to make it, but then he gave América a final frantic shove and they were over the top and sitting in a puddle of water in a place that was as new to him as the back side of the moon, though he'd lived within spitting distance of it all these months. There were no pools here, no rills or falls—there was hardly any water at all. A staggered run of puddles retreated to the next tumble of rock, and beyond that it was more of the same, the canyon a trap, its walls a hundred feet high, unbroken, impregnable. The wind screamed. It screamed for blood, for sacrifice, for *Tenksgeevee*, and the flames answered it, leaping behind them to the height of the ledge with a roar like a thousand jets taking off at once. And then Cándido and América were running up the streambed, stumbling over rocks, splashing through the muck and tearing the flesh of their arms and hands and feet on the talons of the scrub till they reached the next obstruction and went up and over it, and still they kept going.

"Don't stop! No!" Cándido cried, slapping furiously at América every time she faltered. "Keep going! Run, *mujer*, run!" The wind could change direction at any moment, at whim, and if it did they were dead, though he knew they should have been dead already, cremated along with the turkey. He urged her on. Shoved and shouted and half-carried her. The canyon was a funnel, a conduit, the throat of an inconceivable flamethrower, and they had to get up and out of it, up to the road and across the blacktop and on up through the chaparral to the high barren rock of the highest peak. That was all he could think of, up, up and up, that naked rock, high above it all, and there was nothing to burn up there, was there?

They fumbled round a turning in the streambed, the wall falling back and away from them as the gorge widened, and there it was, the answer to Cándido's half-formed prayers: a way out. A second mountain lay at their feet, a mountain of junk hurled over the precipice above by generations of heedless *gabachos*. "Climb!" Cándido shouted, and América, sweating, bleeding, tears of rage and fear and frustration in her eyes, began to climb up over the hood of an accordioned car, her belly swinging out and away from her like an untethered balloon. Cándido scrambled up behind her, knocking aside toasters, water heaters, bedsprings, the refuse of a thousand kitchens and garages. The mass gave gently but held, locked in place by the heavy settled chassis of the automobiles, and as the smell of smoke came to them, as the wind shifted and the flames sent up a demonic howl, they reached a beaten hardpan promontory and struggled through the brush to the road.

The road was chaos. Firefighters ran shouting up and down the length of it, sirens wailed, lights flashed, the police were there, everywhere, the road closed going down, the last straggling automobiles coming up. Cándido took his wife by the hand and hurried up the road to the Chinese store—closed and shuttered and without a car in the lot—and ducked around back, searching along the foundation for a hose bib. They collapsed there, behind the store, gulping water from a hose, precious water, wetting their faces, soaking their clothes. A little water—the Chinamen wouldn't mind, and who gave a damn if they did? Cándido's throat was raw. A big airplane, hunkering low, brushed the treetops overhead. "I'm scared," América whispered.

"Don't be scared," he said, though he himself was terrified. What would they do to him now, what would they do if they found out? They had the gas chamber here in California, didn't they? Sure they did. They'd put him in a little room with cyanide pellets and his lungs would fill with the corrosive fumes, but he wouldn't breathe, wouldn't open his mouth, he wouldn't . . . He took a long drink from the slack hose and thought he was going to vomit. The smoke was blacker now, pouring over them. The wind had changed and the fire was coming up the canyon. "Get up," he said, and his voice was shot through with urgency, with panic, infested with it, a crazy man's voice. "We've got to go. Now!"

She sat there in the mud from the hose, her big maternity shorts soaked through, the big wet folds of the maternity blouse clinging to the perfect ball of her belly, hair in her mouth, her face smudged and bleeding, her eyes wild. "No," she said, "I won't get up. I'm tired. I feel sick."

He jerked her to her feet. "You want to burn?" he shouted, and his grip on her arm was punishing. "You want to die?"

The smoke thickened. There was no one around, no one, and it was eerie, spooky, like some horror movie with the aliens closing in. Sirens wailed in the distance. América snatched her arm away from him, curled her lip to show her teeth. "Yes," she hissed. "Yes, I do."

It was dark, darker than Cándido could ever have imagined it, all the homes in the canyon without electricity, the people evacuated, a pall of smoke closing over the sky against the distant flare of the fire. From here, high up the canyon, the fire sat low on the horizon, like a gas burner glowing under the great black pot of the sky. The winds had died down with nightfall, and the blaze was in remission, settling into its beds of coals to await the coming of day and the return of the winds. Or maybe they would put it out, maybe the *gringos* would keep attacking it with their planes and their chemicals till they'd snubbed it out like a cigarette ground under the heel of a boot. Cándido didn't know what the next day would bring, but as he looked down into the darkened canyon he felt awed by the enormity of his bad luck, stunned by the chain of events that had led from the windfall of the turkey and the simple joy of the campfire to this nightmare of flames and smoke and airplanes that exploded across the sky. Had he really been the cause of all this? One man with a match? It was almost inconceivable, too much for his poor fevered brain to take in.

But he didn't want to think about it. He was in trouble, deep trouble, and he needed to take stock of the situation. He was lost, hungry, with sixteen dollars and thirty-seven cents and a rusted switchblade in his pocket and all their hoard of money, their apartment fund, buried somewhere in the midst of the conflagration, and for the past two hours América had been complaining of pains deep in her gut, pains down there where the baby was, and wouldn't it be just his luck if the baby came now, at the worst possible time? It was the story of his life, pinched like a bug between two granite rocks, and how long before he was squashed?

They were lying in a clump of bushes somewhere halfway up the western rim of the canyon, and he knew now what a worthless plan it had been to try for the top. The fire would have caught them in the chaparral and they wouldn't have had a chance. But he was afraid of the road, of all those *gringo* police and firemen, and he was guilty and scared and ashamed and all he could think of was making it to that peak where they'd be safe. He'd been stupid. Panicky and stupid. But now the fire was back in its lair, at least till morning, and they were in the middle of nowhere and América lay beside him like a shadow, crying out with pain every few seconds. What now? What next? They didn't even have water.

"I'm afraid," América said for the second time that day, her voice pinched and low, coming at him out of the void. All around them the brush crepitated with the tiny feet of rodents and lizards and the shuffling slink of snakes and insects fleeing the fire. There was a crash of bigger things too—deer, he supposed—and a persistent stirring and scratching of dead leaves that could have been anything from a skunk to a bobcat. He didn't answer her, not right away, not until he confirmed what he'd been dreading: "Cándido," she whispered, "I think my water broke. The baby's coming, I can't help it." She paused to draw in a sharp breath. "It's coming."

"It's going to be all right," he told her, and he knelt beside her in the dark and ran his fingers over her face and stroked her brow, but all the while he could feel the little wheels racing inside him. There was no doctor here, no midwife, no apartment, no hospital, electricity, water, no roof even. He'd never delivered a baby. He'd never seen one delivered, except in the movies, and then it always happened off-camera, the honey-skinned actress in a sweat and crying out, a jerk of the camera, and there it was, the baby, clean and healthy and beautiful and wrapped in a snowy towel. América moaned, a deep quavering gasp of a moan that made his legs go weak with fear. She was so small. Too small. This wasn't the way it was supposed to be. "Cándido," she whispered, "I'm thirsty. So thirsty."

He got to his feet. The night clung to him like a stocking. Off in the distance, to the north, there was a string of lights, cars turning back at the top of the canyon, a police cordon maybe, and just to the west of that was the staging area for the helicopters. But that was at least three or four miles as the crow flies, and how could he get her there, and if he did, then what? They'd seize him in a minute, a Mexican coming out of the bushes and the whole canyon ablaze—they'd see it in his eyes, see it in the color of his skin and the way he slouched up to them like a whipped dog, and what kind of mercy could he expect then?

"You stay here," he told her, his own voice as strange in his ears as a disembodied voice talking out of the radio. "I'm going to see if I can't find a house or, or—" He didn't finish the thought. "Don't worry, *mi vida*, I'll be just a minute. I'll find help, I will."

And then he was weaving his way through the scrub, drawn like an insect to the promise of the distant lights. A helicopter clattered off down the valley, its running lights blinking green and red. Something plunged into the bushes ahead of him. He went a hundred feet and called out. América answered him. He couldn't go too far or he'd lose her, he knew that, and he was afraid of losing her, lightheaded with the thought of it, but what else could he do? He decided he would only go two hundred feet, counting out the steps aloud, then double back and go out in the opposite direction. The hills were studded with houses, houses climbing the hills like some sort of blight—there were hundreds of houses out here, hundreds. And roads. Electric poles, water mains, sewers. There were trash cans and automobiles and pavement. There had to be something here, there had to be.

He shouted out twice more and heard América's weak bleat of response, all the while counting higher—*ciento ochenta y uno, ciento ochenta y dos*—as he eased through the brush like a man tiptoeing across a minefield. He was worried about his feet, all the snakes on the move, the son and brother and uncle of that one he'd killed, but he went on, feeling his way, and what choice did he have? He'd rather be attacked by all the snakes in the world than have to deliver that baby out here in the desert of the night, or anywhere, for that matter. He was no doctor—he was a fool, a fool stumbling through an everexpanding obstacle course, the cards stacked against him, the fates howling, and everything that was good or precious or even possible depended on him and him alone. He'd reached a hundred and ninety-five, the wheels racing, despair in his gut, when he saw a faint glow ahead, and then, all of a sudden, it was there and he was pressed against it: a wall, a white stucco wall.

Cándido worked his way along the wall, feeling for an opening. There was no light but for the unsteady glow of the fire in the distance, and the sky was black, as black as the night sky in Tepoztlán during the rains. Gone was the yellow reflection of the city, every last watt of light driven down and conquered by the smoke of his little campfire that had gone berserk. The thought frightened him all over again. All this—the magnitude of it. If they caught him—oh, his *pinche* life would be worth nothing then. But what was he thinking? What did his life matter? América was the one. She'd followed him into this mess and she was out there now, the underbrush rustling with rats and crawling things, out there in the utter absence of light, and her baby was coming and she was thirsty and tired and scared.

The wind had shifted yet again and that meant the flames were

climbing back toward them, relentless, implacable, eating up the canyon despite all that the *gringos* and their airplanes could do. It was
hard to breathe and he could smell nothing but smoke and cinders
and the burning stench of destruction—worse, far worse, than anything the Tijuana dump could offer. Even the smell of the dead burning flesh of the dogs was preferable to this, because this was his smell,
his creation, and it was out of control. He kept going, faster now,
patting furiously at the wall, the copper taste of panic rising in his
throat. And what was behind the wall? Houses, he guessed. The houses
of the rich. Or maybe a ranch—one of those big squared-off places
with a single house set squarely in the middle of it. He wasn't sure
exactly where he was—the flight up the canyon and across the road
had disoriented him—but they wouldn't have built a wall around nothing. He had to get inside, had to find out.

And then the shed was there, announced by a sharp pain in his
knee and the dull booming reverberation of aluminum. He felt his way
around it to the back and the door that opened on the black hole of
the interior. It was hot inside, baked by the sun all day till it was like
one of the sweat lodges the reservation Indians used in their rituals,
and the aluminum ceiling was low. There was a sharp smell of chlorine
and of grass clippings, gasoline and manure—even before he let his
hands interpret the place for him, Cándido knew what it was. He felt
around the walls like a blind man—he *was* a blind man, but a blind
man in a hurry, a rush, life and death—and the tools were all there,
the shovels and the shears and the weed whippers. His hands darted
over the lawn mower, one of those ones you sit in, like a little tractor,
the plastic buckets of chlorine and muriatic acid and all the rest of it.
And then he found the shelves and felt over the boxes of seed and
gopher pellets until, *milagro de milagros,* his fingers closed round the
throat of a kerosene lantern. Half a minute and it was lit, and the shed
was a place of depth and color. He stepped outside with the lantern
and there, tucked in against the wall right at his feet, was a faucet and
a green hose coiled up against the plastic pipe of the irrigation system.

He found a cup in the shed and drank off three cups of water before filling it for América, and then he went off to get her, the lantern puddling light at his feet and throwing a dim halo into the bushes before him. He followed the wall back to where he'd jammed a stick in the ground to guide him and went off at a right angle from that, calling out to her as he went. The dirt was pale, the bushes paler. Smoke rolled over the hill like a deadly fog. "Here," she called. "Over here!"

It was hot. It smelled bad. She was scared. She couldn't believe she was having her baby in a place like this, with the whole world on fire and nobody to help her, no midwife, no doctor, not even a *curandera*. And the pain. Everything was so tight down there, squeezing in, always in, when it should be pushing out. She was in a shed, floating in a sea of rustling plastic sacks of grass seed, the sweat shining all over her like cooking oil and Cándido fussing around with his knife—sharpening it now on a whetstone—as if he could be of any use at all. The pains came regularly now, every minute or so, and they took away her breath. She wanted to cry out, wanted to cry out for her mother, for Tepoztlán, for everything she'd left behind, but she held it all in, everything in, always in and why not out, and then again and again.

She was dreaming, awake and dreaming, but the dreams were full of teeth and claws and the howls of animals. Outside, beyond the thin skin of the shed, the inferno rushed toward them and the winds rattled the walls with a pulse like a drumbeat and Cándido's face was a glowing ball of sweat and worry. She knew what he was thinking: should they run and how could they run with the baby coming now and why did it have to come now of all times and who had elected him the sole target of all the world's calamities? But she couldn't help him. She could barely move and the pains were gripping her and then releasing again till she felt like a hard rubber ball slammed against a wall over and over. And then, in the middle of it all, with the terrible clenching pains coming one after the other, the animals suddenly stopped howling and the wind ceased its incessant drumming at the walls. América heard the fire then, a crackling hiss like the TV turned up full volume in the middle of the night and nothing on, and then a thin mewling whine that was no howl or screech but the tentative interrogatory meow of a cat, a pretty little Siamese with transparent ears that stepped through the open door and came right up to her as if it knew her. She held out her hand, and then clenched her fist with the pain of a contraction, and the cat stayed with her. *"Gatita,"* she whispered to the arching back and the blue luminous eyes, "you're the one. You're the saint. You. You will be my midwife."

3

THE NIGHT CAME DOWN LIKE A HAMMER: NO GENTLY fading light, no play of colors on the horizon, no flights of swallows or choruses of crickets. Delaney watched it from behind the police barrier at the top of Topanga Canyon, his wife, stepson and mother-in-law at his side. Their friends and neighbors were gathered there with them, refugees in Land-Rovers, Mercedes-Benzes and Jeep Cherokees that were packed to the windows with their cardinal possessions, the college yearbooks, the Miles Davis albums, the financial records, the TVs and VCRs, the paintings and rugs and jewelry. Bombers pounded overhead while fire trucks, sirens whining, shot down the road. Emergency lights flashed, strobing endlessly across the panorama of massed and anxious faces, and police stood tall against the strips of yellow plastic that held back the crowd. It was war, and no mistaking it.

Kyra leaned into Delaney, gripping his arm with both hands, her head on his shoulder. She was still dressed for the party. They gazed out on the distant flames and smelled the smoke and felt the wind in their faces while dogs yapped and hastily trailered horses whinnied and the radios from a hundred cars blared out the catastrophic news. "I guess this means we can forget the turkey," Delaney said. "It'll be like jerky by now."

"Turkey?" Kyra lifted her face to fix him with an acid look. "What about the oven, the kitchen, the roof? What about all our furniture, our clothes? Where are we going to live?"

Delaney felt a stab of irritation. "I was just being, I don't know, ironic."

She turned away from him, her eyes on the creeping molten fingers of the fire. "It's no joke, Delaney. Two of my listings went up in the Malibu fire last year, and believe me, there was nothing left, nothing but smoldering ash and metal twisted up out of the ground where the plumbing used to be, and if you think that's funny you must have a pretty sick sense of humor. That's our house down there. That's everything we own."

"What in christ's name are you talking about? You think I think this is funny? It's not—it's terrifying. It scares the shit out of me. We never had anything like this in New York, maybe a hurricane or something every ten years or so, a couple of trees knocked down, but this—"

She detached herself from him then and shouted out to Jordan, who'd been darting in and out of the knots of people with one of his friends, to stay close. Then she turned back to Delaney. "Maybe you should have stayed there, then," she said, her voice harsh with anger, and she went off in the direction of her mother and Dom Flood.

Delaney watched her go. She was throwing it all on his shoulders, making him the scapegoat, and he felt put-upon and misunderstood, felt angry, pissed off, rubbed raw. He'd done his best. He'd managed to get his word processor and discs into the car in the ten minutes the police had given them between the first and final warnings—a pair of cruisers crawling up and down the street with their loudspeakers blaring—but that was about all. Ten minutes. What could you do in ten minutes? He was frozen with grief and anxiety—how could she doubt that? He hadn't meant anything about the turkey—it was gallows humor, that was all, an attempt to break the tension. What did a turkey matter? A thousand turkeys? He was standing there in the garish light, the wind in his face and his entire cranial cavity filled with smoke, angry at the world—What next? he was thinking, what more could they do to him?—when Jack Cherrystone appeared at his side with a bottle of liquor in his hand.

"It's hell, isn't it?" Jack rumbled, and he might have been doing a trailer for the next disaster movie.

"Yeah," Delaney said, his eyes focused on the advancing line of the fire and the furious roiling skeins of smoke. "And what worries me is they evacuated us—which they didn't do last year—and that must mean they think this is worse. Or potentially worse."

Jack didn't have anything to say to this, but Delaney felt the touch of his hand, the hard hot neck of the bottle. "Glenfiddich," Jack said. "Couldn't let that burn."

Delaney didn't drink hard liquor, and the two beers he'd had at Dominick's would have constituted his limit under normal circumstances, but he took the bottle, held it to his lips and let the manufactured fire burn its way down to the deepest part of him. It was then that he spotted the two men walking up the road out of the darkness, their faces obscured by the bills of their baseball caps. Something clicked in his head, even at this distance, something familiar in the spidery long stride of the one in front . . . and then he knew. This was the jerk with the "flies," the wiseass, the camper. Amazing, he thought—and he didn't try to correct himself, not now, not ever again—amazing how the scum comes to the surface.

"Fucking wetbacks," Jack growled. "I lay you odds they started this thing, smoking pot down there, cooking their fucking beans out in the woods."

And now Delaney recognized the second man too, the one with the coiled hair and the *serape*. He was dirty, covered in white dust from his sandaled feet to the dangling ends of his hair, and there were seedpods and burrs and slices of needlegrass clinging to his clothes. They were both dirty, Delaney saw now, as if they'd been rolling through the brush, and he imagined them trying to get up and around the roadblock in the chaparral and then finally having to give it up. He watched the two of them working their slow way up the road toward the flashing lights—no hurry, no worry, everything's cool—and he felt as much pure hatred as he'd ever felt in his life. What the hell did they think they were doing here anyway, starting fires in a tinderbox? Didn't they know what was at stake here, didn't they know they weren't in Mexico anymore?

"Come on, we can't let these jokers get through," Jack said, and he had his hand on Delaney's arm, and then they were moving off in the direction of the roadblock to intercept them. "I mean, we've got to alert the cops at least."

But the cops were alert already. When Delaney got there with Jack, one of the patrolmen—he looked Hispanic, dark-skinned, with a mustache—was questioning the two men in Spanish, his flashlight stabbing first at one face, then the other. Normally, Delaney would have stood off at a respectful distance, but he was anxious and irate and ready to lay the blame where it belonged, and he could feel the liquor burning in his veins.

"Officer," he said, coming right up to them, joining the group, "I want to report that I've seen this man"—pointing now at the glowering twisted face—"in the lower canyon, camping, camping right down there where the fire started." He was excited now, beyond caring—somebody had to pay for this—and so what if he hadn't actually seen the man lying there drunk in his filthy sleeping bag, it was close enough, wasn't it?

The policeman turned to him, lights flashing, the scream of a siren, bombs away, and he had the same face as the shorter man, the one in the blanket: black Aztecan eyes, iron cheekbones, the heavy mustache and white gleaming teeth. "I can handle this," he said, and his voice went cold and he said something vicious and accusatory in rapid-fire Spanish to the two men.

It didn't seem to have much effect. The tall one reached up lazily to twist his hat around so that the bill faced backwards and gave first the cop, and then Delaney, an impassive look. He said something extenuating—or at least that was what it sounded like. That was when Jack spoke up, his voice a magnificent trumpeting instrument that jerked the whole group to attention—the Mexicans, the cop, even Delaney. "Officer," he boomed, "I've seen these men too, I'm sure of it, and I'd like to know what they were doing down there at the scene of a very suspicious fire. Those are our homes down there—that's everything we have—and if arson was involved I damn well want to know about it."

A crowd had begun to gather—Delaney and Jack hadn't been the only ones to spot the Mexicans coming up the road. "That's right," a shrill voice called out at Delaney's back, a female voice, and he turned round on a heavyset woman with muddy eyes and a silver hoop in her right nostril. She wore a shawl over a heavy brocade dress that trailed in the dirt and hid her shape. "And I want to know too," she cried, stumbling over the last two syllables, and Delaney saw that she was drunk.

By this point a second patrolman had joined the first, a ramrod CHP officer with a pale-blond crew cut bristling against the brim of his hat. He gave a quick glance round him to size up the situation, stared down the big woman with the nose ring, and then, ignoring the other cop, said something in Spanish to the two Mexicans, and now they jumped, all right. The next second they were both lying prone in the dirt, legs spread, arms scissored at the back of their heads, and the new cop was patting them down. Delaney felt a thrill of triumph and hate—he couldn't suppress it—and then both cops were bending over the suspects to clamp the handcuffs round their wrists, and the tall Mexican, Delaney's special friend, was protesting his innocence in two languages. The son of a bitch. The jerk. The arsonist. It was all Delaney could do to keep from wading in and kicking him in the ribs.

Somebody's dog was barking, raging in primal fury, and the sirens tore at the air. There must have been thirty or forty people gathered now and more coming. They took a step back when the cops hauled the suspects to their feet, but Delaney was right there, right in the thick of it, Jack at his side. He saw the dirt and bits of weed on the front of the Mexicans' shirts, saw the individual bristles of their unshaven throats and jowls. The tall one's hat had been knocked askew so that the brim jutted out at a crazy angle. The handcuffs sparked in the repetitive light. No one moved. And then the big woman shouted a racial slur and the Hispanic cop's head jerked around.

That was when Delaney felt the tall Mexican's eyes on him. It was like that day out on the Cherrystones' lawn, the same look of contempt and corrosive hate, but this time Delaney didn't flinch, didn't feel guilt or pity or even the slightest tug of common humanity. He threw the look back at the son of a bitch and put everything he had into it, clenching his teeth so hard his jaw ached. Then, just as the blond cop pulled at the man's arm to swing him round and march him off toward the squad car, the Mexican spat and Delaney felt the wet on his face, saw it there spotting the lenses of his glasses, and he lost all control.

The next thing he knew he was on the guy, flailing with his fists even as the crowd surged forward and the Mexican kicked out at him and the cop wedged his way between them. "Motherfucker!" the Mexican screamed over his shoulder as the cop wrestled him away. "I kill you, I kill you, motherfucker!"

"Fuck you!" Delaney roared, and Jack Cherrystone had to hold him back.

"Arsonist!" somebody shouted. "Spic!" And the crowd erupted in a cacophony of threats and name-calling. "Go back to Mexico!" shouted a man in a sport shirt like Delaney's, while the woman beside him cried "Wetbacks!" over and over till her face was swollen with it.

The cops thrust their prisoners behind them and the blond one stepped forward, his hand on his holster. "You people back off or I'll run you in, all of you," he shouted, the cords standing out in his throat. "We've got a situation here, don't you understand that, and you're just making it worse. Now back off! I mean it!"

No one moved. The smoke lay on the air like poison, like doom. Delaney looked round at his neighbors, their faces drained and white, fists clenched, ready to go anywhere, do anything, seething with it, spoiling for it, a mob. They were out here in the night, outside the walls, forced out of their shells, and there was nothing to restrain them.

He stood there a long moment, the gears turning inside him, and when Jack offered the bottle again, he took it.

Ultimately, it was the winds that decided the issue. The fire burned to within five hundred yards of Arroyo Blanco, swerving west and on up the wash in back of the development and over the ridge, where it was finally contained. Night choked down the Santa Ana winds and in the morning an onshore flow pumped moisture into the air, and by ten a.m., after sleeping in their cars, in motels, on the couches of friends, relatives, employees and casual acquaintances, the people of Arroyo Blanco were allowed to return to their homes.

Delaney was hungover and contrite. He'd all but started a riot, and the thought frightened him. He remembered the time he'd participated in an antinuke demonstration with his first wife, Louise, and how it seemed as if the whole world was against them—or worse, when they went up the steps of the abortion clinic in White Plains and the hard-line crazies had yabbered at them like dogs, faces twisted with rage and hate till they were barely human. Delaney had thrown it right back at them, defiant and outraged—the issue was personal, deeply personal, and he and Louise had agonized over their decision, they weren't ready yet, that was all, and why bring a child into a world already teeming with its starving billions?—but the protesters wouldn't let them be, didn't even see them as individuals. Well, he was one of them now. He was the hater, he was the redneck, the racist, the abuser. There was no evidence that those men had a thing to do with the fire—they could have been fleeing on foot, thumbing a ride, walking up the road to take in the sights, *hiking*. As sober as he was, as ashamed and repentant, he couldn't suppress a flare of outrage at the thought—*hiking*, the son of a bitch—but then, he asked himself, would he have felt the same way if the men walking up the road had been white?

They had to show the address on their licenses to get back through the police cordon—the road was open to residents only, as a means of discouraging looters—and Delaney, with Jordan beside him, followed Kyra and her mother down the road, through the as-yet-unmanned gate and into the development. Delaney rolled down his window and the lingering odor of charred brush and timber filled the car with a smell that reminded him of the incinerator at his grandmother's apartment all those years ago, or the dump, the Croton dump, smoldering under an umbrella of seagulls, but the development was untouched, pristine in the morning light. His neighbors were pulling into their driveways, unloading their cars, striding across deep-watered lawns to check the gates, the pool, the toolshed, all of them wearing the faint vacant half-smiles of the reprieved. Disaster had been averted. It was the morning after.

As they swung into Piñon, Jordan began to lean forward in his seat, dangling like a gymnast from his shoulder strap. He was dirty, dressed in the grass-stained shorts, T-shirt and Dodgers cap he'd been wearing when the alarm sounded, and he was wide-eyed from lack of sleep (it had been past midnight when they'd finally decided to get a room at the Holiday Inn in Woodland Hills, the last room available). All he'd been able to talk about was Dame Edith, the cat, who'd managed to vanish just as they were loading the cars yesterday afternoon. "You think she'll be all right, Delaney?" he said now for what must have been the hundredth time.

"Of course she will," he responded automatically, and it had become a kind of mantra, "—she can take care of herself." But even as he said it, he caught sight of the place where yesterday a grove of lemon-scented gum had stood arching and white against the flank of the hill and saw nothing there but a vacancy of ash.

Jordan bounded out of the car before it came to a stop, shouting, "Here, kitty, here, Dame Edith, here, kitty," while Delaney sat there a moment to get his bearings. He'd been prepared for the worst, for blackened beams, melted plastic and twisted metal, for bathtubs hanging in the air and filing cabinets scorched like cookpans. These fires burned as hot as eighteen hundred degrees Fahrenheit, and they would sometimes suck up all the available oxygen in an area, superheating it far beyond the point of combustion until a breeze came up and the whole thing exploded as if a bomb had been dropped. Houses would burn from the inside out, even before the flames reached them, so intense were the temperatures. He'd expected annihilation, and here were the house, the yard, the neighborhood, and not a blade of grass disturbed.

Kyra had pulled in just ahead of him, and now her mother climbed out of the passenger's-side door, looking dazed. She'd spent the night on a cot at the foot of their bed in the Holiday Inn, and since they'd been up early to return to the roadblock and wait for the all-clear she hadn't had time to do her hair and make herself up with her usual attention to detail. She was showing her age, the tragedy of the night etched under her eyes and dug in deep round the corners of her mouth. Kyra, in contrast, had tied her hair back and forgone makeup, and even in her party dress she looked streamlined, girded for battle. Before Delaney could get out of the car she was in the house, striding from room to room like a field marshal, calling out the cat's name while punching numbers into the portable phone. Delaney, cradling a brown paper bag full of indispensable notebooks and essential nature guides, joined her a moment later.

He set the books down on the kitchen table and went to the oven, which still gave off a faint if unappetizing whiff of turkey. And there, inside, was the turkey itself, as tough and desiccated as a piece of camel hide. It had been a hell of a Thanksgiving, Delaney was thinking, the worst he'd ever had, when Kyra strode into the room, gave him a sour look, and reached into the refrigerator for the carton of orange juice. She pinched the phone between chin and shoulder while pouring herself a glass. "Uh, huh," she said, speaking into the mouthpiece. "Uh, huh, yes. Uh, huh."

She was concerned about her properties. As far as anybody knew to this point, the only homes lost had been eight redwood cabins just to the south of Arroyo Blanco in a little enclave of people living alternative lifestyles—hippies, bikers, palm readers, New Age enthusiasts and the like—but she was worried about a couple of far-flung listings, the Da Ros place in particular. She'd been on the verge of hysteria the previous afternoon when they'd had to leave the cat behind to what seemed a horrible and inescapable fate, but now that the fire had passed them by, Delaney could see that she'd automatically shifted her focus to her listings. The cat would be all right, she knew that. It was probably hiding under a bed somewhere, terrorized by the sirens. Or it was out back stalking all those dislocated mice. It would turn up.

"They didn't," Kyra said into the mouthpiece. The juice went untasted from her hand to the counter, a clear orange tube of light. "Are you sure it was the Da Roses'?" And then, to Delaney: "Quick, flick on the TV, will you?" and they were heading in lockstep for the living room. "Channel Seven," she breathed, and spoke into the phone again: "Thanks, Sally. Yes, yes, I'm watching it now."

Full-color scenes of destruction blew by on the screen. The flattened remains of the redwood cabins held center stage a moment, burned-out cars and vans and toppling chimneys raising their skeletal fragments to the treeless horizon, and then the scene shifted to a reporter interviewing people outside Gitello's Market.

"That was Sally Lieberman," Kyra said. "She says they showed the Da Ros place." Her voice caught. "It's gone. She said it's gone."

If this was the case, the reporters on Channel 7 failed to confirm it—at least in this segment—and their counterparts on Channels 2, 4, 5, 11 and 13 didn't report it either. They all showed the blackened rocks, the white ash, the corrugated air rising from the remaining hot spots and the sweaty exhausted firefighters plying their hoses, but already the fire was old news—there had been no deaths and precious little destruction of real property—and they turned to other matters, to the drive-by shootings, the fatal knifings, the traffic gore.

"Maybe not," Delaney said. "Maybe she got it wrong."

Kyra was wearing her frantic look. "I've got to go check."

"What, now?" Delaney was incredulous. "It's dangerous. The thing isn't out yet, you know—it could flare up again. Besides, they've probably got the road blocked."

He was right, and she knew it. She sank into the chair, volitionless, the phone clutched desperately in her hand. She was thinking of who to call next, how to get around the roadblocks, how to make things happen. "There's nothing you can do," he said, "and we've got to get all this crap out of the cars before we do anything. You don't want people stealing it, do you?"

Kit appeared at that moment, still looking a bit disoriented but more herself now—she'd wrapped a turban round her head to conceal her frayed hair and reapplied her lipstick. Delaney saw that she was holding something awkwardly in her right hand, out away from her body, as if she'd found a bit of offal or a dead rat under the bed. But what was it—a belt? A Walkman? Or no, it was a black plastic box dangling from a neatly severed strap. The thing was wrong somehow in his mother-in-law's hand, anomalous, out of place, but powerfully evocative for all that.

"I found this in my purse," Kit said, and her voice rose in surprise and puzzlement. "I can't imagine how it got there."

But Delaney could. It came to him all at once, and he glanced at Kyra and saw that she understood too. "Dominick Flood" was all he could say.

"But why—?" Kyra began.

Epiphany came to Kit with a force all its own and her eyes sank back into her head in shame and hurt—Dominick Flood had been playing a very nasty game with her, stringing her along, waiting his chance. "I can't believe it," she said.

Delaney pictured him, suave and unctuous, Kit clinging to his arm as they watched the spectacle of the fire from the safety of the police line, and the dawning realization coming over him that this was his opportunity. The monitoring device would still be sending out its signal from Arroyo Blanco, even if it wasn't from his own house, and the people at the Los Angeles County Electronic Monitoring Service would have known that he'd been evacuated overnight, that there'd been an emergency—it would probably take them days to sort it out. And Flood? A bank account in the Bahamas? A chalet in Switzerland, a beach house in the Seychelles? He would have had all the eventualities worked out.

Kit drew in a heavy wet gulp of air. She looked as if she was about to break down and Kyra had just crossed the room to sit beside her on the sofa and offer some daughterly comfort when Jordan came tearing into the room, his clothes even dirtier and more disarranged than they'd been twenty minutes ago. "Mom," he panted, and you could see his ribs heaving against the thin skin of his T-shirt, "I looked all over the place and I just can't find Dame Edith anywhere."

4

CÁNDIDO SAW THE CAT THERE AND AMÉRICA CRA-
dling it in her arms like a doll even as her body went rigid with the
pain and then relaxed and tensed all over again for the next contraction.
His first impulse was to shoo it away, but he stopped himself. If it
helped take her mind off the pains, then why not?—and it seemed
lost and hungry just like they were, content in the face of all this
smoldering disaster to curl up and comfort his wife. All right. But
the fire was creeping closer, charged one minute by the winds and
then knocked back again when they ran out of breath. It wasn't safe
here—they were taking a gamble, a big gamble—but he didn't know
what else to do but watch and wait. And pray. Maybe pray too.

He already knew what was on the other side of the wall, and the
prospect wasn't very comforting. In fact, if he let himself think about
it his heart raced so much he was afraid it was going to burst. A
development of big rich houses lay just a stone's throw away—he'd
seen that much from the roof of the shed—and it was as dark as dark
and totally deserted. He knew the place now. He'd worked in there
one day with Al Lopez on a fence, but he didn't remember the wall—
that was new, he was sure of it. What chilled him, though, was the
thought that if all these people had been evacuated, abandoning all
their things, their fine rich houses and their lawns and gardens and all
the rest, then it looked grim for him and América. The fire was coming

this way, no doubt about it, and they would be trapped, burned alive, the fat under their skin sizzling like backmeat in a frying pan, their bones charred and broken. He watched her. He sat with her. And he prayed.

Sometime in the small hours of that insufferable night América called out so sharply it was like a bark, like a dog's bark, and the cat was startled and jumped away from her and she tried to get up from the bed he'd made for her from the bags of seed. "Cándido," she croaked, "I have to go, I have to move my bowels, I . . . I can't . . . hold it in any longer," and as he tried to lift her up, to help her, he saw it between her legs, against her naked thighs and the red paste of the blood: her baby, his baby, his son. The crown of the baby's head was there between her legs, black wet wisps of hair, and he held her down and lifted her legs and told her to push, it was coming, and to push, push, push. Then there was a sound like gas released from a balloon—*Pffffffft!*—and there he was, his son, lying there all wrinkled in a bag of skin, slick with blood and mucus and what looked like curdled cheese. The noise of one of the big bombers came low overhead and there was the whoosh of its load driving back the flames below them, and Cándido smelled the strong human smell of the birth and the placenta coming out too, rich and warm in that shed full of seed and chlorine and manure. América's face was transported. She took the baby in her arms, the blue cord attached to it still, and cleared its mouth and started it breathing, started it crying, a thin mewl like the cat's, and she cradled it, the real thing, alive and healthy.

It was the moment Cándido had been waiting for. He leaned forward with the knife and cut the blue cord that was like a length of sausage and with a rag dipped in water wiped the mess from the tiny limbs and torso. He felt exultant, infused with a strength and joy that made a mockery of his poverty, his hurts and wants and even the holocaust that had leapt out of his poor cookfire in the depths of the canyon. He had a son, the first of his line, the new generation born on American soil, a son who would have all the *gabachos* had and more. And then, moving the rag over the baby's abdomen as América put it to her breast—and there, between the legs, swabbing it clean—he discovered something in the unsteady wash of light that made him pause, hesitate, stop cold with the rag in his hand. This was no son. This was—

But América already knew. "You know what I'm going to call her?" she said in a drowsy voice, the voice of someone in a dream so beautiful they don't want to let it go.

Cándido didn't answer. He was trying to absorb the fact that he was a father, finally a father—the father of a daughter—and his mind was already leaping ahead to the fire and the deserted houses and where they would stay the night tomorrow and the night after that and what would happen to him if the *gringos* got hold of him.

The voice came back to him, sticky with contentment. "I'm going to call her Socorro," she said, "—isn't that a pretty name? Socorro," she repeated, and she nuzzled the baby's tiny red ear with the bridge of her nose and cooed it for her, "Socorro, Socorro, Socorro . . ."

It was dawn. The fire had spared them. It had rushed up over the hill in the night with a flap of beating wings and now the helicopters and the big swollen bombers were diving down out of sight behind the ridge. Cándido hadn't slept, not even for a second. He'd turned the wick down low on the lantern and set it beside América and then he'd gone out to sit on the roof of the shed and watch the war of fire and water. He saw men in the distance, stick figures silhouetted against the blaze, saw the arc of their hoses, watched the planes zero in. Twice he thought the flames would overtake them and he was poised to wake América and the baby and make a run for the road, but then the winds turned on a whim and blew at his back, chasing the fire up and over the hill, and they were saved.

Nothing moved out there in the soupy light of dawn, not even the birds. Smoke hung heavy over the canyon and in the distance the blackened hills steamed and the sirens cried out in exhaustion. Cándido eased himself down from the roof of the shed and stood for a moment looking in on América and the baby. América lay asleep on her side, the baby drawn in under the cover of her arm, as oblivious as if she were in a private room in the hospital with a hundred nurses on call. The cat was there too, nestled in the crook of her leg. It looked up at him and yawned when he reached down to turn off the lamp.

He didn't have much time—two, three, four hours at the most—and he knew what he had to do and how much of him it would take. The first thing was food. He was no looter, no thief, no *pandillero* or *ladrón*, but this was a question of survival, of necessity—he had a wife and a daughter now and they had to eat—and he swore to the Virgin of Guadalupe that he would pay back everything he appropriated. There was a garden in the house directly behind the wall and he climbed silently atop the shed and slipped down over the wall without thinking how he was going to get back up again.

The yard was still, silent, the whole canyon holding its breath in the wake of the fire. No one was home. But they would be back, back soon, and he had to work fast. He wouldn't enter the house—he would never do that, not even if he was dying of hunger in the street—but there was a garden shed here too (a little one, nothing like the big maintenance shed in which América and his daughter lay sleeping as if they didn't have a care in the world), and in the shed some of the things he would need: a hammer, a box of three-and-a-half-inch nails, four burlap sacks hanging from a hook. He stuffed the hammer into his back pocket, filled his front pockets with nails. Then he waded into the garden and weighed down the sacks with cucumbers, tomatoes and squash, topping them off with oranges and grapefruits from the trees that stood in neat rows in the far corner of the yard. What else would he need? He borrowed a bow saw and a hatchet and told himself he would sneak them back in the night and no one would be the wiser.

And how to get back over the wall? A plastic bucket, ten gallons, with a snug green plastic lid, by the doorstep. But it was heavy. Filled with something. He removed the lid and saw the kibbled dog food inside, reddish-brown pellets shaped like stars. His stomach rumbled— he hadn't eaten anything since yesterday morning—and he put a handful of the pellets in his mouth and chewed thoughtfully. They tasted like paper, like cardboard, but if the dogs could eat them so could he, and he decided to bring the whole bucketful along—the people in the house would probably think the raccoons or skunks had gotten to it. He set the bucket at the base of the wall as a stepping stool, tossed hammer, saw and hatchet over the top, heaved the groaning sacks of vegetables up beside him one by one and gently lowered them down on the far side. Then he leaned over as far as he could and just managed to hook the wire handle on the bucket of dog food and drag it up the side of the wall.

He left everything where it lay, his stomach roaring, and dodged away through the brush and on up the hill, just outside the scorched zone the fire had left on the slope. The smell of the burn, rank with sodden ash, dominated everything, even the strong sweet fragrance of the sage that broke off and crumbled beneath his fingers as he hoisted himself up, hand over hand. And there was heat too, the baking heat of midafternoon in the cool of the morning, as if there were a thousand ovens turned up high, and places where persistent wreaths of smoke wound their way up into the sky. Cándido was careful to hide himself. There was movement below him now—the firefighters combing back over the area to douse the hot spots—and helicopters beating overhead every few minutes. He couldn't let them catch him out here—that would be fatal. That would involve explanations, interrogation, handcuffs and billy clubs, and if not the gas chamber, then prison, with its iron bars, *gabacho* guards and high stone walls topped with razor wire. And how would he provide for América then? And for his daughter?

It took him half an hour to find what he was looking for. Zigzagging back and forth across the face of the hill, sharp fragments of stone kicking out from beneath his feet and everywhere rats and lizards and all the other displaced creatures scrabbling away from him with a dry hiss of fur and scales, he came finally to a rock ledge that might have been a fragment of the bank of some ancient stream. It was about five hundred yards up the dry wash that opened out on the development and it afforded him a view of everything that lay below. This was the place. It would have to do. From here he could see anyone approaching from a long way off, and it was close enough to the burn area to discourage casual hikers or joggers—or even the police come to root out Mexican firebugs—and the scrub all round it was thick and tangled, interwoven in a continuous mat of spikes and thorns. They would never find him here.

As he worked his way back down to the shed he ran over in his mind what he would need. He was starting from scratch, like a shipwrecked sailor, everything they had—clothes, blankets, food, a pair of dented pots and a wooden spoon—consumed in the blaze. He thought of the money then, the replenished apartment fund, and what a joke that was—he was no closer to realizing his dream now than he was at the Tijuana dump. At least then he'd had a board to duck his head under in case it rained. But the money would have survived intact, wouldn't it, safe beneath its rock? Rocks didn't burn, did they? The first thing he would do when things settled down was slip into the canyon and retrieve it, but that might be days yet and they needed shelter now, shelter and food. They couldn't risk staying in the shed for more than an hour or two beyond this. The maintenance man would almost certainly be called in to sweep up the ash and clean out the community pool—Cándido could see the big dark brooding mirror of it in the middle of the development, like a water hole on the African plains where all the horned animals came down to drink and the fanged ones lay in wait—but there was still time, because nothing was moving yet on the canyon road. It was cordoned off. They were afraid of the fire still. Afraid of looters.

He didn't wake América, not yet. He made four trips up to the ledge and back, with the tools, the sacks of vegetables—they could use the empty sacks as blankets, he'd already thought of that—and as many wooden pallets as he could carry. He'd found the pallets stacked up on the far side of the shed, and though he knew the maintenance man would be sure to miss them, it could be weeks before he noticed and then what could he do? As soon as Cándido had laid eyes on those pallets an architecture had invaded his brain and he knew he had to have them. If the fates were going to deny him his apartment, well then, he would have a house, a house with a view.

He worked furiously, racing against time, glancing up every few seconds to scan the deserted development for the first cars. The pallets were easy to work with—perfect squares, two and a half feet to the side—and they fit together like children's blocks. Fifteen of them, connected with nails, gave him the frame of his house. The sides and back wall were two pallets long and two pallets high, and in the front he simply left a one-pallet gap for a crawl-in entrance. Then he laid four more side by side on the ground to provide a floor and keep them up out of the dirt in the event of rain, and he saw that he could stuff newspaper and rags into the three-inch gap between the surfaces for insulation. It was a good design, especially for something he'd thrown together on the spur of the moment, his fingers trembling and his heart slamming and one eye on the road, but it lacked the most essential thing: a roof.

No problema. Cándido already had a solution, if he had time, and he had to make time, had to drive himself past the hunger and the exhaustion and get everything he could before the people came back and started looking over their shoulders, looking for thieves, for fire-bugs, for Mexicans. But the first thing was América. The morning was wearing on—it must have been nine or maybe ten—and he couldn't risk leaving her in the shed any longer. He scuttled down the slope, trying to keep his balance and dodge away from the helicopters at the same time, and twice he fell, careening headlong into bushes that scraped his face and showered him with twigs and fibers that stuck to his skin and made him itch all over like the victim of a schoolboy prank. The sky was low and gray, saturated with smoke. There was no wind and the sun was barely strong enough to cast a shadow. "Amér-ica," Cándido called softly from the door of the shed. In answer, the cat mewled and then there was the gagging rasp of the baby's cry, a new sound in a whole new world. "América," he repeated, and when she answered him in that soft adhesive voice he said, "we've got to go now, *mi vida*, we can't stay here."

"I don't want to go."

"Don't give me a hard time, please don't. They're looking for me, you know that."

"I want to go home to my mother," she said, and her face was puffy and red, the eyes sunk deep in their sockets. "I want to show her my baby. I can't live like this. You promised me—you promised."

He went to her, crouched beside her and put an arm around her shoulder. His heart was breaking. He couldn't stand to see her like this, to see his daughter deprived and his wife denied. "It's not far," he whispered, and even as the words passed his lips he was startled by the sound of a car's horn—three sharp blasts—in the distance. "Come on, it's just up the hill."

Cándido grabbed what he could—a few sacks of grass seed for bedding and he'd come back for more later—and helped her up the sharp incline. She was weak still and her hair was like a madwoman's, knotted and filthy and flecked with bits of vegetation. She didn't want to duck when a helicopter suddenly appeared over the ridge and then fell away from them, but he forced her head down. The baby didn't make a sound. She was the smallest living human in the world, a face out of the immemorial past, her eyes clenched against the light, and she rode up against her mother's breast as if she were attached to it, as if she were part of her still. Cándido had to marvel at that—his daughter, and look how well-behaved she was, and not eight hours old yet.

"What is this place?" América demanded when he settled her in the roofless box, and her voice had lost its contentment.

"Just for now," he said, "just till I get this straightened out."

She didn't argue, though he could see she wanted to. She was too tired, too scared, and she sank into the corner and accepted the orange he handed her.

He didn't want to risk going over the wall again—he could see the glint of the first cars on the canyon road as he made his way back down the slope—but he had to, just one more time. There was something he'd seen in the next yard over from the one where he'd got the tools, something he needed to borrow before it was too late. He hit the shed at a bound, then crouched to peer cautiously over the wall and into the yard below, watching the windows of the house for movement. There was no sign of life, though he'd been hearing the cars for a while now—minutes, that's all he had—but this time he wasn't going to leap down behind that wall without a way up, was he? He was. He couldn't help himself. Down the wall he went, crouched low, and he saw the big doghouse in the corner of the yard and the two deep aluminum dishes—one with water, one with kibble—and he stuck his head inside the doghouse and saw the nice green wool-blend carpet they'd put in there for the dog to lie on. They would miss it, sure they would, and the aluminum dishes too, but Cándido was a human being, a man with a daughter, and this was only a dog. Was it wrong, was it a sin, was it morally indefensible to take from a dog? Where in the catechism did it say that?

He threw the whole business over the wall and darted through the hedge into the next yard, and there it was, the thing he coveted, the thing he'd come for: a roof, his roof. It was a single sheet of green-tinted plastic, with corrugations for the rain, and it wasn't even attached to the little greenhouse that sat in a clutch of fig trees just beyond the swimming pool—not even attached, just laid across the top. He stood there a moment in his exhaustion, contemplating it, and the figs seemed to drop into his hands, and then they were in his mouth, pulpy and sweet and with the thick bitter skin to chew on. All the frenzied stinking bad luck and terrible draining exhaustion of the previous day and night began to exact its toll on him then and he just stood there, locked in place, staring stupidly down into the pool. It was a little pool, no more than a puddle compared to the big lake of a thing in the middle of the development, but it was pretty, oval-shaped and blue, cool, clean blue, the water so pure it was transparent but for the film of ash on the surface. How nice it would be to dive in, he was thinking, just for a second, and clean himself of the filth and sweat and black slashes of charcoal that striped him from head to foot like a hyena . . . But then he started at a sound behind him, away and across the street—the slam of a car door, voices—and he sprang for the greenhouse.

The sheet of plastic was unwieldy, too big for the greenhouse, too big for his little shack, but there was no way to cut it to size and the voices were louder now, closing in on him. He gave it a frantic jerk and the next thing he knew he was on the ground, writhing out from under it. The plastic was looser than he'd thought, more flexible, and that made it all the harder to manipulate. Still, he managed to drag it across the lawn to the wall, and he was just working it up the side to tip it over the top when a window shot up in the house next door and he froze. There was a face in the window, a woman's face, gazing out into the yard that now lacked several hand tools, four sacks of fruit and vegetables, a plastic bucket of kibble, two dog dishes and a scrap of carpet.

Cándido didn't dare breathe, praying that the line of bushes separating the yards would screen him from view. He studied that face as he might have studied a portrait in a gallery, memorizing every crease and wrinkle, waiting for the change to come over it, the look of astonishment, fear and hate, but the change never came. After a moment the woman took her face back into the house. Instantly, with a quick snap of his shoulders, Cándido flipped the sheet of plastic up and over the wall, and then fell to his knees in the shrubbery.

"Okay, Butch, okay, puppy," a voice called from next door, and there was the woman at the back door and a huge black Alsatian romping out onto the porch and scuttering down the steps to the lawn. When it started barking—a deep-chested thundering roar of a bark—Cándido thought it was all up and he curled himself instinctively into the fetal position, protecting his head and genitals, but the dog was barking at the woman, who held a yellow tennis ball cocked behind her ear in the act of throwing it. She released the ball and the dog loped after it and brought it back. And then again. And again.

Cándido, buried in the shrubbery next door, flattened himself to the ground. There were shouts in the distance, the sound of engines revving and dying, children's voices, more dogs: they were coming back, all of them, and it was only a matter of time—minutes maybe—till someone returned to this house and saw the roof gone from the greenhouse and came out to investigate. He had to do something and fast, and he was thinking about that, his mind racing, when a further complication occurred to him: he had no way over the wall.

Next door the dog began barking again, a whole frenzied slobbering symphony of barking, and the woman threw the ball a final time and went back into the house. That was a break. Cándido waited till the dog had flipped the ball up in the air a few times, poked its head into the carpetless doghouse and settled down on the lawn to work the ball over as if it were a bone. Then he crawled across the greenhouse yard like a commando, pelvis to the dirt, and wriggled through a gap in an oleander hedge and into the next yard.

This yard was quiet, nobody home, the pool as still as a bathtub, the lawn wet with dew. But he knew this place, didn't he? Wasn't this where he'd worked with Al Lopez on the fence? He remembered that oak tree, sure he did, a real grandfather of a tree, but where was the fence? He got cautiously to his feet and that was when he saw the bare spots in the lawn where they'd set the posts—*gabachos*, they're never satisfied with anything—and then something a whole lot more interesting: a stepladder. An aluminum one. Right there against the wall. In a heartbeat he was up over the top and scrambling along the outside of the wall, hunched low over his feet, angry suddenly, raging, darting on past the plastic sheeting until he found the dog's dishes and the scrap of carpet and tucked them under his arm—and fuck the dog, he hated that dog, and fuck the fat lady who owned him too; they could buy another dish, another carpet, and who cared if a poor unlucky man and his wife and daughter died of want right under their noses? He wasn't going to worry about it anymore, he wasn't going to ask—he was just going to take.

He secreted the rug and the dishes—cookpots, they were his cookpots now—in the underbrush till he could come back for them later, then made his way back along the wall to where the green plastic sheet had fallen in the dirt. His roof. Plastic to keep the rain out, and the rain was coming, he could smell it, even over the stink of ash and smoldering brush. A crow winged past, mocking him. The sun faded away into the gloom. And Cándido, despite his exhaustion, despite everything, began dragging the big balky sheet of plastic up through the unyielding brush, and as the branches tore at him and his fingers stiffened and the helicopters swooped overhead, he thought of Christ with his cross and his crown of thorns and wondered who had it worse.

Later, after he'd flung the roof over the frame and hacked down half a mountainside's worth of brush to stack atop it and hide it from view, he slept. It was a deep sleep, the sleep of utter depletion, but it wasn't without dreams. Especially toward the end of it, when night had fallen and he woke and drifted off again half a dozen times. Then his dreams were the dreams of the hunted—they chased him, faceless hordes with bright Irish hair and grasping hands, and he ran and ran till they cornered him in a little wooden box on the side of the mountain. Then he was awake, awake to the soft glow of the lantern and América and the baby sleeping at his side. He smelled fruit—the smell was so strong he thought for a minute he was fifteen again and working a juice presser in the stand at the *mercado*. With an effort, aching all over from his ordeal, he propped himself up on his elbows and surveyed the little shack, his new home, his refuge, his hideout. There was a pile of peels and rinds in the corner, seeds and pulp chewed for the moisture and spat out again, a huge pile, and then he looked at América, asleep, her lips chapped and her chin stained with the juice.

This was no good. She'd wind up with diarrhea if she didn't have it already. She was nursing, for Christ's sake—she needed meat, milk, eggs, cheese. But how could he get it? He didn't dare show his face at the store, and even if he did, all his money but for sixteen dollars was down there in the blackened canyon, cooling off beneath a blackened rock. Meat, they needed meat for a stew—and at the thought of it, of stew, he felt his salivary glands tighten.

It was at that moment, as if it were preordained, that the cat reappeared, delicate, demanding, one gray foot arrested at the doorframe. "Meow," the cat said.

"Kitty, kitty," Cándido said. "Here, kitty."

5

IT DIDN'T LOOK GOOD. BOTH SIDES OF THE ROAD
were blackened, the chaparral gone, the trees scorched. Kyra drove out
of the normal world and into the dead zone, where the underbrush
had been so completely eradicated she would have thought it had been
bulldozed if it weren't for the crablike clumps of charred sticks here
and there and the pale-gray ash that inundated everything and still,
two days later, gave off heat. The trees that had survived—oaks,
mostly—were scarred all the way up to their denuded crowns and the
ones out on the margins of the fire's path were charred on one side
and still green on the other. She held her breath as she came round
the last turn and caught a glimpse of the skewed remains of the
Da Ros gate.

She was wearing jeans and sneakers and she'd thought to bring along
a pair of work gloves, and she stopped the car now and got out to see
if she could move the gate back manually. It wouldn't budge, what was
left of it. She could see that the fire had swept right up the drive,
scouring the earth and leveling the trees, and that the gate, with its
ornamental grillwork and iron spikes, hadn't been able to hold it back.
The gate had been bent and flattened, the paint vaporized and the
wheels seized in their track. There was no way to drive into the property: she would have to walk.

More than anything—more than the acid stink of the air or the sight of all that mature landscaping reduced to ash—it was the silence that struck her. She was the only thing moving beneath the sun, each step leaving a print as if she were walking in snow, and she could hear the faint creak of her soles as they bent under her feet. No lizard or squirrel darted across the path, no bird broke the silence. She steeled herself for what was coming.

It wasn't her house, not really, she kept telling herself, and she wasn't the one who was going to have to absorb the loss. She would call Patricia Da Ros late tonight, when it would be morning in Italy, and let her know what had happened. If the place had been miraculously spared—and these things happened, the wildfires as unpredictable as the winds that drove them, torching one house and leaving the place next door untouched—it was going to be a hard sell. She'd already had three buyers call up to wriggle out of done deals on houses in the hills, and she knew that nobody would want to even look up here till spring at least—they had short memories, yes, but for the next six months it would be like pulling teeth to move anything anywhere near here, even a horse trailer. But if the house wasn't too bad, she'd have to get the Da Roses' insurer to re-landscape ASAP, and maybe she could use the fire as a selling point—it wouldn't burn here again in this lifetime, and that was a kind of insurance in itself . . .

And then she came over the hill and into the nook where the garage used to be and saw the tall chimneys of the house standing naked against the stark mountains and the crater of the sea: the rest was gone. The leather-bound books, the period furniture, the paintings, the rugs, the marble and the Jacuzzi and the eight and a half bathrooms—gone, all gone. Even the stone walls had crumbled under the weight of the cascading roof, the rubble scattered so far out you would have thought the place had been dynamited.

She'd been prepared for this—she'd seen it before—but still, it was a shock. All that beauty, all that perfection, all that exquisite taste, and what was it worth now? She couldn't bring herself to go any closer—what was the point? Did she really want to see the crystal chandeliers melted into a dirty gob of silica or discover a fragment of statuary pinned beneath a half-charred beam? She turned away—let the insurance adjusters work it out, let them deal with it—and started the long walk down the driveway without looking back.

Her other listing up here, a contemporary Mediterranean on two and a half acres with a corral and horse barn, hadn't been touched, not a shingle out of place. And why couldn't that have gone up instead? It was a choice property, on a private road and with terrific views, but it was nothing special, nothing unique or one of a kind, like the Da Ros place. What a waste, she thought, kicking angrily through the ash, bitter, enraged, fed up with the whole business. It was the Mexicans who'd done this. Illegals. Goons with their hats turned backwards on their heads. Sneaking across the border, ruining the schools, gutting property values and freeloading on welfare, and as if that wasn't enough, now they were burning everybody else out too. They were like the barbarians outside the gates of Rome, only they were already inside, polluting the creek and crapping in the woods, threatening people and spraying graffiti all over everything, and where was it going to end?

They'd held the two Mexicans for the fire—the same two who'd sprayed that hateful filth across the walls of the house—but they'd let them go for lack of evidence. And what a joke that was. They couldn't even be deported because the police and the INS weren't allowed to compare notes. But they'd done it, she knew they had, just as surely as if they'd piled up the brush, doused it with gasoline and set fire to the house itself. It was incredible. Beyond belief. She was in such a state by the time she reached the car her hand trembled as she punched in the office on her phone. "Hello, Darlene?" she said.

Darlene's voice was right there, a smooth professional chirp: "Mike Bender Realty."

"It's me, Kyra."

"Oh. Hi. Everything all right?"

Kyra gazed out the windshield on the wasteland around her, real estate gone bad, gone terminally bad, and she was still trembling with anger, the sort of anger the relaxation tapes couldn't begin to put a dent in, and she took it out on the receptionist. "No, Darlene," she said, "everything's not all right. If you really want to know, everything sucks."

Delaney dropped Kit at the airport on Sunday afternoon, and it was past four by the time he and Jordan got back. He was surprised to see Kyra's car in the driveway—Sunday was open house day and she rarely got home before dark this time of year. He found her in the TV room, the sound muted on an old black-and-white movie, the multiple-listings book facedown in her lap. She looked tired. Jordan thundered in and out of the room, a glancing "Hi, Mom!" trailing behind him. "Tough day?" Delaney asked.

She turned her face to him and he saw in the light of the lamp that she was agitated, her eyes hot, nose red, the petulant crease stamped into her brow. "The Da Ros place is gone," she said. "I was up there this afternoon—they finally opened the road."

His first impulse was to congratulate her—no more nighttime treks to close the place up, one less worry in their lives—but he saw that it would be a mistake. She was wearing the look that had come across her face the day the stranger had locked the dog in the car out back of the Indian restaurant, and in the absence of the stranger, all her firepower would come to bear on him and him alone. "But you knew that, didn't you? I mean, didn't Sally Lieberman call and say she'd seen the house on the news?"

"She wasn't sure." Kyra's voice had grown quiet. "I was hoping, you know? That house really—I don't know, I loved that house. I know it wasn't for you, but if I could have had my choice of any house in all of Los Angeles County, that would have been it. And then, after all the work I put into it, to see it like that—I just don't know."

What could he say? Delaney wasn't very good at consolation—he felt the loss, any loss, too much himself. He crossed the room and sat beside her on the couch, but he sensed he shouldn't put his arm around her yet—there was something else coming.

"I can't believe they just let them go like that," she said suddenly.
"Who?"

"Who do you think? The Mexicans. The ones that burned down my house."

Delaney couldn't believe it either. He'd even called Jack about it and Jack had used the occasion to shoot holes in what was left of the sinking raft of his liberal-humanist ideals. What did you expect? Jack had demanded. You give all these people the full protection of our laws the minute they cross the border and you expect them to incriminate themselves? Where's the evidence? Yes, all right, they determined the thing was started by an illegal campfire in the lower canyon, and these two men were seen walking up the canyon road, fleeing the fire just like everybody else—where's the proof they started it? You think they're going to admit it, just like that?

Delaney had been outraged. The fire had given him a real scare, and though he knew it was regenerative, a natural and essential part of the chaparral environment and all that, this was no theoretical model—this was his canyon, his house, his life. It made him seethe to think of the ruined holiday, the panic of packing up and running, the loss of wildlife and habitat, and all because some jerk with a match got careless—or malicious. It made him seethe and it made him hate. So much so it frightened him. He was afraid of what he might do or say, and there was still a part of him that was deeply ashamed of what had happened at that roadblock Thursday night. "The whole thing is crazy," he said finally. "Just crazy. But listen, it could have been a lot worse. We're okay, we made it. Let's just try and forget about it."

"Look at the Da Roses, look what they lost," Kyra said, lifting the book wearily from her lap, as if the weight of all those properties were bearing her down, and set it on the coffee table. "How can you say 'forget about it'? The same thing's going to happen in these canyons next year and the year after that."

"I thought you said he killed himself."

"That's not the point. His wife's alive. And their children. And all of that artwork, all those antiques—they were priceless, irreplaceable."

There was a silence. They both stared numbly at the screen, where a couple Delaney didn't recognize—B stars of the forties—embraced passionately against a shifting backdrop of two-lane highways and hotel lobbies rife with palms. Finally Delaney said, "How about a walk before dinner? We could look for Dame Edith—"

For a moment he was afraid he'd said the wrong thing—the cat had been missing for three days now and that was another sore point—but Kyra gave him half a smile, reached out to squeeze his hand, and then got to her feet.

Outside, it was overcast and cool, with a breeze that smelled of rain coming in off the ocean. And why couldn't it have come four days earlier? But that was always the way: after the fires, the rains, and the rains brought their own set of complications. Still, the stink of burning embers was dissipating and the Cherrystones' jasmine was in bloom, giving off a rich sweet nutty scent that candied the air, and things were flowering up and down the block, beds of impatiens and begonias, plumbago and oleander and Euryops daisies in huge golden masses. The windborne ash had been swept up, hosed into lawns and off the leaves of the trees, and the development looked untouched and pristine, right down to the freshly waxed cars in the driveways. Fire? What fire?

They were walking hand in hand, Kyra in her Stanford windbreaker, Delaney in a lightweight Gore-Tex backcountry jacket he'd got through the Sierra Club, calling out "Kitty, Kitty," in harmony, when Jack Jardine's classic 1953 MG TD rounded the corner, Jack at the wheel. The car was a long humped shiver of metal and the engine sounded like two French horns locked on a single note that rose or fell in volume according to what gear Jack happened to be in at the moment. He swung a U-turn and pulled up at the curb beside them, killing the engine. "Out for a stroll?" he said, leaning his head out the window.

"Sure," Delaney said. "It's about time the weather changed. Feels good."

"Hi, Jack." Kyra gave him an official smile. "All settled back in? How's Erna?"

"Everything's fine," Jack said, and his eyes dodged away from them and came back again. "Listen, actually—well, there's something I just discovered I thought you might want to take a look at, no big deal, but if you've got a minute—?"

He swung open the passenger door and Delaney and Kyra squeezed in—and it was a tight squeeze, a very tight squeeze, the floor space like the narrow end of a coffin, the head space claustrophobic at best. The car smelled of oil, leather, gasoline. "I feel like I'm in high school again," Delaney said.

"It'll only be a minute." Jack turned the key and pushed a button on the dash and the engine stuttered to life. The car was one of his hobbies. He liked to play with it on weekends, but he reserved the Range Rover for the freeway wars, five days a week, down the canyon road to the PCH and up the Santa Monica and 405 freeways to Sunset and his office in Century City.

They were silent a moment, the thrum of the car all-encompassing, every bump and dip instantly communicated to their thighs and back-sides, and then Delaney said, "So did Dom Flood ever turn up?"

Jack gave him a quick look and turned his eyes back to the road. He was uncomfortable with the subject, Delaney could see that, and it was a revelation—he'd never seen Jack uncomfortable before. "I only represented him in the, uh, the financial matter, the banking case—he has other attorneys now."

"So what are you saying—he ran?"

Jack seemed even less comfortable with this formulation and he shifted unnecessarily to give him an extra moment to cover himself. "I wouldn't call it running, not exactly—"

It was Kyra's turn now. "But he is a fugitive, right? And what he did to my mother, that was inexcusable. She couldn't be charged as an accessory or anything, could she?"

Jack fell all over himself. "Oh, no, no. She had nothing to do with it. Listen"—and he turned to them now, careful to make eye contact—"I really can't defend his actions. As I say, I'm no longer his attorney. But yes, it looks like, from all I hear, he's left the country."

And then they were outside the gate and Jack was pulling over in the turn-around they'd constructed to assist those denied admission to the sacrosanct streets of the development. He shut down the engine and climbed out of the car, Delaney and Kyra following suit. "So what is it, Jack?" Delaney was saying, thinking it must have something to do with one or another of the creatures flushed out by the fire, when he looked up and saw the wall. It had been defaced with graffiti on both sides of the entrance gate, big bold angular strokes in glittering black paint, and how could he have missed it on his way back in from the airport? "I can't believe it," Kyra said. "What next?"

Jack had gone right up to the wall, tracing the jagged hieroglyphs with his finger. "That's what they use, right? It almost looks like the writing on the stelae outside the Mayan temples—look at this—but then this looks like a Z, and that's got to be an S with a line through it, no? Is this what they wrote on that house you were selling, Kyra? I mean, can you read it?"

"They wrote in Spanish—*pinche puta*, fucking whore. They had it in for me because I chased them off the property—the same idiots that started the fire, the ones they just let off because we might be infringing on their rights or something, as if we don't have any rights, as if anybody can just come in here and burn our houses down and we have to grin and bear it. But no, this is different. This is like what you see all over the Valley—it's like their own code."

Jack turned to Delaney. A light misting rain had begun to fall, barely a breath of moisture, but it was a start. "What do you think?"

There it was again, the hate. It came up on him so fast it choked him. There was no escape, no refuge—they were everywhere. All he could do was shrug.

"I just don't understand it," Jack said, his voice soft and pensive. "It's like an animal reflex, isn't it?—marking their territory?"

"Only this is our territory," Kyra said.

And now the thing in Delaney's throat let go and the taste it left was bitter, bitter. "I wouldn't be so sure," he said.

November passed into December, Dame Edith and Dom Flood were given up for lost, the first major storm of the season soaked the hillsides with two inches of rain over a three-day period, and Delaney Moss-bacher discovered his mission. He was a man of patience and resource. He'd spent half his life observing animals in the field, diving among manatees in Florida, crouching outside fox dens in upstate New York, once even roaming the Belizean jungles with the world's foremost jag-uar expert, watching over kills and waiting through endless mosquito-infested nights for the magical photo of the big beast prowling among the lianas. He knew how to be unobtrusive and he knew how to wait. What it all added up to was Judgment Day for those sons of bitches who'd spray-painted the wall—he was going to stake it out, night after night, with a pair of binoculars and a trip-wire camera, and he was going to catch them in the act. Maybe no one had seen them light the fire, but he was going to make damned sure he got the evidence this time, and if the police wouldn't report them to the INS, he would. Enough was enough.

Kyra was against it. She was afraid there'd be a confrontation, afraid he'd get hurt. "Isn't that what we pay Westec for?" she'd argued. "And the guard at the gate?"

"But they're not doing the job," he said. "Obviously. Look: some-body's got to do something."

And he was the one to do it. This was small, simple; this was some-thing he could contain and control. He had all the time in the world. The hills were soaked and the days so short he'd had to cut his daily hikes down to two or three miles, maximum; he'd finished a column on the fire for next month's issue and the piece on invasive species had begun to come together. He sat in his study, staring at the wall, and every time he thought of those Mexicans, especially the one he'd tangled with, the shame and hate burned in him like a twist of pitch, flickering and dying and flickering all over again. And no, he wasn't going to get confrontational—he was just going to record the evidence and call Westec and the Sheriff's Department from Kyra's cellular phone, and that was all.

He set up a pair of cheap flash cameras rigged to a trip wire and positioned them so they'd shoot down the length of the wall on either side of the gate. It was the same rig he'd used a year ago when some furtive creature of the night had been getting into the bag of cat food in the garage. Jack Cherrystone had let him use his darkroom (Jack was an avid amateur photographer, currently working on a series of portraits of "the faces behind the voices," head shots of the unsung heroes who provided vocalization for cartoon characters and did voice-overs for commercials, and of course, the tiny cadre of his fellow trailermeisters), and Delaney, watching the image form in the developing tray, was gratified to see the dull white long-nosed face of *Didelphis marsupialis*, the Virginia opossum, staring back at him. Now he would try the technique on a different sort of fauna.

The first night he watched from ten till past one, saw nothing—not even an opossum or a cat—and dragged through the following morning's routine as if he were comatose, burning Kyra's toast and getting Jordan to school twelve minutes late. He napped when he should have been writing and he curtailed his afternoon hike, unable to focus on the natural world when the unnatural one was encroaching on everything he held sacred. The second night he went out just after nine, prowled around a bit, came home to watch a news show with Kyra, and then went back out at eleven and sat there hidden, within sight of the gate, till two. He slept through the alarm the next morning and Kyra had to take Jordan to school.

During the ensuing week he averaged three hours a night in the blind he'd created in the lee of a ceanothus bush, but he didn't see a thing. He watched his neighbors drive in and out of the gate, knew who was going to the liquor store and who to the movies and when they got back, but the vandals never showed. A second storm rolled in during the middle of the week and it got cold, down into the low forties, and though he knew it was unlikely that any Hispanics, Mexican or otherwise, would be out tagging in the rain, he stayed put anyway, hunched under his parka, experiencing the night and letting his thoughts wander. The rain playing off the slick blacktop at the gate made him think of Florida and the way the roads would disappear under a glistening field of flesh when the Siamese walking catfish were on the move in all their ambulatory millions. He remembered being awed by the sheer seething protoplasmic power of them, their jaws gaping and eyes aglitter as they waddled from one canal to the next, an army on the march. No one, least of all the exotic aquaria importer who brought them into the country, suspected that they could actually walk, despite the powerful intimation of their common name, and they'd slithered right out of their holding tanks and into the empty niche awaiting them in the soft moist subtropical night. Now they were unstoppable, endlessly breeding, straining the resources of the environment and gobbling up the native fishes like popcorn. And all because of some shortsighted enthusiast who thought they might look amusing in an aquarium.

But there were no catfish here, walking or otherwise. The rain fell. Water ran off into the ditches in tight yellow braids. Delaney periodically scanned the shrubbery at the base of the wall through his night-vision binoculars. The graffiti had been painted over almost immediately by the maintenance man—that was the best way, everyone said, of frustrating the taggers—and Delaney sat there watching a blank wall, a clean slate that had to be a gall and an incitement to that shithead with the weird eyes and the hat turned backwards on his head, and he watched as the Christmas lights went on over the entranceway and the sign that announced ARROYO BLANCO ESTATES, red and green lights, blinking against the blank wall in the rain. He didn't mind. This was a crusade, a vendetta.

Then he skipped a night—a clear cold smog-free night that came at the tail end of the second storm—to take Kyra to dinner and a movie. They got back at midnight and the wall was blank still, but when Delaney went to the closet to change into his thermals, jeans and windbreaker, Kyra stepped out of the bathroom in her teddy and Delaney let his vigilance lapse. In the morning, the wall was still unmarked, but Delaney discovered that both cameras had been tripped. Probably coyotes, he was thinking as he took the film over to the Cherrystones', but there was always the possibility that the Mexicans had come back and been scared off by the flash—in which case he'd never catch them now. They wouldn't be back. He'd blown it. His one chance, and he'd blown it. But then, it was probably only a coyote. Or a raccoon.

Jack was at a sound studio in Burbank, but Selda let Delaney in. She'd just had her hair done—it was the most amazing winter-ermine color, right down to the blue highlights—and she was drinking coffee from a mug and pouring words into the portable telephone in a low confidential voice. "Did you get anything?" she asked, putting a hand over the mouthpiece.

Delaney felt awkward. Only the Cherrystones and Kyra knew what he was doing, but in a sense the whole community was depending on him—there might be ten thousand Mexicans camped out there in the chaparral waiting to set the canyon afire, but at least these two were going to get a one-way ticket to Tijuana. If he hadn't blown it, that is. He shrugged. "I don't know."

Jack's darkroom was a converted half-bath just off the den and it was cramped and poorly ventilated. Delaney oriented himself, switched on the fan, located what he needed, then pulled the door closed behind him and flicked on the safelight. He got so absorbed in what he was doing he'd almost forgotten what he was looking for by the time he was pinching the water off of the curling wet strip of film and holding it up to the light.

The face that stared back at him, as startled and harshly fixed in the light as any opossum's face, was human, was Mexican, but it wasn't the face he'd expected. He'd expected the cold hard eyes and swollen jaw of the graffiti artist with the bad dentures, the trespasser, the firebug, caught at last, proof positive, but this was a face come back to haunt him from his dreams, and how could he ever forget that silver-flecked mustache, the crushed cheekbone and the blood on a twenty-dollar bill?

6

AMÉRICA NURSED HER BABY, AND CÁNDIDO BUILT his house. It was a temporary house, a shelter, a place where they could keep out of the rain and lie low till he got work and they could live like human beings. The money—the apartment fund, the hoard in the peanut butter jar—wasn't going to help them. It amounted to just four dollars and thirty-seven cents in coins fused in a hard shapeless knot of plastic. Cándido had waited three days, and then, under cover of night, he'd slipped down through the chaparral and across the road into the devastation of the canyon. There was a half-moon to guide him, a pale thin coating of light that showed his feet where to step, but everything was utterly transformed; he had a hard time even finding the trailhead. The world was ash, ash two or three inches deep, and the only landmarks left to guide him were the worn humps of the rocks. Once he got to the streambed he was on familiar ground, stumbling through the rock-strewn puddles to the dying murmur of the stream in the sterilized night. There was no chirrup of frog or cricket, no hoot of owl or even the parasitic whine of a single mosquito: the world was ash and the ash was dead. He found the pool, the wreck of the car, the sandspit and the stone, the very stone. But even before he lifted it and felt in the recess beneath it for his hoard, the money that would at least get them back to Tepoztlán, if nothing else, he knew what he would find: melted plastic, fused coins, U.S. Federal

Reserve Notes converted to dust through the alchemy of the fire. And oh, what stinking luck he had.

It was beyond irony, beyond questions of sin and culpability, beyond superstition: he couldn't live in his own country and he couldn't live in this one either. He was a failure, a fool, a hick who put his trust in a *coyote* or a *cholo* with a tattoo on his neck, a man who couldn't even roast a turkey without burning down half the county in the process. His life had been cursed ever since his mother died and his father brought that bitch Consuelo into the house and she gave the old man nine children he loved more than he'd ever loved his own firstborn son. Cándido sat there in the ashes, rocking back and forth and pressing his hands to his temples, thinking how worthless he was, how unworthy of América, whose life he'd ruined too, and of his daughter, his beautiful dark-eyed little daughter, and what she could hope to expect. The idea that came into his head in the dark of that obliterated canyon was to run, run and leave América and Socorro in the ramshackle hut with the half pot of cat stew that América thought was rabbit (The cat? She's gone home to the rich people, sure she has . . .), run and never come back again. They'd be better off without him. The authorities would be looking for him, the agent of all this destruction, but they wouldn't be looking for América, the mother of a U.S. citizen, and Cándido had heard over and over how they had clinics and housing and food slips for poor Americans, and why couldn't his daughter get that sort of help? Why not?

He sat there for half an hour, awash in self-pity, as big a fool as any man alive, and then he knew what he had to do and he picked himself up, took the lump of plastic, the bent and blackened remnant of a grill from their old cookfire and the sixteen dollars he had in his pockets and climbed up the hill to the Chinese market, where they wouldn't be so sure to recognize him, and went in to buy cheese, milk, eggs, *tortillas* and half a dozen disposable diapers. There were only two people in the store, a *gringo* customer who ignored him, and the Chinaman behind the counter, who took his money in silence.

Cándido presented the groceries to América as if they were rare treasure and fixed her a meal in the aluminum dog dish on the grill that was the only thing left of their ill-starred camp in the canyon. It was late when they'd eaten and the air was damp and cold and Cándido was thinking of the cement blocks he'd seen out back of the Chinese market and how he could remove a pallet and make a wall of the blocks, with the fire on the inside to warm the place, when América took the baby from her breast and in the shadowy shifting light of the lantern fixed him with a look. "Well," she said, "and what now?"

He shrugged. "I'll find work, I guess."

Her eyes had the look of pincers, that grasping and seizing look she got when she wanted something and had made up her mind to get it. "I want you to buy me a bus ticket with that money," she said. "I want to go home and I don't care whether you're coming with me or not. I've had it. I'm finished. If you think I'm going to raise my daughter like a wild animal with no clothes, no family, no proper baptism even, you're crazy. It's you they want, not me. You're the one."

She was right, of course she was right, and he could already feel the loss of her like something cut right out of his own body, his heart or his brain, a loss no man could survive. He wouldn't let her go. Not if he had to kill her and the baby too and then cut his own worthless throat in the bargain. "There is no money," he said.

He watched her lips form around a scowl. "That's a lie."

Wordlessly, with a brutality that made him hate himself, he dug the nugget of plastic out of his pocket and dropped it on the scrap of wool carpet. Neither of them spoke. They lay there a long moment, stretched out beneath the green sheet of the roof, staring at the little bolus of plastic and the coins embedded in it. "There's your bus fare," he said finally.

She had her baby, and every living cell and hair of it was a miracle, the thing she'd done herself though her father said she was stupid and her mother called her clumsy and lazy and unreliable—her creation, beautiful and undeniable. But who could she show her off to? Who was going to admire her Socorro, the North American beauty, born with nothing in the land of plenty? For the first few days she was too full of joy and too tired to worry about it. She was in a shack, another shack, hidden away like a rabbit in a burrow, and she was alive because of Cándido's bravery and his quick thinking; and she had her daughter at her breast and Cándido had delivered her. That was all for then. That was all she needed to know. But as he went out to scavenge things—a blanket he found on a clothesline one night, a beach towel to wrap the baby in—or left her to crouch in the bushes across from the post office and wait for Señor Willis's car that never came, she began to brood, and the more she brooded the more afraid she became.

This wasn't just bad luck, this was an ongoing catastrophe, and how long could they survive that? Cándido was the best man in the world, loving and kind and he'd never known the meaning of the word "lazy" in his life, but everything he did turned out wrong. There was no life for her here, no little house, no bathroom with its gleaming faucets and bright white commode like the bathroom in the *guatón*'s big astonishing mansion. It was time to give it up, time to go back to Tepoztlán and beg her father to take her back. She had her daughter now and her daughter was a North American, a citizen of *Los Estados Unidos,* and she could come back when she was grown and claim her birthright. But then, how would anyone know? Didn't they have to record the birth in the village or the church? But what village, what church?

"Cándido, what about the baby?" she said one night as they sat before the hearth he'd constructed of cement blocks, laying sticks on the fire while water boiled in the pot. It was raining, a soft discontinuous patter on the plastic roof, and she was lying snug atop the sacks of grass seed, wrapped in the blanket. Cándido had been gone all day, scouring the roadside for cans and bottles to redeem in the machine outside the Chinese store, and he'd come home with sugar, coffee and rice.

"What about her?" he said.

"We have to register her birth with the priest—she was born here, but who's going to know that?"

He was silent, squatting over his haunches, breaking up sticks to feed the fire. He'd managed to make the place comfortable for her, she had to give him that. The slats between the pallets had been stuffed with rags and newspaper for insulation, and with a fire even on the coldest days she was warm. And he'd got water for them too, spending a whole night digging a trench up the hill and tapping into the development's sprinkler system, cutting the pipe and running joined lengths of it all the way to their little invisible house, and then he'd buried it and hidden his traces so well no one would ever suspect. "What priest?" he said finally.

She shrugged. Socorro lay sleeping at her breast. "I don't know— the village priest."

"What village?"

"I want to go home. I hate this place. I hate it."

Cándido was silent a moment, his face like a withered fruit. "We could walk into Canoga Park again, if you think you're up to it," he said finally. "They must have a priest there. He would know what to do. At least he could baptize her."

She dreaded the idea after her last experience, but just the mention of the name—Canoga Park—made her see the shops again, the girls on the street, the little restaurant that was like a café back at home. Somebody there would know what to do, somebody would help. "It's awfully far," she said.

He said nothing. He was staring into the fire, his lips pursed, hands clasped in his lap.

"What did you do with the cord?" she said after a moment.

"Cord? What cord?"

"You know, the baby's cord. The umbilical."

"I buried it. Along with the rest. What do you think?"

"I wanted that cord. For Chalma. I wanted to make a pilgrimage and hang it in the tree and pray to the Virgin to give Socorro a long and happy life." And she saw the tree in her mind, the great ancient ahuehuete tree beside the road, with the crowds of pilgrims around it and the vendors and the hundreds upon hundreds of dried birth cords hanging from the branches like confetti. Socorro would never know that tree; she'd never be blessed. América had to catch her breath to keep from sobbing with the hopelessness of it. "I hate it here," she whispered. "God, how I hate it."

Cándido didn't answer. He made coffee with sugar and condensed milk and they drank it out of *frijole* cans, and then he cut up an onion, some *chiles* and a tomato and cooked the rice, and she wouldn't get up, wouldn't help him, even if he'd tried to force her.

It rained the next day too, all day, and when she went out to relieve herself and bury the baby's diaper, the earth was like glue. For all this time it had been powder and now it was glue. She stood there in the rain, looking out over the misted canyon, the roofs of the houses, the barren scar of Cándido's fire, and the rain smelled good, smelled of release and reprieve—smelled, ever so faintly, of home. She had to get away, even if it meant bundling up Socorro and walking all the way back to the border, and if she starved along the way, then that was God's will.

It was dark inside, dark as a hole in the ground, and when the rain slackened to a drizzle, she brought the baby outside for a breath of air. Sitting there high on the hillside, watching the clouds roll out over the canyon all the way to the sea and the cars creep like toys up the slick canyon road, she felt better. This was America and it was a beautiful place, drier and hotter than Tepoztlán in the dry season and colder in the wet, but she felt that there was peace here if only she could find it. Peace and prosperity too.

She looked down then into her daughter's face and the baby was staring past her, staring up and away into a distance she couldn't possibly contain, and it was in that moment that América felt the naked sharp claws of apprehension take hold of her. She passed a hand over her daughter's face and her daughter didn't blink. She bent her own face to Socorro's and tugged at those dull black irises with her own and they only stared, as if there were a wall between them. And then the baby blinked and sneezed and the eyes stared at nothing.

Cándido told her they were eating rabbit, but rabbit was hard to come by up here. Those other little four-legged beasts, the ones with the bells on their collars to warn away the birds, they were easier to catch. All you had to do was wait till midnight, slip over the wall and whisper, "Kitty, here, kitty." So they ate meat, even if it tasted stringy and sour, and they ate kibble and rice and whatever fruits and vegetables he dared to take. They had water. They had heat. They had a roof over their heads. But it was all a stopgap, a delaying action, a putting off of the inevitable. He'd stared so long and so hard at that strip of road out front of the post office, waiting for the apparition of Señor Willis's Corvair, that it wasn't a real place anymore, but a scene he'd devised in his brain—if he blinked, it wouldn't exist. There were no *braceros* there, not a one, and the word must have been out. Cándido didn't dare show himself and if he didn't show himself how could he get work? And if he couldn't get work, no matter how many things he borrowed from the houses beyond the wall or how many cans he collected in the bushes, sooner or later they would starve. If only he could call Señor Willis, but Señor Willis didn't have a phone. He could go back to Canoga Park, but there was no work there, he knew that already, and a hundred men ready to kill for whatever work might turn up. A little money, that was all he needed—with a little money he might think about going back to Tepoztlán, at least for the winter. His aunt might take them in, and he could always make charcoal, but América—he'd boasted to her, he'd promised her things—América would certainly leave him then, mewed up behind the gate at her father's house till she was a hag scrubbing the floors and Socorro was married off to some *chingado* her old man owed money to.

Cándido took the risk. He waited till the rain began to crackle on the pavement and the hair hung wet in his eyes, and then he stepped out of the bushes, crossed the road and stood beneath the overhang out front of the post office, stamping his feet and hugging his shoulders to keep the circulation going. Surely somebody would take pity on him and bring him home to work in a warm basement, putting up drywall or painting or cleaning out the trash. He waited, wet through and shivering, and every *gringo* who got out of his car and ducked into the post office gave him a look of unremitting hate. If they didn't know he'd started the fire personally, they all suspected it, and where there was once tolerance and human respect, where there was the idea of community and a labor exchange and people to support it, now there was only fear and resentment. They didn't want to hire him, they didn't want to see him warm, they didn't want to see him fed and clothed and with a place to sleep at night that was better than a ditch or a shack hidden in the weeds—they wanted to see him dead. Or no: they didn't want to see him at all. He waited there through the afternoon, and when he couldn't take the cold anymore he went into the lobby of the post office, a public place, and a man in a blue uniform stepped from behind the counter and told him in Spanish that he had to leave.

América was strange that night. He huddled next to her, trying to stop shivering, and she didn't mention going home, not once, though she'd driven him half-mad with it for the past two weeks. Now it was the baby—that was all she could talk about. The baby needed to go to a clinic, the baby needed a doctor—a *gringo* doctor—to look at her. But was the baby sick? he wanted to know. She looked all right to him. No, América gasped, no, she's not sick, but we need to have a doctor check her—just in case. And how will we get to this doctor, how will we pay? He was irritated, feeling harassed, squeezed dry. She didn't know. She didn't care. But the baby had to have a doctor.

In the morning, Cándido put a pot of rainwater on the grill to boil—he'd run a length of PVC pipe off the development's sprinkler system, easiest thing in the world, what with the saw and the cement and all the elbows and connectors right there in the shed for the taking, but he didn't use it if he didn't have to—and he skidded down the muddy slope, keeping low to the cover, and went back to the post office. It was overcast, with a cold breeze coming down out of the mountains, but the rain had tapered off at dawn and that was a relief. Cándido leaned against the brick front of the building, watching the earthworms crawl up out of the saturated earth to die on the pavement and trying his best to look eager and nonthreatening to the *gringos* and *gringas* who hurried in and out the door with Christmas packages in their arms. He could hear the creek where it cut into the bank out back of the post office before whipping round to pass under the bridge and plunge into the cut of the gorge. It was a sinister sound, a hiss that rose to a roar and fell back again as a crippled tree or boulder slammed along the bed of the stream and hung up on some hidden obstruction. They would have been flooded out if they were still camped below, flushed down the canyon like waste in a toilet, battered against the rocks and washed out to sea for the crabs to feed on. He thought about that, watching the earthworms wriggling on the pavement and the postal patrons stepping delicately through the puddles as if dirtying their shoes was the worst tragedy that could befall them, and he wondered if the fire hadn't been a blessing in disguise. Maybe there was a Providence looking out for him after all.

The thought cheered him. He began to smile at the people going in and out, combing his mustache down with his fingers and showing his teeth. "Work?" he said to one woman riding up off her heels like a gymnast, but she turned away as if he were invisible, as if it were the wind talking to her. But he kept on, his smile growing increasingly desperate, until the man in the blue uniform—the same one as yesterday, a *gabacho* with a ponytail and turquoise eyes—came out and told him in textbook Spanish that he was going to have to leave if he didn't have business at the post office. Cándido shrugged his shoulders, grinning still—he couldn't help it, it was like a reflex. "I'm sorry if I'm bothering anybody," he said, relieved to be explaining himself, relieved to be talking in his own language and thinking that maybe this was the break he was looking for, that maybe this man would be another Señor Willis, "but I need work to feed my wife and baby and I was wondering if you knew of anything around here?"

The man looked at him then, really looked at him, but all he said was "This isn't a good place for you to be."

Dispirited, Cándido crossed the road and shambled over the bridge in the direction of the Chinese market and the lumberyard beyond it. He'd hardly even noticed the bridge before—it was just a section of the road suspended over the dead brush of the streambed—but now its function was revealed to him as the churning yellow water pounded at its concrete abutments and the boulders slammed into it with a rumble that was like the grinding of the earth's molars—all through the summer and fall there had been no water, and now suddenly there was too much. Cándido stood for a while outside the Chinese store, though he was nervous about that, and sure enough, the old Chinaman, the one with the goggle glasses and the suspenders to hold the pants up over his skinny hips, came out to shoo him away in his weird up-and-down language. But Cándido wouldn't give up and so he stood just down the street from the lumberyard, hoping some contractor picking up materials might see him there and give him work. It wasn't a propitious place, even in the best of times, and Cándido had never seen a single *bracero* hunkered over his heels here. Rumor had it that the lumberyard boss would call the cops the minute he saw a Mexican in the lot.

Cándido stood there for two hours, trying to attract the attention of every pickup that pulled into the lumberyard, so desperate now he didn't care if *La Migra* picked him up or not, but no one gave him even so much as a glance. His feet hurt and his stomach rumbled. He was cold. It must have been about half-past four when he finally gave it up and started back along the road, looking for cans to redeem and thinking he would watch for his chance to stick his head in the dumpster out back of the *paisano*'s market—he had to bring something back with him, anything. Every once in a while they would throw out a bag of onions with nothing worse than a few black spots on them or po-tatoes that had sprouted eyes—you never knew. He was keeping his head down and watching his feet, thinking maybe there'd be some meat that wouldn't be so bad if you boiled it long enough or some bones and fat from the beef they'd trimmed out, when a car swerved in across the shoulder just ahead of him.

He froze, thinking of the accident all over again, wet roads, *norte-americanos* in a hurry, always in a hurry, and the next car blared its horn in a shrill mechanical curse because the rear end of the first car, the one right there on the shoulder, was sticking out into the roadway and all the endless line of cars coming up the hill with their wipers clapping and headlights glaring had to break the flow to swerve around it. But now the door was swinging open and another horn blared and Cándido was poisoned with déjà vu: this inescapable white, the fiery red brake lights and the yellow blinker, it was all so familiar. Before he had a chance to react, there he was, the *pelirrojo* who'd run him down all those months ago and then sent his gangling ugly *pelirrojo* of a son down into the canyon to harass and torment him, and the look on his face was pure malice. "You!" he shouted. "You stay right there!"

7

"You!" DELANEY SHOUTED. "YOU STAY RIGHT THERE!"

He'd been coming up the road from the nursery on the Coast High-way, the trunk crammed with bags of ammonium sulfate and fescue seed, his view out the back partially obscured by a pair of areca palms for the front hallway, when he spotted the hunched shoulders, the weather-bleached khaki shirt and the pale soles of the Mexican's dark feet working against the straps of his sandals. He slowed automatically, without thinking—could this be the man, was this him?—and then he jerked the wheel and felt the rear tires yaw away from him even as the driver behind him hit the horn, and he was up on the shoulder spewing gravel, his rear end sticking out in the road. Delaney didn't care. He didn't care about the hazard, didn't care about the other drivers or the wet road or his insurance rates—all he cared about was this Mexican, the man who'd invaded his life like some unshakable parasite, like a disease. It was here, almost at the very spot, that he'd flung himself under the wheels of the car, everything come full circle, and this time Delaney wasn't going to let him off, this time he had proof, photographic proof. "You stay right there!" Delaney roared, and he punched 911 into the car phone Kyra had given him as an early Christmas present.

The Mexican stood there dumbfounded, leaner and harder-looking than Delaney remembered him, the eyes black and startled, the thick brush of the mustache making a wound of his mouth. "Hello?" Delaney bawled into the receiver, "my name is Delaney Mossbacher and I want to report a crime in progress—or no, an apprehension of a suspect—on Topanga Canyon Road near Topanga Village, just south of—" but before he could finish, the suspect had begun to move. The Mexican looked at Delaney, looked at the telephone in his hand, and then he just stepped right out into the traffic like a sleepwalker.

Delaney watched in shock as the high blue surging apparition of a pickup cab with a woman's face frozen behind the windshield framed the Mexican's spindly legs and humped-over torso in a portrait of unquenchable momentum, and then, at the last possible moment, veered away in a screeching, rattling, fishtailing blur that hit the guardrail and ricocheted into the back end of his Acura Vigor GS, his new milkwhite Acura Vigor GS with the tan leather upholstery and only thirty-eight hundred and sixteen miles on the odometer, where it finally came to rest in all its trembling wide-bodied authority. And the Mexican? He was unscathed, jogging up the opposite side of the road while horns blared and bumpers kissed all up and down the frantically braking string of cars. It was the commuter's nightmare. It was Delaney's nightmare. "Hello, hello—are you there?" cried a voice through the speaker of the phone.

Delaney didn't call Kyra. He didn't call Jack. He didn't bother with Kenny Grissom or the body shop or even his insurer. As the rain started up again, a blanketing drizzle that seeped into his every pore, he stood at the side of the road and exchanged information with the woman in the pickup. She was in a rage, trembling all over, showing her teeth like a cornered rodent and stamping her feet in the mud. "What's wrong with you?" she demanded. "Are you out of your mind stopping like that with your back end sticking halfway out across the road? And what's with your friend—is he drunk or something, just strolling right out in front of me without even turning his head? You're both drunk, you've got to be, and believe me you're in trouble, mister, and I'm going to demand the cops give you a breath test, right here and now—"

The policeman who showed up twenty minutes later was grim and harried. He questioned Delaney and the woman separately about the details of the accident, and Delaney tried to tell him about the Mexican, but the cop wasn't interested.

"I'm trying to tell you, it was this Mexican—he's crazy, he throws himself in front of cars to try and collect on the insurance, he's the one, and I've got a photograph, I caught him out front of Arroyo Blanco, that's where I live, where we've had all that trouble with graffiti lately?"

They were seated in the patrol car, Delaney in the passenger seat, the cop bent over his pad, laboriously writing out his report in a jagged left-handed script. The radio sputtered and crackled. Rain spilled across the windshield in sheets, drummed on the roof, really coming down now. There were accidents on the Coast Highway, Malibu Canyon Road, 101, the dispatcher's voice numb with the monotony of disaster. "Your vehicle was obstructing the road," the cop said finally, and that was all.

Delaney sat in his car till the tow truck arrived; he showed the driver his Triple A card and then refused a ride home. "I'm going to walk," he said, "it's only a mile and a half."

The driver studied him a moment, then handed him a receipt and pulled the door closed. The rain had slackened, but Delaney was already wet through to the skin, the Gore-Tex jacket clinging to his shoulders like a sodden pelt, the hair stamped to his forehead and dancing round his ears in a lank red fringe. "Suit yourself," the man said through the crack of the window, and then Delaney was walking up the shoulder of the road as the pale shell of his car faded away into the mist ahead of him. He was walking, but this time he wasn't merely walking to get somewhere, as on the torrid high-ceilinged summer morning when his first car was stolen—this time he had a purpose. This time—as he waited for a break in the traffic and dashed across the road—this time he was following a set of footprints up the muddy shoulder, very distinctive prints, unmistakable, cut in the rippled pattern of a tire tread.

Kyra could barely see the road. The rain had come up suddenly, closing off her view like a curtain dropping at the end of a play, and she had no choice but to hit her emergency flasher and pull off onto the shoulder to wait it out. She took advantage of the delay to thumb through her *Thomas Guide* and compare the map with the directions Delaney had scrawled on the notepad by the telephone. It was just past four and she'd taken the afternoon off to do some Christmas shopping—business was slow, dead in the water, actually, and for as long as she could remember she'd been meaning to start making a little more time for her family and for herself too—and she'd volunteered to pick up Jordan at his friend's house. She didn't know the boy—he was a friend from school—and since Delaney had dropped Jordan off, she didn't know the house either. Or the street, which she was having trouble finding.

If she'd smoked, she would have lit a cigarette, but she didn't smoke, so she put in a relaxation tape and listened to the artificial waves soughing through the speakers while the rain, palpable and real, sizzled on the pavement and rapped like a medium's knuckles at the roof of the car. It gave her a cozy feeling, a feeling of being impervious to the elements, sealed in and secure, and she looked at the map and listened to her tape and realized that for the first time in as long as she could remember she was in no hurry to get anywhere. She'd been driving herself too hard for too long, and for what? Even before the Da Ros place went up she'd begun to have days when she just couldn't seem to muster the enthusiasm to stuff envelopes with potholders or write up ads with the same tired old stock adjectives and banal abbreviations—CHARMING Monte Nido Rustic Contemp., Las Virgenes Schools, 2 ac. horse prop., 6 BR/4.5 BA, fam. rm., pool, priced to sell—or even show Mr. and Mrs. Nobody through the eternal hallways of all the eternal houses they had neither the taste nor the money to

buy and then arranging creative financing and holding their hands
through a sixty-day escrow that was as likely as not to fall out. It was
about as exciting as going to the toilet. The deal-making—slipping the
needle in and pulling it out so quickly and painlessly they didn't even
know they'd been pricked—that still got her pulse pounding, and so
did beating everybody else out for a listing, especially a to-kill-for one
like the Da Ros place, but the thrills were all too few and far between.

Ah, there was the problem—she didn't know this part of Agoura as
well as she should have, and she'd confused Foothill Place with Foothill Drive. She was on Foothill Drive now—and there, there it was,
Comado Canyon Road, in the upper-left-hand corner of the map. She'd
never heard of it before—it must be one of those new streets that jog
up and down the grassy hills like roller coasters. Everything was new
out here, a burgeoning, bustling, mini-mall-building testimonial to
white flight, the megalopolis encroaching on the countryside. Ten years
ago this was rural. Ten years before that you couldn't find it on the
map. Kyra was sure there must be some really primo properties up
here, older houses, estates, ranches the developers hadn't got to yet.
The schools were good, property values holding their own, maybe even
rising a bit—and it was just a hop, skip and jump from Woodland
Hills, Malibu and Calabasas. She should look into it, she really should.

The rain fell off as abruptly as it had begun, gray banks of drizzle
bellying up to the hills like inverted clouds, and Kyra started up the
engine, looked over her shoulder and wheeled out onto the blacktop
road. She came to a T and bore left, past a tract of single-family
homes and up into the undulating hills where the houses were farther
apart—nothing special, but they had property, an acre or more, it
looked like—and she saw half a dozen blond-haired children going up
and down a long drive, and a flock of sheep patched into a greening
hillside. The trees seemed to stand up a bit straighter here, their leaves
washed clean of six months' accumulation of dust, particulates and
hydrocarbons and whatever else the air held in suspension. It was
pretty country—real estate—and it made her feel good.

The road forked again and became narrower, a remnant of the cart path that must once have been here, ranchers hauling hay or whatever to feed their cattle, Model T's and A's digging narrow ruts along the inside shoulders of the switchbacks, woodstoves and candlelight, chickens running free—Kyra didn't know what it was, but she was swept up in a vision of a time before this one, composed in equal parts of *Saturday Evening Post* covers, *Lassie* reruns and a nostalgia for what she'd never known. These people really lived in the middle of no-where—Arroyo Blanco was like Pershing Square compared to this. It was amazing. She had no idea there was so much open space out here—and not five miles from 101, she bet, and no more than twelve or fifteen from the city limits, if that. Was it still in L.A. County, she wondered, or had she crossed the line?

It was then, wondering and relaxed, enjoying the day, the scenery, the season, that she spotted the inconspicuous little sign at the head of a blacktop drive tucked away in a grove of eucalyptus just past the Comado Canyon turnoff: FOR SALE BY OWNER. She drove right past it, parting the veil of blue-gray mist that shrouded the road, but then she checked herself, pulled over onto the shoulder and made a U-turn that took her back to the driveway. The sign wasn't very revealing—FOR SALE BY OWNER was all it said, and then there was a phone number beneath it. Was there a house in there? A ranch? An estate? Judging from the size of the eucalyptus—huge pale shedding old relics with mounds of sloughed bark at their feet—the place hadn't been thrown together yesterday. But it was probably nothing. Probably a paint-blistered old chicken shack with a bunch of rusted-out cars in the yard—or a trailer.

She sat there opposite the drive in her idling car, the window rolled down, the sweet fresh breath of the rain in her face, watching the silver leaves of the eucalyptus dissolve into the mist and then reappear again. It was twenty of five. She'd told the boy's mother—Karen, or was it Erin?—that she'd be by to pick up Jordan at five, but still, she didn't feel any compulsion. It was Christmas, or almost Christmas, and it was raining. And besides, the woman—Karen or Erin—had sounded sweet on the phone and she'd said there was no problem,

Kyra could come whenever she wanted, the boys were playing so nicely together—and you never knew what was at the end of a drive if you didn't take the time to find out. The sign was an invitation, wasn't it? Of course it was. Real estate. She pushed in the trip odometer, flicked on the turn signal, took a precautionary look over her shoulder and started up the drive.

She left the window open to enjoy the wet fecund ever-so-faintly-mentholated smell of the eucalyptus buttons crushed on the pavement and let her eyes record the details: trees and more trees, a whole deep brooding forest of eucalyptus, and birds calling from every branch. Half a mile in she crossed a fieldstone bridge over a brook swollen with runoff from the storm, came round a long sweeping bend and caught sight of the house. She was so surprised she stopped right there, a hundred yards from the place, and just gaped at it. All the way out here, on what must have been ten acres, minimum, stood a three-story stone-and-plaster mansion that could have been lifted right out of Beverly Hills, or better yet, a village in the South of France.

The style was French Eclectic, simple, understated, with a tony elegance that made the late Da Ros place seem fussy, even garish, by comparison. From the hipped roof with its flared eaves to the stone quoins accenting windows and doors and the thick sturdy plaster walls painted in the exact pale-cinnamon shade of the eucalyptus trunks and festooned with grapevines gone blood-red with the season, the place was a revelation. The grounds too—the plantings were rustic, but well cared for and well thought out. There was a circular drive out front that swept round a pond with a pair of swans streaming across it, and the pond was set off by casual groupings of birch and Japanese maple. FOR SALE BY OWNER: she'd have to play this one carefully, very carefully. Kyra let the car roll forward as if it had a mind of its own; then she leaned into the arc of the drive, swung round front and parked. She spent half a minute with her compact, ran both hands through her hair, and went up the steps.

A man about fifty in a plaid flannel shirt and tan slacks answered the door; behind him, already trying on a smile, was the wife, stationed beside a mahogany parlor table in a long white entrance hall. "You must be here to see the house?" the man said.

Kyra never hesitated. She was thinking two mil, easy, maybe more, depending on the acreage, and even as she was totting up her commission on that—sixty thousand—and wondering why she should have to share it with Mike Bender, she was thinking about the adjoining properties and who owned them and whether this place couldn't be the anchor for a very select private community of high-end houses, and that's where the money was, in developing—not selling—developing. "Yes," she said, giving them the full benefit of her face and figure and her nonpareil-closer's smile, "yes, I am."

There were places where the spoor was interrupted, the footprints erased by the force of the downpour that had swept over the hills while Delaney was sitting in the police cruiser wasting his breath. That was all right. He knew which direction his quarry had taken and all he had to do was keep moving up the shoulder till the prints became discernible again—and he didn't need much, the scuff of a toe in the gravel or the cup of a heel slowly filling with dirty yellow water. If he could track a fox that had slipped its radio collar and doubled back through a running stream for three hundred yards before climbing up into the lower branches of a sycamore, then he was more than capable of tracking this clumsy Mexican all the way to Hell and back—and that was exactly what he was going to do, track him down if it took all night.

It was getting dark, black dark, by the time he reached Arroyo Blanco Drive, and when he saw by the lights of a passing car that the prints turned left into the road he wasn't surprised, not really. It explained a lot of things—the graffiti, the photo, all the little incidentals that had turned up missing throughout the community, the plastic sheeting, the dog dishes, the kibble. The fire had flushed him out and now the drunken moron was camped out up here, spraying his graffiti, stealing kibble, shitting in a ditch. And then it came to him: What if he was the one who'd started the fire? What if the wetback with the hat was innocent all along and that's why the police couldn't hold him? This one had been camped down there somewhere, hadn't he? Delaney saw the glint of the shopping cart all over again and the trail plunging down into the canyon and the Mexican there in the weeds, broken and bleeding, and he couldn't help thinking it would have been better for everyone concerned if he'd just crawled off into the bushes and died.

But now it was dark and he was going to have to get a flashlight if he was going to go on with this—and he was, he was determined to go on with it, no matter what, right to the end. He was almost at the gate when a car pulled over and the rain-bleared image of Jim Shirley's face appeared in the window on the driver's side. It was raining again, white pinpricks that jumped off the blacktop in the wash of the car's headlights. The window cranked halfway down and Jim Shirley's skin glowed green and red under the blinking Christmas lights. "What in hell you doing out in the rain, Delaney? Looking for horned toads? Come on, I'll give you a lift."

Delaney crossed to the car and stood hunched by the window, but he didn't say Hi, Jim, hell of a night and how are you doing or thanks or no thanks. "You wouldn't have a flashlight I could borrow, would you?" he asked, the rain terracing his cheeks and dripping steadily from the tip of his nose.

Green and red. The colors settled into the big bloated face above the black band of the beard. "Afraid not," Jim Shirley said. "Used to keep one in the car but the batteries went dead and then my wife was going to replace them and that's the last I saw of it. Why? You lose something?"

"No, that's all right," Delaney murmured, backing away now. " Thanks."

He watched Jim Shirley drive through the gate and on up into the development and then he turned and in the haunted light of the red and green blinking bulbs discovered the fresh outrage of the wall, the mocking black hieroglyphs staring back at him, right there, as raw as the paint that was already smearing in the rain, right there under the nose of the guard and the blinking lights and everything else. His car was wrecked, his dogs were gone. He went right up to the wall and pressed a finger to the paint and the finger came back wet. And black. Stained black.

This was the signal, this was it, the declaration of war, the knife thrown in the dirt. First the car, now this. Delaney thought of the cameras then, of the evidence, and he tugged the cord at his feet so the flash would locate him. Only one camera flashed—the near one. The other had been smashed. He couldn't see if any of the pictures had been exposed—the light was too dim—and so he tucked the functional camera under his jacket and worked his way along the wall to the gate.

When he rapped on the glass of the guard's cubicle, the guard—a lugubrious long-nosed kid with a croaking voice and the faintest blond beginnings of a mustache—jumped as if he'd been goosed with a cattle prod, and then Delaney was in the booth with him and the kid was saying, "Jesus, Mr. Mossbacher, you really scared me—what's the matter, is anything wrong?"

It was close. Steaming. Room for one and now there were two. A red-and-white-striped box of fried chicken sat beside a paperback on the control panel, the cover of the paperback decorated with the over-muscled figure of a sword-wielding barbarian and his two bare-breasted female companions. "Your car break down?" the kid croaked.

Delaney pulled out the camera and saw that six pictures had been exposed, six indisputable pieces of incriminating evidence, and he felt as if he'd just hit a home run to win the game. The kid was watching him, his eyes like little glittering rivets supporting the weight of that nose, something sallow and liverish in his skin. They were six inches apart, their shoulders filling the booth. "No," Delaney said, giving him a grin that in retrospect must have seemed about three-quarters deranged, "everything's okay, just fine, perfect," and then he was ducking back out into the rain and jogging up the street toward his house, thinking of the photos, yes, thinking of the wrecked car and the slap in the face of the wall, but thinking above all of the gun in the garage, the Smith & Wesson stainless-steel .38 Special Jack had talked him into buying for "home protection."

He'd never wanted the thing. He hated guns. He'd never hunted, never killed anything in his life; nor did he ever want to. Rednecks had guns, criminals, vigilantes, the cretinous trigger-happy minions of the NRA who needed assault rifles to hunt deer and thought the natural world existed only as a vast and ever-shifting target. But he'd bought it. With Jack. They'd had a drink after tennis one afternoon at a sushi bar in Tarzana, it must have been six months ago now. Jack had just introduced Delaney to Onigaroshi on the rocks and the conversation had turned to the sad and parlous state of the world as represented in the newspaper, when Jack swung round in his seat and said, "Knowing you, I'll bet you're completely naked."

"Naked? What do you mean?"

"Home protection." Delaney watched Jack lift a sliver of *maguro* to his lips. "I'll bet the best you can do is maybe a Louisville Slugger, am I right?"

"You mean a gun?"

"Absolutely," Jack said, chewing, and then he reached for the glass of *sake* to wash it down. "It's an angry, fragmented society out there, Delaney, and I'm not only talking about your native haves and have-nots, but the torrents of humanity surging in from China and Bangladesh and Colombia with no shoes, no skills and nothing to eat. They want what you've got, my friend, and do you really think they're going to come knocking at the door and ask politely for it? Look, it boils down to this: no matter what you think about guns, would you rather be the killer or the killee?"

Jack had picked up the check and from there they'd gone to Grantham's GunMart in Van Nuys, and it wasn't at all what Delaney had expected. There were no escaped convicts or Hell's Angels sifting through bins of hollow-point bullets, no swaggering bear hunters or palpitating accountants running up and down the aisles with their tails between their legs. The place was wide open, brightly lit, the wares laid out on display as if Grantham's was dealing in fine jewelry or perfume or Rolex watches. Nothing was furtive, nobody was embarrassed, and the clientele, so far as Delaney could see, consisted of average ordinary citizens in shorts and college sweatshirts, business suits and dresses, shopping for the tools of murder as casually as they might have shopped for rat traps or gopher pellets at the hardware store. The woman behind the counter—Samantha Grantham herself —looked like a retired first-grade teacher, gray hair in a bun, silver-framed glasses, her fingers fat and elegant atop the display case. She sold Delaney the same model handgun she carried in her purse, the one she'd used to scare off the would-be muggers in the parking lot at the Fallbrook Mall after the late movie, and she sold him a lightweight Bianchi clip-on holster made of nylon with a Velcro strap that fit right down inside the waistband of his pants as comfortably as a second pocket. When he got home, he felt ashamed of himself, felt as if he'd lost all hope, and he'd locked the thing away in a chest in the garage and forgotten all about it. Till now.

Now he came in the front door, water puddling on the carpet, fished the key out of the desk drawer in his office and went directly out to the garage. The chest was made of steel, fireproof, the size of two reams of paper, stacked. There was dust on it. He fit the key in the lock, flipped back the lid, and there it was, the gun he'd forgotten all about. It glowed in his hand, flashing light under the naked bulb that dangled from the ceiling, and the rain crashed at the roof. His mouth was dry. He was breathing hard. He inserted the bullets in the slots so ingeniously designed to receive them, each one sliding in with a precise and lethal click, and he knew he would never use the thing, never fire it, never—but he was going to draw it out of the holster in all its deadly flashing beauty and hold it there over that vandalizing alien black-eyed jack-in-the-box till the police came and put him away where he belonged.

Delaney tucked the gun into his holster and tucked the holster into his pants and then a spasm passed through him: he was freezing. Shivering so hard he could barely reach a hand to the light switch. He was going to have to change, that was the first thing—and where was

Kyra, shouldn't she be home by now? And then the film, and maybe something to eat. The lights had been out at Jack and Selda's as he passed by on the street, but he knew where they kept the spare key, under the third flowerpot on the right, just outside the back door, and he was sure they wouldn't mind if he just slipped in for a minute and used the darkroom—he had to have those photos, had to catch the jerk with the spray can in his hand, catch him in the act. The other picture, the first one, was something, but it wasn't conclusive—they could always say in court that it didn't prove a thing except that the suspect was out there on public property, where he had every right to be, and who was going to say he wasn't on his way to the gate to visit friends in Arroyo Blanco or that he wasn't there looking for work or delivering fliers? But these new photos, these six—Delaney would have them printed and blown up and lying right there on the counter in the kitchen when the police came in . . .

But first, his clothes. His body was seized with an involuntary tremor, then another, and he sneezed twice as he set the gun down on the bed and kicked off his shoes. He would take a hot shower to warm up, that's what he would do, then he'd check the message machine—Kyra must have taken Jordan out for a pizza—and then he'd sit down and have something himself, a can of soup, anything. There was no hurry. He knew now where to find the bastard—up there, up in the chaparral within sight of the wall—and he'd have to have a fire on a night like this, and the fire would give him away. It would be the last fire he'd ever start—around here, at least.

While the soup was heating in the microwave, Delaney pulled a clean pair of jeans out of the closet, dug down in back for his High Sierra lightweight hiking boots with the half-inch tread, laid out a pair of insulated socks, a sweater and his raingear on the bed. The shower had warmed him, but he was still trembling, and he realized it wasn't the cold affecting him, but adrenaline, pure adrenaline. He was too keyed up to do much more than blow on the soup—Campbell's Chunky Vegetable—and then he was in the hallway, standing before the full-length mirror and watching himself tuck the gun into his pants and pull it out again while listening to the messages on the machine. Kyra was going to be late, just as he'd thought—she'd got involved with some house in Agoura, of all places, and she was late picking up Jordan and thought she'd just maybe take him out for Chinese and then to the card shop; he was collecting X-Men cards now. Delaney looked up, dropped the film in his pocket and stepped back out into the rain.

It was coming down hard. Piñon was like a streambed, nothing moving but the water, and he could hear boulders slamming around in the culverts high up on the hill that were meant to deflect runoff and debris from the development. Delaney wondered about that, and he stood there in the rain a long moment, listening for the roar of the mountain giving way—what with erosion in the burn area and all this rain anything could happen. They were vulnerable—these were the classic mudslide conditions, nothing to hold the soil in thanks to the match-happy Mexican up there—but then there really wasn't much he could do about it. If the culverts overflowed, the wall would repel whatever came down—it wasn't as if he and his neighbors would have to be out there sandbagging or anything. He was concerned, of course he was concerned—he was concerned about everything—and if the weather gods would grant him a wish he'd cut this back to a nice safe gently soaking drizzle, but at least the way it was coming down now that bastard up there would be pinned down in whatever kind of hovel he'd been able to throw together, and that would make him all the easier to find.

At the Cherrystones', Delaney found the key under the pot with no problem, and he hung his poncho on the inside of the doorknob in the kitchen so as not to dribble water all over the tile. He fumbled for the light switch, the gun pressing at his groin like a hard hot hand, like something that had come alive, and his heart slammed at his ribs and thudded in his ears. The light suddenly exploded in the room, and Selda's cat—a huge manx that was all but indistinguishable from a bobcat—sprang from the chair and shot down the hallway. Delaney felt like a thief. But then he was in the darkroom, the film in the tank, and that calmed him, that was all right—Anytime, Jack had said, anytime you want. Delaney was so sure of what he was going to get this time he barely registered the reversed images on the negatives—there was something there, shadowy figures, a blur of criminal activity—and he cut the curling strip of film and let it drop to the floor, printing up the first six frames on a contact sheet. When it was ready, he slid the paper into the developer and received his second photographic jolt of the week: this was no Mexican blinking scared and open-faced into the lens on a pair of towering legs anchored by glistening leather hi-tops, no Mexican with the spray can plainly visible in his big white fist, no Mexican with hair that shade or cut . . .

It was Jack Jr.

Jack Jr. and an accomplice Delaney didn't recognize, and there they were, replicated six times on a sheet of contact paper, brought to life, caught in the act. It was as complete a surprise as Delaney had ever had, and it almost stopped him. Almost. He pushed himself up from the counter and in a slow methodical way he cleaned up, draining the trays, rinsing them and setting them back on the shelf where Jack kept them. Then he dropped the negatives on the contact sheet and balled the whole thing up in a wad and buried it deep in the trash. That Mexican was guilty, sure he was, guilty of so much more than this. He was camping up there, wasn't he? He'd wrecked Delaney's car. Stolen kibble and plastic sheeting. And who knew but that he hadn't set that fire himself?

The night was black, utterly, impenetrably black, but Delaney didn't want to use his flashlight—there was too much risk of giving himself away. As soon as he dropped down on the far side of the wall, the faint light of the development's porch lights and Christmas displays was snuffed out and the night and the rain were all. The smell was raw and rich at the same time, an amalgam of smells, a whole mountainside risen from the dead. The boulders echoed in the steel-lined culverts, groaning like thunder, and everywhere the sound of running water. Every least crack in the soil was a fissure and every fissure a channel and every channel a stream. Delaney felt it washing round his ankles. His eyes, ever so gradually, began to adjust to the light.

He started straight up, along the backbone of the slope the coyote had ascended with Sacheverell in its jaws, and there was nothing under his feet. Where the white dust and the red grains of the anthills had lain thick on the dehydrated earth, there was now an invisible, infinitely elastic net of mud. Delaney's feet slipped out from under him despite the money-back guarantee of the boots, and he was down on his hands and knees before he'd gone twenty steps. Rain whipped his face, the chaparral disintegrated under the frantic grasp of his fingers. He kept going, foot by foot, seeking the level patches where he could rise to his feet and reconnoiter before he slipped again and went back to all fours. Time meant nothing. The universe was reduced to the square foot of broken sky over his head and the mud beneath his hands. He was out in it, right in the thick of it, as near to the cold black working heart of the world as he could get.

And all the while he was thinking: I've got him now, the son of a bitch, the jack-in-the-box, the firebug, and the exhilaration that took hold of him was like a drug and the drug shut out all reason. He never gave a thought as to what he was going to do with the Mexican once he caught him—that didn't matter. None of it mattered. All that mattered was this, was finding him, rooting him out of his burrow and counting his teeth and his toes and the hairs on his head and noting it all down for the record. Delaney had been here before, been here a hundred times stalking a hundred different creatures—he was a pilgrim, after all. His senses were keen. There was no escaping him.

And then, just as he knew he would, he caught the first faint reductive whiff of it: woodsmoke. Delaney touched the gun then, touched it there where it lay tight against his groin, and let his nose guide him.

8

"YOU LOOK LIKE YOU JUST SAW A GHOST."

Cándido was feeding sticks into the fire, trying to warm himself, and he didn't answer. A moment ago he'd called out to her in the dark and the streaming rain so as not to startle her—"It's me, *mi vida*"—and then he'd crawled through the dripping flap of rug they'd hung across the entrance, bringing the wet with him. He'd kicked the *huaraches* off outside, but his feet were balls of mud all the way up to his ankles, and his shirt and pants were dark with rain and pressed to his skin. He didn't have a jacket. Or a hat.

América was about to say, *Cándido, mi amor, you need to rinse your feet out the door, this place is bad enough as it is, it's leaking in the corner and that smell of mold or rot or whatever it is is driving me crazy,* but she took another look at his face and changed her mind. He didn't have anything with him, either, and that was strange—he always brought something back, a scrap of cloth she could make into a dress for the baby, a package of *tortillas* or rice or sometimes a candy bar. Tonight there was nothing, only that face. "Is there something wrong?" she said.

He pulled his muddy feet up beneath him in that little space that was like a packing crate, the whole place hardly bigger than the king-size beds the *gringos* slept in, and she saw how thin and worn he'd become and she felt she was going to cry, she couldn't hold it back, and it sounded like the whimper of a dog in her own ears. She was crying, sucking the sounds in before they could escape her, the rain drilling the green plastic roof and trickling down the clear plastic sheeting Cándido had dug up somewhere to protect the walls, and still he didn't answer her. She watched a shiver pass through him, and then another.

"I wish it was only a ghost," he said after a while, and he reached for the aluminum dish of *cocido* where it sat on the shelf he'd built in the corner to hold their poor stock of groceries.

She watched him put the dish on the grill, poke up the fire and lay a few sticks of the bigger wood in under it. *Camping*, how she hated camping.

"It was that *gabacho*," he said, "the one with the red hair who hit me with his car. He scares me. He's like a madman. If we were back at home, back in the village, they'd take him to the city in a straitjacket and lock him up in the asylum."

Her voice was hushed. The rain pounded at the door. "What happened?"

"What do you think?" He curled his lip and the sheen of the fire made his face come back to life. "I was walking along the road, minding my own business—and this was the worst day yet, nothing, not a chance of work—and suddenly there's this car coming up behind me and I swear to Christ on his cross the lunatic tried to hit me again. It was inches. He missed me by inches."

She could smell the *cocido* now—there was meat in it, something he'd trapped—and potatoes and *chiles* and a good strong broth. She couldn't tell him now, couldn't tell him yet, though she'd been working up her nerve all day—Socorro had to have a doctor, right away, she had to—but when he'd finished eating and warmed himself, then, it would have to be then.

Cándido's voice was low with wonder. "Then he got out of the car and came after me—and with one of those telephones in his hand, the wireless ones—and I think he was calling the police, but I wasn't going to wait around to find out, you can bet your life on that. But what is it? What did I ever do to him? He can't know about the fire, can he? And that was an accident, God knows—"

"Maybe he tried to hit you the first time too. Maybe he's a racist. Maybe he's a pig. Maybe he hates us because we're Mexican."

"I can't believe it. How could anybody be that vicious? He gave me twenty dollars, remember?"

"Twenty dollars," she spat, and she jerked her hand so violently she woke the baby. "And he sent his son down into the canyon to abuse us, didn't he?"

Later, after Cándido had cleaned up the last of the *cocido* with three hot *tortillas* and his shirt had dried and the mud that had caked on his feet crumbled and fell through the slats of the floor, she steeled herself and came back to the question of Socorro and the doctor. "There's something wrong with her," América said, and a volley of wind-driven rain played off the plastic sheeting like spent ammunition. "It's her eyes. I'm afraid, I'm afraid—" but she couldn't go on.

"What do you mean, her eyes?" Cándido didn't need this, he didn't need another worry. "There's nothing wrong with her eyes," he said, and as if to prove it he took the baby from her and Socorro kicked out her arms in reflex and gave a harsh rasping cry. He looked into her face a moment—not too hard, he was afraid to look too hard—and then he glanced at América and said, "You're crazy. She's beautiful, she's perfect—what more do you want?" Socorro passed between them again, soft and fragile and wrapped up in her towel, but for all that, Cándido handled her as if she were a bundle of sticks, a loaf of bread, just another object.

"She, she can't see me, Cándido—she can't see anything, and I'm afraid."

Thunder struck his face. The rain screamed. "You're crazy."

"No," and she could barely get the words out, "no, I'm not. We need the doctor—maybe he can do something, maybe—you don't know, Cándido, you don't know anything, and you don't want to." She was angry now, all of it pouring out of her, all the pain and worry and fear of the past few days, weeks, months: "It was my pee, my pee burned, that's what did it, because of"—she couldn't look him in the eye, the fire flickering, the lamp making a death mask of his face—"because of those men."

It was the worst wound she could have given him, but he had to understand, and there was no recrimination in it, what's done is done, but she never heard his response. Because at that moment something fell against the side of the shack, something considerable, something animate, and then the flap was wrenched from the doorway and flung away into the night and there was a face there, peering in. A *gabacho* face, as startling and unexpected and horrible as any face leaping out of a dark corner on the Day of the Dead. And the shock of that was nothing, because there was a hand attached to that face and the hand held a gun.

Delaney found the shack, and his fingers told him it was made of stolen pallets and slats stripped from the chaparral and the roof that had turned up missing from Bill Vogel's greenhouse. There was light inside—from the fire and maybe a lantern—and it guided him, though the mud was like oil on glass and he lost his balance and gave himself away. He thought he heard voices. More than one. He was outraged—how many of them were there, how many? This couldn't go on anymore, this destruction of the environment, this trashing of the hills and the creeks and the marshes and everyplace else; this was the end, the end of it. He blundered into the stolen flap of rug that concealed the entrance and he tore it aside with one hand because the other hand, his right hand, somehow held the gun now, and it was as if the gun were sentient and animate and had sprung out of the holster and into the grip of his fingers all on its own—

And that was when things got hazy. He'd been hearing the roar for a minute or two now, a sound like the wildest surf pounding against the ruggedest shore, but there was no shore here, there was nothing but—

And then he felt himself lifted up from behind by some monstrous uncontainable force and he dropped the gun and clutched at the frame of the stooped-over door of that pathetic little shack, staring in amazement into the lamplit faces there—his Mexican, that was him, at last, and a girl he'd never seen before, and was that an infant?—and the shack was spilling over on its side and floating up on the heavy liquid swell behind him until it fell to pieces and the light was snuffed out and the faces were gone and Delaney was drawn so much closer to that cold black working heart of the world than he'd ever dreamed possible.

And so, in the end, it all came tumbling down on Cándido: his daughter's affliction, the *pelirrojo* with the gun, the very mountain itself. The light was flickering, the rain hissing like a box of serpents prodded with a stick. *She can't see, Cándido, she can't see anything,* América said, and in that moment he had a vision of his perfect plump little daughter transmogrified into an old hag with a cane and a Seeing Eye dog, and before he could assimilate the meaning of that in all its fearful permutations and banish it from his consciousness, there was this maniac with the gun, threatening his life, and before he could even begin to deal with *that,* the mountain turned to pudding, to mush, the light failed and the shack fell to pieces. At first he didn't know what was happening—who would?—but there was no resisting that force. He could have built his shack of tungsten steel with footings a hundred feet deep and the result would have been the same. The mountain was going somewhere, and he was going with it.

He didn't even have time to curse or flinch or wonder about his fate—all he could do was snatch América and his poor blind baby to him and hold on. América had Socorro pinned under her arm like a football and she clawed at him with her free hand as the roof shot away from them and they were thrown in a tangle on the pallets that just half a second ago were the inside wall and were now the floor. The moving floor. The floor that shot like a surfboard out on the crest of the liquid mountain that was scouring the earth and blasting trees out of the ground as if they'd never been rooted, and there was the *pelirrojo*, the white face and flailing white arms, caught up in the mad black swirl of it like a man drowning in shit.

The mountain roared, the boulders clamored, and yet they somehow stayed atop the molten flow, hurtling through the night with all the other debris. Cándido heard the rush of water ahead and saw the lights of the development below them, riding high on the wave of mud that hammered the walls flat and twisted the roofs from the houses and sent him and América and little Socorro thundering into the void. Then the lights went out in unison, the far wall of the development was breached and the two conjoined pallets were a raft in the river that the dry white wash had become, spinning out of control in the current.

América was screaming and the baby was screaming and he could hear his own voice raised in a thin mournful drone, and that was nothing compared to the shrieks of the uprooted trees and the night-marish roar of the boulders rolling along beneath them. He wasn't thinking—there was no time to think, only to react—but even as he pitched into the blackness of this new river that was rushing toward completion in the old river below, he managed finally to curse the engine of all this misery in a burst of profanity that would have con-demned him for all time if he hadn't been condemned already. What was it? What was it about him? All he wanted was work, and this was his fate, this was his stinking *pinche* luck, a violated wife and a blind baby and a crazy white man with a gun, and even that wasn't enough to satisfy an insatiable God: no, they all had to drown like rats in the bargain.

There was no controlling this thing, no hope of it. There was only the mad ride and the battering of the rocks. Cándido held on to the pallet and América held on to him. His knuckles were smashed and smashed again but he held on because there was nothing else he could do. And then they were in the bed of the big creek, Topanga Creek, and the mountain was behind them. But this wasn't the creek Cán-dido had drunk from and bathed in and slept behind through all those punishing months of drought—it wasn't even the creek he'd seen raging under the bridge earlier that day. It was a river, a torrent that rode right up over the bridges and the streets and everything else. There was no escaping it. The pallet bucked and spun, and finally it threw him.

They hit something, something so big it was immovable, and Cándido lost his grip on América and the raft at the same time; he was in the water suddenly with nothing to hold on to and the water was as cold as death. He went under, and it felt as if an enormous fist were pinning him down, crushing him, but he kicked out against it, slammed into a submerged log and then the jagged tearing edge of a rock, and somehow the surface was there. "América!" he cried. "América!" In the next instant it had him again, the furious roiling water forced up his nostrils and rammed down his throat, the current raking him over a stony washboard, hump after hump of unyielding rock, and he saw his mother pounding the clothes back and forth in a froth of suds, he must have been three years old, and he knew he was going to die, *Go to the devil*, mijo, and he cried out again.

Then a voice spoke beside him, right in his ear—"Cándido!"—and there was his wife, there was América, holding out a hand to him. The water churned and sucked at him, throwing him forward only to jerk him away again, and where was she? There, clinging to the slick hard surface of the washboard where it rose dizzily out of the current. He fought with all he had and suddenly the water spat him up in his wife's arms.

He was saved. He was alive. There was no sky, there was no earth and the wind drove at them with pellets of rain and the water crashed at his feet, but he was alive and breathing and huddled in the arms of his wife, his thin beautiful shivering girl of a wife. It took him a moment, interpreting the humped rock beneath him with his numbed and bleeding fingers, before he understood where they were—they'd been saved by the United States Post Office and this was the tile roof and the building beneath them was the cut bank of the river as it swirled round the bend to the swamped bridge and the gorge beyond. "América" was all he could say, gasping it, moaning it, over and over. He fell into a spasm of coughing and brought up the *cocido,* sour and thin, and he felt as if he were being slowly strangled. "Are you okay?" he choked. "Are you hurt?"

She was sobbing. Her body and his were one and the sobs shook him till he was sobbing himself, or almost sobbing. But men didn't sob, men endured; they worked for three dollars a day tanning hides till their fingernails fell out; they swallowed kerosene and spat out fire for tourists on streetcorners; they worked till there was no more work left in them. "The baby," he gasped, and he wasn't sobbing, he wasn't. "Where's the baby?"

She didn't answer, and he felt the cold seep into his veins, a coldness and a weariness like nothing he'd ever known. The dark water was all around him, water as far as he could see, and he wondered if he would ever get warm again. He was beyond cursing, beyond grieving, numbed right through to the core of him. All that, yes. But when he saw the white face surge up out of the black swirl of the current and the white hand grasping at the tiles, he reached down and took hold of it.

READ MORE IN PENGUIN

In every corner of the world, on every subject under the sun, Penguin represents quality and variety – the very best in publishing today.

For complete information about books available from Penguin – including Puffins, Penguin Classics and Arkana – and how to order them, write to us at the appropriate address below. Please note that for copyright reasons the selection of books varies from country to country.

In the United Kingdom: Please write to *Dept. EP, Penguin Books Ltd, Bath Road, Harmondsworth, West Drayton, Middlesex UB7 0DA*

In the United States: Please write to *Consumer Sales, Penguin USA, P.O. Box 999, Dept. 17109, Bergenfield, New Jersey 07621-0120*. VISA and MasterCard holders call 1-800-253-6476 to order Penguin titles

In Canada: Please write to *Penguin Books Canada Ltd, 10 Alcorn Avenue, Suite 300, Toronto, Ontario M4V 3B2*

In Australia: Please write to *Penguin Books Australia Ltd, P.O. Box 257, Ringwood, Victoria 3134*

In New Zealand: Please write to *Penguin Books (NZ) Ltd, Private Bag 102902, North Shore Mail Centre, Auckland 10*

In India: Please write to *Penguin Books India Pvt Ltd, 706 Eros Apartments, 56 Nehru Place, New Delhi 110 019*

In the Netherlands: Please write to *Penguin Books Netherlands bv, Postbus 3507, NL-1001 AH Amsterdam*

In Germany: Please write to *Penguin Books Deutschland GmbH, Metzlerstrasse 26, 60594 Frankfurt am Main*

In Spain: Please write to *Penguin Books S. A., Bravo Murillo 19, 1° B, 28015 Madrid*

In Italy: Please write to *Penguin Italia s.r.l., Via Felice Casati 20, I–20124 Milano*

In France: Please write to *Penguin France S. A., 17 rue Lejeune, F–31000 Toulouse*

In Japan: Please write to *Penguin Books Japan, Ishikiribashi Building, 2–5–4, Suido, Bunkyo-ku, Tokyo 112*

In Greece: Please write to *Penguin Hellas Ltd, Dimocritou 3, GR–106 71 Athens*

In South Africa: Please write to *Longman Penguin Southern Africa (Pty) Ltd, Private Bag X08, Bertsham 2013*

READ MORE IN PENGUIN

A CHOICE OF FICTION

The Ghost Road Pat Barker
Winner of the 1995 Booker Prize

'One of the richest and most rewarding works of fiction of recent times. Intricately plotted, beautifully written, skilfully assembled, tender, horrifying and funny, it lives on in the imagination, like the war it so imaginatively and so intelligently explores' – *The Times Literary Supplement*

None to Accompany Me Nadine Gordimer

In an extraordinary period before the first non-racial elections in South Africa, Vera Stark, a lawyer representing blacks' struggle to reclaim the land, weaves an interpretation of her own past into her participation in the present. 'With great dexterity and force Gordimer combines all these stories – career, colleagues, political struggles, sexual love, identity, family – into a compelling narrative' – *Daily Telegraph*

Of Love and Other Demons Gabriel García Márquez

'García Márquez tells a story of forbidden love, but he demonstrates once again the vigor of his own passion: the daring and irresistible coupling of history and imagination' – *Time*. 'A further marvellous manifestation of the enchantment and the disenchantment that his native Colombia always stirs in García Márquez' – *Sunday Times*

Millroy the Magician Paul Theroux

A magician of baffling talents, a vegetarian and a health fanatic with a mission to change the food habits of America, Millroy has the power to heal, and to hypnotize. 'Fresh and unexpected . . . this very accomplished, confident book is among his best' – *Guardian*

English Music Peter Ackroyd

'Each dream-sequence is a virtuoso performance on Ackroyd's part. In his fiction he has made a speciality of leap-frogging time, so that the past occupies the same plane as the present. Never before, however, has he been so chronologically acrobatic, nor so confident' – *The Times*